Praise for *One*

'A thrilling, heart-stealing hist
M.A. Kuzniar, ***Midnight in Everwood***

'An utterly bedazzling novel, a compulsive page-turner rich in historical detail, and a heart-stopping debut romance.'
Kirsty Capes, ***Careless***

'A heartwarming tale of forbidden love that captured my heart from its opening page... Unputdownable.'
Sarah Ferguson, Duchess of York, ***A Most Intriguing Lady***

'Road trips and secret identities...a beautifully thoughtful and deliciously sweet romance about getting lost in order to find oneself. I loved every moment spent with Penn and Raff.'
Freya Marske, ***A Marvellous Light***

'A beautiful love story and journey of longing until your heart is torn apart and rebuilt.'
Liz Fenwick, ***The River Between Us***

'A heart-wrenching, spellbinding love story, and I couldn't turn the pages fast enough to find out if Raff and Penn would get their happy ever after.'
Cressida McLaughlin, ***The Cornish Cream Tea*** **series**

Emma Denny submitted her first manuscript to a publisher when she was eight and a half, and was astonished when it was rejected. Thankfully, that didn't put her off. After completing a degree in English & Creative Writing, Emma became a professional copywriter and now spends all day – literally – writing. Living on the edge of a forest, Emma enjoys exploring the wilderness while thinking through her latest plot tangle, scouting out exciting craft ales and indulging in historical romances. *One Night in Hartswood* is her debut novel and the winner of the Mills & Boon *Romance Includes Everyone* competition.

ONE NIGHT *in* HARTSWOOD

Emma Denny

MILLS & BOON

This novel is entirely a work of fiction. The names, characters and incidents portrayed in it are the work of the author's imagination. Any resemblance to actual persons, living or dead, events or localities is entirely coincidental.

Mills & Boon
An imprint of HarperCollins*Publishers* Ltd
1 London Bridge Street
London SE1 9GF

www.harpercollins.co.uk

HarperCollins*Publishers*
Macken House, 39/40 Mayor Street Upper,
Dublin 1, D01 C9W8, Ireland

This edition 2023
1

First published in Great Britain by
Mills & Boon, an imprint of HarperCollins*Publishers* Ltd 2023

Emma Denny asserts the moral right to be identified as the author of this work. A catalogue record for this book is available from the British Library.

UK ISBN: 978-0-00-853537-7
US ISBN: 978-0-00-862007-3

This book is produced from independently certified FSC™ paper to ensure responsible forest management.

For more information visit: www.harpercollins.co.uk/green

This book is set in 11.5/15.5 pt. Centaur

Printed and Bound in the UK using 100% Renewable Electricity at
CPI Group (UK) Ltd, Croydon, CR0 4YY

Dedicated to Merry
Written for everyone who has tried to run away

PYLADES: I'll take care of you.

ORESTES: It's rotten work.

PYLADES: Not to me. Not if it's you.

EURIPIDES
(TRANS. ANNE CARSON)

Chapter One

Oxfordshire – 1360

Shafts of bright midday sun pierced through the canopy above, mottling Lord Griffin Barden's retinue with golden flecks of light. A detour through the forest brought an hour's relief for both horses and riders: it had been a long day, and the shade was a welcome reprieve from the blinding winter sun. Raff led his horse along the wide road, thankful for the cover.

Hartswood Forest had been but a dark smear on the horizon as the party approached from the north. Now it was transformed into something huge and imposing, the wide elms twisting above the road, penning them in. Even in early winter, the trees were packed so closely that it posed a near impassable barrier, despite so many of them lacking their leaves. The only way to their destination was on a road through the forest itself, picking around trees older than Raff's father – older than his father's father.

Raff found his mind wandering as he surveyed the area. His experience lay north, in his family's territory, and he pondered what he might be able to find this far south. The trees were pressed so closely together that the heart of the forest was utterly hidden, and he was keen to know what lay between those ancient trunks; what animals he may find here, hidden pools or startling southern wildflowers. The land was protected by royal law – owned by the

King and managed by the Earl their party was travelling towards – which meant it would be rich with game.

'Raff!'

His head snapped around at the intrusion to his thoughts.

'Save it till after Lily's wedding, at least.' His brother laughed.

Raff frowned. 'Save what?'

Ash shook his head at him. 'I love ale. Father loves chess. Lily loves brea—'

'Ash!' Lily warned, twisting in her saddle to glare at him.

'Loves *broadswords*, even though she shouldn't, as a noble lady,' he drawled towards their sister with a mock bow, 'and you, Raff, love your forests. A true hunter, through and through.'

Raff huffed. 'I love *peace*. The only place to find it is in the wilderness when I'm forced to travel beside you for days on end.'

'You wound me, brother.'

'Don't tempt me to make it fatal, *brother*.'

Ash laughed through his nose, the scar on his face pulling upwards.

'If you are intending to explore, you should make yourself useful,' he teased. 'You could catch a pair of rabbits. Lady Cecily,' he drawled, grandly, 'would you deign to wear a fur-lined wedding gown? It may suit, in this weather.'

Lily rolled her eyes at him, but said nothing.

'Maybe they like brides rabbit-furred this far south,' Ash continued. 'I wouldn't know.'

She snorted. 'There's hundreds of things you wouldn't know,' she said, 'both about the south *and* brides.'

Ash continued, unfazed. 'If not a rabbit, a bird, then, perhaps? A circlet of feathers?'

Raff ignored him. He was growing tired of Ash's continual

mocking, already dreading the prospect of a days-long march back to Dunlyn Castle. He wondered how poorly his father and brother would react if he voiced his desire to remove himself from their party and travel elsewhere *now*, rather than waiting to tell them until after the wedding. The temptation to leave was growing stronger every day: the urge to seek his own path, if only for a short while.

It was news that could wait until afterwards, when tensions were less high.

'When this is all over,' Ash was saying, 'we'll be part of the family. Lily, you must ask your husband's father to extend his royal licence to your brother, before he drives us mad with his sour moods.'

'I'm not some hound in need of exercising,' Raff mumbled bitterly, well aware that his brother wasn't listening to him.

He sighed. He *did* crave the solitude of the forest. It would be a relief after so many days on the road, never able to grab more than an hour or so alone. It wasn't the thrill of the track and the hunt he needed, but the peace of the trees, the susurration of nature around him unmarred by the bark of dogs or the stamping of horses or the endless chattering of their party.

Yet these hours they had left were precious, and few. Soon, their family would be lessened by one. Raff could accept his own discomfort if it meant spending time by Lily's side before sending her away to an uncertain future.

He'd stay with her now, and this evening. He'd stay with her through tomorrow's ceremony, through the noise of the feast, and leave in the morning, their entourage burdened with one more ghost.

Raff was dreading the days of feasting for more than one reason. Lily's loss would be a hard blow to them all, but with the wedding came the ever-present need to perform, to fulfil the role that was expected of him as the son of an earl. Twenty-seven years of training had honed not just his skill with the blade, but his manners too, although he was painfully aware that he was poor with people. It was an act, and the performance exhausted him, leaving him feeling inept.

He needed to maintain the ruse, just for a few days. He was not as charming as Lily, but at least he was a better showman than Ash, who had abandoned all attempts at civility some years ago. Ash was too familiar with the cut of steel to feel anything other than contempt for those who'd rather ignore the cost of war in favour of dancing and banquets.

Lily's match had been arranged in haste, and it appeared that his Lordship the Earl Marcus de Foucart hadn't gone to any great pains to announce who he was marrying his son to. It meant they travelled largely unnoticed. This may have been a deliberate choice on the Earl's part rather than an oversight: while the Barden family was an ancient one, well connected in the north, Raff's parents' marriage – a union between an English earl and Marion of Kerr, a laird's daughter – had been met with suspicion. Suspicion had matured into keen distrust, hardened over thirty years, twenty-five of which had been spent embroiled in war with the Scots.

They were known by name alone, too far north for the southern nobles to bother learning their faces. Yet Raff still suspected they were being scrutinised by those around them. The back of his neck prickled, and he realised quite suddenly that they really *were* being stared at.

He turned in the saddle. Two girls – a pair of servants no older than sixteen from the party they'd been travelling with since Tusmore – were watching them with close interest.

Raff gave the girls a curt, courtly nod, sending the elder of the two into fits of giggles. Ash's attention was caught by the noise, and he too peered down at the pair. He scowled at them, the expression twisting his marred face into something more akin to a grimace. The girls paled, falling into a hushed silence.

Ash smirked, clearly pleased with himself.

He had always been terse, his wit more barbed than Raff's. After the ruinous battle that had left him richer only for a scar that snaked down his cheek to his throat, his spiked nature had honed into something with more of an edge.

Raff watched as his brother scanned the carts travelling ahead of them, his scowl deepening.

'I don't trust this match,' Ash said, finally.

'Why not?'

'I don't know enough about this Marcus de Foucart, or his son. I do not even know Lily's husband's *name*.'

'Which is entirely your own fault,' Lily interrupted. 'If you deigned to listen to Father, you'd know more.'

'And do *you* know so much about him?'

She twirled a strand of her long red hair around her finger as she thought. She had inherited her hair from their mother, while Raff and his brother had received their father's darker colouring. They made an odd trio, riding three abreast, the only tell that they shared blood the freckles they had all been blessed with.

'He is named *William*, to start,' she said, as Ash rolled his eyes at her. 'He's the third son.'

'There's at least one elder daughter too,' cut in Raff.

'Unmarried?'

Raff shrugged again. 'I believe so.'

'So why not arrange a marriage for *her*, then? The elder daughter should surely make a match before the younger son.'

Raff hesitated before speaking again. Ash was right: it was unusual.

'She may be infirm,' he mused. 'Perhaps promised to the church, or someone else . . .'

'A convenient excuse. What else?'

'The Earldom is newly established,' Raff said, trying to remember what their father had told him. 'By the King himself. They are close, apparently.'

'Impressive,' Ash intoned, dryly. 'How new is the position?'

'Newer than Father's.'

'That is not particularly difficult.'

Raff pursed his lips. That was true enough; the seat his father occupied had been held by the men in his family for longer than anyone could remember.

'So he's looking to barter favour by tying himself to an old title, is that it?' Ash continued.

'I cannot guess at his motives,' Raff said, 'for the union *or* marrying off the son first.'

Ash snorted. 'It doesn't sit right with me, Raff. It doesn't sit right with you either, and you damn well know it.'

Raff sighed. He'd always been attuned to Ash's moods, more so since his return, and knew there was no reasoning with him. In truth, he *had* heard rumours of the Earl's nature – none of which had been encouraging – but had no way of knowing how accurate they were. Agreeing with Ash would only encourage him, making him more likely to behave rashly.

'I hadn't known you were so keen to wed, Ash,' Raff said instead. 'As the eldest son, it's *you* she would be marrying.'

It was a low blow. Without another word, Ash spurred his horse and sped away towards their father at the front of their travelling party. Together, Raff and Lily rode in silence, the only sound the gentle huffing of their horses. After a while, she spoke, her voice quieter.

'Raff . . .'

He peered at her. Her typical bravado had been softened, an uncertain tilt to her eyebrows. Raff could remember when she'd been a tiny thing, moulded by him and his brother in the way clay was moulded by a potter, bending into the shape it was best suited for, hardened by time. And now, with her steely reserve and strong sense of loyalty, her brittle shape was being forced to change. It was either that, or shatter.

'Ash is too suspicious,' he said, answering the question she had failed to put to words. 'No doubt there's good reason for the daughter to be unwed.'

'Marriage is a convenient way to remove an inconvenient child,' she said, slowly. 'He could be a scoundrel.'

'Then you two will get along.'

She glanced at him, darkly. 'Not quite in the way he hopes we will, I fear.'

'Cecily . . .'

'I know, I know.' She rolled her shoulders. Her poise was sure, but her knuckles had turned white where she gripped the reins of her horse. 'If he *is* a scoundrel, at least I've had plenty of practice with them.'

She laughed, but her hands were shaking around the worn leather. The impending marriage pained her, Raff knew, but she was locked into it by duty and expectation, by the respect she had for their father, and her trust that he'd never knowingly hurt her. She had no desire to be married to a stranger, a union with wholly political motivations, but neither would she refuse, even if she could.

Lily was braver than him, of that much he was certain.

He didn't want to see her go, and their chilly home would be quieter without her. But neither of them had a choice, and with her wed, there would come a chance for his own freedom too. He'd vowed to keep her safe until she left, and now that time was upon them.

After Ash had ridden to war, Raff had picked up the duties of the firstborn son, keen to ease the burden on his father's shoulders. Ash had returned a changed man years ago, yet Raff had still yet to restore those duties to his brother. The resentment prickled at them both: Raff for the years shackled to a role that was never made for him, and Ash for the responsibilities he didn't want. If Raff chose to leave, Ash would have no choice but to accept them.

Part of Raff hoped that the sudden accountability would soothe his brother's temperament. Ash could make a good earl: one who was *loved* rather than *tolerated*. But only he could make the choice as to which he would be.

As Raff continued to muse, the party finally broke through the southern border of the forest, the road bathed in light once more. He lifted his arm to shield his eyes, peering around at the pastures, the rows of fields and the enormous keep that loomed ahead of them. He couldn't help but wonder whether Lily's future father-in-law was loved, or merely tolerated.

It didn't matter, he tried to remind himself. An intolerable lord would not necessarily mean the son was similarly burdened. Lily could be correct in her assumption that the marriage could be to remove him from the familial home. That could be a blessing or a curse: he could be cruel, and forcing him into marriage was a neat way to impose him upon somebody else. Equally, he could be ill-suited for court, yet unfit for monastic life. That, too, could be concerning, but Raff would sleep easier knowing that his sister's husband was foolish instead of vicious.

There was another reason for an untraditional match, of course.

Raff considered his own position beneath his father's roof, and how precarious his perch would be under the rule of someone less tolerant than Lord Barden. Lily's wouldn't be the first marriage hastily arranged with a distant, unfamiliar family as a way to douse the fires of other, far less acceptable relations. Perhaps a servant. Perhaps another man.

Raff shook his head, trying to rid himself of the thought. Although, if it *did* transpire that William was indeed tolerable, but either too free or misplaced with his affections, such a union may yet work; one of necessity and mutual understanding rather than love. Lily could find happiness like that, and Raff would be able to let her go.

There was no way of knowing. That was the worst of it, for them all. The wedding feast was less than a day away, and all they could do was wait to see what sort of man fate had handed them.

The dark bird wheeled across the sky with a screech, barely moving its wings as it dived across the expanse of blue. It was a kite, the pointed tips of its forked tail swivelling as it directed itself against the barely-there breeze.

Penn watched, shielding his eyes from the sun, as the huge bird soared above before diving, ducking out of sight behind the towering outer wall. Perhaps it had found something to eat beyond the thick stone curtain. He wished he could get a closer look, to watch it pull the carrion apart and see it take off again once it had eaten its fill.

There was a shout from the gatehouse, breaking him from his thoughts. One of the guards was gesturing, then another, and then the doors were being heaved open, the portcullis ahead lifting.

Beyond the metal bars, he could see half a dozen carts, flanked by servants and horses. The covered carriage that led the party had a familiar coat of arms sewn into the fabric, one which Penn hadn't seen in over a year. There was a distant flurry of footsteps, and suddenly Johanna was at his side, tucking loose strands of long, dark hair back into her net.

'She's here?' his sister said, smoothing her skirts.

'She's here,' Penn replied. He watched as the cart entered the courtyard. 'I suppose that's all of us, then.'

'I suppose it is.' Jo reached out and took his hand. 'Are you all right?'

Penn gave her hand a perfunctory squeeze before pulling away.

'Why would I not be? Father has finally found a use for me.' He cocked his brow, staring forwards. 'Although I suspect he would have preferred this role was Henry's.'

'*Penn—*'

Before she could properly reprimand him, there was a shout, and the rosy face of their sister appeared from the back of the cart. With some difficulty, she clambered down the steps and into the yard as Penn and Jo rushed forwards to greet her.

'Ros!' Penn said, forcing himself to smile as she awkwardly embraced him. 'I hadn't expected you to come, surely—'

She cut him off with a wave of her hand. 'My physician says I've at least four months left, and it's not so long a journey. I wouldn't miss your wedding for the *world*, William.'

He winced, but she missed the expression, continuing to talk.

'When I received Father's message, I was afraid I'd be too late. It's all happening so quickly!'

Penn gave a half-shrug, not trusting himself to say anything that didn't betray his feelings. Thankfully, Jo stepped in, looping a hand around Ros's arm.

'Penn and I were—'

'Oh!' Rosalind cut her off, turning back to Penn. 'You're *still* going by that name?'

He held his chin higher, a foolish attempt at defiance. 'I am.'

'And is that what your wife will address you as?'

'If she's willing . . .'

She laughed. 'My sweetling, you've much to learn.'

He scowled at her, a retort already on his lips, but she just gave him another of those smiles, speaking before he could even choose his words.

'I *am* glad to see you married, Will—' she sighed, 'Penn, if you insist. Truly, I am. It's . . . well, it's unlike anything else.'

She smiled again, the corners of her eyes crinkling as she did. Had she been Jo, Penn would have assumed she was teasing him, but Ros spoke so *genuinely*, like she really believed it. Perhaps she did: her marriage, by all accounts, was a complete success, even if her noble husband had been too busy to join them for his brother-in-law's wedding.

When she'd gone to marry Lord Peter, it had felt like a loss. They'd never truly seen eye to eye, and time and distance had done nothing to solve those differences, but her absence gnawed at him regardless. He'd grown used to the three of them, bound by blood more than anything else, made close through the simple and sure knowledge that there was no one else to cling to.

Yet she had found someone else, and she had left.

The thought of his new wife and their impending marriage twisted bitterly around Penn's grief. It was a cruel irony that the one person forced to stay by his side was a stranger to him. He was not so cynical to hate his sister's happiness, but the resentment rubbed: he would never find that for himself.

'Well,' he said, trying to sound flippant, 'I shall have to hope you are right, Ros. I cannot say I'm convinced.'

She laughed again, like it was just another joke, then took his arm as they crossed the yard towards the hall. The three of them were aligned once more, easily falling back into step. Even all these years later, he still felt the yawning gap where Leo and Henry should have been.

Rosalind nestled closer, as if reading his thoughts.

'Soon you'll realise how wrong you are,' she said. 'You need someone to love, Wi—Penn.'

He placed his hand over hers. Her skin was warm, and soft. 'Where's Robin?' he asked, attempting to move the conversation on. 'You *did* bring him, didn't you?'

Penn knew this was a low tactic, as Ros loved nothing more than to talk about his nephew, but it was fair if it made her forget the topic of his impending marriage. Penn listened to her chat, her fingers squeezing around his arm. For a moment, absorbed in her stories, he could forget it too.

'I knew it!'

Raff sighed into his cup, already regretting not taking the evening for himself. 'Ash,' he said, attempting to keep his voice level, 'there's nothing to know. You're fretting needlessly.'

'I'm *right*.'

'Lily is with Father,' he said, 'she'll be fine.'

'Don't you care that they're refusing us boarding? We're her brothers!'

Raff shrugged. 'I've no desire to be beholden to de Foucart any more than we already are.'

'So you'll leave her there? Alone?'

'She's not *alone*. Father—'

'Father arranged this! She needs someone with her, someone who understands. If one of us could just—'

Raff was struck with the image of Ash forcing his way into the keep and demanding hospitality and a place at her side. He could imagine the reception such a demand would have, and the repercussions.

'I will not have you ruin this.'

'What is there to ruin? You know this isn't right for her.'

'And *you* know how precarious our position is in the south.'

'I'd rather be ruined than do as they ask us.'

'Then ruin *yourself*. Do not do what she hasn't asked of you.'

Ash's rage, fuelling him onwards, was a double-edged blade. It forced him to act for what he believed was right, but always came chased by consequences beyond his control. He gave in so *easily*, while Raff was forced to keep a tight rein over himself, always aware of how much could go wrong.

He tried to keep his face impassive. 'There's nothing we can do.'

'We could go in there and get her.'

'We can't.'

'Why not?'

Raff wished he had a better answer. He wished he didn't have to battle against what he wanted and what he knew they had to do.

'We *cannot*. And you know it.'

There was a prolonged silence before Ash spoke again.

'Do you even care, Raff? Or are you so ready to be free of her that you'd rather sit here and do nothing?'

The fury inside him boiled over, his self-control spent. In that hot, sparking second he considered taking a swing at Ash, knocking him to the ground, throwing him down.

But he didn't. He clenched his fists at his side, taking a long breath.

'I care,' he spat. 'I *care*. I'm done with this argument.'

'Then—'

'I'm *done*.'

Raff turned on his heel, pushing past Ash and out of the tent before he could do something he'd regret. Ash shouted after him, but he ignored him, trudging onwards through their camp and towards Hartswood Forest.

Penn spent much of the afternoon with his sisters, or playing with Robin, amazed at how much he'd grown in so short a time. His intended, he learned, had arrived a few hours after Rosalind, but despite his requests his father had refused a meeting between them.

'There'll be time for that tomorrow,' he'd said, waving an impatient hand.

Usually, Penn would have argued. For once, he hadn't had the energy.

When Ros had married, there had been feasting for days. He could still remember the music they'd played on the eve of the wedding, the ever-moving troupe dancing around the room, the palpable sense of energy that had settled over them all, even his father.

He could remember the way Ros had stared at her betrothed across the hall, as well. She'd been enamoured from the start. Penn knew he wouldn't have such a moment with his own intended, given that his inclinations had only ever been towards men, but he hoped at least to meet her. Yet it was not to be, and that evening he'd found himself hunched at the long table picking at an uneventful meal with the remainder of his family: his sisters and nephew, his father's second wife Isabelle and their two children, Ellis and Ingrid.

No one had mentioned his father's absence, or the fact that Penn *still* hadn't met his soon-to-be wife, and the meal passed quickly, their echoing voices the only sounds in the huge chamber.

Penn returned to his rooms in a daze. He pulled off his tunic then washed and shaved his face, just for something to do, staring at himself in the mirror above the basin. He didn't recognise his reflection. He hadn't slept properly in a week, and the face in the metal betrayed that. There were dark bags beneath his eyes, and his curly hair was a wild tangle where he'd run his hands through it so many times.

Instead of retiring to bed, he took the opportunity to pack the remainder of his things, ready to be moved into the small manor that would be his new home.

Most of his meagre possessions had been packed already. In the process of arranging his things into chests, Penn had come to realise exactly how little of what he'd come to think of as *his* he actually owned. All the furniture in his chambers belonged to the house, and therefore his father. His effects amounted to little more than his clothes and shoes, a few trinkets, and the single book he'd been able to salvage from his mother's things after she had died: a collection of Arthurian tales.

He hoped his wife, whoever she was, liked such tales. He hoped she liked *him*, what little of him there was to like. He had no desire to rule with a fist like his father, casting a shadow larger than himself over their home.

Penn didn't even know what she looked like. When he'd expressed a similar sentiment to his father, his steward had barked a harsh, ringing laugh towards him across the expansive wooden table.

'They all look the same under the coverlet, boy,' the steward had chuckled, as if espousing some brilliant philosophy.

Penn hadn't even been *thinking* about that. He didn't care if she was beautiful or not; to do so would make him a hypocrite once they were sharing a bed and she saw all of him. He'd just wanted to imagine her face.

Now, standing in the centre of what was going to be his bedroom for one more night, he could only imagine a blur. He gripped the book he'd been packing more tightly, his fingers trembling.

He peered out of the window and across his father's land. The de Foucart keep itself was nestled on the edge of Hartswood Forest – the expansive kingswood that his father managed but didn't truly care for, named for the red deer found within it. Beyond that he could see the rolling fields of farmland, bare for the winter, illuminated by the growing moon and the golden dash across the horizon where the sun was sinking. A whipping breeze danced across the pastures, making the treetops shudder. It buffeted through the window, barely touching the heavy curtains but ruffling Penn's hair, bringing with it the smell of pine and smoke.

It was late, and his father had no further need of him. He could allow himself one last indulgence before shackling his life to another.

He placed the book onto the bed, then heaved open the closest chest and pulled out an old tunic. It had been Leo's, once, passed onto Penn despite its age. The fabric was thick and dark, if a little worn, ideal for riding or hunting.

He tugged the garment on, followed by his cloak, then headed for the door.

It was locked.

Penn pushed harder. Panic coiled in his chest. The last time he'd found himself in this position had only been two months or so past, after . . .

After he'd been caught. It had only been once, but it had been enough. Arthur had been removed from his role in the stables – his safety traded for his silence – and Penn had remained, trapped.

He'd hoped, foolishly, that with the impending marriage his father would have trusted him. He'd been wrong. Wrong *again*.

He pressed his head against the wood, allowing himself a moment to breathe – a moment to hold the hot little ember of anger that flared in his chest. When his breathing had calmed and his fingers stopped shaking, he turned away from the door and towards the opposite wall.

As he ran his fingertips over the tapestry that hung from floor to ceiling, he couldn't help but acknowledge that his father was correct not to trust him.

The narrow door behind the thick wool opened easily, and he quickly slipped behind the drapery and through onto the tightly winding staircase beyond.

Penn wasn't sure what this passage's original purpose had been. After a childhood devouring tales of courtly romance, he'd hoped it was for romantic trysts and daring escapes. As he grew older, the more he realised that it was probably a disused servants' passage, built when the room belonged to someone more important. In any case, the stairs let out into the vaulted undercroft beside the kitchens, so unless his ancestors were fumbling amongst filthy linens and vegetable peelings, it was likely a passage for practicality rather than pleasure.

He'd taken this route hundreds of times since discovering the hidden door when he was only seven years old. It was a useful shortcut, even when his door *wasn't* barred, the quickest and easiest way from the keep without being spotted.

This evening he would have to be cautious. He dashed down the stairs, and paused on the third step from the bottom, listening for footsteps. The hallway below apparently empty, he scurried on.

Thankfully, it was still quiet. No doubt the servants were still making preparations for tomorrow. He ducked through another door and out into the shadowy courtyard beyond, a wide space between the outer wall of the keep and the side of the kitchens.

This was a servant's space, and laundry hung on strings, slowly drying in the winter breeze. Soon, the linens would be collected by the laundress and her girls and placed beside the kitchen hearth. Penn wove his way between the sheets, hurrying as he heard voices approaching, then finally out through the door built into the outer wall.

This wasn't an entrance: simply a quick way for the laundress to dispose of spent water. He sidestepped the worst of the mud, glanced around to make sure no guards had spotted him, then dashed towards the forest.

He knew what he was feeling was borne of panic, the shock of being caged. All he needed was time.

He remembered Leo, and the expression on his brother's face the last time Penn had seen him. He wished, desperately, that he was with him. Leo would have known what to do. His advice would have been the sort that Penn wanted to hear, not Jo's platitudes or Ros's assertions that *everything would be fine.*

But he had neither time nor his brother. He had the fistful of hours before dawn, and the impenetrable dark of Hartswood Forest. It would have to be enough. Tomorrow he'd wake to a new day, and a new life.

Penn tugged his cloak tight, set his shoulders, and slipped between the trees.

Chapter Two

The silence of the forest only served to louden the echoes of the argument that still rang in Raff's head. Fresh, cool air filled his lungs but did little more than fuel the anger swirling in his belly as he marched ever deeper into Hartswood, looking for relief from his own thoughts.

It had been a low insult, even for Ash.

Raff knew that he needed to be reasonable, be mindful of his brother's tempestuous nature. Ash had spoken more through anger than the belief he was right; an attempt to wound him. His ire was to be expected.

But Raff was finished with being reasonable. He'd been reasonable since Lily was born, since Ash rode off to war, and even more so since his return and refusal to resume his duties. Ash had brushed against the truth without meaning to: Raff *did* want his freedom, from all of it, even though that thought pained him. It made him feel like a traitor.

He cursed into the silent forest, his own voice but a soft echo.

His chest burned. But beneath that was the promise of relief. Within the day, Lily would be married, and the heaviest of the burdens upon his shoulders lifted. He would be free at last to leave Dunlyn Castle, if that was what he chose.

It would be an unusual decision: there were expectations of him, even as the youngest son, and he would be dashing them all. There had been talk that Raff's eventual fate would mirror Lily's – a marriage bartered for profit – but when Ash returned from war with a scar on his face and his cynicism honed, all talk of matches had been dropped.

Regardless, it would not take long after Lily's marriage for lingering eyes to turn back to Raff. Soon he would find himself at the centre of the machinations of neighbouring lords with unwed daughters.

He tried to push weddings and family and duty from his mind. He'd come to the woods to escape his turbulent thoughts, not to dwell on them. Raff would have time to tie himself in knots tomorrow during long hours of ceremonies and feasting and – he realised with sudden horror – getting to know his newly acquired family.

He'd forgotten it wasn't just *Lily* marrying into the de Foucart family. It was all of them. He'd only heard unfavourable things about the Earl but knew little of the rest. There was an air of mystery that hung over the whole household, and while he was keen to clear it for Lily's sake, he didn't want to find himself swept up in it either.

No doubt he'd be pressed beside a stranger, and that would be his evening: talking. He dreaded it. He hoped that Lily's betrothed really *was* tolerable, if only so the conversation would flow more easily between them.

As her brother, it would be expected of him to treat her new husband with suspicion at best and hostility at worst. Ash was better suited for that role; no doubt he would relish the chance to frighten the young nobleman. Hopefully Raff could instead find an elderly relative to tell him about some fifty-year-past battle and could drink through the story while not really listening at all.

He was allowing himself to *think* again. Lost in introspection, he'd already wandered into the deeper part of the forest, the trees around him taller and thicker, the ground darker. Another man might panic, fearing himself lost. Raff took a moment to peer around, gauging his location, before heading south-west towards the setting sun that he could still see through the spaces between the leaves.

He breathed deeply through his nose, focusing on the smell of the trees. Even in winter it smelled alive: the fresh tang of pine needles, the scent of the leaves underfoot and the soft, damp dirt beneath those. It made *him* feel alive. Like those leaves were filling his lungs, like his blood was turning to sap.

Raff pressed a hand against the trunk of a tree, stepping over a deep-looking puddle, and paused to feel the bark beneath his palm.

Deeper in the forest, he could hear a fox calling, a faraway reply coming from somewhere even further beyond. There was no silence here, not really: the absolution of solitude without ever being truly alone.

He walked for half an hour, keeping south-west, even after the sun was no longer visible through the trees.

And then—

The air felt closer. The breeze, once rich with the smell of the forest, was tinged with something else. Something like iron. Something like blood.

He ducked around a tree, his foot connecting with an old branch that gave way beneath his boot with a horrible crunch, and there was a brief, strangled cry from somewhere ahead.

He froze instinctively but knew immediately that it wasn't the sound of another human. He moved quicker, throwing himself forwards. *There.* Half-suspended above the leaves was a struggling doe, her leg caught in a snare.

Raff swore. His anger had somewhere to go at last.

He crept closer, keen not to startle the deer. Her back leg, caught in the tight rope, was clearly broken: he could see white splinters of bone jutting from the fawny fur.

He spat at the ground. This was *wrong*. The deer must have been there hours, judging by the state of her leg and the sheen of sweat across her neck. Raff knew there were men desperate enough to break poaching laws and trap animals on their lord's land, but such carelessness was not the sign of someone trying to feed their family. It stank of fur trappers, or someone with a grudge against the Earl.

He pulled out his dagger to cut her down.

There was a snap behind him. Raff stilled, his hands hovering over the rope. It was likely just an animal sniffing about in the woods, but if the poachers had returned, he could find himself outnumbered. Clutching his knife tighter, he prepared to step back into the shadows.

There was another rustle, followed by further cracks. The sounds were too heavy for an animal, but it wasn't the footfalls of several men. It could be a single poacher hoping to provide for his loved ones, only interested in the next hot meal. A person like that might be content to leave Raff alone, if Raff granted him the same courtesy.

Still he kept his eyes trained to where the noises were loudest. A twig snapped beyond the next tree, and then a figure emerged.

It was a man. He met Raff's gaze, and froze.

This was no poacher.

He was slender, with sharp features and wide eyes, his curly brown hair a shaggy mess crowning his head, worried by wind and hand. He was dressed oddly for one exploring a forest, his clothes of high quality but certainly not the finery worn by a nobleman.

Raff met the stranger's eyes, and in the low light they looked almost entirely black. There was a clench in Raff's chest – something close to fear. He swallowed. This man wasn't a threat, of that much Raff was certain. Beyond that, he couldn't say.

He sheathed his dagger and raised his hands in surrender, indicating that he, too, wasn't hostile.

Raff was expecting the intruder to sensibly retreat, to grant him a curt nod of recognition and move on. But he didn't. He stepped closer, emerging from the safety of the trees.

'Ah—' the man said, which by way of an introduction was very poor. 'I did not—' His eyes landed on the deer, widening. He stumbled backwards.

Clearly he thought that this was Raff's doing. His expensive dress meant he likely worked for some lord: if not one of the many who had arrived for the wedding, then for de Foucart himself. Raff had no desire to end up with a noose around his neck for a crime he hadn't committed, and he couldn't trust this man not to sprint back to his master and tell all.

'Wait!' To his surprise, the man actually stopped. 'I was going to free her.'

Confusion marred the stranger's features. He glanced back at the deer. Perhaps Raff had misjudged: perhaps he was simply running from what he'd seen.

'What . . .?' He took a slow step forward.

'A snare.' Raff gestured to her leg, hoping he could trust the stranger's judgement.

'A snare? But this is my—' the man stuttered, before continuing, 'this is the King's land. There's a law against poaching.'

Raff snorted. 'Rightfully too. This is needless.'

'Needless?'

'An arrow through the chest would have been quicker. This way, she either dies slowly, or something comes along and finishes her off.' He shook his head. 'It's cruel.'

'What do we do?'

That was a surprise. He didn't even know this man's name. 'We?'

'Yes, *we*. You said this is cruel. You don't expect me to leave her here like this, do you?'

Raff shrugged. 'I rarely expect anything from anyone. You're willing to help?'

The stranger set his shoulders. 'Of course.'

Raff hesitated. He couldn't free the deer alone.

'. . . Thank you. I can cut her down, but I'll need your help. If you take some of her weight . . .'

The man stepped forwards as Raff pulled out his knife. He didn't appear to be particularly strong: no doubt he was a household servant, not a soldier or a hunter. But he took a breath, set his stance and hoisted up the deer as best he could.

Raff tugged at the rope, giving it more slack. It was thick, and difficult to cut. He sawed at it with the knife, the deer shuddering beside him.

'Steady . . .' he muttered, more to the deer than the stranger, who said nothing. '*There—*'

The last thread snapped, and the deer dropped. Her weight was more than the stranger had been anticipating, and he stumbled down. The doe fell beside him, but where Raff was expecting her to bolt she simply lay panting. Her leg was a bloodied mess, the rope digging into the limb.

Raff looked down at the stranger. 'You can get up now.'

The man rose, brushing himself off. He stared at the deer.

'What do we . . .' He twisted the edge of his cloak between his fingers. 'What about her?'

'What *about* her?'

'Do you intend to kill her? Or to leave her, like this?'

'You told me this land belongs to the King. Killing her is a crime.'

'Surely she won't survive a wound like that?'

'She will not.'

'So it is fine to let her die, but not to kill her yourself?'

'It's the *law*.'

The stranger scowled. 'Give me your knife.'

Raff hesitated before responding. 'Why?'

'If you won't do it, then I will.'

Raff looked him up and down. He was tall – taller than himself, Raff realised, now they were standing so close – but skinny, and his soft hair and clear, unmarked skin made Raff surer that this man was a household servant, *not* an outdoorsman. He was probably a member of the chamberlain's staff, or even the chaplaincy.

'Have you killed a deer before? Or *any* animal?'

The man's frown deepened. 'I have,' he said, voice unwavering. 'I . . . only a few times, if you need the truth of it. But yes, I have.'

'And you're content with breaking the law? If de Foucart's men catch you, they could kill you.'

There was a steely glint in the man's eyes. Raff felt the sudden urge to step back.

'Are you going to give me your knife or not?' he asked.

Raff handed the dagger over. It was an old, practical thing, broken and re-made dozens of times over. It had been his father's knife, once, and his grandfather's before him, the blade honed by three generations of Barden hands. It wasn't a small weapon, and in the stranger's grip it looked unwieldy and wrong: entirely out of place.

He held it heavily for a moment, as if weighing it up – weighing up what he was about to do – then took a sure step forwards, kneeling by the doe's side. He placed a gentle hand to her neck, took a deep breath—

And stopped. Raff could see a tremor in the hand that held his dagger. The stranger's fingers were wrapped too tightly around the hilt, his knuckles pale even in the dark.

Raff got to his knees beside him. He gently took the blade from his hands. The stranger didn't resist.

'Put your hands here, and here,' he said, gesturing with the tip of the blade to the doe's neck and head.

The stranger complied, pressing his palms to the doe's skin. Raff whispered a brief prayer, then flicked the knife.

Blood stained the stranger's hands like ink. But he didn't flinch as Raff had expected him to, staying steadfastly in place until Raff indicated he could let go.

The man pulled back, and worried his bottom lip between his teeth before he spoke again.

'It's Penn,' he said, quietly.

It took Raff a moment to realise he was giving his name. He wiped the blade on the grass, slid it back into the sheath, and turned to face him.

'Raff.'

Chapter Three

There was blood on Penn's hands. Self-consciously, he rubbed them against his cloak, although the stains were already dry. It would take more than itchy wool to remove them.

He hadn't lied: he *had* killed an animal before. But his hunting skills, such that they were, lay predominantly by bird. It was rare that he would wield the knife himself.

After the doe had stopped moving, her blank eyes staring at nothing, he'd expected the stranger – Raff – to tell him to leave, or perhaps leave himself. But he hadn't. He'd risen, placed the knife back in the sheath on his hip, and thanked him.

Raff's voice was low and dark. He was northern, that much was immediately clear, but there was a Scottish twang to his accent that Penn found irresistibly intriguing. It was probably just the closeness of the trees, the canopy above and the horror of what he'd seen, but his voice reminded Penn of hidden secrets. Of shadows.

He'd expected Raff to demand to know what Penn was doing in the forest, but his presence wasn't questioned. He wasn't being endured, either; Penn was sure that if Raff wanted him gone, he would have felt no hesitation in telling him so.

There was the predicament of what to do with the deer. Both of them saw the waste in leaving her, but there was twofold danger in taking her: the risk of being caught and accused of poaching, and the risk of running into whoever had set the snare. Penn knew from a single look that Raff would be able to defend himself against an attacker, but neither of them had any desire to court needless violence.

They left the cooling body half buried in the leaves, and without speaking headed the same way into the forest, away from the evidence of the crime they'd been forced to commit.

Penn didn't know why he followed Raff through the forest, to attach himself to his side despite being a stranger to him. But when he had emerged accidentally into the little clearing and spotted the snared deer and the bearded man beside her, he'd thought he'd stumbled into a dream; a vision from one of the stories his mother used to tell him about the Norsemen and their strange gods. He'd been noticed instantly, of course, and had frozen, as caught as the deer with her broken leg.

Raff's face had been half-shadowed, his long hair spilling in dark waves across his shoulders. Penn had felt immediately like he was intruding, like he'd walked into something sacred and dangerous. It *was* dangerous: at first glance Raff had appeared to be a poacher, and Penn's father had drummed into him how cruel the lawless men who stole from his lands could be.

He'd intended to leave, but Raff had spoken, and that *voice*—

He couldn't.

He couldn't leave, and there now was blood on his hands and beneath his fingernails, and he was walking side by side through his father's woods with a man whose bloodstains matched his own.

'So,' Raff stepped over a fallen tree, 'who are you? Besides *Penn*.'

Penn was shocked at his bluntness. 'Just Penn will suffice.'

'An interesting name.'

'It's for the bird,' Penn said, truthfully. 'The peregrine. But as I said: Penn will suffice.'

Raff hummed. 'I would like to know the man who could throw me to the King's law, if he saw fit.'

Penn snorted. 'As could you, if *you* saw fit. I aided you in killing her. We are both guilty.'

'I wielded the knife. I am the one who would face the more severe punishment.'

'Forgive me for not trusting a stranger not to lie to the Earl to save himself,' Penn responded. 'You could tell him it was *I* who struck the killing blow.'

'It would be your word against mine.' Raff paused, and turned to meet Penn's eyes, expression sombre. 'I wonder which holds more weight.'

There was a tension in the air. Penn shrugged his shoulders, as if attempting to heave it off.

'I suspect they'd be equal,' he said, wryly, 'if only in the sense that de Foucart would choose not to listen to either of us.'

Raff granted him a small smile, and Penn felt a little bubble of relief in his chest. They walked a few more yards before Raff spoke again, his words measured.

'You're with the de Foucart family?'

Penn took a moment to control his voice. 'I am,' he said cautiously.

'What—' Raff stammered as if suddenly self-conscious, 'what are they like?'

'The family?' Penn frowned.

'No,' Raff kicked aside a hunk of rotten wood, 'their hounds.'

It would have been funny, if it was not for the way he was glaring at the trees. Penn wasn't sure how to answer that without giving himself away. Raff noticed his hesitation.

'I find them difficult to keep track of,' Raff said, tone lighter. 'I am here for the wedding of de Foucart's son, yet I don't know the family whose hospitality I have taken advantage of.'

'Oh.' Penn tried not to trip over his own feet as he pondered the best direction to take their conversation. Raff was clearly a hunter, or a tracker; it was unlikely that his own lord would have given him more than the barest details. 'It's a fair question, I suppose.'

'I hear the Earl is . . .' Raff said, his tone careful, 'formidable.'

'That's one way to describe him.' It slipped out before Penn could still his tongue. Raff's gaze snapped to him. 'That is . . .' Penn shuffled, pinned under his steady stare, 'he is . . . strict.'

'Strict?'

'Perhaps needlessly so.'

'With servants?'

'With *everyone*.'

'What about William?'

Despite the wool of his cloak, there was ice in Penn's lungs.

'What about him?'

'Is he . . . strict?'

'No.' It was a quiet, simple statement; but it felt like a confession. If Raff had noticed Penn's stiffness, he didn't show it.

'No? Then what *is* he like?'

The ice cracked.

'William is . . .' What *was* he? Really? He swallowed, and the ice split, and the truth came spilling from his mouth in a torrent. 'William is different. He's unlike his father. As unlike his father as one can be.' He punctuated that with a harsh laugh, which made him wince. 'He is unsuitable for the Earldom. I think both he and his father fear him inheriting it.'

Raff was staring at him, but he couldn't dam the words again.

'He is not keen to wed. He disappoints de Foucart, but with the elder brothers gone—' there was a lump in his throat like a stone, but he forced himself to continue, 'he's no choice but to tolerate him.'

'Hence why he's being married before his sister.'

It was half the truth. The better half. The rest of it was too risky.

'That is what we suspect, yes. Besides, de Foucart needs this union. He has had the title for so long, but—' Penn clamped his mouth shut. He was speaking too freely.

'But?' Raff's eyebrows rose.

'But . . .' Penn glanced away. 'He is still not yet established. He needs to join himself to a family with ancestry.'

'So he intends to use his son to bargain for power.'

The simple statement didn't need a response. Besides: Penn had said far too much already. It was a while before Raff spoke again.

'What happened to the elder brothers?'

'You aren't aware? But you know of de Foucart's daughters?'

'I know of one of his daughters. There are more?'

'Two elder than William – Rosalind and Johanna – and one younger – Ingrid – by his second wife. He's another son with her,' Penn added, shortly, 'Ellis.'

'And the elder brothers?'

Penn couldn't avoid it, then. He stared at the ground, willing his voice not to shake.

'Henry,' he said slowly, 'and Leo. Henry died squiring for a neighbouring lord. They were hunting. He was injured, and the wound turned.'

'And Leo?'

'Gone.'

'Dead?'

'I cannot say. He was removed from the household some time ago.'

'Removed?'

'There was . . .' *Leo's face. His pleading eyes. His father's dismissal, cruel and perfunctory.* 'A servant,' Penn managed. 'De Foucart was displeased. That was several years ago.'

'One son dead, one son *removed*—' he repeated Penn's own word back to him, but it didn't sound like mockery, 'and William merely tolerated.' Raff finished with a low chuckle.

'What?' Penn snapped. Raff schooled his expression into one more serious.

'You reminded me of a thought I had during our journey, nothing more,' he said. 'I am sorry for the family's losses. Two sons and a mother . . . it is a tragedy.'

Penn's hand stilled on the tree he'd been using to balance his way across the uneven ground. He hadn't mentioned his mother's loss, not in so many words. No one spoke of the Countess Eleanor de Foucart anymore. Not, at least, where they could be overheard.

'Yes,' he said quietly. 'It is.'

'What about *you*?'

'What about me?'

'Do you find the son – William – merely tolerable? If he is so unlike his father?'

'Me?'

Raff shrugged, but there was tension in his shoulders. 'As a servant I'm sure you're close enough to cast judgement. I won't spill your secrets.' He nodded towards Penn's bloody hands. 'Not when you could ruin me, if you chose to.'

'I certainly tolerate him well enough.'

'Only well?'

Penn felt like he was playing some kind of one-sided game; one to which he didn't know the rules.

'As I said, he is unlike his father. Utterly. That is all one needs to know, if one wishes to judge his character.'

'Is that—'

'Although de Foucart is correct on some accounts. He is lazy. He is foolish to the point of distraction. He is *far* too free with his words. He is unfit for court or war or even a monastery.' Penn ran a hand through his hair with another short laugh. 'It would have been better were he born a peasant, or a merchant's son. He wouldn't have been tied to the title or the keep, and de Foucart would have been gifted a more suitable heir.'

'Is that an unfair judgement?'

Penn looked away. 'Unfair or not, it is accurate.' He sighed, then continued before Raff could press further. 'Enough of de Foucart. If I wished to talk about my Lord, do you not think I would have returned to the keep, instead of wandering about the forest with a stranger?'

Raff had the grace to look guilty. 'Forgive me. I've asked too many questions.'

Penn dismissed him. 'You have, but I *will* forgive you, if only for the interesting company I've found in you. I had been looking for . . .' He trailed off. What *had* he been looking for?

'Respite within the forest?'

'Exactly. And what I found was a tracker with a snared deer looking like he might kill me for standing too close.'

Raff laughed. 'Do I still look as if I might kill you for standing to close?'

Penn stepped around a bush, deliberately aiming wide, and shoved into him with his shoulder.

'No.'

Raff treated him to another one of those small smiles, and Penn felt something flutter between his lungs. This was utterly foolish, he knew, and dangerous besides. This manner of attention was what had found him so suddenly betrothed. If he was caught again, his father could find a more permanent solution. It would be no hardship to him, Penn knew, especially with Ellis ready to step into the title: his father's third chance at a suitable heir after the blow that was Henry's death.

In any case, the chances of Raff being similarly inclined were so slim that he surely thought the gesture was camaraderie; good-faith teasing, the sort that Penn saw between his father's soldiers.

The blood under his fingernails itched. If Raff *did* work him out – like he'd already teased so much from him – perhaps he would be hesitant to condemn the man who could throw him to the King's wrath too.

Raff hadn't even appeared to have noticed the friendly gesture. He certainly hadn't baulked at the touch. Penn's shoulder burned beneath his cloak and tunic, and he tried not to think about it as they continued deeper into the woods. After a while, Raff asked Penn where he'd been intending to go, and at Penn's vague dismissal had laughed again.

'What about you?' Penn demanded. 'Are you not similarly lost?'

'Lost?' Raff leaned against a tree. 'I am not lost. I'm following the sunset.'

The sun had set hours ago, plunging them both into an eerie, moon-speckled darkness.

'Not lost, but mad, then.'

Another smile. Another flash of teeth. 'Something like that.'

As they walked, they spoke. Raff had taken Penn's words to heart, and dropped the subject of the de Foucart family, but within the pauses of his words Penn could see him thinking. He felt like he was being examined, plucked and pulled apart. Unbidden, he thought of the kite he'd seen earlier that same day.

Raff spoke of his own family, and Penn learned that he had a brother and a sister. He spoke of his sister fondly and his brother in clipped curses, but there was no malice behind the insults, just exhaustion. He told him that his mother was Scottish, by way of explaining his strange amalgamated accent; not quite Scot, but not quite northern either. He was vague about his role in his lord's retinue, and Penn knew better than to force him to speak. After all, he'd lied himself. He could not expect better from a man he didn't know.

Penn broached the subject of the deer. 'You were furious,' he said. 'Why?'

Raff had stopped, examining the dark red berries adorning a holly bush with an interested eye.

'She did not deserve to die at my blade,' he said. 'And now she will be wasted. To hunt, and eat, and use the skins . . . there is nobility in that. To catch an animal and leave it to rot in the woods . . .' He shook his head. 'It is cowardly.'

'The poachers may yet return. They may have *already* returned.'

'Maybe they have, God curse them all. It is a cruel death, and sad. She would have died whether trapped or released.'

'You seem to care very much about the laws of the kingswood,' Penn suggested. 'The King's land?'

'Hah!' The sound was quick and sharp, sending something small and skittering running for cover in the brush ahead of them. 'The divine right of kings, is it?'

Penn nodded.

'The land deserves more respect. I would wager that the King has not set foot in this forest since his coronation.'

Penn had to concede that he was correct, but did not voice the admission out loud.

'But tell me,' continued Raff, 'what about you? I find you out here, alone and unarmed, and forgive me: unprepared for hunt or track. Why?'

'Why?'

'Why explore the forest alone, when no doubt the keep is warmer and safer?'

'I needed a moment's thought. And out here . . .' Penn mused, 'it's never *silent*, not really. But it is a different kind of noise to the one you find behind stone walls. I would rather listen to foxes screech and birds sing than the cook clattering about, or the soldiers training, or de Foucart ordering his men to do his bidding.'

Another smile, as if he'd said something poetic. 'You speak well.'

Penn shrugged. 'I can only say what I know.'

Raff peered around the woods surrounding them: the high trees, the moonlight scattered roughly across the bark.

'It *is* different,' he agreed. 'I fare better in the wilds, as my brother so often reminds me.'

He sighed, his shoulders stiffening.

'Come,' Raff said. 'We've walked far enough. If we don't go back now, neither of us will return in time for tomorrow's festivities.'

He turned on his heel, retracing their steps and marching back the way they'd come. Penn could only follow helplessly after him.

'How do you know the way?'

'I told you,' Raff said, 'I am following the sunset.'

Penn could hear the sweet, trilling sound of early birds, the dawn chorus fluttering to life. The canopy above was thick, but through the sparse spaces between the leaves the once-black sky was a deeper shade of blue, signalling the encroaching dawn.

A new day was beginning to split the sky. The beginning of the end. They'd been walking for hours, and Penn had barely noticed. Penn could not recall the last time he'd been in company he didn't find strained. Moments alone with Jo were becoming shorter and further apart, especially after the engagement was announced. He was increasingly aware of a gap between them – one he suspected was hewn by their father.

But there was no such gap with Raff, despite their obvious differences. Nor did Raff treat him with the same nervous detachment that everyone else did: those who did not wish to incur the wrath of Penn's father by speaking too freely or out of turn. By Raff's side, he could be *Penn* for one long night, rather than *William*.

He was still waiting for Raff to tire of him, or to berate him for being incompetent. Yet it never came. If anything, he allowed Penn's inexperience with good-natured amusement.

His attention did nothing to dampen the heat in Penn's belly, or the tightness in his chest. It stirred up those feelings until he was beginning to doubt his assumption that Raff's inclinations were unlike his own. When they approached a fallen tree, Raff heaved himself onto the enormous, broken giant like it was nothing at all. Sensing Penn's hesitation, he reached down, and after pulling him up beside him held onto his hand for a fraction longer than necessary before twitching away, as if remembering himself.

Penn's skin tingled in a way that was entirely unrelated to the blood itching between his fingers. It was intoxicating, addictive. So he pushed. An extended hand over uneven ground, a step too close, the brush of shoulders. Nothing that would damn him. Raff didn't extend the same tentative touches – it would have been odd for someone so familiar with the wilds to require assistance from a household servant, after all – but he didn't brush them away, either.

Raff could have moved away if he wished to. It would take a single step to put enough distance between them that he was no longer subject to Penn's attentions. He could have refused to offer help when, for the fourth time, Penn extended a hand as he stepped around a murky-looking half-frozen puddle.

But Raff didn't. He took Penn's hand, guiding him, and let the touch linger too long as dawn broke above them.

Soon Penn would need to return to the keep, creeping back into his own home like a criminal. He'd snake up the empty staircase, emerge from behind the tapestry and fall into a bed that had never felt like his.

And Raff would remain. Raff would stay in the woods, sharpening his knife, learning the land. He'd return to his lord's retinue with the rest of the servants. No doubt he'd be given some mead and meat to celebrate the noble marriage so far removed from his own life, and then they'd be off again to whichever northern kingdom he hailed from.

He wasn't free, not really. No man was truly free, not when there were mouths to feed and families to keep and burdens to carry, both big and small. But when night fell he'd be on his way home, the wind on his back. He wouldn't be trapped.

Another bird – a thrush, Penn thought – began to sing from somewhere high above.

It wasn't Raff that made him do it; not really. It wasn't his easy smile or his intense eyes or the broadness of his shoulders. It was what he had: a freedom that Penn was reaching for, but could never take for himself.

Perhaps he could take this. Just once, just tonight. Just *this morning*, really, with the sun already threatening to rise.

Penn turned, and collided with Raff's chest. He hadn't realised how close Raff was standing. He stared into a pair of deep blue eyes.

The air around them smelled of moss and rotting wood and blood.

He shouldn't. He could be caught. He could be *killed*.

Yet . . .

There was no space at all between them. He surged forward, powered by adrenaline and grief, and crashed their lips together.

There was a second where Raff didn't move, and Penn was doomed.

And then he was being pushed against a tree, the bark pressing into his back, his head knocking against the wood.

Penn had shared furtive kisses in hidden corridors before – he'd shared them in these very woods – but their quickness had come with uncertainty, the gentle touch of lips that may need to part at any moment, with little warning.

This was not like those. It was rough, and sure, and their lips moved like a fight. Raff's hands slid under the fabric of Penn's cloak, grasping at his tunic, the touch confident and desperate.

The rough tree scraped Penn's back, but he didn't move away. He pushed back against Raff's lips, opening his mouth beneath the yearning movement. He gasped into the kiss as Raff licked into his mouth, hot and wet, trailing the line of his bottom lip with his tongue.

He shouldn't. But he *wanted*, urgent and without direction. His hands made their way to Raff's sides, bunching in his tunic, slipping beneath—

There was a noise from behind; a rustle in the leaves, the sound of a heavy branch cracking. Raff stilled. He pulled back.

'We're not alone.'

It was barely even a whisper. Penn's insides curled. 'What?'

'Run.'

'What?'

'Run!'

By the time Penn made it back to the keep, there was no denying that dawn was breaking. He spoke a silent prayer of thanks as he found the door he'd escaped through still unlocked. This early, there was no one to catch him, and he made his way into his chambers unimpeded and fell backwards onto the bed.

There was still a fire smouldering in the hearth, but it did little to warm his prickling skin. There were twigs and leaves caught in his hair from his flight through the forest. He would need to comb them out, clean the mud from his face and the blood from his hands. He rose with a groan, and stood before the basin and mirror where he'd shaved that evening. His face was darkly shadowed. He scrubbed his skin with soap and water, removing the evidence of his flight.

When he was done he glanced at his own reflection once more. There was a glimmer of recognition, now: a light in his eyes that hadn't been there before.

He turned away from the mirror with a sigh. He'd have only a few hours to sleep before his room would be full of servants, readying him for the day ahead. He tugged off his boots and tossed them carelessly aside with his cloak. He struggled beneath the thick coverlet, still in his muddied clothes.

He closed his eyes. He did not sleep.

Penn could still feel Raff beneath his hands, taste him on his lips, still feel the scratch of his beard against his jaw and the press of him to his chest. He wondered if he was still out there. Raff had told him to run. Penn hoped he was safe from whatever he'd been running from. *Whoever*: that sound hadn't been a deer.

Penn rolled to his side, pulling the coverlet over his head, and tried not to dwell on it. Raff was armed, at least. Had Penn been caught by whoever had stumbled upon them, he'd be dead, or worse. It was sheer luck that Raff hadn't recognised him. There were hundreds of people with a grudge against Penn's father who'd have been keen to rid him of another son, or barter an absurd price for his freedom.

Freedom. He laughed into the pillow. This was not freedom. Perhaps he'd fare better with a poacher or a kidnapper than he would with a wife.

A breeze came through the window, bringing a winter chill into the room. He thought again of Raff. He wondered where his path would take him next, where his Lord would need him most.

He drifted in and out of uneasy sleep. The long walk over rough ground had made his legs ache, and the bed was soft, although his thoughts were rough. He wandered through hazy, uncertain dreams with the smell of grass in his nose and the warmth of the doe's neck beneath his hands.

Penn opened his eyes, and it was dark. A shadowed shape with sparkling eyes and near-black hair leaned over him, pressing him to the bed. A mouth, soft and hot and urgent, moved against his own.

He opened his eyes again. He was alone, and he had made a decision.

Chapter Four

Five men. Five men, moving through the forest with all the noise of a dozen. Raff pressed himself closer against a wide tree trunk, stilling himself as the poachers made their way past his hiding spot.

Thank God, they were heading west, the opposite direction to the way he'd pushed Penn. They didn't seem well organised, but they *were* well armed; even in the shadows he could see that.

Raff gritted his teeth as he watched. They chattered as they walked, presuming themselves alone. He waited until their voices had been entirely muffled by the rest of the forest before moving on.

The bark had left indentations in the backs of his hands. He flexed his fingers as he walked, following the direction that Penn had taken, keeping his steps swift but silent as he left the forest – and the poachers – behind.

An angry-looking bird soared through the violet sky as Raff emerged from the treeline and picked his way back towards camp. He'd been gone far longer than he'd intended, and he was hoping that Ash's sour mood may have at least lost some of its acidity. His older brother would never be fully placated – that wasn't in his nature – but perhaps he would learn to tolerate the perceived slight.

Some of the weight of his family and the impending wedding had lifted, and he walked with a lighter step as he headed through the camps towards the familiar colours of his father's flags. He'd only snatch a few hours of rest, but the burden of sleeplessness was one he was willing to tolerate for today, so long as he didn't fall asleep during Lily's vows.

His tent was silent and still, and he made his way to his pallet without disturbing his sleeping brother. He tugged off his boots and surcoat, burrowed beneath the blankets, and was asleep in moments, his mouth rich with the taste of someone else's tongue.

Raff awoke to the feeling of a boot to his back, a sensation he'd grown used to when travelling alongside Ash for such an extended period of time.

'Wake up,' his brother grumbled. 'He's gone.'

Raff rose, blinking in the sunlight that filtered through the thin walls of the tent.

'Who's gone?'

'William.'

Raff's head was heavy with too little sleep, a dull throb behind his temples. 'Ash, what are you—'

'He's gone, Raff! We just got word from the keep. Father and Lily are still there with de Foucart, trying to figure this out.'

Raff tried to swing from the pallet, but found his way was impeded by Ash throwing his boots at him. They hit him in the chest, winding him, but it was no use arguing. He tossed them aside, standing up.

'Ash—'

'I *said* it wasn't right. I *told* you. No one listened.' He threw his hands in the air. 'They'll think this a slight against Lily. No one will marry her now.'

Raff stretched his neck, trying to ease the pain in his shoulders. 'I thought you didn't wish to see her married?'

Ash spun around. His face was red. 'That's not the point. This is an *insult*. To us, to Lily, and Father.'

There was a jug of water on the table at the other side of the tent, and Raff pushed past Ash, reaching for it. He drank straight from the vessel, not bothering to dig through their things for a cup. The water was cold and crisp, dribbling down his face and into his beard.

'So,' he said, wiping his mouth with the back of his hand and placing the jug down with more force than he intended, 'what do we do?'

'We've been invited into the keep.'

'No doubt to stop Father or Lily calling off the match,' Raff muttered. 'Fine. But let me dress, at least. If this de Foucart is the man people say he is, I've no desire to show up to his home dressed in yesterday's clothes.'

Ash eyed him. 'You slept in your clothes?'

'What of it?'

He shrugged. 'Nothing. You were gone for some time.'

'It took *some time* to calm myself after your squawking.'

Ash gave him another of those looks, which Raff chose to ignore. 'My squawking proved correct, though.'

Raff started to pull off his tunic. 'Not yet.'

The keep was smaller than Dunlyn Castle, yet far grander. Wherever they walked there were staff underfoot. They ducked out their way with lowered gazes in perfect silence. Raff couldn't help but find his eyes lingering on those they passed by, looking for a crop of curly hair and a pair of dark brown eyes.

They were being shown to de Foucart's solar. His steward – an older man with white hair and a pinched face – led them through close corridors, scattering servants in his wake. He did not speak, save from bidding them good day when they first stepped through the wide gates and informing them that they would be speaking with the Earl and their father shortly.

He didn't ask for their names. He didn't tell them anything of their sister. Raff could see Ash's hand flexing at his side, and placed a warning grip below his shoulder. This was a time for diplomacy, not aggression.

They were shown into a huge high-ceilinged chamber, their father standing to one side. It was a relief to see him again, although he was visibly exhausted, a line between his brows.

In the centre of the solar, at a table piled with documents and neatly stacked reams of paper and parchment, sat a man who Raff immediately knew was Earl Marcus de Foucart.

He was roughly their father's age, but he looked younger. He was a broad, well-built man who clearly had experience with blade and battle. His square jaw was dusted with stubble and his hair was shorn short, only exacerbating his severe expression. He didn't look up when Raff and Ash entered. Silence hung over the room.

'So,' he said, adding a mark to the paper in front of him before finally looking at them, 'my son is missing.'

It sounded like an accusation.

'As I have heard,' said Raff, speaking before Ash could get a chance. 'We extend our sympathies to you, my Lor—'

'None of that.' De Foucart waved an impatient hand. 'I do not want your sympathies. I want my son returned.'

'Of course,' said Raff, willing himself to sound level. 'It must be worrying for the household.'

De Foucart gave him a withering sneer before turning back to the paper in front of him. 'I have men searching for him. He will be found.'

'As you say.'

'Given the circumstances, you will stay here until he is returned.' He put the pen down. 'Do you understand?'

'Completely, my Lord.'

'My Lord—'

Both brothers turned to their father. It was the first time he'd spoken since they had arrived.

'If I may, Raff is the best tracker in our household. He could be of use . . .'

De Foucart grimaced. 'My son is not *game*, Barden. I have enough of my men searching. His efforts will not be needed.'

'But—'

'If William does not return soon, then I may reconsider. You may leave.'

There was nothing else they could do. The three Barden men trudged from the chamber, the steward shutting the door behind them.

'That went well,' grumbled Ash, as soon as they found their way back to the chilly courtyard.

'De Foucart is keen for his son to come back,' said Lord Barden, diplomatically. 'He is worried.'

'Was that worry?' spat Ash. 'He was acting like his son's disappearance was an inconvenience.'

'That's because it *is* an inconvenience.' Their father sighed, rubbing his eyes. 'William was not in his bed this morning. There's no knowing what time he vanished. If it was during the night, he could be long gone by now. Forgive me for volunteering your services, Raff. I thought it would be good to make ourselves appear useful.'

'I don't even know what the man *looks* like. How you might expect me to find him, I do not know.'

'De Foucart certainly doesn't expect you to find him. But we can say that we offered.' He pinched the bridge of his nose. 'I must return to camp and inform the others of what is happening. I need you two to stay here.' He shot a warning look at Ash. 'We need our own people in the keep, lest de Foucart decides to call the wedding off entirely. I will not leave Cecily alone in this nest of adders.'

Before Raff could say anything else, their father gave them a curt nod and strode towards the gates.

'What a mess,' Ash groaned.

'Indeed. What should we—'

'Raff! Ash!'

They turned to see Lily running towards them, her skirts gathered in both hands. She'd been standing beside a severe young woman with dark hair in a plain net at the back of her head, who watched Lily with interest as she bolted across the yard.

'You're here,' she panted, looking relieved.

'We're here. How are you?'

'They've been keeping me distracted, I fear, so I don't ask too many difficult questions.' She glanced over her shoulder at the woman, who gave her a nod before walking back inside. 'What did they tell you?'

'Only that William has vanished,' said Raff.

'Your dear brother has volunteered to find him,' added Ash, with a smirk.

Lily squinted at Raff. 'Is that right?'

'I did not volunteer. Father offered my services to de Foucart.'

'And *will* you find him?' Her gaze was steely.

Raff looked at his feet. 'If de Foucart asks me to, then I must.'

'Raff—'

'My skills lie in tracking *animals*. How they expect me to find a man amongst the trees I truly do not know. But I will try. I will not have your reputation ruined like this.'

'You think I care—'

'I do *not*, Cecily, and that's the problem.' She fell silent, face drooping. 'I love you. I want you to be happy. But this will affect *you*, not him. I have reason to believe that de Foucart's son is not as bad a match as you believe him to be. If we can find him, your reputation will not be ruined, and you may find him more bearable than those willing to strike a match with a failed engagement behind you.'

'You're telling me to settle for unhappiness rather than misery?'

'I wish I could offer you more. You *deserve* more. But . . .'

'Why?'

They both turned to face Ash. 'Why what?' Raff asked.

'Why do you think the son is a suitable match? Yesterday you agreed that de Foucart is aiming to be rid of him. What's changed your mind?'

Raff looked between them; Lily confused, Ash accusatory. He could not lie to them.

'We need to speak,' he said. 'Privately. Lily, where might we talk?'

'There are private rooms beyond the main hall,' she said. 'But, Raff, what—'

'I shall explain when we're not being listened to,' he said. 'Show us the way.'

Raff's siblings didn't question his motivations for spending so long in the forest with a servant. He never gave them Penn's name, nor the late hour of his return, and they listened mostly in silence as he told them what he'd learned.

'You trust this stranger?' asked Ash, when he was done.

'I do. What would he gain by spreading disrepute about his lord?'

'And his lord's son,' mused Lily. 'It's odd that he told you so much.'

'And nothing at all,' cut in Ash. '*Not like his father*. He could have been more specific.'

'You *met* de Foucart,' said Raff. 'Before, I would have agreed with you. But now . . .' He looked at Lily. 'A man unlike the Earl can only be a good thing.'

'It's not much to go on,' Lily acknowledged. 'But it sheds more light, I think.' She sighed. 'It hardly matters, with William lost.'

'Could we find this servant?' Ash said. 'He must be in the keep *somewhere*. You said he seemed close to William, perhaps he—'

There was a rap at the door. The face of the dark-haired woman appeared.

'Johanna,' Lily said. The three of them stood as she came in. 'Has he returned?'

Johanna's face fell. 'Not yet,' she said. 'But Father asked me to find you. He didn't wish for you to be without a woman's company.'

All three of them winced. That was a clear insult; de Foucart was afraid that Ash and Raff would convince Lily to call off the match unless there was a mediator present.

'Oh,' said Lily, slowly. 'Do you wish to join us . . .?'

'I thought you could join *me*, actually,' Johanna said. 'I wondered if you wished to accompany me on a walk of the grounds?'

The siblings shared a look. It would not do to refuse a lady, certainly not the daughter of their host.

'Of course,' said Lily. 'I would love to.'

Johanna smiled – a genuine smile, Raff thought.

'Your brothers have leave of the keep,' she said. 'We've lit the fire in the great hall, and I'm sure they can find some way of entertaining themselves.'

That was less of a suggestion and more of an order. Raff stepped forwards, tugging Ash with him.

'Thank you,' he said. 'For you and your father's hospitality.'

Johanna gave him another smile, but this one didn't quite reach her eyes. 'You're welcome.'

By late afternoon, Raff had grown impatient. The Earl had sent out dozens of men to find his son, and all of them had returned empty-handed.

Raff knew better than most how easy it was to get lost in a forest. He and Ash mused on the possibility that William was merely suffering a case of nerves, and would return once calmed, but as the hours dragged on it seemed more and more unlikely.

'What are we going to do?' Raff said after winning his fourth game of dice against his increasingly irate brother.

Ash threw his own dice to the table. 'Go home?' he suggested. 'Take Lily and return north and never come back?'

It was a tempting prospect. Raff doubted William would return, and was keen to set off home without further delay. There was work to be done, mouths to be fed, land currently standing without a protector. It was unusual for the whole household to leave the ancestral home at once, and the idea of it standing empty worried him.

Part of him – a part that he was doing his best to silence – wanted to search de Foucart's keep for someone quite different. Penn was here, somewhere, working.

It would be best not to hunt him out, especially after lying to him. Knowing that he'd told such secrets to the brother of William's betrothed would no doubt panic him. Besides, he was a servant. In the forest, they'd been equals, but within these walls Raff was painfully aware of the power he held over him.

Raff set his jaw. All he could do was wait. He tried to push yesterday's diversions from his mind, and goaded Ash into another game of dice.

By the time night fell, Raff was looking forward to returning to their camp, despite the freezing weather. Unfortunately, de Foucart had different ideas. Raff and Ash found themselves sleeping in the great hall on thin pallets, warmed by the roaring fire.

Lord Barden had returned just before their evening meal – a simple affair, considering the lush feast that should have been taking its place – and they ate in near silence. Lily was staying in the room adjacent to Johanna's that she'd been given the previous night, and it soon became clear that this was William's elder sister. Raff had been keen to press Lily for more information on the lady, but there were no opportunities to speak privately, and they were forced to retire early.

Despite the anxiety in Raff's stomach and the uncertainty of what would face them tomorrow, when he lowered himself onto his pallet he was struck with exhaustion. He'd barely slept for more than a few hours the previous night, leaving his limbs – and his mind – slow and leaden. He drifted asleep partway through one of Ash's particularly virulent complaints, the words burying him, blanket-thick.

Dawn came all too soon, failing to bring news with it. The keep had descended into a stony silence, the wedding preparations finally brought to a halt, the Earl locked in his solar like a sullen king. The other guests had been informed, and before the sun had reached halfway across the sky many were already leaving, returning to their own responsibilities.

There had been an argument to which Raff had not been privy, but had been held at such volume that he – and the rest of the castle

– knew it in intimate detail regardless. Lily and the retinue would be returning north with Ash as chaperone. Lord Barden would stay in her stead and return home as soon as William was discovered or the search called off.

And Raff was now pulling the final few things onto his back ready to spend two days traipsing through Hartswood Forest in search of the lost lordling.

He suspected the hunt would be futile. The previous night had been bitterly cold, and one of the first true winter frosts had settled on the ground as they slept. Even a man used to travel and sleeping hard would have struggled.

De Foucart had informed him that William's rooms had been searched, and he'd only taken a handful of things. He was travelling light, clearly, or he'd simply packed and absconded in a panic. He did not seem well prepared.

Knowing that William was unprepared hadn't been much to go on, especially considering that Raff had never met the man. When pressed, the Earl had granted him a curt portrayal of his son: surly, perhaps even boorish, completely senseless, and selfish besides.

It wasn't until after Raff had been dismissed that he realised the Earl had failed to give him a physical description. Yet his words had painted a clear enough image in his mind, and he could distinctly picture the sort of person he was searching for. He wondered whose description had been more accurate: De Foucart's, or Penn's.

Raff couldn't delay any longer. He adjusted his bag once more and set his eyes on the edge of the forest, somehow looking far less welcoming than the last time he'd walked through the treeline.

Two days of searching, maybe three, and then he could follow his siblings. Perhaps not: perhaps he really *would* only search for two days, then drag out the journey home, allowing himself the freedom he longed for if only for a few weeks. It would be an easy lie, once he returned.

'Raff—'

There was a grip around his hand that broke him from his treacherous thoughts. He turned to see Lily, her eyes wide beneath the shadow of her hood.

'Can we talk?'

Raff nodded just once and allowed her to lead him closer towards the trees.

'You'll find him, then?' Her eyes were wide, expression steady.

'I cannot say.'

'But de Foucart has asked.'

'He has, unwillingly. But I don't even know if he's there to be found. He could have—'

Lily's grasp tightened and she tugged him around to face her, his feet skidding against the damp grass. Her eyes were blazing. 'I am not de Foucart. Nor am I our father. Do not patronise me like you're some diplomat, Raff, it doesn't suit you. De Foucart asked you to find his son. I am . . .' she hesitated, her voice faltering for only a moment even though her eyes remained locked on his, intense, 'I am asking you *not to*.'

The dangerous words hung between them. Raff pulled his gaze and his arm away, peering over her shoulder to ensure they weren't being overheard.

'Lily . . .'

'Raff.' She stuck her chin in the air. She looked like she had when she was a tiny child, when she was a petulant, stubborn youth.

He didn't speak. He took Lily's hand, rubbing his glove-clad fingers across her knuckles. He pressed a quick kiss to her cheek, then turned his back and strode into the forest.

Chapter Five

'God's *teeth!*'

The treetops above him shook with startled birds, and Penn gripped the useless flint so hard his fingers shook.

His attempts at building a fire had been rather lacking. He didn't want to count how many times he'd tried and failed to keep himself warm. That first evening in the forest he'd lost his temper, kicked away the pile of dry twigs and hurled the flint through the trees. It had taken him an age to find it again, half buried beneath fallen foliage.

He'd felt stupid, which had only served to make him angrier. He was hungry, too, having realised that he lacked the creeping footsteps needed to hunt and instead settling for a handful of mushrooms he'd found beneath a twiggy shrub just before dusk. They had tasted like dirt, with an unpleasant chewy texture, but they'd filled him enough to stave off the pains of hunger.

He had been so weighed down with exhaustion that he'd simply burrowed into the leaf litter beneath the gnarled roots of an enormous tree and had attempted to sleep, with only the moss growing from the wood and his cloak – which he had learned wasn't suited for such weather – to keep him warm.

He had woken with the dawn and moved deeper into the forest, intending to hide in the trees for as long as possible. If he could make it to the furthest edge of Hartswood without being found, he would stand a better chance of escaping.

This assumed that anyone was looking for him. He had no way of knowing if his father had sent out search parties or simply accepted that he'd gone, sending Ros, the visiting lords and his unfortunate betrothed back home.

It didn't matter. Penn was *out,* he was free, and—

He was hopelessly lost, and starving after spending a second day walking through the dense trees. He glared at the meagre bundle of twigs he'd managed to gather, half hoping they would simply burst into flames beneath his stare, when there was a *crack* from a few yards away.

Penn scrambled to his feet, his hand going to the dagger on his hip that he'd dug out from the very bottom of one of his chests.

'Stay—' His voice quivered, and he felt like a child. 'Stay back, whoever you are! I'll kill you!'

The dagger – a long, slender thing with an intricately carved hilt – shook in his hand.

'Penn?'

He knew that voice. A shadow detached itself from the trees, stepping forwards.

It was Raff, hands raised in surrender.

Penn went rigid, his fingers tightening around the hilt of the dagger, not dropping his arm. Had Raff somehow found out who he really was? Had he ripped a description of him from his father and set out to find him? Perhaps he was furious that he'd been deceived. Perhaps he simply didn't care, and was only here to drag him back.

'What are you doing here?' Penn demanded.

Raff didn't lower his arms, although his expression was amused;

clearly he didn't find Penn's threat particularly concerning. 'Looking for the Earl's son,' he said. 'What are *you* doing out here?'

So they *were* hunting for him. But Raff was looking for William, not Penn. Penn's lungs deflated, his knees shaking where they were locked so stiffly. He slid the dagger back into the sheath on his hip and gave his bundle of sticks a bitter kick.

'Attempting to start a fire,' he huffed. 'With little success, as you can see.'

'But . . . why?'

'So I don't freeze my bollocks off?'

'I mean, why are you out here? Are you searching for William too?'

Penn settled back down on his knees and started to rebuild the would-be fire.

'Something like that,' he muttered.

Raff apparently took it as an invitation to talk, and sat down heavily beside him. He reached across, taking the flint, and despite the unimpressive bundle of tinder he quickly had the fire burning. The yellow light cast weird shadows over his face.

'Your lord tasked you with finding William, then?' Penn asked, throwing out the dangerous question before Raff could interrogate him further.

'I was sent by de Foucart himself, for what good it will do.'

'You don't think you'll find him?'

'I am hardly the best suited for it. How should I find a stranger in lands I do not know? It's a futile task.' He paused. 'I suspect de Foucart knew that. Besides, it's been two days. Were William intending to return or be found, he'd have done so by now.' Raff poked at the fire. 'I would not be surprised to learn that he was dead.'

Penn stilled. There was a faint, low ringing in his ears. 'You think he's dead?'

Raff shrugged. 'De Foucart claims very few of his possessions were taken. He sounded ill-prepared. Perhaps he fled, unaware of what he was running into. No one has seen him since, and if they have, I've not heard word of it.'

'Oh.' There was an echoing emptiness between his ribs.

'Penn . . .'

He glanced at Raff warily, who looked as if he was struggling to find the right words.

'The Earl's son. William. You said you were looking for him. Did you . . .' A long, pregnant pause. 'Did you know him?'

Penn took a moment to think before responding. It was a foolish question: he'd told Raff more than enough about William – about himself – the other night. It was obvious, even to a stranger, that he'd known the Earl's son. But there was something else hidden behind those words. *Did you know him?*

Then it struck him. Raff had taken his strange familiarity with the man who was supposed to be his master, along with his sullen mood, long silences, and escape into the forest, and had reached a conclusion about the imagined relationship between the two of them; between master and servant.

'I did know him,' he said, voice hollow. He was quite sure it was the truth.

There was a vast space between them suddenly, despite how close they were sitting beside the tiny fire.

'Are you giving up?' Penn asked, finally. 'If William is dead, will you stop searching?'

'I suppose I must. I cannot spend the rest of my life in Hartswood, looking for a corpse.'

Penn pictured his own face, lifeless amongst the leaves. The visceral image made him shudder. Raff didn't miss the unconscious movement, eyebrows twisting into something like sympathy.

'I'm sorry,' he said. 'For speaking so harshly. And for . . .'

He didn't finish that sentence, leaving the implication unspoken.

'Thank you.' It was all Penn could say – gratitude for an apology not meant for him.

His words hung between them, saying more than either of them could plainly. Eventually, Raff spoke again.

'Come,' he said, 'we need more firewood. This is *pitiful*.'

With the added weight of his pack on his back and the conflicting requests from both de Foucart and Lily on his mind, Raff had found his going more difficult as he made his way through Hartswood Forest for the second time.

De Foucart had demanded he join the search because he had no other choice, despite how little he clearly thought of his son. To refuse Lord Barden's offer would have betrayed him as the vain, self-important man Raff knew him to be. Lily had asked him not to because she was desperate. She'd asked him not to for the same reason Raff had first entered the forest: because she longed for something more, if only for a short while.

He cursed himself. He cursed de Foucart, and his blasted son. He would struggle to refuse his sister, even if the dissolution of her betrothal would force him to return to the role he wanted to leave behind.

In any case, he was sure that he would not find William regardless. De Foucart's men knew the lay of the land and the habits of the son better than Raff ever could. If they hadn't found him, then it was unlikely he would ever *be* found.

It was selfish, the urge that made him press deeper into the woods. It was a fine excuse to snatch more time alone, to linger for as long as he needed till his lungs were clear and his burdens lifted. He could claim a sudden burst of altruism, lie to his siblings upon his return and tell them he'd decided to add his eyes to the search for a full week before giving up.

The easy way with which he'd decided to lie to his family turned his gut. He didn't enjoy lying – he wasn't even *good* at lying – and he'd not lied to his siblings since he was a boy stealing sweets and blaming it on his father's hounds. It made him feel false.

Raff had ploughed onwards through the trees, following winding paths left behind by deer or hunting parties. Several times he paused, concentrated, then followed the sound of a chirruping bird or the crack of a twig, just to see what he could find.

What he found was Penn, pointing a dagger at him in a shaking hand. A lost servant, alone in the woods, searching for someone that Raff suspected to be dead. He was half-starved, nearly frozen and completely morose.

Raff acted without thinking. He lit the fire, fuelling it with something more substantial than the twigs Penn had found. He even snared them a pheasant, the King's laws be damned.

Penn ate little, but quickly, and in the flickering light of the fire Raff could see dark, wide circles beneath his eyes and dirt muddying his face and hair. He looked nothing like the man he'd first met.

He looked lost. Before, he'd been unafraid even when coming across a potentially dangerous man. Now he was curled in upon himself, shoulders hunched. There was an expression in Penn's eyes that Raff recognised, but couldn't understand. It was similar to the hollow mask his father's face had become in the weeks after Lily was born; after Raff's mother had died.

Raff suspected why. Penn had been wary when describing the older de Foucart brother's disownment. Could it be that he'd come across another servant who'd entangled themselves with one of the Earl's sons? He'd spoken about William with an exasperated fondness that didn't match the clipped words de Foucart had used to describe him. Did that fondness go beyond the typical care of a servant unused to being treated well? Had Raff somehow managed to meet the person to whom Lily's betrothed's heart truly belonged, and more than that, had he *kissed* him? It was farcical.

Raff's life was one marked by constant work. He didn't dwell on things like *love* beyond what he felt for his father and siblings, and the memory of his mother. There'd been a handful of trysts, nothing more than brief dalliances with both men and women. He had never missed his lovers, and he was content to find relief at his own hand when he was alone again.

It didn't particularly pain him. He had been there when his mother passed and his father slipped into seemingly endless grief, and Raff – not even seven years old – had vowed to look after his newborn sister: a promise he'd kept ever since. He'd sat by Ash's bedside when his brother returned half-dead from war with a name on his lips that Raff didn't recognise, shouted into the night when the fever was at its peak. If *that* was love, Raff was content with his lot. To act recklessly for it – as Penn and William must have done – seemed foolish, and needlessly dangerous.

After they had eaten, Penn rubbed his hands on his cloak, staring at the fire. He seemed brighter for the food, even though the purple marks beneath his eyes had only darkened.

It was Raff who broke the silence first.

'Were you truly going to kill me?' he asked, trying to bring some levity to Penn's sullen stillness.

Penn's fingertips brushed the hilt of his dagger.

'I'd have tried,' he said with a sigh, 'if it had been anyone else.'

It was almost enough to make Raff laugh. 'I suspect you wouldn't have been very successful.'

'I—' Penn turned on him, all outrage. But it dropped quickly. 'Perhaps,' he muttered.

'Did no one train you to fight?'

Penn shrugged. 'They *tried,* but I don't think it was worth the time or money to keep my skills honed.' He stared at the flames with a rueful smile. 'And I resisted, of course. The clash of steel never appealed to me, even as a boy.' He laughed. 'I should have listened.'

'Not everyone is cut from the same cloth,' Raff said. 'Combat comes easier to some than others.'

Penn eyed him. Raff couldn't quite read his expression in the low light. 'So it seems.'

'What will you do now?'

The thought had been plaguing Raff since finding him. If he *had* been searching for William, he would need new plans if the Earl's son was truly gone.

'I do not know.'

Raff had been afraid of that answer. 'I'm not intending to insult you, but . . .'

'But?'

'. . . but if you insist on staying out here, you are *going to die.*'

Penn spluttered. 'You cannot say—'

'You couldn't even light a fire!'

'That's just a matter of practice!'

'And what would you have done if I hadn't found you? Frozen to death?'

'I'd have survived another night . . .'

'You *barely* survived last night.'

'You don't know that.'

'You can see it just to look at you. And what about tomorrow night? What about the one after that?' Raff pinched the bridge of his nose. 'Do you even have any food?'

'. . . No,' Penn admitted, 'but I would have—'

'Would have *what*? Begged at doorsteps? Did de Foucart give you leave to go?'

'. . . No.'

'And do you not think he'd find it odd that you vanished the same night as his son? His son who is likely dead?'

Penn's silence betrayed him.

'If you return now, willingly,' Raff continued, 'and explain that you were simply looking for William, perhaps he might—'

'I'm not going back.' Penn's words were *steel*. Raff fell silent, and Penn continued. 'I refuse. I'd rather die.'

He pulled his legs closer, resting his chin upon his knees.

'Do you have anywhere to go?' Raff urged. 'Any family?'

'No.'

The fire crackled, sparks shooting into the air above like stars. Another dry stick popped. Every noise made Penn jump.

Raff thought of his sister, released from the marriage she'd only accepted to keep their father happy. He thought of his *own* freedom, snatched away by the very thing that had released her. Perhaps he could gift that freedom to someone else; perhaps, for once, not everyone needed to live in misery.

And perhaps he *could* avoid the burdens that awaited him back at Dunlyn Castle, for a little while longer. A reason to delay his return home had landed shivering at his feet.

'Penn.'

'Raff . . .'

They both spoke at once. Penn relented, immediately. 'Go on.'

'No, I . . .'

They spoke over each other again, fumbling with the words.

'Come with me?' said Raff, just as Penn spoke— 'Take me with you.'

They stared at each other.

'What?'

'Penn—'

'You would take me with you? That is—' Penn stuttered, the words coming too fast, 'you don't have to take me to your home, just . . . just somewhere else. Far enough away so I can start again—'

'I understand it's an odd request. You don't have to—'

They both stumbled into silence again, but there was a smile threatening to crack Penn's face, no matter how much he was attempting to hold it back. Raff wanted to see him release it.

'Come with me. As far as you need . . . as far as you want. You'll die on your own, and I refuse—'

'Yes,' said Penn, quickly. 'I . . . I thought you would dismiss me. Tell me this was my problem to solve.'

'My . . .' Raff faltered, 'my *Lord* has chosen to remain with de Foucart,' he said. 'The rest of his retinue are moving north as we speak. I'll be making the rest of the journey alone, and—'

He cut himself off, the lie already too heavy. Penn turned to him, intrigued. 'And?'

'And I had not intended to hurry back regardless. At least . . .' he rubbed his face once more, 'at least for a while. I *will* need to return, but it needn't be *soon*.'

'Your lord has given you leave to return so late?'

Raff shrugged. 'He has. But I cannot simply leave. I need to tell de Foucart I couldn't find his son.'

'And face the consequences for that.'

Raff set his shoulders. 'If he sees fit.'

'And then?'

'And then I'll head north.' He turned to look at Penn, expression curious. 'You have no plan? No direction? Anything?'

Penn shrugged.

'Then you *are* a fool, truly. Perhaps that's the kind of work you should seek next. A court jester.'

Penn spluttered with laughter. It was a sweet sound, his eyes sparkling darkly, the fire reflecting from them.

'I *will* find you somewhere to go,' Raff said. 'You have my word.'

'I . . . thank you,' said Penn, unfurling from himself. 'Truly. You've nothing to gain by helping me, you realise; I've no money, no family. Nothing.'

'I'm not looking for what I might gain,' Raff said. 'We want similar things, I think. I would regret standing in your way.'

Penn stared at him. 'What—'

'We should sleep.' Raff spoke before he could ask him a difficult question. 'We'll rise early,' Raff shot him a dark look which he hoped implied that if he were not awake, he would be left behind on the forest floor, 'and tomorrow I will return to de Foucart and inform him that I have abandoned the search.'

'He'll be furious.'

'No doubt he will. We'll head north from there.'

'Then what?'

Raff shrugged. 'Then we'll keep heading north until we find someplace for you.'

'Right.' Penn tapped at his legs, fingers twitching. 'Well, then.'

There was no end to that thought. Raff rose to his feet in a quick, easy movement.

'Well, then,' he agreed. 'Sleep. You need all the rest you can get.'

Unlike Penn, who had apparently fled with little more than his bag and cloak, Raff was more suitably prepared for a night in the woods. He removed his pack, unstrapping a tightly wound roll of haphazardly sewn deer skins, before kicking the leaves at his feet into a hasty pile. He threw the skin on top and manoeuvred himself into a sleeping position, pulling his cloak over his shoulders like a blanket, aware of Penn's eyes on him.

He rolled onto his back, staring upwards at the gently moving trees, listening to Penn readying to sleep on the other side of the fire. He should bid him a good night. He should say *anything*. But he found the words trapped.

It had been so easy to lie, allowing Penn to believe he was another servant – just a tracker, not nobility in his own right.

Before, he hadn't told Penn who he was, happy for a moment's respite from being the son of Lord Griffin Barden. With Penn, under the canopy of leaves, he could be free of the burdens he'd been carrying along with him for so many weeks; his sister's marriage, his brother's suspicion. He didn't have to think about the state of the home he'd be returning to, or the blow he'd be landing on his family when he left them, whether or not Ash was ready to take on the role he'd shirked for years.

The trees rustled. Far away, an owl called into the night. Penn sniffed. Beside him, the fire crackled, a merry accompaniment to the rest.

Chapter Six

Frost coated the grass at the edge of the forest in sparkles, crunching beneath Penn's boots. He'd woken with ice on his shoulders, yet despite the bitter cold he was feeling brighter than he had in days.

He'd eaten real food last night, and the warmth of the fire along with the gentle reassurance of Raff nearby had meant that he'd slept soundly. Even the ache in his spine from slumbering on the hard ground couldn't dim the lightness in his chest.

It all was thanks to Raff, a man Penn barely knew. But he had offered to help, and Penn had to admit that Raff was right: he was more likely to find death than freedom on his own.

Beside him, Raff stood with his arms folded, staring towards the keep. He didn't seem anxious to return. In the sunlight, Penn could see him more clearly. His hair and beard were so dark they were nearly black, his pale skin littered with freckles, and there was a bump to his nose where it had been broken long ago.

'We could leave,' Penn suggested. 'No one needs to know we were here.'

Raff sighed. 'I promised the Earl I would return, whether or not I had word of his son.' He unfolded his arms. 'Besides, my effects and my horse remain in the keep, and I have no desire to see them fall into his hands simply because I wished to avoid a difficult conversation.'

'I thought you were a hunter.' Penn glanced at him with a coy half-smile. 'De Foucart is an elderly man in a crumbling keep. He should make for easy quarry.'

'I *am* a hunter,' Raff agreed with a smirk. 'If he were a deer or a bundle of pheasants dressed in an ermine robe, perhaps he would be easier to deal with.'

'An arrow through the chest? It would be quicker.'

Raff frowned, the expression more troubled than offended. 'That it would,' he mused. 'I will admit I am not well-suited for diplomacy.'

'Neither is de Foucart. You could use that to your advantage. Shout at each other till one of you goes hoarse.'

'Perhaps *you* should speak to him.'

'We both know that's impossible.' Penn took a step towards the trees. 'De Foucart is not the most attentive man, but he *would* recognise me. I have no wish to be subjected to questions on the whereabouts of his son.'

Raff nodded. 'No,' he said, 'I should think you would not.' He sighed again. 'I won't be long. The message is brief, after all.'

Penn seized the opportunity. 'Will you tell him William is dead?'

'I wouldn't tell a father his son was dead unless I held his body in my arms,' Raff said. 'I will broach the subject, although I suspect it is a discussion he's had already. Maybe they have already found him.'

Penn nodded. 'Maybe they have.'

'Penn,' Raff turned to him, a neat line between his brows, 'if William has returned . . . will you stay in the keep?'

'I—' Penn started, then quickly stopped short. He needed to find a balance; would Raff be more likely to help him if he saw Penn as a lovelorn fool, or as a desperate runaway?

The lies were already threatening to trip him up. It was best to go with the truth – or *a* truth.

'I have no desire to return,' he said.

Raff raised his eyebrows at him but did not press the matter.

Penn couldn't say more when the chance for freedom had been granted so easily, yet could be so easily taken away again. He felt low, snatching the opportunity so greedily, but Raff seemed practical above all else. He was helping him through nothing more than a sense of chivalry and displaced empathy. He didn't *care*, not about Penn. As soon as it was safe to do so, Raff would bid him farewell in a stranger's court, and never see him again.

Besides, Penn wouldn't be taking advantage since Raff had *offered* his services. It would be best to think of himself as a package, a dog being sold to a new owner. He would move on, and Raff would move north. He would not grow attached.

Raff flexed his shoulders, pulling them back as if preparing for a fight, then strode towards the keep. Penn watched his departing figure with interest.

Raff was *intriguing*, of that much Penn was certain. He was realising that his initial impression of him in Hartswood Forest had been incorrect. Raff was a little gruff, perhaps, but beneath that he appeared to be deeply thoughtful. More to the point, he hadn't baulked when Penn had kissed him. That meant a great deal. It meant even more that he had kissed him back.

He tried to push that thought down. Raff had offered to help him, and he couldn't risk losing that help when he needed it so badly.

Penn was forced to trust Raff's word, but it was still with fluttering nerves and a growing sense of dread that he waited on the edge of the forest. What if Raff had been lying? What if he knew who Penn really was, and had returned to the keep not to fetch his things but to fetch de Foucart's men? Penn had been too quick to accept Raff's help, too easily won over by his company, too absorbed in the memory of the kiss to consider that it could all be a trap.

When Raff finally emerged, leading a gelding carrying several packs, Penn considered simply turning and running.

But he didn't. Raff was alone, and moving at too leisurely a pace for a man about to spring a surprise attack. Penn breathed again.

He waited, and when Raff approached he stepped into the winter sunlight, raising his hand in greeting. Raff didn't stop walking, but gave him a tight-lipped nod: a clear indication for him to follow.

Despite his prickling nerves, Penn did.

They kept close to the treeline, and soon found themselves on the winding, shadowy road that wended through the forest. The way was quiet, but Penn kept his hood low over his face regardless.

'How fares de Foucart?' he asked, as soon as they were away from the keep.

Raff shot him a look, weighing him up. 'To talk to him, one would not realise he's lost his son.'

'Is that so?'

He was lucky, Penn supposed, that Raff assumed he was already attached to the Earl's son. It made it easier to know he didn't have to entirely restrain the emotion in his voice.

'He's behaving more as if a horse has bolted.'

'It's very inconvenient for him, I'm sure.'

'Inconvenient?' Raff repeated, aghast. 'His son could be dead. I told him that myself, and I was not the first. Yet he acted as if I'd told him his hound had pissed on my boots.' He shook his head. 'I will be glad to be away from here.'

Penn swallowed. 'Will he continue to look for William?'

Raff shrugged. 'He claimed the hunt would continue. A pointless endeavour. But if he wishes to waste resources, so be it.'

That would complicate Penn's escape. He had hoped that his father would accept him as dead and establish Ellis as the heir in his place. Penn couldn't help but wonder why he would continue the search: it certainly wasn't affection that was making his father act.

'Perhaps . . .' he mused, more to himself than to Raff, 'perhaps it is for show.'

Raff raised an eyebrow at him. 'For show?'

'Word of William's flight will have spread by now,' said Penn, slowly. 'Every town five miles from here will know. And de Foucart is . . .'

He hesitated, looking for the right word. Raff provided one for him.

'Strict?'

Penn's lip quirked. 'He is not the most popular man. A frantic search for a missing son could win him favour.'

'You think this could be about consolidating power?'

Penn gave a half-hearted shrug. He had said too much, especially considering how freely he had spoken in Hartswood.

Raff mused on this. 'I've seen powerful men do worse for less.'

'You have a low opinion of men in power.'

'You're a servant,' said Raff. 'Surely you see worse every day?'

'In a way.'

'Regardless. De Foucart – and his son – are of little importance now. I'm glad to be rid of them. We must decide what to do with *you*.'

Penn felt Raff's gaze on him. 'I must leave the county, at least,' he said.

'Do you have a horse?'

Penn thought ruefully of the fine mare he'd left in the keep. 'No.'

'Then that will be our first task. Do you know of any stables in the area?'

Penn did, of course, but he was known to them too. Word would travel that he was alive and well on horseback before he'd crossed the county border.

'I have no way of acquiring a horse,' he said, instead of the truth. 'I've very little money.'

'We can find you something cheap,' said Raff, dismissively. 'And I can pay. We're always wanting for horses in my Lord's keep. He will consider it an investment.'

'You cannot—'

'I can. We'll take twice as long by foot.'

'You said yourself you were willing to draw the journey out.'

Raff was clearly biting back a smile. 'I did. Choked by my own noose. *Yes*: I am in no hurry to return, but I will not stand to ride while you walk beside me. We will find you a horse.'

'The nearest stables all know me,' Penn insisted desperately. 'I can't just walk in and—'

'Then *I* will walk in.' Raff paused. 'They know you?'

Penn set his shoulders. 'If you assumed I was an under-servant, then that was your mistake, not mine.'

Another smile. Penn was growing fond of these smiles; he would have to seek them out less.

'Well spoken,' Raff said. 'Fine. *I* will find you a horse. I hope you ride well.'

'I ride exceedingly well.'

'In that case, I hope you have the opportunity to prove it,' Raff said. 'Come. Lead me to where I can find you a horse, and we can take the road north before midday.'

They walked for another mile or so before Penn directed Raff towards a town where he knew of a well-kept stable.

Penn leaned against the trunk of an elm tree in the pale sun. He resolved that once they'd passed the county line, he'd strive to make himself a more valuable travelling companion. Raff had admitted that he didn't have the skill for diplomacy; Penn's experience at court could be to their advantage.

He hoped it would be enough. They wouldn't survive on charity alone, and he'd left in a rush, blind to all else beyond throwing a few things in his bag and escaping the high, thick walls of the keep. There was a meagre pouch of coins at the bottom of his bag, which had been all he could find at the time: his father kept money under tight control, and he was lucky to have the few pennies he did. There was always the dagger, too, which he could sell for a good price. It wasn't as if he was adept in using it.

Raff took longer than Penn had anticipated in returning, leading a chestnut gelding behind his own horse. It had a pack slung over its back, along with a cheap yet serviceable saddle. Penn idled beside the tree, keen not to draw too much notice to himself.

'Did you find the stables suitable?' he asked, when Raff finally joined him.

'More than,' Raff said, handing him the reins. 'This is a good horse, for a fair price. I acquired some supplies too. Usually we – I – would rest in towns or homesteads. Locals are generous towards travellers. But for now,' he looked Penn up and down, making him feel self-conscious, 'we'll need to make camp, lest you are recognised.'

'That sounds wise.'

'I warn you, you will find it unpleasant.'

Penn forced himself to shrug. 'I likely will,' he said, 'but better than remaining where I was. What do you intend us to do? I find myself rather . . .' he swallowed, 'at your mercy.'

Raff's expression was unreadable.

'We will remove you from the county, first,' he said. 'Do you have any preference on where you wish to go? There are dozens of places that may be suitable in Leicestershire or Derby. You will not be recognised so far removed from de Foucart's keep.'

Penn fiddled with the horse's tack as he contemplated. He had never truly considered where he would go next, too focused on simply escaping. Thoughts of his future had been extinguished after Henry had died. Since then, he'd only planned as far as the next day, one foot ahead of the other. Now he had a choice, he didn't know what to do with it.

'I had not thought so far ahead,' he admitted, not looking up. 'To get even this far – I had tried not to hope for it too much, knowing how unlikely it was.'

'Had you planned with—' Raff cut himself off. Penn was sure he could guess at the unspoken question: *had you planned with William?*

Penn could already feel the lie tightening around his wrists, binding him. He didn't feel guilt at lying, but he would have to take pains not to become too entangled in its threads, lest it fall apart and damn him.

'In a way,' he said, choosing each word carefully. 'In truth, it was his idea more than mine. I am quite sure he had a plan, but – but I did not ask, and he did not tell me. Perhaps to spare me if my—' he swallowed down the word *Father*, 'if de Foucart discovered his plans and attempted to question me.'

If Raff found the lie unbelievable, it didn't register on his face. He nodded.

'It is easier to plan for a certain future,' he said. 'It will be some time before we find somewhere safe enough for you. By then you may be surer of what it is you want.'

Penn peered at him. He hoped he was right. For now, he would continue as he had done since becoming heir: one foot ahead of the other, trying not to trip.

It was a long, cold day of riding. They kept as close to the forest as possible, and Penn found himself pressed between the trees to one side and Raff to the other: a dual barricade, hiding him.

Another reason for his father's continued search had struck him as they rode. Penn's flight had ruined his father's plans to secure power. He would have to be punished. But he would have to be found, first. The lightness that had flared when Raff had agreed to help him dulled. Now he could only feel fear.

He kept his hood up around his face, feeling phantom eyes on his back. They passed very few people on the road, but whenever they did Penn was sure that this time would be his undoing.

Recognition never came, but neither did his anxiety cease. By the time they stopped to rest after a full day's riding, Penn's shoulders ached and his head was pounding where he'd sat hunched over and too tense, unable to relax. Every footfall of the horse beneath him had sent a stabbing pain through his temple. If this was how the rest of the journey would go, he would be mad long before they'd made it across the county line. He should turn around, give himself up and bear the punishment his father delivered.

But he didn't. Raff built them a fire – Penn didn't even realise he'd done it – and handed him something warm to eat sometime later. Penn forced himself to nibble at the food, utterly silent.

Raff moved around him, setting up camp, stoking the fire, never speaking.

Or perhaps he *did* speak, but Penn didn't register his words.

He was about to succumb to sleep when Raff stopped him.

'Here,' he said. 'You will need this.'

He passed him a tightly wrapped bundle. A bedroll. Penn thanked him, the words tumbling from his mouth in leaden syllables. Raff gazed at him, all sympathy. Penn hated the expression. He wanted to drown in it.

He placed himself a safe distance from the fire, unfurled the bedroll, and collapsed onto it, pulling his cloak around himself.

It wasn't until he felt something heavy drop around his shoulders that he realised he was shivering. Raff had placed something over him. Penn reached up, and his fingers brushed against thick cloth. Was it a blanket? Penn couldn't tell, but it was warm: warmer than his cloak. He tugged whatever it was closer, too tired to think, and squeezed his eyes shut.

Chapter Seven

It was late the next morning by the time Penn awoke. Raff had been up for some time, and ruefully thought back on his unspoken threat to leave Penn where he slept the previous day if he didn't rise early.

He wouldn't leave him now. As they'd moved from the de Foucart keep, Penn's anxiety had only grown. Raff had wished he could help, but was keenly aware that there was nothing he could do. He was only a stranger. He didn't know what to say.

He'd thrown himself into the tasks he *could* do: finding a clearing in which they could camp, lighting a fire, snaring game. He relished feeling useful, but it also gave him something to keep him distracted. A way to stop his mind drifting back to Penn.

When he let his thoughts rest on him for too long, they inevitably wound their way back to the moments shared in Hartswood Forest. The kiss, of course, was the most urgent memory, but he also found himself remembering how pleasant – how *easy* – Penn's company had been. Somehow, the two recollections tangled; the kiss and the companionship, mingling in a way he couldn't name.

Both made him feel guilty. He shouldn't think about Penn like that, not when he was so clearly struggling.

Raff was kicking out the fire when he finally heard Penn stir, and turned to see him sitting on the bedroll, holding the cloak Raff had placed over him with a look of confusion on his face.

'My spare,' Raff said.

Penn glanced up at his words. 'Thank you,' he said, his voice hoarse. 'That was . . . very kind. You did not need—'

'You were cold,' Raff said, quickly. 'And I have no use for it.'

'Oh. Yes, well . . .' Penn sat up properly as Raff continued to pack up camp. 'Forgive me,' he said. 'You have treated me kindly, and I have repaid you with sourness. I am not a pleasant travelling companion.'

Raff finished strapping his bedroll to his horse and squatted beside Penn on the hard ground.

'You were scared,' he said. 'I am not so selfish as to demand thrilling conversation from a man who carries so much fear.'

Penn worried the cloak between his fingers. 'I cannot risk being caught.'

'Then we will not risk it.'

Penn just stared at him.

'I gave my word to help you,' Raff said. 'And I will. Whether or not you are a pleasant travelling companion.'

Penn gave him a soft smile that didn't quite reach his eyes, then rose to his feet, bundling the cloak in his hands.

'Thank you,' he said, offering it back. 'Truly. For all of this.'

Raff waved a hand at him. 'Keep it,' he said. 'Or at least borrow it, until we find you somewhere safe. You will need it on the journey. I had not realised that your own clothing is so—' he winced, realising he sounded insulting, 'unsuitable,' he finished, lamely.

Penn raised an eyebrow. 'Indeed,' he said, appearing faintly amused. 'Onwards, then? Towards Warwickshire?'

Raff nodded. 'Onwards.'

✡

The day's ride was easier than the previous had been. Penn didn't think too much about his destination, still half-believing that he would be caught at any moment by a winter-bundled traveller. But even a day away from his father's keep was further than he'd dared to hope for. His anxiety hadn't lifted, but it had abated enough for him to breathe again.

The clouds above them were growing grey and heavy, the threat of snow more likely than the threat of discovery. The sky burst as they were moving on from an early afternoon rest, and soon they were travelling through thick, swiftly falling flakes.

The snow was a relief. It veiled Penn in swirling white, obscuring him. When a particularly severe gust of icy wind blew what felt like an entire snowdrift into his face, he laughed – the sudden sound causing Raff to twist in the saddle to stare at him.

It couldn't last, of course. His spirits remained high, but the biting chill soon made his nose sting and his eyes water as they rode into the wind. The wool cloak kept him warm and dry, but his face was exposed, red-raw. It took several hours for the snow to abate, and by then the road was buried so deep that they were forced to dismount.

By the time they came to rest, Penn was desperately looking forward to the warmth of the fire and a good meal. Snow could either curse or bless a hunt, Raff explained: fresh tracks were easier to follow, but in such harsh weather anything small enough to make a suitable meal was likely burrowed underground or hidden away.

'We could have put that deer to good use after all,' Penn said, rubbing his hands together.

Raff glanced at him. 'Indeed we could.'

Raff was successful despite the thick snow, and it was with a smug smile that he returned to the camp, boasting a pair of plump partridges in one hand.

'We are lucky,' he said, as he sat beside Penn and began to pluck the first bird. 'Fowl are stupid creatures.'

Following Raff's lead, Penn took the second bird and began to work. He moved more slowly than Raff, who swiftly finished off his own bird before taking Penn's, too, completing the job with far more speed and care than Penn could have managed.

The partridges cooked quickly thanks to their small size, and Penn realised he was ravenous after the trek through the snow and the scant amount he'd eaten the previous day. As he chewed, he felt his fingers slowly coming back to life, warmed by the hot meat.

Raff had been right, curse him: Penn wasn't built for this sort of outdoor travel. Even with Raff's spare travelling cloak wrapped around him he was shivering. He'd learned that his own clothing wasn't as heavy, hardy or warm as the tracker's garb that Raff wore, and it was another small disappointment: further evidence that he was unsuitable.

He wished he could have refused the cloak. It was a generous gift, and kind, and Raff was already doing so much for him. He hated feeling indebted to him, even though he knew that had Raff not stumbled across him he'd be dead.

Penn felt a little guilty for his fears that Raff was tricking him, or had planned to turn him back to de Foucart. Raff wasn't like that. He was *honest,* and clearly intended to fulfil his promise.

The meal finished, Penn wrapped the borrowed cloak tighter around his shoulders, sinking into it. It smelled of Raff: he must have worn it on the journey south. It was a good smell – all sweat and muskiness – and every time it sent him hurtling back to those intense moments in the forest before he'd had to run. Today, with his spirits lighter but conversation muffled by snowfall, he'd spent several moments lingering on the memory, imagining how it might have gone were they not interrupted.

He had tried in vain to ignore it. The recollection was made stronger by the smell clinging to the wool. Every time he adjusted the fabric, the memory of the taste of Raff's mouth burst onto his tongue.

It was maddening. Raff was as handsome and intriguing as he had been when Penn had first found him. More so now he had time to really study him; the way his dark hair framed his bearded jaw, the bright blue of his eyes, his freckled face. Penn couldn't help but wonder if the rest of him was freckle-flecked too. In Hartswood Forest, he'd been strength and power and desire. Out here, as they traipsed along in the stark sunlight, he was strikingly beautiful.

Neither of them mentioned the kiss. Penn thought that he caught Raff staring, spotting his gaze on him for longer than necessary, but his eyes always darted away before he could be sure. He knew well enough that *he* was looking at Raff: he couldn't help himself. That tight, hot *want* hadn't ebbed.

Maybe it had, for Raff. Helping Penn escape may have dampened those fires for him. Penn wouldn't blame him, of course: he was under the impression that Penn was a servant with an unsuitable attachment to his master's son, lovelorn and grieving. It was likely a mess he didn't wish to entangle himself in, even if Penn had surprised him by confessing his intentions to leave with or without his apparent lover.

Penn told himself that Raff's interest had both flourished and died in the forest, and yet, there it was again: a furtive glance over the fire as Penn rubbed his hands together before the flames.

Perhaps it was the rush from managing to evade capture. Perhaps it was the warmth of the fire, or the satisfaction of a good meal after a day of starving. Perhaps it was just how cold the night promised to be.

'Raff,' he said, edging closer, 'the night we met . . .'

Raff stared into the fire. Penn shuffled along the cold ground till their shoulders knocked together.

'That is,' he continued, 'when we *first* met . . .'

He pulled off his gloves, ventured out a bare hand, and rested it gently upon Raff's knee. Raff didn't move away.

'I find myself wondering what may have happened were we not disturbed.'

Finally, Raff looked at him. His eyes were dark. 'Is that so?'

It was as good as an invitation. Penn moved his hand higher, feeling the coiled muscles of Raff's thigh beneath his palm. He knelt in front of Raff's crossed legs. Still Raff didn't move, just watched him, as if waiting to see what he would do next. It felt like a challenge, and when Penn placed his second hand upon Raff's other knee he could hear his own pulse drumming in his ears, eagerly terrified.

He wasn't sure what he was so afraid of. In Hartswood, Raff had been just as enthusiastic as Penn, kissing him with a fierce, wild hunger. They both had more to lose now, he supposed, but it was hard to care when he could feel the strength of Raff's legs beneath his hands and see the firelight flickering in his eyes, a blue that defied the darkness.

He moved forwards, sneaking one of his hands higher; over Raff's hip, drifting up his torso and settling between his surcoat and the thick wool of his cloak. He was so *warm*. Raff sighed at the touch, his eyelids lowering a fraction, and Penn felt a smug twinge of satisfaction, eager to hear the sound again.

Penn rose to his knees. He tilted his head to close in not on Raff's lips, but his neck, obscured by the fold of his cloak. He brought both hands forwards, fiddling with the cold metal clasp that kept the garment in place. Raff shifted, and as the clasp unhooked beneath Penn's fingers Raff grabbed his waist, tugging him nearer.

It was Penn's turn to gasp as Raff held him gently in place. He let one hand drift into the warmth beneath Raff's cloak, the other lingering on his shoulder. He wanted to rip away the layers of wool and linen to see the skin beneath, to trail his fingers across the jut of his collarbone, to press his lips to the curve between neck and shoulder.

'You know,' Penn leaned forwards till his lips were brushing against Raff's neck, 'I have not been able to properly thank you for helping me. I wish there was some way I could . . .' he burrowed closer, feeling Raff's rapid heartbeat beneath his lips, breathing out the final words, '*repay* you.'

Raff froze. He released Penn's waist, leaning away from the touch of Penn's lips on his skin.

'We should not.' His voice sounded strained.

Penn went still, his pulse thundering. Slowly, attempting to regain a little dignity, he slid backwards.

'Oh.'

'It is . . .' Raff started, his face flushed even in the firelight, 'it may not be right. Like this.'

'No,' Penn said, hastily. 'Of course. We shouldn't.'

He didn't add more to that thought, none too sure what it was that was preventing Raff from finishing what they'd started in the forest. Things had changed, that much was clear. He didn't fault Raff for his new-found hesitance; helping him escape was taxing enough. Being forced to spend so long at Penn's side may have made him more aware of the sort of man he *really* was: the sort of man he might not truly desire. The lingering looks were no doubt just the remnants of that night. Penn had simply let his imagination get the better of him.

He moved away, pulling his cloak tighter, cheeks smarting. The fire was now burning low, and the moon hung in the sky above them like a watchful eye.

'It's late,' he whispered. 'I should try to get some sleep before we set out again tomorrow.'

Raff nodded. 'There's a long way to go, yet.'

Penn glanced at him briefly before huddling down onto his bedroll, moving closer to the dying embers of the fire.

'Yes,' he agreed. 'There is.'

Penn's eyes were shut, yet Raff was sure he wasn't asleep.

He shifted, his crossed legs numb beneath him. He tried, rather unsuccessfully, to focus on the small flames, the sounds of animals in the undergrowth, the soft huff of Penn's sleepy breaths.

Anything to distract him from his hardened prick.

He glanced again at Penn. He couldn't. But, oh, how he wanted to.

He thought of Penn's whispered words. *I wish there was some way I could repay you.* No: Raff wanted him, but not like that. He didn't want Penn to feel he owed him anything, to think that his help hinged on sexual favours. He had the sudden, terrible thought that Penn believed Raff was only doing this to get something out of him.

Raff couldn't help but suspect that to give in to the heat settling low in his stomach would be to take advantage. Penn had told Raff himself when they set off that he found himself *at his mercy,* and besides, he was still grieving, balancing that against the stark shock of escape. No doubt his attentions towards Raff were spurred more by heartbreak and relief than anything else.

Raff knew what grief could do to a person, even the sturdiest of people. He would not benefit from Penn's misery, even if Penn *had* chosen his freedom over a reunion with the man he'd tried to escape with.

He could still feel Penn's hands on his knee, on his chest. The way his mouth had brushed against his neck. He could hear the softness of his voice, making his skin erupt into gooseflesh. Raff rubbed at his face. He could not. He *would* not.

His body seemed to disagree with him. Fairly certain Penn wasn't watching him, Raff rose awkwardly to his feet. If he *was* awake, at least the darkness should conceal his arousal. After throwing more fuel onto the fire, aware that the night was only going to grow colder, he pulled out his own bedroll and lay down without bothering to prepare the hard ground. The discomfort would give him something else to think about.

Trying to ignore the tingling feeling of Penn's lips on his neck, Raff drifted into a fitful sleep.

Chapter Eight

The next day, the road was easy and – more importantly – quiet. They both ignored Penn's offer, and the thing that had come so close to blooming between them. They had woken that morning as if nothing had changed, yet it hung between them, unacknowledged. Just thinking of it was enough to make Raff's skin tingle, to light an urgent heat in his belly that even the snow couldn't smother.

They were nearly at the county border, further from de Foucart's grasp. With each mile that passed beneath them and each step further away from the Earl's lands, Raff could see a change come over Penn. He was lighter, the tension in his shoulders looser.

He wasn't safe, not yet, and still chose to ride with his hood covering his face, but now he could keep pace with Raff, spitting jokes and discussing where they would be heading next. The planning fell largely to Raff, more experienced with the lay of the land and the journey north, but Penn helped where he could, describing notable locals and lords, men whose alliances with the Earl were tense and those whose connections were built more on mutual interests or respect.

It was a relief to see Penn so *free*. Raff had watched him float along on the maelstrom of his own emotions, tossed about and battered as he struggled to stay afloat. Now those feelings were calming, he was catching more glimpses of the sort of person Penn really was.

Raff *liked* the person he really was. The pointed humour he'd displayed when they'd lingered outside the keep hadn't gone, but it had tempered. Raff suspected that Penn had a sharp tongue when he chose to use it, and hoped that he wouldn't be on the receiving end of a verbal lashing.

When Penn laughed – which he did often – his pleasant face became startlingly handsome, lines appearing beside his eyes and wrinkling his nose. It was easy to make him laugh: Raff suspected that part of it came from how little he'd had to laugh at until now.

He was skinny, made more apparent by his height, with near-permanent bags beneath his lively eyes no matter how much he laughed or how long he slept. Raff could guess that laughter wasn't the only thing he'd been lacking.

Penn hadn't propositioned Raff again, but he still stole glances at him, eyes wide. He still let their fingers brush when passing over food or equipment or bundles of sticks when they were setting up camp.

Raff could have told him to stop. He could have moved away countless times. But he didn't. He sat closer, allowing the touches to linger, gazing back when Penn wasn't looking. There was a door there that neither of them had shut yet, and he suspected that neither of them wanted to.

He would not dwell on it. Penn's companionship was more than enough, and he would not act on his desire and send this new, tentative friendship into ruin. He would not put Penn in a position where he felt he couldn't say no, or worse: a position where he felt he couldn't change his mind later.

It helped that winter was truly upon them, and the freezing winds that nipped at his skin every time he stopped to relieve himself by the side of the road made him desperate to wrap himself in layers and never even *consider* the body beneath. Frost and ice and snow did not make for a romantic setting, even if the sparkling dawns were beautiful.

It was painfully cold, and the weather was only growing worse. In truth, the frosts and ever-present threat of snow didn't give him cause for great concern. It was certainly unpleasant – there were much better places to sleep than the frozen ground – but it was bearable. It reminded Raff of the time he'd spent training and squiring as a younger man before being called back to Dunlyn Castle after Ash had ridden into battle.

Penn, however, was not so untroubled. During the day, he moved around enough to hide the shivering in his shoulders and the chattering of his teeth, but in the evenings it couldn't be concealed. Raff had given him his spare cloak the first night they'd spent together, and had taught him the best way to fuel and stoke a fire, yet still his gloved hands shook.

Until they had passed across into territory where Penn was unlikely to be spotted, they were confined to the hard ground rather than the inns and rooms that Raff favoured this time of year.

Penn had not been forthcoming with details about his role in de Foucart's keep, but it was clear that his position was visible enough to make him recognisable to those who knew the family. Raff knew not to pry. No good could come of asking questions Penn didn't want to answer, and he'd told him once already that he asked too many. Raff would not do so again, suspecting that if he interrogated too much, Penn would simply leave.

He didn't *want* Penn to leave. He told himself it was because it was unlikely Penn could survive alone, whether he chose to remain on the roads or seek out new work. He needed someone to guide him so he wasn't robbed at knifepoint or eaten by wild animals or frozen in his sleep.

It was because it was Raff's duty to help him, no more. It wasn't because he enjoyed his company, as sharp as it could be. It wasn't because he kept snatching glances at him, his light brown hair curling in the damp weather and eyes bright as he laughed at his own jokes. It wasn't because that damned kiss was still playing on Raff's mind at inopportune moments.

It wasn't. And yet of course it was – and Raff forced himself to remember that he could not think that way, or at the very least couldn't act on those thoughts when they did come.

They were resting beside a fire – this one constructed nearly entirely by Penn, who was learning quickly – when the weather finally proved too much to bear.

'Curse this miserable season,' Penn exploded, his hands pressed beneath his armpits, his face a picture of misery. 'I cannot understand how you tolerate it, Raff.'

Raff simply shrugged. 'I am more used to it.'

'Perhaps they breed their children not to feel the cold in the north,' Penn mumbled. 'You said your mother was Scottish? Maybe she had some ice faerie magic in her veins, and passed it on to you.'

Raff let himself smile. From anyone else that would have been a jab about his parentage, but Penn was too unserious for that.

'Then surely my skin would be icy cold, as well?'

Penn looked at him for a moment, then was upon him, pulling his glove off and resting his palm against Raff's jaw.

'You are quite warm,' he said. 'Which proves it.'

'Proves what?'

'That you northerners are simply made for colder climes, and I must sit here and suffer in silence.'

He moved away, and Raff immediately missed his touch, watching as he tugged the glove back on.

'I beg *you* to suffer in silence,' he said, raising his eyebrows. 'I have had to listen to your complaints for several nights.'

Penn huffed. 'My heart bleeds for you,' he said. 'How sad, to be forced to listen to my anguish as I slowly succumb to the cold.'

'You could have remained with de Foucart,' said Raff. 'Warm hearths, plenty of food, stone walls and thatched roofs . . .' He tossed a couple more sticks into the fire, gauging the heat. 'Yet you chose to follow me.'

'You *asked* me to come.'

'As you asked me to take you with me. Next time I am approached by a runaway in the forest I shall remember to leave them behind, lest they deafen me with their complaining.' He rose to grab the kettle, considering the fire warm enough to cook. 'Or their chattering teeth.'

'How noble of you.'

'I never claimed nobility.'

Raff filled the kettle, noting that he would need to refill his waterskin from the nearby stream before the night was out, then placed it on the hook above the fire. Penn watched for a moment, then scrambled to his feet towards the packs that Raff had leaned against the fallen tree that served as a windbreak.

Without being asked, he pulled out a couple of turnips and began to slice them into uneven chunks with his dagger. Raff winced at the casual use of the fine blade, but did not chastise him. At least he was helping.

'I think,' Penn said, eventually, 'that I would prefer to freeze by your side in the wilderness than live one more day beneath de Foucart's roof, thatched or not.'

Raff stilled, the rabbit he'd snared earlier clutched in one hand. It was a simple admission of how poor Penn's life had been in de

Foucart's domain – how desperate he was to escape. Still, it felt like more: *I would rather freeze with you. I would rather* die *with you.*

He shook that thought from his head. Penn was determined to find freedom, that was all. He was lost, freezing, and grieving besides.

And yet . . . Penn had mentioned de Foucart – weaving tales about his explosive temper – far more than he'd spoken of the man he was supposed to meet in the woods. Raff supposed this could be self-preservation, an attempt to hold onto deniability if Raff questioned him, but he was sure Penn had understood that he'd known, and hadn't cared.

Aside from his quips and biting remarks, he was buoyant and loud and brash, particularly for a man who had apparently lost part of his heart.

Raff was beginning to suspect that he had overestimated Penn's heartbreak. A dalliance with the son of the Earl could have been a means to an end: a way to escape with safety guaranteed. He had assumed that the gap between Penn and de Foucart's descriptions of the man had been brought about by infatuation, but what if Penn had attached himself to a brute just to secure his freedom, only to find himself freed from *him* too?

It was not his burden. Penn's relationship with William – be it sincere or something more calculated – was not his to explore.

When the turnips were prepared, Penn tossed them messily into the boiling water, followed by the skinned rabbit and a handful of oats. It was no feast, but it would warm them both well enough that they could keep the cold at bay and ensure they had energy enough to walk the miles between their camp and the next town.

Tomorrow, they would pass across the county border. This would be the final night they were forced to spend outside. That thought alone was enough to warm Raff, even if he wasn't looking forward to the crush of strangers.

They sat in companionable silence as the food cooked, the camp soon thick with the smell of rabbit. When the meal was ready, Penn edging closer to the fire to warm his frozen feet, Raff scooped out sizable helpings into bowls. They ate quickly, and the hot broth thawed Raff's stiff fingers, warming him from the inside out. He watched as Penn blew on the steaming stew, holding it close enough that there was a fine sheen of sweat across his face as he greedily drank it down.

When the bowls and kettle were both empty, the last remnants mopped up with the heel of bread that Raff had managed to save from the loaf they'd shared yesterday afternoon, he headed for the stream. The surface had frozen, and he stamped through the ice to get to the freezing water beneath, washing out the bowls, refilling their waterskins, then finally returning to the clearing and allowing himself to slump against the fallen tree with a low sigh.

After a moment, Penn moved from his position beside the fire and leaned next to him, their shoulders brushing.

'I realise,' he said, breaking the silence, 'that I may have been overly dramatic.'

Raff glanced at him. 'Oh?'

'I do not expect to freeze by your side.'

'That is reassuring.' Raff moved against the wood. 'I would not wish to bury a body in this weather. The ground is far too hard.'

He thumped his boot against the already frozen earth to prove his point, and Penn barked out a short, sharp laugh.

'No,' he said, 'I would fully expect you to leave me where I lay. After retrieving your cloak, of course.'

'It is a fine cloak. I would not see it go to waste.'

Penn laughed again. 'At least wait until I *am* dead,' he said. 'Judging by the frosts, it could be this very night.'

'We will have worse nights to come.'

'Somehow I do not find *that* reassuring.' Penn rose, then made his way to where his bedroll was strapped to his horse's flank. He nudged the blanket over the animal back into a better position, giving him a quick pat. He mumbled something in soft tones that Raff couldn't catch, stroking the horse's nose, before returning to the patch they'd cleared beside the fire.

He kicked a pile of damp leaves into a reasonable mound as Raff had shown him, far enough away from the fire that they wouldn't ignite, then placed the thick roll atop them before slowly lowering himself down onto the makeshift bed with a grimace that Raff did not miss.

Raff watched for a few more moments before getting up himself and finding a spot for his own bed. He too stayed a sensible distance from the fire – burning would be far worse a fate than freezing – and was quickly ready to sleep, bundled with a rolled tunic beneath his head and his cloak tight around his shoulders.

He muttered a quick goodnight to Penn, who was still and silent several metres away. Now that Raff had stopped moving, he could feel the true chill in the air, set to only worsen as the night drew on.

Damn his desire for solitude, he wanted a warm hearth more. A fireplace, and good food. A tavern with stone walls; a log farmhouse. He'd be content with a barn and a pile of straw, after this. Raff pulled his cloak tighter, breathing hot air down towards his chest.

The fire, low as it was, crackled. The treetops high above rustled in the winter breeze. Their camp was otherwise silent. Silent, save for a strange noise on the edge of Raff's hearing that he couldn't quite place. After lying still and straining to listen, he realised it was coming from his companion's huddled form.

Penn was shivering. His teeth really *were* chattering, a whole army drumming in his mouth. Raff opened his eyes in time to see Penn roll onto his other side with a groan, the movement only serving to let in more of the cold air.

Raff hesitated. He thought of Penn's words, even though they were little more than a joke: *freeze at your side*. Before he could change his mind, he sat up, wincing at the sudden bite of frigid air.

'Penn.'

At first, Penn did not respond. Then— 'Yes?' He sounded muffled, as if speaking directly into the fabric of the cloak draped over him.

'Come here.'

There was a shuffle, a mumbling sound, then Penn's tousled head emerged from beneath the fabric. 'What?'

'You were right. It is dangerously cold. We—' He sought the right words. We should? We need to? *I want to?* 'We should share heat,' he chose, finally.

Penn was staring at him, the low fire reflected in his eyes. 'Share heat?' he repeated. 'You mean to say—' He gestured with a hand, still gripping the cloak, towards Raff's bedroll.

'It's common, on the road,' Raff hurriedly explained, glad that the darkness was hiding the flush no doubt building across his face. 'When travelling in groups, during the winter . . .' His words were failing him, damn it. 'No matter. I simply thought, if we are both so cold—'

'No, I—' Penn spoke over him. 'I agree. Neither of us will sleep well if we are shivering all night.'

Without another word he stood and grabbed his bedroll,

scattering the leaves beneath. He hurried to Raff's side then paused, as if unsure.

'Here—' Raff reached for the roll, which Penn handed him mutely.

Truthfully, they did not need to rest that close to one another; even an adjacent body would be enough to warm them both enough to sleep. Raff knew this, and yet he still went to his knees, spreading the roll so close to his own that they overlapped.

If this displeased Penn, he didn't show it. He knelt on the roll beside him, keeping his eyes down. For a moment, neither of them moved. Neither of them spoke. Raff's chest squeezed in anticipation.

'Well, then,' Penn said, looking up at last.

'Well, then.'

Penn chewed at his lip, then lay upon the roll, tugging his cloak around him.

Raff lowered himself down behind him, their bodies barely touching. He grabbed the edge of his cloak in a trembling hand, ready to cover them both. He stilled.

'May I?'

Penn gave a brief, mumbled word of assent. Raff moved swiftly, tugging the fabric over Penn's body and pulling him closer.

But instead of relaxing into the touch, Penn froze, his shoulders stiffening. It had been too much. Raff had pushed too far. He went to move his arm away, warring with the urge to curse, the urge to *run*. As if sensing what he was about to do, Penn wriggled back, chasing him. *Stay.*

'Wait—' Penn said, quietly. 'I just – I am not used to—'

He fell silent again beneath Raff's arm.

'Do you wish me to move?' Raff asked.

A soft pause. 'No.'

Thank God. Raff edged forwards till their bodies were flush. This close, their difference in height was even more apparent, and Raff found his face pressed to Penn's shoulders.

He could feel him breathing, the rise and fall of his body. Raff kept his hand balled in the fabric of his cloak rather than resting it against Penn's chest, resisting the urge to splay his fingers above his sternum to feel his heartbeat too.

They fell into silence again, but Raff could no longer hear the crackling of the fire or the rustling of the leaves over the sound of Penn's gentle breaths.

Sleeping on the frostbitten earth had proven a difficult task since leaving the keep. But Penn still fell asleep every night, praying that his fingers and toes would remain attached, and woke every morning stiff but whole.

Now he felt like he might never sleep again. Raff's body was warm where it was curled around his own, but the comfort which should have lulled him into a deep sleep was battling against the sudden, overwhelming closeness. Penn had never been held like this before; hadn't known what it could feel like to *be* held.

Even with the cloak wrapped around him he could feel Raff's breath on his neck. Raff's arm, heavy against his side, pinned him down. His chest against Penn's back penned him in.

Penn's skin was alight, every nerve tingling, his hearing attuned to Raff's breaths and the sound of the leaves crunching beneath him when he moved. They hadn't been travelling together long, but Penn had already learned the shift in breathing that indicated Raff had slipped asleep. It still had not come.

Penn couldn't object, of course; he hadn't fallen asleep either. They were both lying awake, pressed together on the unforgiving ground.

He was thankful for the layers of fabric between them. Had it been summer, and they were dressed more lightly, he wouldn't have been able to resist making a fool of himself. Raff's body curved around him, broad and warm and, more than the rest, *safe*. The desire to feel more of that body tangled with how secure Raff made him feel.

Like this, even in the middle of a blasted forest and trapped beneath a sky heavy with unspilled snow, he felt protected – like no harm could come to him.

He desired Raff, that much he knew. He wanted to turn on the bedrolls bunching beneath them and press their lips together and *taste* him, to feel Raff's body hard against his own. But Penn's impulsiveness could lose him his companion, and thus his safety.

He shuffled back, eyes closed. Behind him, Raff sniffed but didn't move away, wrapping his arm a fraction tighter around him. Penn wished he would release the fabric and press his hand to his chest instead, but Raff appeared to have better restraint than he did.

Penn thought of the gifted cloak, and the heady scent that had clung to it. Now he was buried in that smell – drifting in it, lost in it. It was wonderful, and it *stung*.

Tomorrow, they would cross the county line. He should have felt relief, but all he could think of was the painful realisation that this night they were sharing wrapped beneath Raff's cloak would be the first and only night they slept so closely.

There was the rejection too. Raff didn't want him; not like that. This was a practical choice on a freezing evening, nothing more.

Penn inhaled deeply. He would need to remember this night to keep him warm on the many lonely ones to come.

Chapter Nine

When Raff awoke, more comfortable than he'd felt in weeks, it was to the movement of Penn's lips against his neck as he mumbled quietly in his sleep. He'd turned around in the night, tangling their legs together, even snaking one of his slender arms around Raff's torso, clinging to him. Raff's heart skipped, a perilous pressure beneath his lungs. His arm was still wrapped around Penn's waist.

He could have laid on the ground for hours longer. But the air was cold, and the sun was high: they'd already slept too long. He shifted, moving away from the tempting brush of Penn's lips, and Penn suddenly started awake, his eyes fluttering open.

They stared at each other for a long, warm moment.

And then the moment passed.

They rose swiftly and silently, packed away their camp, and were on the road in less than an hour.

As they rode, finally crossing the county line, Raff found himself unable to shake the feeling of Penn within his arms. He couldn't forget the smell of his hair pressed beneath his nose. The way his breath had danced hotly across his neck. Every time he closed his eyes he was assailed with the vision of Penn's half-awake little smile, the one he'd gifted so easily before realising where he was and quickly pulling away.

It would only happen once. Now they were away from Oxfordshire and Penn was unlikely to be recognised, it would not happen again. Their way from here onwards would be easier – they'd be able to beg hospitality in villages and towns and farms – but the relief of even the warmest bed would be overshadowed by the comfortable memory of something he couldn't have again. There would be no need to bundle together when sleeping indoors, dry and sheltered from the biting winter winds.

He couldn't help but wonder how it might have gone had he given into Penn when he offered. To push past the voice telling him that he was taking advantage, and let Penn kiss him; let him slip his hand beneath his clothes, brush against his skin. He wondered how he would have felt beneath him, hard kisses exchanged without the threat of being discovered.

He wondered what Penn would sound like.

No.

It was a dangerous line of thought. Penn was vulnerable; his safety resting solely on Raff's good feelings. The more Penn had told him about de Foucart, the more Raff was sure that his discovery would end in violence, and however fast a learner Penn may have proven to be, Raff knew he would struggle to survive alone on the road. Should Raff give in, only for one or both of them to change their minds, Penn may feel it necessary to set off alone. It was better to resist if it ensured Penn stayed safe.

Besides, the guiltiest part of Raff whispered: Penn didn't know who he was. Who he *really* was. That was the true danger, of course: part of him didn't care. Penn saw him in the wild, saw him at his most free. He saw him without the close control he had to wield as the son of an earl. He didn't see the weight Raff bore for his family. When Penn looked at him, he saw a tracker. He saw a man who cared about the animals he hunted, and those hunted by others. He saw a man who'd help another with nothing to gain from it.

A man who'd accept a kiss from a stranger in the middle of the forest.

Penn didn't need to know who he was: his family, his history. He knew he was Raff, and that was enough. More than enough.

It felt far more honest – and therefore more vulnerable – for him to be known this way. And that was the crux of it, because if the lie was only in his name, then he would be able to give in; to accept if Penn ever offered more than just this steady, unexpected roadside companionship.

The horse brayed beneath him, cutting him from his thoughts. He realised that he'd been pressing his heels into the animal's flank and pulling too tight on the reins. He relaxed, giving the horse an apologetic pat.

'Raff?'

He turned. Penn was watching him.

'It's nothing,' he said, catching the question before Penn could voice it. 'I was lost in thought.'

'Good ones, I hope.'

Penn in his embrace. His lips against his skin. His heavy, sleepy breaths.

'They were fair.'

Penn gave him a faint smile. 'Do you know this place?' he said, nodding towards the encroaching walls.

Raff trained his eyes on the walls of the small town ahead of them.

'I am unfamiliar with the county,' Raff said, regretfully. 'We will have to ask when we arrive.'

Truthfully, even now Raff was a little nervous as they approached the town's walls. This was the first time they'd been around such a number of people, avoiding villages and farms for fear that Penn would be recognised. The risk had passed, but the tension had not, and he could not shake the knowledge that discovery would carry with it dire consequences for them both: Penn would be dragged back to the keep, and Raff would face the ramifications of aiding his escape.

Raff sighed. He didn't enjoy busy towns regardless, and his lingering anxiety only exacerbated those feelings. He endured them well enough, but the throng of so many people unsettled him, making him feel incapable. The frustrating part was that he knew he *wasn't* incapable: he fared perfectly well with his family, or on the road, or even with Penn, a thought he was trying not to examine for too long.

It was an unremarkable settlement, and they soon found a stable where they could leave their horses for a small fee. The stablehand watched them curiously, but without malice.

'Where is this place?' Raff asked, handing the coins across while avoiding his stare.

'Arlescote,' said the boy with a frown. 'You been travelling far, masters?'

'Terribly far,' Penn said, before Raff could respond. 'Have you been caught with the snow yet?'

The boy started on a long story about the blizzards that Penn and Raff had managed to miss, telling them how the thatch of the farrier's shop had collapsed under the weight and *still* hadn't been replaced. Raff let the words wash over him as he tied up the horses, Penn nodding along and occasionally interjecting with an affirmation or a sound of polite shock.

By the time they left, the boy had forgotten about the unusual appearance of two travellers with no idea where they were, happily stroking down Penn's horse.

'What was that?' said Raff, as they walked towards the town centre.

Penn shrugged. 'We passed the farrier's workshop as we entered town. The thatch *is* ruined, you can see where it collapsed. It's darker around the damage too; likely it froze and rotted. I assumed a boy who worked in the stables would know all about an incident at the farrier's, and in a town this small—' he gestured around, 'the news would be impressive gossip, especially for strangers.' Raff stared at him, speechless. Penn pursed his lips. 'It distracted him from questioning how we had managed to find a town without knowing its name.'

'Oh.' Raff blinked. He had assumed Penn was being friendly, engaging the stablehand in meaningless conversation to pass the time. 'Penn—'

'Yes?'

He swallowed. 'I . . . It is nothing. Come, we need supplies for the road ahead, and to find somewhere to sleep.'

It was growing late in the day, so they went separate ways; Penn seeking respite for the night while Raff found supplies. He immediately missed Penn's presence – especially after witnessing the ease with which he had engaged the stablehand – but it would be quicker, and he didn't want Penn to think him inept.

The town was small but well-stocked, and he bartered for food easily. He was feeling pleased with himself, heading back towards the centre crossroads to wait for Penn, when he heard a commotion coming from the makeshift square.

There was a horse tied to the well in the place where the two roads met, stamping at the ground and snorting in distress. Snapping at its hooves was an enormous tan-coloured dog. Raff was familiar with this sort of behaviour; he often saw it in the dogs his father brought home to train into well-heeled hounds before selling on. It was waiting to strike.

No one else in the square paid notice, giving both animals a wide berth, deliberately ignoring the bloodshed that was sure to happen. Raff glanced around, and failing to see Penn lingering anywhere, stepped forwards. He had no desire to see a horse injured in the middle of the street, especially not by a rogue hound that clearly lacked proper training.

Raff had barely made it halfway across the space when the dog leaped, aiming for the unfortunate horse's throat with a snarl. Suddenly, Raff was running.

He didn't know who the animals belonged to. Nor did he care. The exertion alone could kill the horse, let alone the wounds left by the dog's shining teeth. Raff pulled the dog away before he could shout for help, grabbing it by the muzzle and sending it tumbling to the ground.

The dog took only a second to recover itself, scrambling to its feet and jumping again. For a moment Raff thought it would turn on him, but it aimed once more for the horse. Raff grabbed it around the scruff of its neck, pulling it back before it could gain good purchase around the horse's skinny foreleg.

The horse was snorting and squealing, tugging at the rope that kept it tethered to the well. The dog writhed in Raff's grasp, snapping at him. Raff needed to act quickly; the dog would not stay restrained for long, but the horse could still bolt.

He reached to his hip, grabbed the hilt of his dagger, pulled it from the sheath, and—

'What in God's name are you doing to my dog?'

Distracted, Raff's hold on the beast loosened, and it jerked from his hand, running to the voice. Raff got to his feet, gripping the blade tighter. A man was rushing towards him, broad and red-faced, wearing the expensive garb of a town official; most likely an alderman. The dog bounded to his feet, circled him a couple of times, then wheeled back towards the horse. Raff swiftly stepped between them.

'Unhand that blade!'

'No.'

The alderman scowled, the anger on his face transforming into something more malicious.

'I tell you, unhand it!'

The dog was barking, low to the ground. Behind Raff, the horse was huffing. The hound tried to lunge again, and Raff put out a foot, blocking it. The alderman spluttered, furious.

'My *dog—!*'

Raff ignored him. He spun around, trying to keep the beast back with his boot. With a single, swift slash he severed the rope. The struggling horse immediately pulled free, galloping through the gathered crowd and towards the fields beyond the town. With any luck, its owner would appear and Raff could direct them to it, warning them against leaving their horse so exposed again.

He pushed the dagger back into the sheath at his hip and turned to face the still-shouting man. Without something to chase, the dog had fallen back to his master's heel.

'Who are you,' the man said, voice loud and low, 'to ignore me? To do as you will when this town falls under *my* jurisdiction?'

Raff set his feet. 'Nothing but a tracker,' he said. 'Keen not to see unnecessary bloodshed.'

The man's face purpled. 'You attacked my dog—'

'Your dog is a poorly trained beast. I stopped it from killing that horse.'

'*You attacked my dog,*' the man repeated, yelling over him, 'and you think you can tell me how to keep my animals?' He spat at the ground. 'You're no more than a filthy Scot!'

This was not the first time Raff had experienced hostility on the road. All he could do was weather it, and wait for it to ebb.

'If my actions saved that creature, I am content,' he said, slowly. 'Your dog is unharmed.'

'That is beside the point! You had no right to lay your hands on *my* property.'

Raff bristled. The alderman took a step forward, the dog following, keeping its pin-point sharp eyes fixed on Raff. He didn't speak, aware that the wrong words could leave him dead.

He wondered if Penn was in the crowd, or if he'd slipped away as soon as he'd seen the danger that Raff had walked into – walked them *both* into. He cursed his own foolishness. He had not got Penn this far just to have them caught by an alderman with inflated pride and a hatred for Raff's lineage.

Part of him hoped Penn *had* fled. He faced the alderman down alone, and the dog snarled.

It seemed a welcoming town, in Penn's opinion. He'd managed to find a place to sleep, paying for meals and beds in a shared room for the night. He'd faltered only once, when he realised that he'd need to part with most of the paltry money he had, but managed to cover his slip with a lie about hiding his purse at the bottom of his bag after a near-miss with a bandit on the road.

He was feeling cheery as he headed back to the town square, the sun settling behind the forest that bordered the town's wall. Even the winter air, which promised to soon turn freezing, could not dampen his mood.

No one had even looked twice at him. He suspected that Raff

had been nervous, too, and had felt the way their shared anxieties had fuelled each other, intensifying. Hopefully Raff had also put his mind at ease during their short time apart, and they would finally be able to properly sit down for a meal together. An untroubled night's rest would also do them both good, although rousing in Raff's arms had been one of the more pleasant ways Penn had awoken in a long time.

It was a shame that it was unlikely to happen again.

The pleasant memory carried him along until he reached the crossroads at the centre of the town and noticed the people gathered there.

He pushed through the crowd, trying to get a better view of what was going on, wondering where Raff had got to.

Until, suddenly, he didn't need to wonder anymore. He edged past a woman covered in flour and spotted Raff standing beside the town's well. Another man stood a few metres from him, bellowing something Penn couldn't make out.

There was a large dog at the stranger's feet, hackles raised, growling at Raff. The light feeling in Penn's chest quickly turned tight and icy.

The dog snapped. Raff didn't even move, but Penn stepped back instinctively.

He turned to the floury woman, who was watching enraptured.

'Excuse me—'

The woman peered at him.

'What's happening? Who is that man – the one shouting?'

'Everard,' she said, with a poorly concealed grimace. 'The alderman. *One of* the aldermen.'

'Oh?' said Penn, sensing there was more to the statement. 'Does he fancy himself the *only* one?'

The woman smirked, but swiftly fixed her face to hide the expression.

'His dog was worrying a horse,' she continued, talking quickly as if to cover the facial slip. 'The other man – forgive me, I do not know him – saw off the dog and freed the horse.'

'And Everard takes offence at being chastised by one lower than him?'

The woman neither confirmed nor denied the guess, but simply added: 'And a Scot, at that.'

Penn should have expected this. There was still bubbling discontent between the two countries, but he had hoped they would not directly run into anti-Scottish sentiment on the road.

'And what happened to the horse?' he asked.

The floury woman pointed, and Penn craned his neck to see the creature now standing unsteadily in the field beyond the crossroads.

'No one has attempted to claim it?'

She shook her head, expression set. Penn read her easily: *no one dares.*

Penn glanced around. The street was full of onlookers, locals and traders, keen for the snatch of excitement. None of them were moving, more than happy to watch Raff face down the shouting man alone. He prickled with anger at their callous indifference before realising that were he not with Raff – had he not *known* him, as he did now – he likely would have been happy to stand and watch as well.

He scowled, edging forwards cautiously. He needed to see how this would play out. If he threw himself into the fray too soon, he could get Raff killed.

He drew close enough to hear what, exactly, they were saying.

'We are here to trade and rest,' Raff was explaining. 'Nothing more. Simply one night—'

The alderman took another step forward, his dog at his heels, and Raff fell silent. In the low winter sun, Penn could see a flash of steel at the alderman's hip. Surely Raff must have noticed too.

'I don't need your money, Scot.'

'We are simply passing through,' Raff said, his voice shockingly level for a man being threatened.

Penn knew that Raff's father was English, and wondered why he wasn't leading with that, trying to placate the man's anger with misdirection. Perhaps it hadn't occurred to him; he could be used to such treatment, as well as his attempts to argue his case being dismissed. Penn watched, keeping low. The dog at the man's heels let out a deep, rumbling growl.

'You should be thankful I did not cut you down where you stood for your insolence,' said the alderman, one hand reaching for his dagger, the other poised with splayed fingers above the dog in a clear command to *stay*. 'Grateful I spared you for these few, pathetic minutes. I will—'

Penn couldn't delay any longer. He shoved the people standing in front of him aside and burst onto the crossroads. Both Raff and the alderman turned.

'My good man!' he shouted, pulling himself to his full height. 'Might I ask what all this noise is in honour of?'

'This does not concern you.'

'If you intend to use *that*—' he glanced darkly to the dagger, 'my apologies; it does. What seems to be the problem? I leave my tracker for but a moment, and I return to . . .' He gave the man a pointed look, and was pleased to see he looked cowed.

'Your tracker?'

'Oh, forgive me,' Penn said, as if suddenly remembering. 'My appearance and choice of travelling companion must seem unusual.

I am heading north, indeed to Scotland, where I hear tell that there are some ferocious boar which are as delicious as they are notoriously hard to kill. I consider it a personal challenge.'

He grinned, the lie coming easily and smoothly the more he spoke.

'Of course, they are no more than a *rumour*, but I have hired this man—' he gestured carelessly towards Raff, 'to guide me. I thought I would make a winter hunt of it. I find myself bereft of purpose after my father's death.'

The man blinked at him, clearly struggling to take in so much information.

'My sympathies,' he said, his face still set in a frown that showed just how little sympathy he really felt.

Penn ignored the glower, brushing him off and continuing in a haughty tone.

'It is my brother you must reserve your sympathies for. Thrust into a Lordship quite unexpectedly, while I escape into the wilderness. Much more comfortable than the Honour of Wallingford during this . . .' he winced, a deliberately overblown expression, 'time of unrest,' he settled on, praying that this man didn't know the true Lord.

The alderman nodded. He'd taken the lie, but his expression had not softened and his hand still clutched the dagger. The dog continued to growl.

'This Scot—' he spat, not to be deterred.

'Is part of my retinue,' Penn interrupted. 'The *only* part of my retinue, so I would rather he remain alive. He thinks I am mad, choosing to venture so far with such a small party, but I am afraid I have rather taken him hostage. He has little choice in the matter, considering how far we have already come. Besides,' he grinned,

'I relish the challenge. Akin to a pilgrimage, wouldn't you say?' Penn watched the man's mouth open and close indignantly. 'Anyway, he is only *part* Scot. His mother's side, I believe.'

The alderman scowled. He clearly disapproved of Penn's choice of companion, but mentioning a *lordship* had made him aware of his place. If this came to violence, it would be difficult for him to avoid the consequences of his actions. Still, he did not let go of the blade at his hip.

'I want you gone. Both of you.'

'My friend—'

'I am *not* your friend,' the alderman growled. 'This man threatened my dog and dared speak to me as if I were no more than *muck*.'

Your dog was out of control. Your dog was attacking that horse. Raff saved *that poor, abused creature, while you and all your men stood by and did nothing.*

Penn choked it all back. 'Truly, we need to stay but a single night and we'll be moving along.'

'No.'

'I – no?'

'No. No stopping. By rights I could have your tracker in the stocks for presuming to lay his hands on my property. But I will not; so long as you both remove yourselves.' The dog took a step closer to Penn. *'Now.'*

Penn swallowed. 'As you wish,' he said, quickly. 'Raff? I believe we've spent as much time as is useful here. Shall we . . .?'

Raff nodded, his expression as set as it had been during the rest of the encounter, and strode forwards. Together, they hurried back towards the stables, aware of the gaze of the alderman on their backs.

'Penn . . .' Raff started, once they were out of earshot.

'Not yet.'

They readied and mounted their horses with haste. Penn kept his eyes downwards, his fingers slipping as he tightened the straps of the saddle and bags. He dared not turn around.

They left the stable at a trot – not too fast, lest their speedy exit paint them as guilt-ridden men, running from a crime. They both knew Penn had lied, spinning the words so easily, and if they left without raising further suspicion then it was likely they wouldn't get caught in the web.

Penn stared ahead at the road, his lips tight shut, his skin prickling. The eerie feeling of wariness stayed with him till they were well away, following the bending road. They were safe, he knew, yet he couldn't shake the sensation that they were being watched. It was the first dangerous encounter they'd had since leaving his father's keep, and it sent him back to the memory of raised voices, of threats that always saw themselves to bloodied completion.

He thought he'd freed himself from that violence. He'd been wrong.

All at once, the weight of what they had so narrowly avoided came crashing upon Penn's shoulders.

Raff was talking to him, he was sure, but his voice sounded far away, the low tone warbling as if he was speaking underwater. Penn's fingertips tingled. His back itched.

'Raff—' It was all Penn could manage before dark spots burst in front of his eyes.

He couldn't remember getting down from the horse – he *certainly* couldn't remember Raff guiding him to a low farmyard wall to sit. There was a waterskin in his hand, and he drank greedily, the cool water reviving him.

'My apologies,' he said, once he'd regained control of his tongue. 'But I just realised how close we came to being torn apart in the street.' He tried to laugh, but the sound was choked. 'He would have killed you. He would have killed *me* for defending you. My God . . .'

Raff didn't speak, but laid a gentle hand on Penn's shoulder. Penn resisted the urge to lean his cheek against it.

'I have never feared for my life like that before,' Penn said, squeezing the skin between his hands and feeling the water sloshing inside. 'And . . .' he swallowed, looking away, 'your life too. You just *stood* there.'

'What else was I to do?'

'Curse it, Raff, you should have fought back! Would you have done, had he attacked you?'

'I would have had to.'

'You would not have chosen to, though.'

'I would not.'

Penn shook his head, running his hand through his hair with a sigh as Raff continued to speak.

'I am forced to admit, though—'

'Yes?'

'I was impressed with how you dealt with him. *Very* impressed. I merely stood there—'

'Waiting for him to set his dog on you.'

'Waiting for him to set his dog on me, if it pleases you.' Raff chuckled, and the warm sound went some way to settling Penn's nerves. 'Yet you twisted him in words so thoroughly he forgot which way was up.'

'There was not much else I could do.' Penn sniffed. '*Had* he set his dog on you, or used his knife . . .' he winced, even at the thought, 'I doubt I would have been much help.'

The truth of that statement stung. He had vowed to make himself useful – and he *had* – but it was luck more than skill that had saved them.

They sat in silence for a few moments. Penn shivered, the cold biting at him once more now his panicked heart was settling.

‘We should make camp,’ said Raff, at last.

Penn shook his head with a huff.

‘We should be sleeping in comfort tonight,’ he said, allowing Raff to pull him up so they were standing side by side. ‘And we find ourselves in the wilds once more.’

Raff squeezed his hand.

‘There are worse places to be.’

Chapter Ten

When they finally stopped, the sun had sunk behind the horizon, rendering the sky a deep, luxuriant purple. Raff set Penn to building a fire and prepared to head into the woods to catch them something to eat.

'Rabbit or pheasant?'

Penn turned to him. 'What?'

'We've no wild boar,' Raff continued, grinning. 'A disappointment for the Lord of Wallingford, I know.'

'It's the *Honour* of Wallingford,' said Penn, grandly. 'The Lord owns the Honour.'

Raff shook his head. 'Southern nobles are fools.'

Penn snorted. 'Perhaps.'

'I hope you'll be content with whichever unfortunate beast I can catch first?'

'More than content.'

Raff left him to the fire and headed between the trees. As he walked, keeping his footsteps light, he thought of Penn's actions in town. He'd risked both his wellbeing and his hard fought for freedom to keep Raff out of harm. It set a strange, fluttering feeling in his stomach. Penn could have fled, leaving Raff to his fate. He'd chosen not to.

He considered Penn's words on the road: *What if he had set his dog on you, or used his knife?* Raff had suspected Penn was devaluing the importance of his intervention, but now he was alone he could see that he was right. If it *had* turned violent, it was unlikely that Raff could have kept them both safe.

Penn had told him that he had no training. He had a dagger, but could not use it for more than slicing turnips. Raff was suddenly struck with the image of Penn, unable to protect himself, falling beneath a dog's jaws or an attacker's blade.

The thought made his blood run cold.

When he returned to camp with a scraggly pheasant, he found Penn meticulously chopping carrots. He discarded the blade as Raff approached, and together they made quick work of preparing the meal. Once the kettle was boiling, Raff took Penn's dagger from where it lay on the grass, wiping it on the edge of his cloak and examining it with a critical eye.

'This is a fine blade,' he said, turning it over in his hand. 'You truly have no combat training?'

Penn shrugged. 'Only a little. I do not think my station required the skill.'

'You're not in the Earl's keep anymore,' said Raff, handing it back to him. 'We are on the road. You were right: had the alderman chosen violence, it would have ended in bloodshed. You should learn how to use it.'

'Oh.' Penn blinked at him, sheathing the dagger. 'I had intended to sell it, in truth. I thought the money would be more valuable to me than the blade.'

'A few extra coins won't serve you if there's a man with a knife to your throat, or an arrow between your eyes,' Raff said. 'Keep the blade, even once you are settled in a new household. *You* should know that a lord's protection cannot always be as thorough as one would hope.'

'How am I to learn, then?' Penn asked.

'I will show you how to use it.' Raff turned to face him. 'Use it *properly*, should you need to. I am a hunter, not a fighter, but I can teach you enough.'

'You do not need—' Penn began, but Raff cut him off.

'You are right. I do not need to. But I will. The incident today was deftly handled, but it was a breath away from ending in violence. I will not have you placed in a situation where you are unable to defend yourself.'

'I defended myself – and you – very well,' said Penn, insulted.

'You did,' Raff said, 'and I am grateful for it. But next time you may face a more unreasonable man. Or do you propose to charm your way out of a bandit's grasp? Will you convince a wolf not to rip out your throat?'

Penn glowered at the fire.

'I am not trying to insult you,' Raff said. Penn didn't look at him, and he resisted the urge to place a hand upon his knee. 'Let me teach you. At least how to defend yourself.'

Penn's shoulders slumped. 'I warn you,' he said, 'I am no great warrior.'

'How fortuitous.' Raff smiled. 'Neither am I.'

It was growing late by the time they'd eaten. Raff knew he should wait until morning for their first lesson, but he saw a nervous sleeplessness in Penn that was mirrored in himself. He suspected that any attempt to slumber would be blocked by visions of what they had escaped in Arlescote. A good lesson – a *thorough* lesson – would tire them both sufficiently that they wouldn't be able to linger on it.

A cool breeze blew through the camp, and Penn shivered beside him. That was another thought Raff tried to ignore: it would freeze again tonight.

He unsheathed his own dagger, turned it over in his hands a few times, then passed it across to Penn. He took it cautiously, examining the gleaming blade.

'This is likely too heavy for you,' Raff said, 'especially as you're not used to using a knife at all. It's designed for hunting, not combat; killing and skinning, rather than seeing off an attacker.'

'I see.'

'Your blade,' he pointed to the one at Penn's hip, 'is more decorative, yet still useful. In truth, it is not well-suited for self-defence, but it is what we have. Any blade is better than none at all. Remove your gloves, feel the weight. Compare the two.'

Penn did as he asked, unhooking the dagger and laying it on his lap beside Raff's. Raff's was larger, yes, but Penn's finer: a well-made rondel with a carved bone handle, the shining steel completely untarnished. Raff wanted to ask where he'd acquired such a blade, considering his station, but suspected he would not care for the answer.

A stolen blade was a small price to pay. A snatch of revenge, as well as freedom. Even more of a reason not to sell it: it was far too conspicuous not to draw notice, and would no doubt wend its way back to de Foucart.

They talked through the very basics first, Raff aware that he was likely insulting Penn's intelligence by pointing out the difference between hilt, pommel and grip. But Penn listened intently anyway, following Raff's hands with his eyes as Raff explained why Penn's dagger had only a single edge and his had two.

He listed the merits of a leather grip versus bone, demonstrating on their own knives, bidding Penn feel the difference. When Penn grabbed the hilt of Raff's blade, Raff was so lost in the lesson that he reached out instinctively, curling his hand around Penn's fingers to demonstrate the best grip. He realised too late what he'd done. Penn's skin was warm beneath his, softer than his own calloused grasp. Neither of them pulled away. They were so close, shoulders pressed together, knees knocking.

He heard Penn take a shuddering breath and immediately let go. When he had suggested that he train Penn himself, he'd been thinking practically: Penn needed tutelage, and he was a willing teacher. He'd not considered what training him would actually entail. Close moments, fingers wrapped together, bodies locked in combat. His skin tingled.

Raff swallowed heavily. The night had truly drawn in. Somewhere beyond their camp an owl began to hoot – a low, mournful noise that echoed dully through the trees. They should sleep; get rest where they could before moving on early next morning.

But this thing – this odd, close thing – was too much to resist.

'Let me see your grip again,' he said, 'on your blade, now.'

Penn grasped the hilt. Raff adjusted Penn's fingers, moving his hands and wrists to demonstrate the best position. Penn allowed himself to be moved, copying Raff's gestures, a soft, irresistible smile on his face whenever Raff praised his technique. Penn's blade was more delicate, trickier to maintain a sure grip on, but he worked hard, half-lidded eyes sparkling.

'Up,' Raff said eventually. 'We'll see how you fare on your feet. The stance is different, and you're more likely to be attacked standing up than you are sprawled on the floor.'

Penn scrambled upwards, leaves clinging to him. When standing, his grip was looser, his posture unbalanced. Standing with his legs planted in such a haphazard way, it would be easy for even an inexperienced attacker to disarm him and knock him down.

Raff told him this, demonstrating the correct stance, and Penn *laughed* at him, almost daring.

'My stance is poor?' he repeated, eyes glinting in the low light. 'Come, then. Disarm me.'

'Penn . . .'

'You cannot?'

'You are not *trained*.'

'Well, if you are such a coward—'

Raff jumped forwards, taking him by surprise. He hooked his foot around the ankle closest to him, tripping Penn backwards, then threw an arm around his back and shoved the other elbow first into his wrist, making him drop the dagger as he fell with an undignified shout.

But he did not hit the ground. He stumbled directly into Raff's arms, staring up at him, his face flushed.

'A scoundrel would have let you fall,' said Raff, tightening his hold around Penn's shoulders, leaning over him.

'Then I should count myself lucky,' Penn breathed, steadily maintaining Raff's gaze, 'that you are not a scoundrel.'

'Only if you do not continue to goad me.'

Penn grinned. His dark eyes were made of fire and starlight. He shuffled, steadying his footing amongst the piles of leaves, but he did not move away from Raff's touch. He edged closer, drawing himself forwards and upwards without ever leaving Raff's grasp.

Their faces were barely a hand's breadth apart.

Raff's arms were steady, but his pulse was racing. He could close the gap in an instant. It would take no effort to lean in and press their lips together, to feel Penn's mouth once more, to lock him in an entirely different kind of fight; one in which Raff was sure that Penn had the upper hand.

Somewhere nearly beyond hearing, there was a screech – a fox or a deer. In the shadowy night, it sounded almost like a dog.

They both froze. Penn's wide eyes glazed, his breath hitching. Raff edged back, heaving him onto to his feet.

'You . . .' There were hundreds of things he could say. Hundreds of things he needed to say. 'You are a quick learner.' He swallowed. 'We should sleep. It is late, and . . .'

Penn nodded wordlessly at him as he trailed off, before moving back towards their horses to get their things. He passed Raff's bedroll towards him, but when Raff went to take it, he found it stuck in Penn's grasp.

'It is another cold night,' Penn said, without letting go. 'Dangerously so.'

They stared at each other over the proffered bedroll. Something unspoken simmered between them.

'Yes,' Raff agreed. 'It is.'

Chapter Eleven

They slept deeply, and awoke early the next day with the cracking yellow dawn. Penn opened his eyes to find his face against Raff's broad chest, his hands balled into fists between them. Raff's arm was loosely slung around him, now fallen to his hip. The gentle touch, however casual and unbidden it was, sent a shiver down Penn's spine, sparking a heat lower in his belly.

He clenched his fists harder and tried not to think about it. He shuffled on the rolls, their cloaks heavy over his shoulders, attempting to put a little more space between them lest he embarrass himself.

He pulled back, lifting his head, and with sudden horror realised that not only was Raff awake, but he was staring at him, his expression alert and amused. It was not a dissimilar expression to the one he'd been wearing yesterday, when they had nearly—

'You talk in your sleep.'

Penn blinked, the memory dissipating like smoke. He tried to remember what he'd been dreaming of, in case it was something that would incriminate him. His dreams of late had either been nightmares or sweet, torrid things, and Raff would surely baulk to know of either.

'What of?'

'I could not tell. Your pronunciation is poor.'

Relief washed over him as Raff smirked and sat up, finally moving his hand away from Penn's hip. He looked dishevelled in the early morning light, his dark hair in chaos around his head. He stretched with a wince – clearly so long sleeping on the ground was leaving him stiff and sore as well. Penn surreptitiously tracked his movements, unable to pull his eyes away.

'Come.' Raff stood, dragging his cloak with him and leaving Penn shivering on the rolls. 'We ought to move on. Let us pray the next town is more friendly towards travellers.' He wrapped the cloak around his shoulders. 'And *I* shall pray that you are as fast a learner as you seem.'

As they moved on, Raff told Penn the full story of the alderman, Penn's face twisting into an angry grimace. Raff thanked him again for calming the situation – or at least guaranteeing it did not end with his blood being spilled – before finally voicing the question that had been playing on his mind since the previous evening.

'Why do it?' he asked, carefully. 'You took an enormous risk.'

Penn gave him a sceptical look. 'Because no one else was going to act,' he said. 'Because I *need* you. And . . . because I feared losing you more than I feared that stupid man.'

'Penn—'

Penn's cheeks had turned pink. Surely just the biting winter wind.

'Come,' he said, spurring his horse into a canter. 'It is freezing, and the next village is some way away. I am desperate to eat something not cooked over a campfire.'

Raff could only follow helplessly behind, Penn's words ringing in his ears.

They *did* find a good meal in the next village, as well as directions to an inn that could put them up for the night. Raff watched as Penn charmed a kitchen girl into exchanging far fewer coins than they ought to for two slices of a rich-smelling date loaf, still oven-warm, which they shared by the roadside. The girl had seen Penn off with a wink and a giggle, enquiring if he would be in the village long. Something bitter coiled in Raff's gut: a feeling he couldn't name that stuck with him till they fell asleep in the shared sleeping quarters above the inn.

The next morning, Raff was half expecting Penn to announce that he would remain in the area to seek work. But he didn't. He was up before Raff, waiting impatiently to get back on the road.

It was not the last time they passed somewhere suitable. They had hurried across the Oxfordshire border, but now they had journeyed into the counties beyond they were taking a longer, more meandering route. As they travelled, Raff knew that they should be enquiring for keeps looking for staff, yet neither of them did. Penn could just be waiting till they were further north. No doubt he was enjoying his freedom: even under a compassionate lord's rule, he would still be a servant, bound to one keep for – potentially – the rest of his life.

Raff sympathised with his desire to cling to independence for as long as he could. And if Penn stayed a little longer, even if it was only for a few days, then Raff was happy to have him. He could ignore the emptiness he knew he would feel when Penn finally chose to leave.

As William de Foucart, Penn had hated travel. Journeys with his family seemed to last for ever, leaving him with aching limbs, saddle sores, and blisters where he'd worried the leather of the reins between his fingers.

As Penn, the journey by Raff's side felt like it would last for ever too. He hoped every day that it *would*, coming to dread the moment when Raff would leave him behind.

He tried not to dwell on it. If he was in a melancholy mood, then Raff would likely leave him even sooner. It wasn't as though Raff had spoken about finding him somewhere to stay. Penn could hold onto this, for just a little longer.

Raff had been correct, and they found hospitality easily now they were away from Oxfordshire. On nights where beds were unavailable or the next town too far, they had fallen into an unspoken arrangement, sleeping close together beneath their cloaks. Penn would wake with their legs tangled and his heart fluttering.

They continued to train, whether sleeping outside or staying in an inn or rest stop. Raff was an inexperienced but attentive tutor, entirely unlike the men who'd attempted to teach Penn as a boy, and he was coming to keenly anticipate each evening's lesson.

They were sparring in the courtyard of a bustling inn after growing bored of a game of dice, garnering a small crowd of onlookers. When Raff was distracted, Penn managed to land a lucky blow to his wrist, making him drop his blade and eliciting a cheer from their meagre audience.

It was the first effective move he'd managed to strike, and he couldn't hold back his delight. For a moment, he was concerned that Raff would take offence at the loss, but instead he leaped over the fallen dagger with a beaming smile and pulled Penn into a hug so tight his feet lifted from the floor.

Heart racing, Penn promised to buy Raff a drink to make up for the defeat. In the end, he didn't need to: as they sat in the far end of the room, shoulders brushing, they were joined by a wealthy-looking man with warm brown skin and a broad smile carrying three slopping tankards of ale. Penn stiffened, fearing discovery, but it transpired that the man – Benedict, a merchant turned alderman – had watched them spar and was eager to make their acquaintance, even going so far as to offer them a night's room and board in his home when he heard they were travellers.

They had treated his kindness with caution at first, but it soon became clear that he was well-liked in the town and hungry for gossip. All he required in exchange for food and a place to sleep were stories about their journey, and they eagerly accepted.

As if by some unspoken agreement they ignored the more tantalising news of the lost lord, speaking instead of the harsh weather. Penn gave him the boar hunt story, and Raff added a couple of tales which Penn didn't recognise, assuming they were from his journey south. Benedict had been thoroughly enraptured, and after they'd eaten had even offered them use of his bath.

'You both appear to need it,' he said, laughing over the rim of his tankard. Penn was forced to admit that he was correct.

The tub had been placed in the kitchen beside the largest hearth in the house, the room emptied. Penn had settled himself on the bench at the long table, insisting that Raff use the water first, feeling distinctly that he deserved it.

Penn had lost count of how many days ago they had kissed, but he was still dwelling on how Raff's body might look beneath all those layers of winter clothes. They'd undressed around each other, of course: it couldn't be avoided on the road, no matter how much Penn tried to hide his own body. The winter weather had made it a brief, perfunctory affair, and Penn hadn't seen anything more than flashes of skin: a glimpse of pale back or sturdy thigh. Once, still playing in Penn's mind, the defined curve of Raff's chest and the jut of his hipbones as he'd pulled his tunic up and over his head, taking his undershirt with it.

And now Penn knew. Raff had peeled off his clothes without a second thought, and Penn was unable to look away. He was broad, his arms wide and well-defined. His skin was as pale and freckled as his face, hidden under dark hair that trailed down his chest and lower, over his stomach.

The days of hard travel could be seen in his body, but he wasn't slender, either. His torso looked temptingly soft, although Penn had seen enough of him on the road to know that there was strong muscle beneath.

Penn let out a low breath as Raff lowered himself into the water. As he washed himself, he spoke easily, apparently unaware of Penn's staring. The only sound was their voices, the crackling fire, and the slosh of water lapping against Raff's skin. Penn could almost pretend that Raff wasn't so thoroughly naked, so maddeningly close.

Penn really did look away when Raff finally emerged from the water and began to dry himself on the clean linen sheet their host had provided. Penn needed to rein himself in, to focus on something – *anything* – else, lest he give himself entirely away when it was his turn to strip and Raff noticed how obvious his attraction was.

A hand clapped to his shoulder. Penn looked up to see Raff – his hair wet and his undershirt clinging to his skin – standing patiently beside him. He passed him the hard soap, and for a moment his fingers lingered on Penn's palm. Penn swallowed, feeling far too warm even for the humid space. Without thinking, he hastily rose from the bench, throwing off his clothes and getting into the tub before Raff could look too closely.

The bath was already murky after Raff had washed. Under another circumstance Penn would have felt discomforted by that thought, but this evening he was thankful for the cloudy water as he splashed in, pulse racing. Raff sat on the bench as Penn quickly ducked under, wetting his hair. When he emerged, Raff abruptly spoke.

'What are those?'

Oh, no. His back. In his haste, Penn had completely forgotten to hide it. He froze, a horrible weight in his chest. He wanted to sink back down and conceal himself beneath the water, but it was too late. Raff had already seen. There was a scrape as the bench moved across the stone floor and then Raff was behind him, staring.

The last time Penn had attempted to look at his scars was the night his father had told him of the marriage. He'd gone to his room in a daze, ripped away his clothes and twisted around, trying to look over his shoulder to see their full extent. He'd been appalled, then, at the idea of someone else seeing them.

He cursed himself for forgetting them.

Raff was silent. Penn was sure he was about to turn away, disgusted, when there was a soft noise behind him, and then – a gentle touch on his back. It felt like a brand. Penn flinched, jerking forwards, water splashing over the side of the tub.

'*Don't—*' It was all he could say, ducking lower till the water and the wooden rim concealed him.

Raff snatched his hand away.

'Have you never been disciplined?' Penn's mouth was barely above the surface.

'Not like this.'

'Clearly I am more poorly behaved than you.'

'*Penn—*'

There was sudden, misplaced pain in Raff's voice. Penn didn't deserve it. 'It's fine.'

'It's *not—*'

'I do not wish to talk about it.'

Raff fell silent, hastily stumbling back to the bench. 'I'm sorry.'

Penn didn't speak. His scars were normal, he knew. They were expected. But he had also known, even when he was young, that his outnumbered those of his peers. As children, they had been among the first to ask about them, to push and prod and demand to know the stories. To ask what he'd *done,* to be so punished.

They had been the first to wince and turn away, revolted.

They had not been the last.

He wasn't supposed to talk about them. After Leo had gone, all of Penn's companions – never friends, just his father's allies' heirs – were chosen for him. Chances to socialise were chaperoned. He'd asked another lad, older than himself and stoically serious, if he too was so punished. He had shaken his head, and quickly changed the subject.

Later that day, his father had taken him aside and warned him not to mention them again. He'd left with another mark on his back and his lips tightly shut.

No doubt he *had* deserved them. He *was* more poorly behaved than his peers, or than Raff had been when he was young.

If he hadn't deserved them, someone would have put a stop to it.

The water around him was growing cold, and he could hide no longer. He grabbed for the sheet lying beside the tub and swiftly rose, tugging it around his shoulders.

He shivered, and the fabric clung to the broken landscape of his back.

Raff stared at the wooden beams above the bed, resolutely awake, feeling Penn's warm, slow breaths against his skin through the thin fabric of his undershirt.

When they had lain down to sleep – the agreement to share the bed entirely unspoken – Penn had placed himself a careful distance away. But in sleep, as ever, the space between them had closed. Penn had twisted till he slumbered beside him, almost on top of him, one arm slung across his torso and the other folded between their bodies, fingers clutching Raff's undershirt. His cheek was pressed to his chest, his lips parted.

Raff held Penn there, his arms looped around his shoulders and back. He could feel every place their bodies touched in knife-edge sharpness.

He willed his heart to quieten; surely the noise would wake him.

Despite how exhausted Raff felt, sleep refused to come. Every time he closed his eyes, he saw Penn's back.

Raff could remember the tradition of boasting about injuries with the other lads he was training with, before his squiring was cut abruptly short. They'd all been green boys, but had shown off their scant scars as if they were warriors returned from battle. So young, and so fresh, many of his peers' most impressive scars had been dealt at the hands of their parents or teachers.

All of them paled in comparison to the criss-crossing mess of raised skin that marred Penn's back. Raff wasn't a fool – it was a father and master's right to punish those within their household however they saw fit – but he'd never witnessed brutality to this extent before. He wondered at whose hand those marks had been made: father or master.

He needed to *fix* it, but he couldn't fathom how. His efforts could be a pointless attempt to soothe a hurt so deep that there *was* no soothing it.

He squeezed his eyes shut, trying to focus on his breathing, and was assailed again with that terrible image. Something squeezed in his breast, a snare twisted around his heart.

Overwhelmed with the pain of it, he ducked down and pressed his face to the crown of Penn's head, breathing him in. He smelled of soap and smoke and *Penn.* His damp hair was warm and soft against Raff's lips.

Raff was struck with the sudden, blinding urge to place a kiss there.

But he didn't. He sighed against Penn's hair, holding him tighter. Everything else fell away – their journey, the room, the bed beneath them – until all that remained was the feeling of Penn in his arms, and his gentle breath against his skin.

Chapter Twelve

Penn awoke to a rumble beneath his ear and a hand on his back. Once again, he'd slung himself against Raff in his sleep. His cheek was pressed against Raff's shoulder, their legs linked, his hand clutching Raff's undershirt. Raff's arms were wrapped around him, although his grip was loose. He was snoring.

Penn wanted to close his eyes and return to the blissful peace of slumber. He wanted to lie awake and listen to Raff snore, to move with the rising and falling of his chest. To feel his heartbeat. But Raff's hand was on his back, and Penn's undershirt was only thin linen, and panic was already swirling in his belly, frosting across his skin.

Carefully, he pulled away from Raff's grasp. Raff stirred, but didn't wake.

Penn edged across the mattress, his skin prickling coolly in all the places where their bodies had touched.

When dawn came, Penn was on the very edge of the bed, clinging to the woollen blanket. Raff lay an arm's reach away, his lips slightly parted. The space between them had opened up. Penn had forced it open.

Keen for distraction from his own turbulent thoughts and – more pressingly – how temptingly soft Raff's mouth looked, he slid from the bed.

He dressed quickly, feeling foolish. He and Raff had slept just as closely before, and he'd never been left feeling discomforted then. But before, sleeping outside and fighting off the cold, he'd been protected by linen and thick wool. Beneath the blankets of the bed, the only thing between Raff's loose touch and his scars was a single layer of fine, thin fabric.

And Raff had *seen* them. He knew. Something in Penn's core had been exposed, struck open for Raff to examine.

By the time Raff woke, Penn was ready to leave.

They left Benedict with their thanks, and in turn he wished them luck on the road, gifting them supplies for the journey ahead.

'I have more than I need,' he said, passing Raff a pack stuffed with food. 'Good luck with your journey, and your hunt.'

As they rode out, the weather held, and the heavy clouds that hung on the horizon never quite reached them. It proved to be a fine day for travel, and they made good progress.

Penn feared that Raff would bring up the subject of his back, perhaps to ask how he'd come to acquire his scars. The thought made him nauseous. Most people found them hideous, but many had treated their hideousness with fascination. If Raff asked, it would not have been the first time Penn had found them – and himself – being scrutinised. People loved stories, especially ones that ended in blood.

Something told him that Raff wouldn't want to know the long, drawn-out details of the dozens of times Penn had been punished at his father's hand, or at his father's command. He wouldn't demand the grim retellings of the story behind each lash. He'd wear that expression of soft sympathy, his voice laced with pain, just as it had been when he'd seen them.

In a way, that was worse. Penn had earned each and every scar.

When they stopped to rest just after midday, Raff's usually affable expression had melded into something more sombre.

'Penn . . .' he began, looping his horse's reins over a branch and turning to face him.

Penn went cold. His back itched, the skin sensitive and stinging. So this was it: this was the conversation he'd been dreading.

Raff took another step closer. Penn wanted to run.

'Get out your dagger. We should train, while the weather holds.'

The fear had been for nothing. The tightness around Penn's ribs loosened again.

'Of course,' he said, able to breathe once more. 'What do you intend to teach me today?'

Raff dropped his pack to the ground beside a fallen tree and walked towards him, stretching out his shoulders.

'All I can.'

As they journeyed further north, Raff continued to insist on training, throwing himself into Penn's tutelage with an intensified vigour that left Penn exhausted. After a long day's ride, or when the weather turned poor, he would hope that *this* day Raff would let him rest, yet he was always there, dagger in hand.

'You need to defend yourself,' he would say, heaving Penn up to his feet. 'You need to be able to protect yourself, if I am not here.'

Raff's concern was frustrating, but he made a fair point. If Penn was alone and attacked, it would be a short fight. So he allowed himself to be pulled up, his stance corrected, his dagger knocked from his hand. It wasn't entirely a burden: their sparring forced them together, breathless and panting, the warmth of Raff's body igniting a different kind of heat in Penn's core.

He felt it in moments of stillness too: in the gentle way Raff moved his grip on the hilt or pressed himself against Penn's back as he demonstrated the best way to hold his arm. Penn even watched, enraptured, as Raff taught him how to treat his blade, honing the edge with a whetstone then daubing the steel with slick-looking oil to prevent it rusting.

He wondered – the thoughts coming further apart the longer they travelled – if his father's men were still hunting for him. When he *was* allowed to rest, he pictured what might happen if they found him. He imagined himself fighting them off, his dagger in his hand and Raff at his side. It was a foolish dream, but when he managed to land a blow or Raff praised his technique it almost felt like it would be possible.

They were travelling late, pressing on past sunset towards a town that Raff had stayed in while heading south, when they found the way blocked. A river had burst, engorged with meltwater, flooding the road and severing their route. The short journey to a place to sleep became a further day's ride as they were forced to find an alternative path.

The diversion was no great hardship – they still had supplies enough for another day on the road – but it would be the first time they'd made camp outside since leaving Benedict's home. There was a tension in Penn's shoulders and a fluttering in his belly as they found a suitable clearing in the trees away from the roadside: it would be the first night they'd slept close together after Raff had seen his scars, and Penn had forced himself to pull away from Raff's arms.

There was no way he could adequately explain his unusual silence, so it was a relief when Raff suggested Penn head into the trees to fetch kindling. A few minutes alone would give him time to gather his thoughts.

As he moved between the trees, occasionally grabbing a dry-looking stick, he considered his position. The weather was freezing. If they *did* fall asleep tangled together as they had so many times before, he would be wearing such thick layers that his scars may as well not exist.

If. His apprehension was borne of nothing more than an assumption. Raff might not even suggest such sleeping arrangements. As Penn bent to grab a likely-looking branch, he smiled ruefully. If Raff didn't suggest it, he almost certainly would himself. He was weak, and he craved Raff's touch more than he hated his scars.

Penn tucked the branch under his arm, satisfied that he'd found enough. He was about to head back when there was a rustle from the trees beside him. He froze.

There: a crack. Footsteps. Someone moving between him and the clearing.

Penn edged through the trees, trying to keep to the shadows. They'd encountered lone travellers before, but those times he'd had the comforting presence of Raff at his side, and even a desperate bandit wouldn't take on two men.

But now he was alone. No doubt it was just another traveller, hurrying home before the worst of the winter weather set in. There was no reason for him to think that they were a criminal, or someone who would recognise him. Yet that fear burrowed in him regardless, making his pulse race and his breath stop, as his eyes fell on the shadowy figure of a man ahead.

He'd *prepared* for this, he reminded himself, or at least he was more prepared than he had been when he left the keep. He grasped the hilt of his dagger. With any luck, the man wouldn't even know he was there. They would go their separate ways, and he would return to Raff unharmed with kindling under his arm and a tale of a stranger in the woods.

The man moved around a tree, heading in the opposite direction to their camp. Penn sagged with relief, took a sidestep away from him, and stepped directly onto a rotten branch. He winced as the crunch echoed from the trees around him.

The man turned.

His face was partially obscured in the low light, but Penn could see enough. Dark hair, a smattering of stubble, and a deep scar webbing down his right cheek to his jaw before disappearing beneath the collar of his cloak. It tugged the corner of his mouth upwards.

In a slow, deliberate movement Penn unsheathed his dagger.

'Stay back,' he warned, trying to keep his voice even. 'I want no trouble.'

The man raised an eyebrow. He *smirked*.

'Aye,' he said. 'Nor me. So how about you put that thing down?'

He sounded Scottish. Penn clutched the dagger tighter, a clear refusal. 'I would prefer not to,' he said, far more calmly than he felt.

'Is that so?' The scarred man turned properly, taking a step closer. 'A shame.'

He darted forwards. Penn dropped the firewood and raised the dagger, but the man was quicker. They swiftly descended into a messy struggle. Penn slashed at him, trying to recall Raff's lessons, but those moments had been easy and safe. Now he was panicking, moving instinctively without calculation or form.

He ducked under the man's arm and brought the dagger around in a sweeping curve. He missed his target by several inches, stumbling as he overshot the movement. As he attempted to right himself, the man grabbed at one of his flailing arms and yanked him up with such force that there was a bone-deep wrench in his shoulder. Penn yelped, and the man squeezed, pressing his thumb into the inside of Penn's wrist. Pain flared through his palm to his fingertips, and he dropped the dagger.

The blade gone, Penn's attacker spun him, kicked at his ankles and sent him tumbling to the ground. Penn fell heavily, his temple colliding with a rock buried beneath the leaves, making his vision pop in white spots. The man sat atop him, keeping him pinned, one hand tangled painfully in his hair.

'Now,' the stranger said, 'let's not have any more trouble. I'm sure we both mean no harm.'

Penn struggled uselessly. 'Says the man who has me pinned.'

The scarred man laughed, then reached with his free hand to grab Penn's dagger from the ground.

'Says the man who turned a knife on me,' he said, waving the tip dangerously close to Penn's nose.

'But—'

Before he could plead his case, Penn found his face being pressed into the leaves, words muffled. Frustratingly, the man was right: Penn had started this fight, even if it had been an act of self-defence. He held his tongue.

'So,' the man continued, 'can we agree to be—'

A snap echoed through the trees, followed by frantic footsteps. The man fell silent, tugging Penn's hair even tighter. Another snap – someone hurriedly moving through the forest – and then, at last, a voice: clear and loud and instantly recognisable.

'Penn?'

Penn's attacker went still. Penn twisted his head around, spitting out a mouthful of damp leaves.

'Raff?'

The pressure on his back lessened. The man shifted, and taking advantage of his distraction Penn pushed against him and called again.

'Raff!'

Before the scarred man could act, Raff burst through the trees. He immediately spotted Penn and leaped forwards, reaching for his own weapon.

Then he saw the man straddling Penn's back. To Penn's dismay, he lowered his hand.

'Ash?'

Penn dumped the kindling into the small circle of stones Raff had arranged in the centre of the clearing. His head throbbed where it had struck the rock, and his back ached. He kicked the sticks into a haphazard pile before straightening and stretching out his shoulders, pulling his arm across his chest where the stranger's attack had jarred the joint.

He flexed his fingers with a wince. Not a stranger. Ash. Raff's *brother.*

Close behind him, the pair were loudly talking. Ash's tone was lighter now he was no longer being threatened.

'So you failed to find William, I take it?' Ash was saying, as Raff knelt beside the firewood.

Raff struck the flint with more force than was necessary, throwing up sparks. 'I did.'

'What a shame.'

Penn looked up to spot Ash sneering. He kept his mouth shut. Ash glanced at him, before edging around Raff towards him. For a moment, Penn feared he was discovered – that somehow, Ash knew who he was – but Ash merely smiled, extending his hand. He was still holding Penn's dagger.

'Here,' he said. 'I believe this is yours.'

Penn went to reach for the blade, but Ash snatched it back before he could take it.

'You must promise not to threaten me with it again.' He smirked.

Penn resisted the urge to scowl. 'What if you deserve to be threatened?'

Beside the fire, which was now smoking, Raff laughed. Ash's teasing expression held for a moment, before he too grinned.

'Aye,' he said, taking the dagger by the blade and pressing the hilt into Penn's hand. 'Then you may hold me down and slice my bollocks off, if it pleases you.' He paused, his fingers still pinched around the steel. 'And if you can best me.'

He let go. Penn tucked the blade back into the sheath on his hip. Ash gave him another sly smile and took a step back, walking straight into Raff, who'd risen without either of them noticing. Raff shot his brother a look which Penn couldn't read before moving past him – not *quite* pushing him aside – to stand beside Penn.

'So,' Ash said, gesturing towards them both with a lazy hand, 'how did you two come to be travelling together?'

Penn swallowed. Since Arlescote, they'd been using the same lie whenever a stranger asked them who they were or where they were going, the story about his apparent Lord brother and desire to hunt wild boar growing more elaborate every time he told it. But Ash was no stranger. He wasn't a nosy traveller or a curious alderman. He was Raff's brother. Penn had no idea how much would be safe for Ash to know.

He looked to Raff, a silent plea for help.

'We are heading north,' Raff explained. 'Penn is – he *was* a servant, in de Foucart's keep. I found him in Hartswood Forest, the night after—' he stumbled over his words, 'after William disappeared. He asked for my help finding work elsewhere. Or, rather . . . I offered my help when it became clear that he'd be dead within the day if I left him.'

Ash's eyebrows crept higher. 'You fled your master's keep?' he said, addressing Penn directly.

Raff spoke before Penn could. 'You met de Foucart. Would *you* wish to stay?'

Something hung in the air between the two brothers. Penn wasn't sure what had happened, but a challenge appeared to have been laid down.

Ash ceded first. 'No,' he said. 'I would not.'

'Exactly. And nor would I.'

'I am not sure that is reason enough to steal a servant, Raff.'

Penn bristled. 'He did not *steal* me,' he snapped. 'I *left*. I could not very well ask de Foucart for permission, could I?' He sighed, attempting to relax his shoulders. 'Raff is right. If he had left me, I would have died. I couldn't even light a fire.'

Ash's expression wavered.

'Still,' he said, 'I do not—'

'*Ash*.'

Penn's head snapped around. He'd heard Raff be *stern*, but there was steel in his tone that he hadn't heard before. Ash fell silent.

'It is what it is,' Raff continued, leaving no further room for debate. 'How about you make yourself useful and catch us something to eat if you intend to bless us with your company? Make amends for wounding Penn.'

It appeared as if Ash was about to argue, but he sighed, scowled, and strode back into the woodland. It was only after the dark green of his cloak had vanished into the shadows that Penn even registered what Raff had said.

He lifted his hand and carefully felt at the spot above his eyebrow, wincing as his fingers brushed against the bump forming on his temple. They came away bloodied. He must have cut his head when he cracked it on the rock. He cursed under his breath.

'Let me—'

Penn turned to see Raff hovering, nearly – but not quite – reaching for him. Penn gave him a quick nod before settling down beside the fire. Raff grabbed his waterskin and a scrap of cloth from his pack before sitting beside him, their knees pressed together.

Penn ducked his head, allowing Raff better access. Raff leaned forwards, gently brushing Penn's hair away and tucking it behind his ear. Penn felt himself relaxing, allowing himself to breathe for the first time since finding Ash.

'Does it hurt?' Raff asked.

Penn sighed. 'Yes.'

'Do you feel unwell?'

Penn shook his head, the movement making his head pound.

'Good. I just need to . . .'

Raff trailed off as he dampened the cloth and got to work. He curled one hand around the back of Penn's head, keeping him still. The touch was warm and comforting.

'So,' Penn said, peering down at him, 'your brother attempted to kill me.'

Raff smiled. 'If Ash had been attempting to kill you,' he said, 'you would know.'

'Oh *good*.' Penn sniffed. 'I shall keep that in mind for next time.'

'I, ah . . .' Raff stilled, the cloth held to Penn's temple. 'I am sorry,' he said. 'For Ash.'

'He didn't know who I was. It was reasonable of him to assume I meant him harm. I thought the same.'

'And yet *you* are the one whose wound I am cleaning.'

Penn attempted to shrug. 'I overestimated my own abilities.

I thought I would be able to see off an attacker.' Raff laughed, and Penn scowled at him. 'What?'

'You barely know how to hold a dagger correctly. Ash has been sparring for *years,* since he was old enough to wield a sword. He's—' He hesitated, a moment, lowering his voice and continuing to wipe gently at the cut. 'Ash has been in *battle.* I suspect you would struggle to best him even after years of practice.'

Penn hummed, unwilling to concede.

'One day you will be experienced. For now, it is enough that you tried.' Raff frowned. 'Although next time you find yourself threatened, I would prefer you run.'

'And why is that?'

Raff retracted the hand that was cupping the back of Penn's head.

'Because I did not bring you all this way for you to be killed by a bandit.'

'How thoughtful of you.'

'Indeed.' Raff stopped dabbing, looking at the injury with a critical gaze. 'There,' he said. 'That will suffice.'

His fingers lingered on the side of Penn's face, the edge of his hand pressed lightly against Penn's temple. His eyebrows were still tilted into an expression of genuine, soft concern. He was so *close,* near enough that their breaths mingled, forming clouds in the space between their chests.

Around them, the trees creaked, and the fire spluttered sparks into the darkening sky. Penn allowed himself this moment of peace, the pain in his head slowly abating.

From far away, there was a muffled crash. Raff rolled his eyes with a fond smile. He removed his hand from Penn's cheek and stood up, the bloodied cloth still in his hand.

'I should see if Ash needs assistance,' he said. 'I have always been the better hunter.'

Penn's skin tingled where Raff's hand had been.

'Of course,' he said. 'I shall prepare the camp.'

It took no time at all for Raff to find his brother, following his heavy footsteps and muttering, cursing both the forest and the animals within it. He hadn't lied; Ash *was* the poorer hunter, too impatient to track with any real success, but that wasn't why he needed to find him.

When he and Penn had been travelling alone, Raff had been able to maintain the façade that he was little more than a tracker. Now, the lie – which had never been well constructed – would topple at a single word from his brother. He needed to ensure it wouldn't.

He caught up with him at a jog. 'Ash—'

Ash turned to face him with a beleaguered sigh. 'What?'

'I need a favour of you.'

'Oh?' Ash raised his eyebrows, his disinterested expression turning into one of curiosity.

'I would appreciate it if you did not . . . if you didn't tell Penn about our father. Or Lily's betrothal.'

Ash's eyes widened, intrigued. He watched Raff carefully. 'Why not?'

Raff looked away, breaking Ash's probing gaze. 'He doesn't know who I am.'

'*What?*'

'When I found him, he assumed I was a tracker, working for one of de Foucart's guests.'

'You *lied* to him?' Ash said, aghast.

Raff darted forwards, panic swirling in his chest. 'Be *quiet*, for God's sake,' he said. 'I did not *lie*. I just . . . failed to correct the assumption.'

'And what is the difference?'

'I—' Raff began. 'There is no difference,' he conceded. 'Christ. You think I ought to tell him?'

Ash shrugged. 'That depends entirely on what you intend to do with him.'

'Would *you* tell him the truth? Were it you?'

'Raff.' Ash stepped closer, and clapped a hand to Raff's shoulder. 'I would not have lied to him to begin with.'

He shook his head, clearly amused, then strode onwards.

'After all these years,' he continued as Raff caught up, 'we have finally discovered what it takes to get a lie out of you.'

'And what is that?' Raff asked, darkly.

'A lovely face and a warm body.'

'Shut your mouth,' Raff hissed. 'It is not like that.'

Ash's lip quirked. 'Truly?' he said, disbelieving. 'There is nothing between you? At all?'

A kiss in the woods cut short. Penn's breath on his neck, his hands on his chest, their limbs twisting together as they slept. An offer, refused.

'No,' Raff snapped.

'And nothing has happened? Not *once*?'

Raff faltered for a moment too long. Ash pounced immediately.

'I knew it. You are incapable of lying to me. Tell me, then.'

'There is very little to tell.'

'And yet still I want to hear it.'

Raff sighed, aware that his brother would not drop the subject. 'Fine,' he relented. 'But it *was* just once. The first night we met. It will not happen again.'

Ash looked back at him, his hand resting against the trunk of a tree. 'The *first* night you met? But . . .' He paused, working it out. 'The servant in the forest,' he said. 'The one who knew about William.' He began to laugh. '*Raff—*'

'I said, be *quiet*—'

'You never did explain to us why you spent so long with a stranger.' Ash's grin deepened, twisted by the scar. 'You spent all night with him, did you not? You returned to camp at dawn.'

Raff remembered that morning, what felt like an age ago now. The lightness he'd felt in his chest as he'd made his way back into their tent. He could still recall the kiss – the taste of Penn's lips and the huff of his breath – as if it had happened that same day.

'You were awake,' he said sourly, glad that the encroaching darkness hid his heating face.

'*You* woke me,' Ash countered. 'But as a loyal and dutiful brother—' Raff snorted at that, but Ash continued undeterred, 'I chose not to pursue the matter, considering the mood you left in.'

'How kind of you.'

'This *does* explain the lie, I suppose. Why didn't you tell him?'

Raff swallowed. 'He didn't know who I was. It was easier. It was a – a *relief*. To be someone else for a night. Besides, he is a *servant*.'

'And? I thought you didn't agree with that nonsense about lesser classes of men?'

'I don't, but that does not mean I didn't have power over him. That I still do.'

'Which is why you have resolved that nothing more will happen between you?'

'Exactly. I will not hold myself over him like that.'

Ash smirked. 'I am sure he would be quite keen for you to hold yourself—'

'*Ash!*'

Ash raised his hands in surrender. 'Fine. I will not tell him.' He shook his head, exasperated. 'I cannot believe that you're begging me to lie for you. This is unlike you, Raff.'

'I did not *beg*,' Raff said, ignoring the rest.

'So you would be perfectly content with me telling him exactly who you are?'

Raff spluttered, 'You said—'

Ash laughed. 'I thought as much. I will not tell him; you have my word. But your secrecy seems pointless if you really have no intentions to bed him.'

'I do not,' Raff said, quickly.

'Even if you want to?'

I do not. It would be easy to repeat himself. It would be easy to deny, to tell Ash he was seeing something that wasn't there. That Penn didn't want that, either. But Raff had been quiet for too long. Ash raised his eyebrows.

'I know you better than you know yourself, it seems,' he said. '*And* your friend. As I said, I am sure if you were to—'

'Why are you here?' Raff snapped, unwilling to listen to any more of what his brother had to say.

'Keen to be rid of me already?' Ash gasped, placing a hand over his heart. 'How cruel of you.'

'Of course not,' said Raff, suspecting it was not entirely the truth. 'You should be home already. Why are you not?'

Ash kicked the leaves at his feet.

'I left the retinue a few days ago,' he said. 'We stopped in a tavern at the roadside, and I remained.' He spotted Raff's expression, and hastily added, 'Only for a few days! You find me on my way back.' Raff continued to scowl. 'Truly. I am not lying to you. I *am* heading back. I was cut off by the floods.'

They too had been waylaid because of the burst river, yet still it felt like a convenient excuse.

'I do not like that you left Lily alone,' Raff said.

Ash raised an eyebrow at him. 'Like *you* did?'

'I left her with her *eldest brother.* I left her with the man who one day will inherit our father's title. The man who is *supposed* to be—'

'Enough!' Ash grumbled, throwing his hands up. 'I concede. I should have stayed with her.'

'And what about Father?' Raff pressed. 'Has he returned yet?'

Ash shook his head. 'He did not re-join the retinue. But he could have returned to Dunlyn during my absence. Lily is probably home already.'

Raff frowned. 'Odd. De Foucart must have kept him longer than he anticipated.'

'Then he'll have my sympathies when he *does* return,' Ash said. 'I would not wish to spend a day longer in that place than I had to. I suppose they've much to discuss.' He sighed. '*Did* you receive news on William?'

'I suspect he is dead,' Raff said. 'I told de Foucart as much myself, although he didn't seem to take me seriously.'

'A fine example of a doting father.'

'Indeed.'

As they walked on through the trees, Raff wondered if he ought to tell his brother about Penn's relationship with the Earl's son. He could finally voice the belief that Penn's attachment to William had been more opportunistic than genuine. Ash's cynicism may be useful for once; he would be better poised to see through the act, if that was all it was.

But it was not Raff's story to tell. Ash would not baulk at the idea of Penn being with another man, but no doubt he would question him where Raff was content not to press the matter. For Ash, William's disappearance was a convenient way to free Lily from a marriage she didn't want, and Penn's relationship with William would be no more than an amusing afterthought.

It held more weight than that, for Raff. What if he was wrong, and Penn's feelings for William had been real? There was a lurch in his stomach: the unnerving feeling that he was being weighed against a ghost.

He set his shoulders, and kept the secret behind his teeth.

'Whatever has befallen William, I am glad Lily is out of it,' Ash continued blithely, ignoring Raff's silence. 'I would not wish to be tied to that family.'

'No,' Raff agreed, trying to clear his head of thoughts of Penn's erstwhile lover. 'Nor I.'

Chapter Thirteen

They returned to the clearing richer for a pair of unhappily startled rabbits, and with Ash's horse, which he'd left hitched to a tree not too far off. Ash loudly made clear his intentions to stay with them for a couple of nights, claiming that he wished to spend time with Raff after so long apart. Raff doubted his sincerity – to his mind, it had been no time at all since they'd parted – but agreed regardless. It *was* good to see him again, even if he kept shooting Penn looks that Raff was struggling to interpret.

Penn had coaxed the fire into something they could cook over, and a heap of foraged mushrooms rested on his cloak alongside the last of a particularly hard loaf of bread. He was still treating Ash with caution, but as the night drew in Raff could see his shoulders relaxing and the tension in his back slipping away.

'That wound is neat,' Ash said as they ate, gesturing to the mark above Penn's eyebrow. 'It may not even scar. A shame; we could have matched.'

Ash waved in the direction of his own face. Penn stilled. Raff waited to see how he would respond.

'If you wish to match, you will need to do worse than throw me against a rock,' Penn said, impassively.

Raff looked to his brother. For a moment, his expression was blank. And then he laughed – quick and sharp and loud.

'Indeed I would,' he said. 'I cannot help but notice you have not questioned how I came to be so handsome. Aren't you curious?'

Penn shrugged. Raff watched the lift of his shoulders, the shift of his cloak on his back.

'Does it matter how it happened?' he said, quietly. 'Or is it not enough to simply know that it did, and say no more about it?' He sat back, tilting his head. 'Unless you *wish* me to ask, of course, and this is an attempt to boast.'

For once, Ash was speechless. 'No,' he said at last, 'but I am used to strangers subjecting me to their questions.'

'And *I* have no intentions to do so,' Penn responded. 'Tell me, if you wish. But I am not asking you to.'

With that, Penn skewered a hunk of meat on the end of his knife and shoved it into his mouth, effectively ending the conversation. Ash stared at him, before finally continuing his own meal. His silence did not last long; soon he was loudly complaining about the thinness of the broth, and any tension that had settled over their meagre camp lifted.

When the meal was over and the air around them crisp with the promise of frost, Raff began to prepare for sleep, banking the fire and seeing to the horses. Ash muttered unhappily about sleeping outside, but Raff kept back the retort he wanted to throw at him: *if you wished to sleep comfortably, you should have remained with the retinue.*

Ash had never been well-suited to the road, especially without the guarantee of a pallet and tent. Raff wondered if he had complained as much when he'd marched off to war, or if he'd managed to hold back his grievances.

He somehow doubted it.

Raff ignored his brother, preparing his bedroll with a weight in his stomach. When they'd found their path blocked that afternoon, he had allowed himself to imagine the sort of night he and Penn would find themselves spending together, already anticipating the warmth of their embrace as they slept under their shared cloaks.

He'd missed Penn's gentle touch, these past few days. He hadn't realised how much he came to enjoy it – and subsequently crave it – until he no longer had it.

Penn was not too far away, setting up his own bedroll beside the fire. His eyes were down, shoulders hunched against the biting breeze. He was trembling again, despite the thick woollen cloak. Raff had told him that sharing heat was typical when travelling on the road, and it was. Yet this was different.

He could accurately claim that Ash – a man who'd ridden with an army in all weathers – would understand. He *would* understand, but he had also known without even asking that something had happened between them, and had pushed Raff to dwell on it again. He would be able to see that for Raff there was more to the gesture than simply staving off the frosts.

He couldn't do it, and shuffled beneath his blanket and cloak, trying not to think of how cold it would be without Penn pressed beside him.

Next to him, Penn buried himself beneath his makeshift blankets. Between the thick wool and the dark mass of curls, all Raff could see were his eyes and the tip of his nose.

'Goodnight, then,' Penn said, voice muffled.

Raff pulled his own cloak up. If he closed his eyes, he could almost pretend that the empty space between his arms had been filled.

'Goodnight.'

✡

Raff woke to ice on the ground and a boot to his back. He rolled over with a curse, bitterly recalling why he'd been keen to set out alone. Ash, it appeared, was eager to get back on the road. Raff sat up as Ash complained about the cold, and beside him he could see white strands frosting through Penn's curls as he too rose with a grimace.

They moved on quickly, and without the shadow of Ash and Penn's first meeting hanging over them conversation came smoothly and easily.

Apparently forgiving him, Penn had warmed to Ash, countering his smugness with edged cynicism of his own. Ash's sharp tongue and sharper nature was matched in Penn's acerbic wit, and Raff soon found them both talking over him.

Ash asked, in a pointed tone that Raff did not miss, what they had been doing on the journey north; why a trip that should have taken two weeks at most was dragging on so long.

Penn had shrugged, expression casual. Raff was unsure if he'd missed Ash's implication or was choosing to ignore it.

'We have decided to take a longer route,' he explained, 'to find me work without relying on the keeps we come across on the main roads. I am less likely to be recognised that way.'

It was entirely a lie – they hadn't stopped at a single keep at any point on their journey thus far. Ash nodded along anyway.

'Very sensible,' he drawled. 'But do you not find yourself growing bored at my brother's side? The evenings are long, this time of year, and the nights even longer. You must be wanting for ways to fill your time.'

There was a slight pause before Penn responded. The tips of his ears were pink.

'I am well distracted,' Penn said, carefully. 'Raff has been teaching me to fight. Rather, he has been *attempting* to teach me. I suspect I am not built for combat.'

Ash smirked. 'So *that* explains why you felt prepared to attack me?'

'I did *not*—' Penn cut himself off, shaking his head. 'Yes,' he sighed. 'That is why.'

'And it also explains why you were *not*.'

Penn frowned. 'What do you mean?'

'If it is *Raff* who is teaching you . . .' Ash grinned, 'I would be surprised if you could take on much more than a wounded rabbit.'

'That is unfair. Raff is a good instructor.'

'I would wager that he goes easy on you.'

Penn grimaced. 'It certainly doesn't feel that way.'

'Have you ever been trained in combat before?'

'Only briefly.'

'Then you have no way of knowing. No one to truly compare him to.'

Raff could see where this conversation was heading. Before he could put a stop to it, Penn spoke, sitting up straighter.

'What are you suggesting, then?'

'When we reach the inn, give my overworked brother a rest and spar with *me* this evening.'

'And you will *not* go easy on me, is that it?'

Ash gave a non-committal shrug. 'I will try not to.'

Raff tried again. 'I do not think—'

'Fine, then.' He and Penn had spoken at the same time. Raff fell silent as Penn continued, 'If you are so confident in your abilities.'

Ash turned in the saddle, and shot a smirk over his shoulder towards Raff. Raff felt a flare of anger, hot and sudden. Ash grinned wider as the feeling twisted in Raff's stomach, tingling down his arms to his fingertips, making him grip his horse's reins tighter as he was thrown back to the moment he'd found Penn pinned to the ground between Ash's legs.

Penn's head flicked around, following Ash's gaze. Raff attempted to fix his expression, but had clearly been too late. Penn's eyebrows quirked.

'Come,' he said, 'you told me I have much to learn. And you *do* deserve a night's respite from my ineffectual attempts at sparring. You are already doing too much for me.'

Raff hunched his shoulders. 'It is no burden.'

Ash dismissed him with a wave of his hand. 'And it is no burden for *me*, either. It has been some time since I've had a sparring partner; you will not deny me this opportunity, will you?'

Raff was pinned beneath their stares: Ash's of smug victory, Penn's of genuine concern.

'Fine,' he said with a sigh, aware that he had no reasonable excuse for denying them. 'But do not injure him again. It will not do to show up at a stranger's court with a servant with a broken arm.'

'Do not worry yourself.' Ash smirked. 'I will ensure he returns to you in one piece.'

As he turned back to the road, Raff scowled. Somehow, his brother's promise did not bring him any comfort.

Raff leaned against the low wall that surrounded the inn, watching Ash and Penn circle each other in the outer yard. As Raff watched, trying to focus on the stone beneath his hands instead of the quickness of Penn's breathing, he realised bitterly that Ash had been right: he *had* been going easy on him.

Penn had yet to land a single hit, and was behaving more recklessly the longer they practised. Raff was only able to watch, lips tight, as Ash landed blow after blow against Penn's weak guard. Penn was taller, but Ash was broader and stronger. There seemed to be no advantage that Penn could win from him.

'Again,' Penn said, stubbornly pushing his hair back from his face and fixing his grasp on the dagger.

Ash didn't give a word of assent, simply lunged forwards, sidestepped around him and grabbed Penn's wrist, jerking his hand till he released the blade. Before Penn could break free, Ash twisted his arm around, forcing Penn's hand between his shoulder blades until he stumbled forwards. Ash moved with him, keeping his chest pressed to Penn's back, one boot planted firmly between Penn's feet. Ash wasn't even out of breath; Penn was flustered, hair wild, his face flushed. Sweat was beading on his forehead.

Ash leaned over Penn's shoulder.

'Do you yield?'

Penn winced, struggling even harder. Ash didn't let go. He wasn't exerting any effort at all to keep Penn precisely where he wanted him.

The sickening twist in Raff's gut suddenly crashed against something else: something rational and *real*. Fear. He'd intended to teach Penn all he knew, promising himself that he would keep Penn safe, even when he wasn't there. He'd seen the mess of his back and sworn to give Penn a chance next time – if there *was* a next time – to save himself.

But it wasn't enough. It wasn't *nearly* enough, and he could see the proof in front of him. Ash was an accomplished fighter, but more so, he didn't hold himself back. If Penn was confronted alone, by a real attacker, he would be doomed.

Ash pressed forwards, tightening his grip, pushing Penn down. Penn made a cut-off noise, a sharp inhale between his teeth. Ash *laughed*.

'Well?' he said, his lips dangerously close to Penn's ear. 'Do you—'

'Enough.'

At Raff's voice, Ash immediately released Penn, letting go of his arm and stepping back. Penn righted himself, rubbing his wrist.

'You're going to injure him,' Raff said as Ash approached. *'Again.'*

Ash did not appear remorseful. 'A danger of sparring.' He shrugged.

'I'm *fine,*' Penn sniffed, giving his fingers a quick flex before bending to grab the dagger.

'See?' Ash headed through the gate, Penn following close behind. 'Do not be so dramatic.'

'You have always been heavy-handed.' Raff tossed Penn's cloak back to him, who draped it over his arm with a sullen expression. 'Even when we were boys.'

Ash shot him a sly smile. 'And *you* have never been so cautious. You're growing soft, little brother.'

Raff ducked out of the way as Ash attempted to ruffle his hair. 'Forgive me for not wishing to spend my evening cleaning up blood.'

'It won't come to that,' Penn said, forcing his way between them and pushing past into the inn.

'No?' Raff followed him inside. 'It has before.'

Penn finally turned to look at him. His expression of annoyance was replaced with one of interest. 'Oh?'

'Ash is the one who broke my nose,' Raff explained, gesturing to his face as he guided them towards a table in the corner of the room.

Penn's eyebrows rose even higher, and he let himself drop onto the bench beside him. *'How?'*

'We were jousting.' Ash sat opposite, leaning his arms on the worn wooden tabletop.

'With broom handles,' Raff put in. Penn stared at him, and he added, 'We were young, and it was Ash's idea. Ash missed, hence . . .' He gestured again to his nose.

'I did not *miss*,' Ash said. 'I hit my target well enough.'

'And you wonder why I am hesitant to subject Penn to your *sparring*,' Raff said, with a shake of his head.

'You are just still bitter that I bested you.'

'Yes,' Raff sighed, unwilling to let Ash pull him into a years-old argument. 'I resent that you won, and still carry the grudge with me.'

Penn shot Raff a sidelong glance, clearly trying not to laugh. Ash grinned even wider.

'Good,' he said, 'I am glad to hear you finally say it.'

'And because you are such a noble and accomplished knight—'

'Yes?'

'You can enquire for a room for the night, and find us something to eat.'

Penn snorted, his shoulder colliding with Raff's as he attempted to smother the laugh.

'And something to drink,' he added, breathlessly. 'To celebrate your victory.'

Ash scowled at them, but rose from the bench and went to seek out the owner regardless.

It was a pleasant evening, and Raff was warmed by both surroundings and company. The coiling tension in his stomach from watching Penn and Ash spar had begun to loosen. It was reassuring to have Penn beside him once more, their shoulders brushing and knees knocking beneath the table.

Ash had managed to secure them a room in the roof which contained four cots, squeezed close together into the small space. The fourth bed had not been filled, so they had the room to themselves: a small luxury. Ash lowered himself onto the pallet closest to the door, tugging off his boots with a grimace.

Penn dumped his pack unceremoniously on the floor. He reached inside for his waterskin before moving to Raff's bag and pulling out his as well.

'I shall get these refilled,' he said, tucking them under his arm. 'Ash?'

Ash tossed his waterskin over, and Penn headed back down to the room below, the floorboards creaking beneath him. When he'd gone, Raff grabbed Penn's things and placed them on the cot closest to the stone wall before settling himself on the one in the middle. Ash watched him, eyebrows raised.

'What?' Raff said, taking off his cloak and leaning back on the pallet.

'He is a free man, thanks to you,' Ash said. 'A free man who can do as he likes.'

'I am aware.'

'Are you?' He heard the pallet creak as Ash rolled onto his side. 'Raff . . .'

Raff sighed, ready to tell him to drop the subject. But when he looked at his brother, the smug expression he was expecting wasn't there. His eyes were low, face sincere.

'You seem fond of him,' Ash said, voice measured. 'And I do not want to see you hurt.'

'I . . . value his company,' Raff conceded.

'You *value his company*?' Ash mimicked with a snort. 'Aye, and this—' he gestured to his scar, 'is but a scratch.'

Raff wanted to argue. To claim, again, that Ash had it

wrong. But he floundered, the denial clanging behind his teeth. Ash watched him closely.

'It is odd.' He looked down. 'He reminds me a little of Oliver.'

Raff froze. Ash *never* spoke of Oliver; none of them did.

'It is not like that,' he said, far too quickly. 'I—'

He was cut off by a sound from outside: the floorboards creaking. Penn reappeared, the waterskins dangling from one hand.

'Here . . .'

Penn threw Ash his skin, before handing Raff's over as well. Their fingers brushed; Penn's were still damp. He lowered himself to the pallet Raff had left free, settling on the lumpy, straw-stuffed mattress without passing comment on the fact that Raff had chosen his bed for him. He noticed the silence.

'Have I interrupted?' he said, glancing between them.

'No,' Raff said hurriedly, Ash adding, 'Not at all.'

Penn's eyebrows rose, but he didn't press the issue further as he pulled off his boots and slid beneath the woollen blanket.

There was a hole in the roof where the thatch had been damaged. Moonlight was streaming through the gap, palely illuminating the room. Pinpricks of light danced through the air like stars where dust drifted from the ceiling. Raff was resolutely awake, his head reeling.

He couldn't let go of the image of Penn held against Ash's chest, face flushed with exertion and adrenaline.

He wondered if Penn looked like that when *they* were sparring. His cheeks red, his eyes wide, his chest heaving. If his skin took on a fine sheen of sweat when it was Raff pressed against him.

The image of Penn sweaty and panting beneath his own hands was entirely too tempting, but one that was forced aside by the memory of Ash's smug expression as he'd kept Penn in place. It was an unpleasant image, and the more Raff lingered on it the more he wished he'd forced them apart.

There it was again: that twist, opening up an angry hollow in his chest. And then he realised, with dawning horror, what it was. He was *jealous*. He feared for Penn's wellbeing when sparring with his impulsive brother, but more than that, he didn't want Ash near him to begin with. He didn't want him *touching* him, pressing their bodies together, ghosting his lips over Penn's ear.

The jealousy was tight, hot, and unutterably dangerous. It would not do. Beneath could lie something far more damning, a pain he couldn't stand to touch. Raff tried to think back to the kiss. *That* memory carried with it an entirely different kind of pain, but one that was familiar and manageable.

He *had* managed it – taking himself in hand in brief moments of solitude he'd stolen, sneaking off into the trees like a youth. Those moments came wrapped within shame and guilt; the furtive feeling that he was doing something wrong exacerbated by the images that flitted through his head as he sought release: Penn, always Penn.

There was no relief for this other pain; no way to make it abate. There was no substitute he could find at his own hand for the feeling of Penn against him as they slept, or the twitch of his fingertips against his arm, or the smell of him as Raff buried his face into his hair, his chest, the crook of his neck. If he was truly desperate, he could seek satisfaction with someone else, but he knew it wouldn't suffice. It wouldn't come close to what he sought, and would leave him all the more wanting for it.

You seem fond of him. Raff tried to scrub the conversation from his memory, to ignore Ash's gentle questioning that was so much more painful than his teasing. With a muffled groan, he rolled onto his side, trying to silence his thoughts so he could sleep.

His breath caught. Penn was awake and watching him, his eyes shining in the sparse moonlight.

'You cannot sleep?'

Penn's voice was little more than a whisper. It was lucky their pallets were so close. Raff silently shook his head.

Penn sighed. 'Nor I.'

'Aren't you tired?'

Penn frowned. 'I *am,* and that is the worst of it. I am unable to let go of my thoughts.'

Raff swallowed. 'I find myself in a similar position.'

'Anything you wish to share?' Penn asked, moving to reveal more of his face.

Raff wished he could. 'No,' he said instead. 'It is . . . I am overthinking things.'

Penn smiled. 'As usual, then.'

'Exactly.'

Penn nodded, looking away.

'So . . .' he continued, eventually, '*that* is your brother. You are not dissimilar. Although . . . very different too. Not in any way that matters, I suspect.'

Raff smiled. 'Is that not true of all brothers?'

Penn granted him a true smile. 'Yes,' he said, 'I found—' He cut himself off, the smile faltering.

Raff peered at him. 'What is it?'

Penn pulled the blanket tighter. 'It does not matter.'

It was as if a cloud had covered his expression. In the low moonlight, Raff could see him frowning.

He was about to ask again when he was suddenly cut off by a snore from Ash's pallet so loud that dust fell from the rafters.

Penn burst into stifled laughter, pressing a hand over his mouth. Raff couldn't help it; he too had to force himself to stay silent, biting his lip so as to not laugh out loud and wake his cacophonous brother.

'I—' Raff was interrupted by another snore, rumbling from Ash's chest like thunder. 'I suspect neither of us will sleep now.'

Penn's lips quirked. 'Should we wake him?'

'If *you* wish to wake him, you may try,' Raff said. 'But I have no desire to have my nose broken again.'

'Perhaps we could go, and leave him here,' Penn whispered. 'I would sleep better outside with only the owls to disturb me.'

Raff paused. He *would* sleep better outside, though it had little to do with the comparative peace of the woods.

'I agree,' he said, keeping the rest of that thought to himself. 'Much better.'

Penn shot him a soft smile, almost like he understood.

'We shall just have to struggle through tonight,' he said. 'And tomorrow—' he swallowed, as if catching himself before continuing, 'tomorrow we may have more luck.'

Raff imagined what tomorrow night could bring. What he would be granted, if they were once again forced outside. He ducked his head, turning away from Penn's piercing gaze.

'I can only hope we do.'

When Raff woke the next morning, flakes of snow were drifting through the hole in the roof, dusting across Penn's still shoulders.

As they left the inn and rode on the weather held, but the dark skies promised that it would become a blizzard soon enough. Ash and Penn chatted as they followed the path north, the conversation turning to Raff's childhood: shared mischief, tales of their sister and parents. True to his word, Ash didn't mention their father's position, nor the family's noble lineage, carefully guiding the conversation back to safer topics whenever it seemed like Penn might ask one question too many.

Raff was grateful for that. His brother thought the lie was a step too far, but he was keeping it regardless.

They stopped at the fork that split the road; the direct path to Dunlyn heading north, and the longer route winding west. This would be where they parted.

Penn shot a look towards Raff before leading his horse away, giving them privacy to speak. It was an unasked for but appreciated gesture, and when Raff turned from watching him rearranging the straps of his horse's reins he noticed Ash staring too. There it was again: that unpleasant twist of jealousy in his chest as his brother's curious gaze bore into Penn's back.

'I hope your journey home is swift,' Raff said. 'Try not to linger, this time.'

Ash rolled his eyes. 'You do not need to chastise me again. I'll head back to Dunlyn.'

'Good.' Raff sighed. 'I won't always be there, Ash.'

'No.' Ash frowned. 'I think I am beginning to see that. But really, Raff. You worry too much. It's only a short way from here, and Lily is perfectly capable—'

'I *know*,' Raff snapped, before reining himself in. 'I know. But I would feel better knowing that you were home regardless.'

'Soon I will be. As should *you*.'

'I'll return as soon as I am able.'

'And when will that be?'

Raff forced himself not to look at Penn. 'It is hard to say,' he said, absent-mindedly stroking his horse's neck. 'I do not expect it will be long. A fortnight, perhaps.'

Ash raised his eyebrows at him. 'So soon?'

'There are dozens of keeps between here and Dunlyn. One of them will be wanting for staff.'

Ash snorted a laugh through his nostrils.

'What?' Raff huffed.

'There are an equal number of keeps and courts between here and Oxford,' Ash said. 'Were none of them "wanting for staff"?'

Raff made a non-committal noise, staring at his hands.

'Or was it that you did not think to check?' Ash continued.

'It is still too close—' Raff began, before being cut off by another laugh.

'Aye, of course,' Ash said, rolling his eyes. 'Too close, too dangerous. Or just too soon?'

'Meaning?'

Ash shook his head, and once again his eyes landed on Penn. He was watching them, too, and quickly looked away.

'You know exactly what I mean,' Ash said. 'Even if you choose not to think about it.' He lowered his voice. 'Why not bring him with you, when you return home?'

'I *told* you, he does not know—'

'All right,' Ash spoke over him, 'but if you *were* to tell him . . .' He trailed off, giving Raff a long, searching look. 'In any case. It is not my place. Good fortune on your journey; to both of you.'

'Thank you. And send my love to Lily and Father, when he returns.'

'I will,' Ash said. 'And I shall let them know to expect you in – what was it? A fortnight?'

Raff nodded, lips tight.

'I look forward to your return.' Ash walked his horse forwards a few paces and called to Penn. 'I am glad to have made your company, Penn. I hope my brother takes good care of you, as he promised.'

Penn turned. 'I am sure he will,' he called back.

Ash nodded at him. He gave Raff a final smile and a brief wave, then turned the horse towards northern road, his shadow thrown large by the still-rising sun, snow swirling around his shoulders.

Chapter Fourteen

It didn't take long for the weather to truly turn. They travelled through thick snow for hours, sometimes riding, sometimes leading the horses on foot when the flakes grew too dense to see the road ahead.

Raff had been acting oddly since Ash left, and the weather meant that Penn hadn't been able to ask if he was all right. As the day passed, Penn began to fear that Raff's mood was to do with Ash himself.

Raff had seemed perfectly at ease around his brother, and as Penn had watched them tease each other he'd felt a mingling sense of joy and jealousy. It made him happy to see Raff so freely comfortable with someone else, and it was clear they cared for each other despite the endless jokes, but it made him remember his own lost brothers; the relationships he would never have.

Penn too had enjoyed Ash's company – when he wasn't pinning him to the ground – but his affability could have been an act. He'd only caught the very end of the conversation that they'd been having in his absence, and found himself dwelling more than once on who Oliver could be; if the comparison was an unfavourable one.

Penn attempted not to linger on those thoughts, instead focusing on the difficult way through the snow. No doubt Raff had simply slept poorly, just as he had, and would be happier for a good night's rest.

They finally came upon a tiny farmstead, appearing slowly from the thick snow. It was too early to stop, but the roads were nearly impassable and the little progress they were making in the blizzard was not worth the effort.

An imploring tale about their journey to the farmer found them sleeping in a sturdy barn for the night. He had even allowed them to leave their horses in the stable and insisted on them sharing supper with the family in their tiny home. His two young children had been wary of them at first, until Raff had asked about the shining black mare in the stable and they'd both started babbling at once.

Penn had smiled at him across the table, amused at his ease with children. Warmed and fed, Raff's mood lifted, and by the time they retired to the barn Penn had all but forgotten his anxiety.

The farmer had been keeping a handful of cows, all recently slaughtered for the winter, so they had the space to themselves. Penn dropped down onto a pile of dry hay while Raff heaved the heavy wooden bolt across the doors, ensuring they would not be forced open by the wind.

The straw prickled at Penn's scalp and stuck in his hair as he stretched out with a long yawn. It wasn't as warm as it had been in the farmhouse, but without the bite of the wind it was bearable. He pulled the thick cloak from his shoulders, lying on it above the hay.

After securing the doors, Raff wandered over, peering down at him where he lounged.

'Get up,' he said, shoving him with the side of his boot as he removed his own cloak and surcoat. 'We should take this opportunity to train.'

Penn grumbled at him, sitting up. 'Did Ash not teach me enough yesterday?'

Raff scowled. He quickly tempered the expression, but Penn caught it regardless.

'You still have more to learn,' Raff said, turning away as Penn got to his feet. 'Your skills *are* improving, but you are not yet experienced enough to defend yourself without employing other techniques.'

'Other techniques?'

'Distraction. Weaknesses and advantages. Learning how to turn a fight in your favour. The other day, you managed to get the upper hand on me because I was distracted. That will be your boon, while you are still unpractised.'

'Are you proposing to teach me how to fight unfairly?' Penn teased. 'I thought you were honourable.'

'There is no honour in death. You need to learn to survive before you can learn to fight in a way which upholds your *virtues*. Besides, it is not cheating to understand another man's weaknesses, or your own advantages against him.'

'And what advantages are those?' Penn leaned heavily against the beam in the middle of the barn. 'You said yourself I'm inexperienced.'

'Not all advantages are obvious,' Raff said, walking around him. 'You are tall, but slight. That makes you fast, and it would be easier for you to escape if you needed to. You rely more on instinct than experience or form, which may throw off a more seasoned attacker if you behave in a way they are not expecting.'

'And weaknesses?' Penn smirked, before adding, 'Not my own, I'm well aware of them.'

Raff smiled. 'Watch. *Learn.* This is harder, as if you are being attacked you likely have had no warning. Watch for someone favouring a certain side. Note which hand they use to hold the blade. Every person you encounter will have a weakness. You have to find it, and exploit it.'

Penn moved away from the beam, drifting his hand to the hilt of his blade.

'And what about you?' he said. 'What is *your* weakness?'

Raff grinned. 'You must work that out yourself.'

Not waiting for Raff to make the first move, Penn surged forwards, unsheathing the blade as he did. He had hoped to take Raff by surprise, thus ensuring the upper hand, but Raff stepped backwards swiftly. Penn stumbled straight past him, feet slipping on the straw-strewn floor.

He righted himself quickly, spinning on his heel and turning back.

'Good,' said Raff. 'Now—'

They launched into the dance, their feet ever-moving, Penn trying to win an advantage. Raff anticipated his every step, leaping aside or blocking him with ease. When they'd first started training, Penn had found this ability intensely aggravating, but now he was beginning to enjoy the challenge.

He jumped forwards once more. Raff dodged again, sidestepping the kick that should have hooked around his ankle. Penn slid behind his back and attempted the movement again from his left side, but Raff was far too quick. He attempted to land a blow, which Penn countered, blocking Raff's hand with his arm before twisting around once more.

He was pushing Raff backwards rather than attempting to land a hit on him. Raff was right, he *was* quick on his feet, and his slender build made it easier for him to pivot around Raff's larger body. If Penn could back him into a corner – or against a wall – then he'd be trapped, and Penn would have the advantage.

It was a good tactic – or at least one he could maintain. Raff's footwork was more practised, his stance surer, but he was correct in his assumption that Penn's lack of experience made him unpredictable. He was only awarded a brief look of shock in Raff's eyes two or three times, but each time made his heart flutter with pride.

It was the pride that felled him. Feeling smug, he moved too quickly in an ill-prepared attack. Raff grabbed him around the waist, spun him, and restrained his arm until he was forced to drop the dagger.

'Swift,' he said, releasing him. 'But thoughtless. Again.'

Penn grabbed the dagger and took a wild swing forwards, launching himself up. Raff easily dodged the blow, ducked under Penn's arm, grabbed him, and pinned him with his chest against the barn wall.

'Have you worked it out yet?' he muttered over his shoulder.

Raff was pressed against his back, unbearably hot and close. Penn felt his breath on his skin, his hand wrapped around his wrist. Penn huffed against the wall, trying to think, but all he could focus on was the way their bodies touched. He was trapped beneath him, one of Raff's feet sliding between his own, and he wanted nothing more than for Raff to pull him around and kiss him.

He didn't. Of course he didn't. After a drawn-out moment, Raff released him, and the yawning, tingling space between their bodies returned. Feeling flushed, Penn shrugged off his tunic, throwing it to the floor as Raff backed away.

Raff had appeared to have the same thought, tossing his own tunic aside as Penn turned to face him. His undershirt was made of little more than thin linen, tight around his arms. His cheeks were ruddied. Penn found himself staring.

He took a single step forwards, stretching his arms. Raff's gaze, which had been trained on his eyes, snapped downwards, watching him. Taking him in. Penn licked his lips, his mouth suddenly dry.

Raff watched *that* movement, too, and Penn felt something hot flare in his stomach.

He took another step, tightening his grip on the dagger with a cocky grin. This time he moved more slowly, edging around, forcing Raff to follow his footsteps. He needed an opening – a single lowering of Raff's defences. He slunk in a circle, his fingers flexing around the hilt of the blade that he held low to his side, near his hip.

Raff watched him, closely, one eyebrow raised. 'Well?'

Now. Penn sheathed the blade and pushed forwards. He wasn't attempting to land a blow, just force him back. Raff tripped as Penn collided with him, and now both of Penn's hands were free he could bundle them in the fabric of Raff's undershirt, forcing him exactly where he wanted him.

He could feel the heat of Raff's skin through the material, his breath against his cheek, hear the unbidden noise of shock he made as Penn shoved against him with all his weight, slamming him against the wooden support beam. Penn's heart was pounding, his lungs constricting, his skin flushed and slick with sweat—

And then he was kissing him, fierce and hot, his hands clutching Raff's shirt.

Raff gasped, but he didn't pull away. His hands came around Penn's waist, tangling in the fabric of his undershirt. Penn opened his mouth beneath Raff's lips, eager to taste him, and Raff let out a low growl before Penn felt the hot brand of his tongue against his lip.

Penn ran his hands down Raff's torso, fervently pulling his shirt aside to reach the skin beneath as Raff deepened the kiss. He slid his hands under the cotton, digging his fingers into Raff's flesh with a needy moan as Raff sucked his bottom lip into his mouth, nipping it between his teeth. Raff's skin was warm and soft and reassuringly solid beneath his palms; better than Penn had anticipated all those nights ago when he had pushed him away.

Penn knew he shouldn't. He knew that it could have damned him, especially after Raff's rejection. He hadn't thought, merely acted, giving into the blistering *want* which had finally overwhelmed him. But he didn't care that he *shouldn't,* not now Raff was kissing him back with an intensity that made his head reel. All his doubts and fears were pushed aside as the taste of Raff exploded into his mouth: the salted meat they'd eaten at supper, the beer their host had provided them. He tasted of *heat*; of something spiced and heady and intoxicating.

When Raff pulled back, Penn let out a low whine, attempting to chase his lips. Raff didn't extract himself from Penn's grasp or move away; just peered at him, expression steady.

'Penn . . .'

Penn kissed him again, tasting his own name on Raff's tongue. 'Yes?'

'Do you . . .' Raff paused. 'Are you *sure*—'

'Yes,' Penn spoke before Raff could finish the sentence; before either of them could come to their senses. 'Raff, *yes.*'

That appeared to be all Raff needed to hear. He ducked forwards again, pressing a line of kisses across Penn's jaw and down his neck, towards the place where his undershirt bunched at the base of his throat. He pulled the fabric aside with his teeth, his beard scraping against Penn's skin, before licking a heated, open-mouthed kiss against the sensitive spot where shoulder met neck.

Penn suppressed a groan, shuddering beneath the touch, feeling himself stiffening in his breeches. He arched back, urging Raff closer, pressing himself against Raff's thigh. Raff chuckled against his skin and squeezed him tighter, moving him minutely, till Penn could feel the unmistakably hard line of Raff's prick pressed against his hip too.

'My God, Raff—' he gasped, feeling the scrape of Raff's teeth against his skin. Raff laughed again – a low noise that only further inflamed the heat in Penn's belly – before leaning back.

Raff's eyes were dark, his lips kiss-bruised. His hair, which he'd tied back to train, was falling in dark strands about his face. When Penn had first seen Raff in Hartswood Forest, he'd thought he looked almost like a fabled god. He could see that in him again: in the curve of his smile, the arch of his brows.

Raff hesitated for just a moment before grabbing Penn's hand and guiding him backwards until Penn felt the crunch of straw beneath his feet. Then there was a boot behind his ankle, and he was stumbling down.

He landed with a soft thud onto the cloak and the thick layer of straw beneath it. Raff stood above him in the low light, eyes dragging down Penn's body, before easing on top of him, his knees either side of Penn's hips, his hand to his jaw.

Penn remembered Raff's words in the woods: *a scoundrel would have let you fall.*

He'd fallen, now.

Raff examined him with a hungry look that he didn't attempt to conceal. The hand that cupped Penn's cheek was hot, making his skin flush even deeper. Raff paused there for a moment, eyes searching Penn's face, before kissing him again.

Penn squirmed beneath the kiss, jerking his body upwards, sending tendrils of desire tingling down his spine, pooling in his stomach. Raff muttered something against his lips, the noise making his chest tighten, then pulled at the fabric of Penn's shirt. Penn froze, his muscles tensing, his heart skidding to a halt.

His scars.

'Raff—'

Raff had also frozen. 'I'm sorry—' He moved back, the gap between them suddenly vast. 'I forgot—'

He tried to move away, his expression clouded with guilt. There was no disgust or discomfort on his face, only earnest remorse. He *cared*, Penn realised, the thought sudden and wholly unexpected. He cared more about Penn's comfort than his own pleasure; cared so much that he was leaning back as if to leave.

The realisation made the ache within him flare even more urgently. Penn surged forward, pushing himself from the straw, and crashed their mouths together. It was a sharp, desperate kiss: an unspoken plea. His hands moved to the back of Raff's head, tangling in his hair. Raff didn't resist, and Penn pulled him down till they were sprawled on the cloak. Raff's hands were finally back on him, although now moving with more caution, warm despite the cool air of the barn.

Penn stroked down Raff's back, tugging at his shirt, and in a swift movement he pulled it away to reveal his bare chest and broad shoulders, his skin a constellation of freckles. Captivated, he leaned forwards, trailing kisses along Raff's neck, over his collarbone, to his sternum. Raff shuddered under the touch, so Penn opened his mouth wider, lightly pressing his tongue against his hirsute skin.

Raff hissed, and Penn was about to gloat when Raff grabbed him boldly by the shoulders, spinning them around so he was once again on top and Penn beneath. Penn's bragging was forgotten as Raff kissed him into the straw, running his hands up his arms till their fingers were twined together above Penn's head.

Raff's kisses strayed, trailing across Penn's neck, lathing his skin with his tongue, nipping with his teeth. Penn couldn't stop the moan that passed his lips, or the way his hips jerked upwards, seeking relief.

When Raff finally released his hands, Penn was breathless and keen, desperate for more. Raff dragged his hands down Penn's arms to his shoulders and chest, his fingers catching in the fabric of Penn's undershirt as he stroked down his body. He pressed his thumb into the divot of Penn's hip, sending shudders down his spine, then cupped him boldly through his breeches.

Penn made a sharp noise of pleasure as a familiar, urgent pressure built inside him. Raff pressed a final, fluttering kiss to his neck before moving down his body. Penn could feel the heat of his breath through the fine linen of his undershirt, the press of his lips as they edged down his skinny frame and towards his belly.

At Penn's waist, Raff nudged the hem of his shirt aside then lowered his mouth to his hips. He licked a hot line above the ties of Penn's breeches, making him shudder and writhe beneath him. Raff made a low, eager noise before pressing a kiss to the bulge of his cock through the linen.

Penn whimpered, his voice echoing in the high, empty space. '*Yes*—'

That was all he could say before Raff tugged at the cord, pulled down both breeches and hose and took Penn boldly into his mouth.

'Oh, *God*.'

Raff grabbed at Penn's waist, pinning him. Penn jerked his hips, reaching out and tangling his hands in Raff's hair, twisting against the cloak. Waves of pleasure coursed through him, making the hair at his nape stand on end, his skin erupting into gooseflesh.

All thoughts of teasing or joking were lost as Penn arched against the straw, only able to keen and curse and murmur Raff's name beneath his expert ministrations. Penn squeezed his eyes shut, pulse racing, skin aflame. Nothing else mattered besides Raff, the warmth of his hands on his hips, the movements of his mouth, and the brush of his hair against Penn's skin.

The building, coiling pressure grew and tightened as Raff quickened his movements until, at last, the final wave crashed over him. Penn let out a strangled moan, the sound wrapped around Raff's name.

Raff stilled, then gently released him and pulled away, his hands lingering around Penn's waist. Penn lay trembling against the tangled cloak, heart thundering. He stared down at Raff, chest heaving, trying to regain control over his breathing.

'Raff—'

Raff crawled back up his body. When he was close enough, Penn grabbed him by the shoulders, pulling him into another frantic kiss.

'Christ,' he murmured, still panting. 'That is, I— Good *God*, Raff.'

Raff grinned at him, clearly trying not to laugh. Penn softly batted his shoulder before kissing him again, and when Raff didn't pull back he deepened the movement with a satisfied hum. He could still feel Raff's cock pressed against his leg, and when Penn slid his tongue into his mouth, Raff groaned and thrust slowly against him.

Penn smiled into the kiss, trailing his hand down Raff's torso, his nails grazing against his skin before moving lower, tugging at the waistband of his breeches. Raff moved back to grant him better access, and Penn eagerly untied the cord and swiftly slid his hand beneath the fabric.

Raff was desperately hard beneath Penn's hand, and he huffed into the crook of Penn's neck as he wrapped his fingers around him. Raff moaned, body stiffening, his hands clutching tight around Penn's waist as he drew him out. Penn stroked quickly and urgently, leading Raff towards his own climax. Raff opened his mouth against Penn's skin, and as Penn guided him over the edge Raff sunk his teeth into his shoulder with a muffled groan.

Penn gasped, releasing him, and together they fell back onto the cloak.

Penn trailed his finger across Raff's skin, tracing the pattern of his freckles as they lay beside each other, foreheads touching, breathing each other in. Raff's skin was warm, shining with sweat, and his breath caught as Penn's fingertips danced over his collarbones. One of his hands rested lightly against Penn's side, bunching in the fabric of his undershirt.

Penn finally looked up, meeting Raff's gaze. His dark hair was a loose mess of waves around his head, framing his sparkling eyes. Penn felt his cheeks heat, his breath catch.

Something had changed. They had both lost their grasp on their restraint, finding something sweeter to reach for. Something had changed, and Penn didn't know how to put it into words, or if he even should: as if putting a word to it would ruin it.

Cautiously, careful not to shatter this new, uncertain thing, he slid a hand across Raff's shoulder and laid his head against his chest in a mirror of the way they'd slept together outside, curled around each other to stave off the cold.

'Well, then.' It was little more than a whisper; a gentle exhale against Raff's skin.

There was the slightest pause. Then Raff's grip on his side tightened. He pulled the second cloak over them, protecting them from the chill that was becoming more apparent as their breathing calmed, then wrapped his free arm around Penn's back, tugging him closer.

'Well, then.'

Chapter Fifteen

Sharp dawn sunlight was pouring in through the gaps in the barn door. Raff blinked, waking slowly. They would need to move on soon, especially considering how little progress they'd made in yesterday's blizzard.

He turned on the straw, watching Penn sleep. The cracking yellow light spilled across his face, making him glow. His expression was soft and gentle, free from the troubles that burdened him while he was awake, his lips still darkly red from Raff's desperate kisses. He shifted in his sleep, eyes squeezing, mouth parting in a breathy sigh.

Raff edged closer. He swallowed. He wondered how it would feel to wake Penn not with a sharp word or a shake of his slender shoulders, but with a kiss.

It would be too tender. Raff could only guess at what had spurred Penn to act last night, but he would be foolish to think it was anything more than lust: desire and desperation, a mutual yearning for a different destiny.

Before he could act – kiss or back away – the decision was made for him as Penn's eyes slid open. He spotted Raff staring, and his face split into a warm, genuine smile.

Raff felt his stomach flip. Before the tingling feeling could take him over, he quickly sat up, sending straw flying.

'We should move on,' he said. 'It is already growing late . . .'

Penn blinked at him. 'Of course.'

Penn sat up as Raff rose to his feet, grabbing his undershirt where they had tossed it aside and pulling it over his head. He could feel Penn's eyes on his back, watching him, before he too rose from the straw and began to gather his things.

They had finished what they'd started that night in Hartswood. That should have been enough. It should have satisfied the urge that had been swirling in Raff's chest since then. But it hadn't. Raff already knew how it felt to kiss Penn, but now he knew the rest as well. Knew the softness of the skin on the inside of his wrists, knew the feel of his hands, knew the noises he made when his pleasure peaked.

He wanted to hear them again.

'Penn . . .' Fully dressed, Raff reached down and grabbed his pack from the floor. 'Last night . . .'

Penn turned. He too was ready to go, his pack on his shoulder, standing in the doorway of the barn. He was smiling, although the expression did not reach his eyes.

'Are you about to tell me that what passed between us was a mistake?' he said. 'That however much pleasure we found in each other, we cannot do it again? That you regret behaving so recklessly?'

Raff knew he should. He knew that to give into this would make it easier to give into the rest; the feeling he'd tried to bury when he'd named the pain in his chest as jealousy.

'You *are* too reckless,' he said, fondly.

Penn looked away. 'Before you found me in Hartswood I had accepted that my escape might mean my death. Now I realise that I may yet survive this. And . . .' he set his shoulders, staring out at the snow-buried fields, 'and soon you will leave me. What else should I do but be reckless?'

He turned when he noticed that Raff was not by his side. 'Well? Are we leaving?'

The sun illuminated him. The breeze whipped in his hair. His cloak – Raff's cloak – moved around his ankles. Something broke. The final thread of Raff's self-control snapped, the ends irreparably severed.

'Damn you, Penn.'

Penn's eyebrows knitted in confused outrage. 'What have I—'

Raff stepped swiftly forwards, wrapped an arm around Penn's waist and pulled him into a kiss. Penn softened into the embrace immediately, threading his hands over Raff's shoulders with a quiet sigh.

'Oh,' he said, their lips brushing. 'I see.'

Raff had struggled to define the thing that had been growing between Penn and himself since their first kiss beneath the trees. That first night, he would have said it was desire; a too-hot flame destined to burn itself out.

Travelling by Penn's side for so long had changed that. That desire had given way to something far more tender, and far more hazardous. It was a feeling that made his stomach lurch and his head spin. It made his fingertips tingle whenever their hands brushed. It made him *jealous*. When Penn had fallen asleep against him, with his damp hair and ruined back, it made Raff want to pull him close and breathe in the smell of him and never let him go.

But he could ignore that perilous, fragile feeling. He could force it down and pretend it didn't exist; focus on the desire, the memory of Penn's lips, the lines of his body. *Desiring* Penn was safe, even if he told himself nothing would ever come of it.

And then he had given into it – despite swearing he wouldn't – and he had become unsteadied.

They met in brief, frenetic moments: under the cover of trees in the middle of the day, in the empty stables of a run-down inn. Scraps of time alone often ended in a hectic mix of hands and mouths, whispered curses and bitten-off words. Raff delighted in learning Penn's body, where he liked to be touched.

Raff's previous partners had rarely stayed, and this was entirely new: not simply sharing a night together, but sharing their *days* too. It was more than just seeking pleasure, but comfort as well: soft companionship that he'd never sought before.

Penn would drop down behind him, loop his long arms around Raff's middle and rest his chin on his shoulder to watch as he plucked a bird or sharpened their blades. Raff would lean against him, press against Penn's chest, lay his head in his lap. Often, that was all it was: easy closeness that never went beyond a simple embrace. In those moments, Raff didn't *want* anything else, either.

Raff's determination that Penn should be able to protect himself had intensified, although progress was made slower by lingering looks turned fierce and touches turned urgent. Raff knew that he should be stricter, but his self-control cracked every time Penn gave him so much as a smile.

They were sparring in a woodland clearing a little way from that evening's rest stop on the edges of a town concerningly close to Dunlyn Castle. Raff was intending to send them straight past; Penn would never even know how close they came to his ancestral home. The decision made guilt swirl in Raff's stomach, but it was a feeling he could better ignore when gifted with another one of Penn's sharp smiles.

It had only taken a single step and a deliberate brush of skin before Raff found himself pressed against a tree with his breeches tugged down and Penn on his knees between his feet.

Raff regretted turning Penn away when he'd first propositioned him. They'd lost precious time together, and each of these encounters had to be hurried, lest they were discovered. As his head knocked against the tree and his fingers caught in Penn's hair, he wanted very much to repay him, to reciprocate until Penn was left a gasping, wordless wreck. He wondered if it would be worth suggesting forgoing the inn to spend the evening outside, where they would be alone.

But it was a cold evening, and it promised to snow, so it was with reluctance that they made their way to the rest stop.

The inn was more crowded than Raff would have liked: clearly other travellers had also anticipated poor weather. After securing two pallets in a shared room, they placed themselves at a table by the far wall, sharing a jug of ale. Settling opposite Penn, basking in his smile, Raff didn't care about how loud or busy the room was. For the first time in too long, he felt content.

They were talking vaguely about the journey, Penn lamenting the snow with increased irritation, when he abruptly stuttered silent. His eyes went wide. He ducked his head.

'There is a man across the way – do not look.' Raff's eyes snapped back to Penn. 'He has looked this way several times. I'm sure I don't know him, but—' he shrank down on himself, 'what if he knows de Foucart?'

Dread sank in Raff's chest. Surely they were too far from Oxfordshire for Penn to be recognised. Surely not *now*, not when they had got so far.

'Penn . . .'

But Penn was frozen, eyes down. There was a heavy hand on Raff's shoulder. He turned, half expecting a sword to his throat.

'Raff Barden, I thought I recognised you!'

Oh, no.

Lord Roland: a local nobleman, and firm friend of his father. Raff had known him since he was a boy, and as a man had often dealt with trades and petty village squabbles with him in his brother's stead when their father was busy elsewhere.

'Are you returning to Dunlyn?'

'I am,' Raff lied.

'Good,' Roland said, sitting at the bench beside him. 'I'm sure there is much to do. This blasted weather is wreaking havoc in the villages. I am overrun with people begging for help. I am sure your father's tenants are much the same.'

'You are probably correct,' Raff could only continue the conversation, feeling Penn's eyes on him.

Roland turned, spotting Penn for the first time.

'Forgive me,' he said, jovially. 'I am being rude. Lord Roland—' he extended his hand across the table, 'I have known Raff here since he was a boy.'

Raff watched as Penn shook Roland's hand, feeling himself pale. Penn didn't even hesitate.

'Penn Wallingford,' he said, swiftly. 'I must admit, I have not known Raff quite as long.'

Roland smiled. 'What brings you north?'

'Wild boar,' Penn said smoothly as Roland burst into laughter. 'My brother granted Raff hospitality during a storm. We got to talking, and he promised to guide me to Scotland for a hunt.'

'In this weather?' Roland looked aghast. 'At this time of year?'

Penn shrugged. 'Wallingford is very dull,' he said. 'And I desire a challenge.'

Roland shook his head. 'What have I told you?' he said, turning back to Raff. 'The southern nobles are mad.' Raff gave him a small shrug as he continued. 'Especially that fool who spurned your poor sister.'

Raff grimaced. 'Word has spread, then?'

'It has. We were surprised to see her return. It is a shame, being so publicly rebuffed will go against her.'

'I fear the same,' Raff said. 'But Cecily is strong. She will find another path.'

'We best pray she does,' Roland said. 'I will keep her in my thoughts, and hope you can untangle this mess.'

Raff raised his cup. 'As do I.'

'It is especially difficult without your father,' Roland continued. 'Your brother must find himself quite snowed under.' He laughed. 'Not even to speak on this cursed weather, of course.'

Raff frowned. 'Father is not at Dunlyn?'

Roland paused. 'You were not aware? We have not seen him since you left for Oxfordshire.'

The noise around them died away. Raff's stomach sank. 'Oh,' he said, uselessly.

Someone from across the way called – clearly Roland was needed elsewhere. He rose, clapping his hand to Raff's shoulder once more.

'It has been good to see you again,' he said. 'And a pleasure to meet you too, Wallingford. I hope you can find your wild boar.'

Penn gave him a curt nod as he left, heading back to his own table at the other side of the inn. As soon as he was gone, Raff turned to Penn, heart thundering.

'Penn—'

Penn rose to his feet. 'We need to talk,' he said. 'Outside.'

He strode towards the door, and Raff could only follow.

✡

The cold air outside the inn hit Penn like a slap to the face. Of course Raff wasn't a servant. He carried himself too well, and he hadn't baulked at the cost of Penn's horse or food along their way. Penn had been a fool not to see it all this time. It had barely been a lie: Penn had assumed that Raff was a tracker, and Raff had failed to correct him. The shock of it was already ebbing away, replaced with swirling sickness; Raff had made his own assumptions too. Ones which Penn had been more than happy to indulge.

He led Raff towards the stables at the far end of the field, pulling him behind the stone building so they were hidden from view.

'Penn—' Raff started, but Penn spoke over him.

'What is this?'

'Penn, *please*. Forgive me—'

'*Well?*'

'I lied to you,' Raff said. 'I am not a tracker.' He took a deep breath. Penn waited for him to speak. 'My name – my *full* name – is Raff Calum Barden. My father is Lord Griffin Barden.' He hesitated again. '*Earl* Griffin Barden. My home is Dunlyn Castle. I had not intended to lie to you. But you—' his face twisted, 'but *I* wanted . . . Damn it, I wanted my freedom. I didn't want to be beholden to my father and siblings, just for a few days. And if you knew who I really was . . .' he sighed, looking away, 'this would have been an impossibility. It would have been *wrong*.'

'Wrong?'

'I'm an *earl's son*, Penn. My word here is powerful, just for the circumstances of my birth. I didn't want that hold over you.'

There is no hold, Penn wanted to say. *Not like that. My father*—

He couldn't.

'What about your sister?' Penn didn't want to know, but he needed to ask. 'What did Lord Roland mean about the southern fool?'

Raff's gaze dropped. 'Cecily was William's betrothed.'

Penn's head turned dull and hollow. Cecily. He hadn't even known her name, then.

'Oh.'

He'd run from his future only to find himself thrust back towards it. He'd escaped a wife he didn't want and run straight into the arms of her brother. It was a farce; a bawdy tavern joke told in drunken huddles.

Guilt struck at him. He should confess. He needed to tell Raff that he'd let himself get tangled with the very man his sister was supposed to be marrying; the man de Foucart had sent him to find; the man he presumed dead.

Yet Raff had made no attempts to leave him yet. Raff wanted to be free, just as Penn had, and this thing between them *was* that freedom.

And it wouldn't last, Penn reminded himself. Raff had agreed to find Penn somewhere else to go. They *would* be parted; it was inevitable. But if Raff knew who Penn really *was,* that parting would only come quicker.

Penn could see his choices: a crossroads ahead of him. 'Raff . . .'

Raff's expression was tight, like a man being led to the gallows.

Penn's resolve splintered. Honesty hardly seemed to matter when he knew this would end so soon.

'I understand,' he said, slowly. 'I *do*. That urge to run . . .' He cast his eyes down. 'I do not blame you,' he said. 'And I forgive you for the lie. Perhaps you can blame me for not questioning you earlier.'

'I don't want to blame you.'

'No,' Penn smiled, 'I imagine you don't.'

'If you want to leave—'

Penn cut him off with a wave of his hand. 'Why would I leave someone who, by his own admission, holds power in the northern counties we're currently traipsing through? I would be a fool to leave now.'

'Penn—'

'I started this,' Penn spoke over him, 'before I knew who you were. You do not have to fear that you're taking advantage of me.' He took Raff's hand. 'I suspect the opposite might be true. I have more to gain than you do from our travelling together.'

Raff gave a doubtful snort, so Penn continued.

'You pulled me from the control of a violent man. You have fed me, and kept me warm, and taught me how to survive and protect myself. We both know that without you I would be dead.'

'Yes, but—'

'Do not assume *you* are taking advantage of me just because *I* enjoy taking you in my mouth.' Penn shot him a coy smile. 'I would have done that anyway, were we not interrupted in Hartswood.'

Raff fell silent, blushing furiously. Content that he'd won, Penn ducked forwards, kissing him.

'And, perhaps . . .' he pulled back, 'perhaps you could still be Raff – *just* Raff – until we part.'

Raff stared at him, their hands still linked. Reluctantly, Penn let him go.

'Come,' he said. 'It is freezing out here. We should return inside before we begin to look suspicious.'

As they moved onwards, Penn noticed a change come over Raff. He lapsed into silence more often, distracted and difficult to rouse. He still reached for Penn when they were alone, still leaned against him as they rested and pulled him into soft, lazy kisses when he could, but there was a part of him that was always elsewhere.

They had been forced to make camp after arriving late to an already full inn. Raff was silent again, the flickering firelight making his frown more apparent.

And then Penn realised. Raff's sister had been rejected, his brother was irresponsible and his father had *still* not returned. He was worried.

Raff needed to return to his home and aid his siblings in his father's absence. Every day his anxiety grew, and Penn could not bear to see him so troubled. But if he *did* return, it would force them to reconsider their arrangement, and the tentative thing that had flourished between them. Penn could lose him after so long fighting to keep him, maintaining the lie which had begun to snap at him with glistening teeth.

He looked back at Raff. His set expression. The nervous way he was clasping his hands together. He thought of the man who had given Penn his cloak when he was freezing cold and too anxious to talk.

'You should return to Dunlyn,' Penn said, breaking the silence.

Raff's gaze snapped up. 'What?'

'You are worrying about them,' Penn said. 'You should return.'

Raff stared at him. 'I . . . have thought of it,' he admitted at last. 'But I swore to help you.'

Penn reached out for him around the fire.

'From the start, we have said that you would help me find work elsewhere. Perhaps at Dunlyn—'

'No.'

Penn baulked at the sudden seriousness of Raff's voice, flinching away. Raff immediately chased him, grabbing his hand.

'No, I—' He shook his head. 'Damn it, I don't want you with me as my servant, I want you with me as my—'

Raff cut himself off. Something lodged in Penn's throat.

'As your what?' he said, half-choked.

'As my *equal*. I told you before, I do not want that power over you. I don't want you to feel like your security depends on my *interest* in you.'

'I do not feel like that.'

'I know.' Raff let go of Penn's hand. 'But if you decide you no longer want this, I need you to be able to tell me. If I am your *master*, that will be so much harder.' He groaned. 'Besides, I do not want to have to hide you away in the servants' quarters and sneak you out every time I wish to see you.'

Penn sighed. Raff *was* far too noble; too concerned with the imbalance that didn't even exist between them. Again, he was struck with the urge to tell him who he really was, but he swallowed that back down.

'You *must* go home, or you will drive yourself mad with worry,' he said instead. 'Which means you either take me with you, or . . .' Penn stopped, terrified that Raff would agree to what he was about to suggest. 'Or we find somewhere else for me to go.'

Raff stared at him across the fire. His expression – always far too loud on his face – was one of mingling pain and indecision. The air was full of sparks. *Please*, Penn thought, wondering if Raff could read *his* emotions on his face as well. *Take me with you. Do not toss me aside yet.*

Finally, Raff spoke.

'Perhaps . . . if just for a few days,' he mused. 'To ensure all is well . . .'

Something snapped in the fire. Penn didn't move. Didn't speak.

'Ash knows who you are,' Raff continued, talking more to himself than Penn. 'And he must have told Lily. But we could tell the servants the boar hunt story . . .'

'Raff?'

'I will return to Dunlyn. You are right: I will make myself sick with worry if I do not. And . . .' Raff looked up, his expression open and sincere, 'will you come with me? Or do you wish to go elsewhere? You have more to risk through this than I, and I am sure we can find somewhere before we reach Dunlyn.'

Penn's heart tripped over itself. He wondered if Raff knew what question he was really asking.

'I would be honoured to go with you,' he managed. 'If you would have me.'

Raff stared at him. 'Of course I would.'

Penn's gut twisted. He should feel elated; this was all he wanted. But instead he felt like a traitor. He needed to say something true. Something that would *remain* true, and not forsake him.

'You're a good man, Raff,' he said. 'Your family is lucky to have you.' *I am lucky to have you.*

'Hah,' Raff laughed. 'You'd not think it, to talk to Ash. I'm a fool.'

Penn grinned. 'Perhaps you can be both.'

Raff glanced across at him, as if seeing something just beyond his shoulder. 'Perhaps I can.'

Chapter Sixteen

Dunlyn Castle was close by, although they were forced to turn back the way they had come.

'You intended for us to pass without me knowing?' Penn asked, when he realised the route Raff was leading them on.

Raff looked cowed. 'I did,' he admitted. 'I am—'

'It was a difficult choice.' Penn stopped him before he could apologise again.

Raff peered at him. 'It was.'

The journey to Raff's home would only take them a few days, and Penn could already see Raff holding himself straighter, his mood brighter. Penn had never felt any real attachment to the keep in which he'd grown up, but Raff clearly cared a lot for the place where he'd been born. Taking him to Dunlyn, Penn realised, truly *meant* something to Raff. Penn was being granted access to the space Raff loved so much it felt almost sacred.

Raff was taking him *home,* making him part of that sacredness, instead of leaving him elsewhere as he so easily could. The thought made butterflies erupt in Penn's stomach, made his heart beat faster. Raff wanted him there.

As they drew closer, Raff spoke of his family, clearly keen for Penn to know more about them. He talked about Cecily – Lily, he called her – with such fondness that it made Penn's chest squeeze, for more than one reason.

He was walking towards the woman he'd spurned, and on the arm of her brother. He hadn't considered how his flight could have impacted his intended wife: she had barely seemed real when he'd fled the keep. But now she was suddenly, startlingly solid. She was the person Raff talked about so often and with such fondness. He'd damned someone Raff loved. Lord Roland was correct: being so publicly rejected would go against her. It could make her unmarriable.

It was a painful little thought, and the guilt bit at him sharper the closer they got to his intended bride.

There was another anxiety building within him too. The road had been quiet, granting them privacy enough for closeness. Penn had never felt so content as he did with Raff leaning against his shoulder, their fingers linked as Penn listened to him breathe.

But it would not be the same at Dunlyn. Once they arrived, Raff would be *Raff Barden* once more, and the thing between them would be forced into the shadows.

They were sheltering from torrential rain in a disused barn when he mentioned this fear, his head resting gently against Raff's thighs as Raff leaned against the wall, his hand playing in Penn's hair. It had been the gentle movement that had spurred him to speak: he would miss this when it ended.

He'd been expecting Raff to tell him in sombre tones that it was how things were, that the thing between them would be a secret that they would have to hide. That no one could ever know.

But he didn't. Instead, he laughed, fingers tangling in Penn's hair.

'The Barden family is unusual,' he said. 'You do not need to worry.'

Penn sensed there was more he wasn't saying, stories that were not his to tell.

'Besides . . .' Raff's hand stilled, and Penn looked up at him, 'I suspect Ash will realise the moment he sees you.'

'Oh?'

Raff looked abashed. 'He encouraged me to act.' He quirked his lips. 'He said I should bring you home.'

Penn wasn't sure how to respond, his breath catching as Raff smiled at him. Ash had seen something in his brother that Penn had missed. It meant that Raff *wanted* this as much as he did: that it wasn't just Penn's impulsive decision to kiss him as they sheltered from the blizzard that had led them to this moment. It gave more weight to that night in the barn, and everything that had happened since. Raff wanted him, and Ash had been able to see that where Penn had been too scared to even look.

Penn's chest felt tight, unbearably full.

It was early the next morning that Penn first spotted the castle in the distance. The landscape had changed drastically as they had travelled, the rolling fields he was used to giving way to steep hills. It was beautiful, even if it left his legs aching and his lungs burning when they dismounted to allow the horses an easier journey.

He complained halfway up a steep incline about *mountains,* and Raff laughed at him.

'This is a hill,' he said. 'One day I shall take you to see *real* mountains.'

Penn had grinned, despite the pain in his thighs. It wasn't until later, when they were riding again across a blissfully flat stretch of road, that he realised the unspoken implication of Raff's words.

They approached the gates of the castle just after midday. The keep was larger than his father's, and far older, the stones a weathered, white-veined grey. It was staffed far more sparsely too, with only a single pair of guards watching the gate as they approached.

There was no announcement as they made their way across the drawbridge and into the wide central courtyard, just the quiet day-to-day goings-on of household staff. Suddenly there was a cry from the direction of the main building.

'Raff!'

They both turned to see a young woman dashing towards them, her skirts held up in her hands as she ran across the muddied yard. Her hair, tied in a pair of loose red plaits, danced around her face. She was upon them in an instant, flinging her arms around Raff's neck. He caught her instinctively, lifting her into a crushing hug.

'You should have been home *days* ago,' she said as she released him, dropping back to the ground. 'Ash said—' She spotted Penn, half-hiding behind Raff. Her eyes widened. 'Oh.'

'*This* is why I am so delayed,' said Raff. He beckoned for Penn to step forwards.

Penn knew who this woman must be, who she *could* have been. He forced himself to move.

'Cecily Barden,' Raff said, giving his sister an exaggerated bow, 'may I introduce you to—'

'Penn?'

Raff didn't even hesitate. 'Ash told you, then.'

Cecily grinned, and something flashed across her pale, freckled face that Penn couldn't read. She glanced between them, and he suddenly suspected that she knew exactly why Raff had brought him home.

If she was displeased, she didn't show it, and swept forwards in an equally exaggerated curtsey, offering her hand. Penn took it and placed a quick kiss to the back of her fingers. She flashed him a wicked smile.

'I assume this means that Ash returned?' Raff said as she straightened.

'He has.'

'And Father?'

She shook her head. 'No. We were growing worried about you both.'

Raff frowned. 'Has he sent word?'

'None.'

The frown deepened. 'I am sorry, Lily,' Raff said quickly. 'I should have come home sooner. I just—'

'*Raff.*'

Raff fell silent as she spoke.

'Does it appear as if the keep has crumbled without you? Did you and your friend ride through burning fields and rioting tenants?'

Penn watched, amused, as Raff seemed to shrink beneath his sister's hard gaze.

'No,' he muttered.

'We are faring without you,' she said, not unkindly. '*Yes,* I would prefer Father were here, but we all would.' She peered again at Penn, that little smile still curling her lips. 'You did not need to rush home on my account.'

'You are far too certain of yourself,' Raff said, shaking his head with a sigh.

'Better than being uncertain,' she countered. 'Come, let's get you inside. You are a *host,* after all. We cannot leave our guest standing in the yard.'

Cecily led them into the keep, down a wide corridor towards a set of side chambers warmed by a roaring fire. It was a small, cosy space utterly unlike anything in the de Foucart keep. Ash was sprawled on a chair by the hearth. He looked up when they entered, his eyebrows raised, but he did not stand.

'So,' he said, looking smug, 'you *did* bring him home.'

'It is good to see you too,' said Raff, shaking his head as he moved them both towards the fire.

Ash ignored him, turning to Penn.

'And *has* he taken good care of you?' he asked, innocently. 'As he promised?'

Penn felt himself turning scarlet, his suspicions that Raff's siblings knew the nature of his relationship with their brother feeling bluntly confirmed. He ignored his burning cheeks, standing straighter.

'Yes,' he said. 'He has.'

Ash's smirk cracked into a smug grin. 'Oh *good*.'

'*Ash*,' Raff warned.

'What?'

'I came back to see if Father had returned, *not* to subject us to your teasing.'

Ash rolled his eyes. 'Worrying, then, as ever,' he said. 'We are *fine*. Truly: Lily has done a remarkable job in our absence.'

'But she should not have had to.' Raff sighed, rubbing his face.

Penn watched him, carefully. He was relieved to be home, that was immediately clear, but was still wracked with worry and guilt. He needed this time with his family, and Penn felt distinctly like he was intruding upon their reunion.

Ignoring Ash's intense stare, he moved forwards, grabbing Raff's hand.

'I shall go and see to the horses,' he said. 'Find me when you are finished here.'

Raff gave him a quick, thankful smile and after briefly nodding to

Ash and Cecily, Penn wandered out towards the yard. Their horses had already been stabled – as he had expected – so he returned to the empty hall and sat at the low table with their packs.

In the silence, he finally had time to think. He was safe, safer than he'd been in *years,* and Raff was glad to be home, but guilt was curdling in Penn's stomach regardless.

He had lied. He was *still* lying, with every word he said, every action. There was no reason for Raff to see through the deception, but its existence alone was enough to make his insides knot.

When Raff had found him in the forest, the lie had come easily and had been easy to keep. But it had twisted, since: the lie was the same, but the reason for telling it had shifted. For those first days, it had been to keep himself safe. But now, so far from his father's keep, it was to keep Raff by his side.

Now it was poison, slowly destroying him, and Raff too – unknowingly succumbing to the rot. Raff had brought him *home,* and Penn was repaying him with deceit. Penn stared around at the walls between which Raff had grown and thought of his own home, his own childhood. His father had been right to punish him. His flight and the lie were proof enough of that.

He sat on the long, empty bench and waited.

'You told him who you are, then?' Ash said, sprawling in the chair.

'I had little choice,' said Raff. 'I was recognised.'

Ash snorted with laughter. 'Serves you right for lying to him.'

Raff found it difficult to disagree.

'So what now?' Ash folded his arms across his chest. '*Do* you intend to put him to work? Or will you keep him as a guest?'

'We will claim he is a guest until Father returns. We can tell the staff he is the brother of a lord, their father recently died. His brother granted me hospitality during a snowstorm, and we got to talking. I have agreed to guide him across the border to hunt boar, but we wish to rest before moving on.'

Both Ash and Lily stared at him.

'Did you just now invent that?' Lily blinked.

'It's a lie we have used before,' said Raff. 'It is Penn's, not mine.'

Ash looked impressed, pursing his lips. 'That does not surprise me.'

'He isn't what I expected when you told us you'd found a man in the woods all those weeks ago,' said Lily.

'No,' Raff agreed. His face flushed under his siblings' gaze. 'He isn't.'

Lily grinned, slyly. Raff quickly continued, keen to move the conversation on before she could attempt to scrutinise him.

'So,' he said, 'what is there to be done? We ran into Lord Roland – it was he who recognised me – and he told me that his tenants were struggling in the snow. Tomorrow, should the weather hold, we will need to visit the villages, and ensure they are—'

'It has been seen to.' Ash cut him off.

'What?'

'Lily and the steward dealt with the worst of the damage upon her return,' Ash explained. 'And I have been working with the aldermen to ensure they are prepared should the weather worsen.'

'That is good,' Raff said, thoughtfully. 'That means I can spend tomorrow ensuring the winter trade routes are still—'

'There is no need.' Ash suddenly stood. 'They have also been seen to. Perhaps not to the standards *you* are used to, but they *have* been seen to, while you were tarrying in the woods with a stranger.'

Raff blinked. 'Oh,' he said. 'Thank y—'

Ash raised a hand. 'There is no need to thank me,' he said,

although his tone was a little sour. 'It is my duty, after all. Go, show your guest around the keep, if he *is* to be staying.'

Raff wanted to ask more about the winter trade routes – how often they would be, and which roads they were taking – but he found himself being pushed towards the door. Clearly, he had little choice in the matter.

When he left the room, sure that Ash and Lily were gossiping about his arrival and unexpected guest as soon as the door had shut, he found Penn still sitting in the hall, face pale, eyes down.

'Penn?'

Penn's head snapped up. 'Is everything all right?'

'We should . . .' Raff glanced around. They were unlikely to be overheard, but he wanted that guarantee. 'Give me a moment.'

He arranged for Penn's few belongings to be taken to a guest chamber on the same floor as his own rooms before guiding him out of the keep, through the gates and out towards the grounds. Alone, and sure they weren't being watched, he took Penn's arm as they walked.

'It is good to finally meet Cecily,' Penn said, as their shoulders knocked together.

Raff smiled. 'I am glad that you *have* met,' he said. 'Although I dread to think what Ash told her about you. About *us*.'

'She seems to know,' Penn said, his words carefully vague.

'She almost certainly does,' Raff agreed. 'She and Ash are likely talking about it at this very moment.'

Penn grimaced.

'She means well. They both do.'

'Raff . . .'

Raff turned. Penn was looking uncertainly out across the misty landscape. 'Yes?'

'What will happen to her,' he asked, 'with the marriage dissolved?'

'It *will* go against her,' Raff said. 'William will have escaped lightly, if he's still alive. It could be likely that no one else will accept her hand now. Yet . . . Lily won't look upon it as a reputation ruined. Made unmarriable by circumstances out of her control? That will suit her.'

'You were looking for William, when you found me.' Penn turned. 'What would you have done if you had found him?'

Raff hesitated. 'I don't know.' He looked towards Penn. 'I am glad that I was not forced to decide.'

Penn didn't respond. Raff led him around the outer wall of the keep, pointing out landmarks, the village nestling in the valley below. Penn was warm and reassuring beside him, his steps falling in pace with Raff's own. Seeing him there lit a warmth in Raff's chest hot enough to melt the lingering snow that piled by the stone. It felt good to be home, and for a moment he couldn't recall why he had been so keen to leave.

'How long do you intend to stay?' Penn asked, as Raff led them back into the yard and towards the stables. 'Is there much to do?'

Raff swallowed. Clearly his absence had not been too hard on his siblings, but he was loath to go before their father returned. Yet he had promised Penn they would only stay a few days, at most.

Penn noticed his hesitation.

'You are still worried about your father,' he said. It was not a question.

'I am,' Raff admitted.

Penn squeezed his arm just once before letting go, flexing his fingers. 'Then we will stay until he returns.'

'But—'

'I am sure I can bear to be a Lord's brother for however long it takes,' Penn said. 'How terrible, to be forced to accept your hospitality as a guest, instead of working on hand and knee as a servant.'

'You do not mind?'

'Of course not. As I said, I cannot stand to see you so troubled. I can – *we* can – stay for as long as is needed.'

Raff proceeded to take Penn around the rest of the keep. He took his arm once more and guided him around the yard and the lower floors: the stables, the armoury, the kitchens and the cold, echoing basements. He took his time, and Penn absorbed it all with interest.

Everywhere they went, Raff found jobs to be done. There was food that needed to be restocked, staff to hire, dwindling supplies that would take traipsing through three separate towns to replenish. Before, he would have been taking note of each task, but now, with Penn chatting by his side, they felt less urgent.

He had no way of knowing when his father would return, and they would head back out on the road once more. They could have weeks together, or only mere days. That suddenly felt like no time at all.

They hadn't even made it to the upper floors by the time Raff had decided. He would not waste their time together on duty and work, not when Ash and Lily had clearly been able to manage the keep without him. For the first time, he would do what he *wanted,* not what he was expected to do.

It was with a little squeeze of surprise that found him gripping slightly tighter to Penn's arm that he realised: he'd never *wanted* like this before, either.

They were about to climb the staircase when Lily appeared, looking for them to inform them that the evening's meal was ready.

Ash joined them, brushing snow from his shoulders and muttering bitterly about an argument he'd been having with the marshal, and together they made their way into the great hall where their tiny party would be eating.

Despite how well Ash and Penn had got along when they'd met, Raff was nervous that something would have changed now that Penn was in their home. What if his siblings disapproved? What if there was tension there, or Lily did not care for him, even though he had chosen not to tell her of the relationship between Penn and William?

He sat anxiously beside them, waiting. But his fears were almost instantly abated.

A serving girl carried up a jug of beer and four cups, placing them on the table. She was about to pour, when Ash stopped her, taking the jug from her hands.

'I'm sure we can manage,' he said, with a smile that was as sincere as Ash ever got.

After she vanished through a narrow doorway, Ash turned to Penn.

'My brother seems unwilling to take you on as a servant,' he said, 'for reasons I don't understand. But he does not run this keep, nor—' he shot Raff a knowing look, 'is he the heir. which means the decision does not fall to him.' He handed Penn the jug. 'Make yourself useful and pour, if you are truly here seeking work.'

Lily bit back a laugh. Raff glared at him, unsure of how to respond. Before he could, Penn smiled sweetly, rose from his seat, and made an exaggerated, deliberate mess of pouring Ash a cup of beer, spilling it over the table and Ash's lap. Raff leaped out of the way to avoid the worst of the mess, but Ash was far too slow to avoid it.

'I am not that kind of servant,' Penn said smoothly, returning to his seat.

Ash stared at him for a long moment.

'I would wager you're not,' he said, with a sure smile and a raised eyebrow.

'Please,' Lily said, grabbing the jug. 'I *beg* you not to fight over him. I will not be able to bear it.'

And that was it. Any potential tension was gone, replaced with laughter. Raff could even put aside his father's absence for one evening, happy that their lands had been managed without either of them there.

Lily immediately warmed to Penn, and soon their conversation drifted again to the topic of her broken betrothal.

'Everyone is treating me as if I am ruined,' Lily said, rolling her eyes. 'It is tiresome. Father's allies are taking me even less seriously than before we left.'

'What will you do?' Penn asked, refilling both their cups with far more care than he had demonstrated towards Ash.

She shrugged. 'I could stay here,' she said. 'Look after Father and keep him—' she nodded at Ash, 'out of trouble.'

'If we cannot marry you off by the time I inherit,' Ash said, taking the jug, 'I will send you to a convent.'

Lily gasped in imagined outrage.

'Oh *no*,' she breathed, 'how *dreadful*. All those women and not a single man, I shall go quite mad.'

Penn laughed along, his hair falling in his face. 'Indeed,' he said. 'It sounds awful.'

After the meal was finished and they were sipping on strong honeyed mead from across the border, Raff rose to relieve himself. When he returned to the great hall, chilled by the winter winds, his eyes fell to the long table and the three figures occupying the end nearest the fire, huddled together. Penn said something that Raff didn't catch, and all three of them burst into laughter. The light from the fireplace, blazing strong enough to heat the whole room, painted them in oranges and yellows, warming them.

Raff realised he was staring. Penn looked up, and their eyes locked. He beamed across the room at him – a true, blinding smile – before being pulled back into the conversation by Ash.

Something deep between Raff's ribs constricted. Penn looked like he belonged. Like he was—

Oh.

Like he was home.

Raff sat at the table beside Ash as if in a dream. Across the worn, well-used surface, Penn grinned at him again, and nudged his foot beneath the table where no one else could see. It made Raff's heart skip, his skin ignite.

He smiled back, but there was a throb in his chest. He didn't want him to leave. They'd snatched this time together in the safety of his father's keep, but eventually they would move on again. He would have to fulfil his promise.

Ash made a joke. Raff barely caught it but laughed along anyway. Across the table, Penn's eyes sparkled.

When they were finished, Raff led Penn up the winding stairs to the upper floor, their fingers warm where they were linked. They stopped briefly at the guest chambers before heading down the hall to his own rooms.

Raff's chambers were exactly as he'd left them. Two adjoining rooms, both feeling excessively large after spending so long on the road. He shut the door behind them, feeling himself relax in the secure, familiar space.

The smell of dust hung in the air, so Raff flung open the balcony door. A cool winter breeze blew in, fluttering the canopies around the bed.

There was a small gasp behind him.

He turned to see Penn staring and stood aside so he could make his way out to the balcony. He watched as Penn stepped onto the stone, although now the sun had set he likely couldn't see anything beyond the looming shadow of the hill behind the keep.

'You have full use of the guest chambers,' said Raff, coming up behind him. 'But if you wish to stay . . .' He placed his hand around Penn's middle and leaned in towards him.

'Do the guest chambers have views this fine?' Penn said, glancing over his shoulder at Raff.

'They do not.'

Penn relaxed against him. 'Then I suppose I'll have to stay here.'

Chapter Seventeen

Penn shut the balcony door behind him as he turned, folding into Raff's arms. Ash and Cecily, the two most important people in Raff's life, had *liked* him. They'd laughed at his jokes. They'd included him in theirs, like he belonged.

He knew he didn't, but he wouldn't allow himself to chase that thought, not tonight.

'That went well,' he said, as Raff pulled him closer.

'Hmm.' Raff pressed a warm kiss against his neck, then higher, to his jaw. 'They will miss you when you leave.'

It was like a split, cracking his sternum. 'They barely know me.'

Another kiss. 'They will miss you anyway.'

Words formed and died in Penn's throat. The room was warm and close and safe, and anything he could say now could break that and hurl him into the darkness outside.

He tilted his head down so their lips met. Raff melted beneath the touch, his hands clutching at Penn's waist as Penn smoothed his hands down Raff's back, feeling the thick fabric of his tunic beneath his palms, then lower to where his leather belt was still slung around his waist.

Without breaking the kiss, Penn quickly tugged the belt away and dropped it to the floor. Raff smiled against his lips, so he continued, unlacing the tunic with quick fingers and manoeuvring it over Raff's head.

Raff's linen undershirt was thin beneath Penn's grasp, and he swiftly removed that as well. Raff stood bare-chested and beautiful before him, dark hair in disarray around his head. Penn pushed him backwards till Raff's legs collided with the bed and he dropped against the pile of blankets and furs, then chased as Raff clambered back, following him to the centre of the mattress.

Penn's own tunic was fastened at the back, so Raff eagerly pulled him between his legs to access the knots that Penn had inexpertly tied that morning. He swore against Penn's nape, and Penn couldn't help but laugh.

'You could cut them,' he said, over his shoulder.

'And pay for new lacing?' Raff responded, managing to tug the cords free. 'I would prefer not to.'

Raff loosened the ties, then grabbed the thick fabric of the tunic and pulled it over Penn's head in a single, deft movement. Penn's undershirt clung to the material, and with a bite of panic Penn realised *that* was sliding up, too, and his back was to Raff and his skin was exposed and—

He grabbed at the hem of the shirt and tugged it down as Raff quickly dropped the tunic to the floor.

'Forgive me,' Raff said, alarmed. 'I did not mean to—'

Penn twisted his fingers in the shirt, still kneeling between Raff's legs. Raff cautiously shuffled forwards, sliding his hands across Penn's stomach until they reached the place where he grasped the linen. Penn relaxed into the touch, letting go of the fabric as Raff's fingers laced between his own.

He lifted their clasped hands and pressed a kiss to Raff's knuckles. His skin was warm, and a little calloused. He thought of the lie.

He'd given so much to Raff, without ever meaning to. He'd turned over part of himself, while keeping the rest locked away, untouchable and unknowable. But Raff was *good,* and kind, and treated him with such gentle care that Penn feared he would shatter. Raff deserved more. He deserved the truth.

Penn couldn't give him that. But he wanted to.

'I—' He stopped, regained his breath. Tried again. 'I want you to take it off.'

'Are you certain?'

Penn kissed his fingers again. 'I am.'

Raff let go of his hands, moving slowly. He didn't pull the shirt away with the frantic movements they'd undressed each other with before, but carefully slid his hands beneath, brushing his fingers lightly against Penn's skin. The touch sent irrepressible shivers down Penn's spine, his skin prickling into gooseflesh as Raff's hands moved, drifting over his hips, his stomach, his chest.

Still he didn't make any motion to remove the garment. One of his hands moved upwards, the tips of his fingers dancing lightly over Penn's nipple, and Penn's breath hitched as the graze sent another shudder over him, fuelling the heat in his belly, making his cock stiffen in his breeches. Raff huffed a warm breath against Penn's back and Penn wriggled closer, feeling Raff's own erection pressed hard against him.

Raff clearly wasn't in any hurry to do anything about it. He drifted his hands up and down Penn's torso, moving with the familiar gentleness that Penn had come to expect from him. He splayed his fingers across Penn's skin, tugging him close, holding him. He waited, letting Penn breathe, before kissing his neck, taking the hem of the undershirt in one hand, and slowly pulling it away.

The room wasn't cold, but Penn still shivered as the air touched his skin, feeling remarkably exposed. Raff dropped the shirt but didn't let him go. Penn realised that he was using his own body to shield him – to hide his scars.

'Are you all right?' Raff muttered, his voice drifting over Penn's ear, his beard tickling his back.

Penn nodded, unable to do much else. Raff hummed, then replaced his voice with his lips, leaning up and leaving gentle kisses along the shell of Penn's ear before taking his lobe in his teeth with a little tug that made Penn gasp.

'May I . . .?'

Raff's arm around his middle loosened. One of his hands moved to Penn's shoulder, waiting.

'I . . .' Penn took a steadying breath. 'You may.'

The warm press of Raff's body behind him moved away, opening the space between them in a rush of cool air. Penn's skin burst into gooseflesh, his heart thundering.

'God . . .'

Raff's hand stilled. Penn should have known it would be too much: even a hunter like Raff was disgusted by the reality of it – or the realisation of the sort of person Penn really was, to earn such punishment. Penn went to pull away, to wrap himself in layers once more so Raff wouldn't be forced to look, when he felt himself being tugged into a crushing embrace.

He froze, his pulse thudding horribly in his ears.

'Raff?'

Raff rested his head against Penn's shoulder, trying to regain control over his breathing. He hadn't seen the scars since the night Penn had flinched away from him as he bathed. He had forgotten their true extent.

'Raff?' Penn's voice sounded small and far away.

'I *hate* this,' Raff said against Penn's back, 'I hate that this happened to you. That no one stopped it from happening.'

'Why would anyone have stopped it?' Penn's voice was a whisper. 'I told you: I was – I *am* – more poorly behaved than you. I deserved—'

'*No.*'

Penn fell silent. Fury boiled in Raff's chest, his ire utterly and frustratingly directionless.

'You did not deserve this. No matter what you did. This is *cruel.*' He clung around Penn's middle, his cheek pressed against the scars. 'No one will do this to you again. No one.'

Penn *laughed*. 'You cannot promise that.'

Raff's arms flexed tighter. 'For as long as I am able, Penn. No one will hurt you. Not like this.'

Penn sighed, but didn't speak, and Raff leaned back to better examine his skin. This close, he could see the criss-crossing marks more clearly, the raised edges where they'd healed poorly. Some were a hair's breadth wide, no more than faint, white lines. Others were angrier; dark red tracks that bumped across his back. Several, Raff realised in horror, were no more than a few years old.

The wide canvas of Penn's back was irreparably torn, the marks like great, fluttering wings. He ran his hands down Penn's spine, feeling the raised lines beneath his fingertips.

Raff could imagine Penn, no more than a boy, his back bleeding and his eyes filled with tears. Worse, he could imagine him but a few years previous: a stubborn, reckless young man whose back still bled but who held his head high in an act of defiance.

He couldn't bear it. He pressed a kiss between Penn's shoulder blades, where the scars mingled tightest. Penn drew in a small intake of breath, but didn't pull away, so Raff repeated the movement, covering the ridged landscape of his back with light, delicate kisses.

Raff moved slowly – reverently – leaning Penn forwards so he could reach the marks that snaked down his back in stiff, uneven lines.

'Penn,' he breathed, his lips not leaving his skin, 'they are—'

'I know what they are,' Penn murmured. 'I *know* they're hideous.'

Raff winced, ducking his head. He had not been intending to call them hideous; the thought hadn't even occurred to him. They were *raw*, and they pained him. But clearly not as much as they pained Penn. He wondered who had seen them before, what they had said.

'They are a sign of your strength,' he said. 'Of your endurance. You were strong enough to survive this. You endured it, because you had to.' He moved away from Penn's back, pressing his lips to his neck, pulling him closer. 'I swear, you will not have to endure it again.'

There was a choked noise. Raff loosened his grip, and Penn twisted around between his legs to face him. His eyes were shining, and tears shivered on his eyelashes. Raff raised his hands, cupping his face and leaning forwards to rest their foreheads together. Penn's breath caught, and Raff wiped away the tears with the pads of his thumbs before they could spill down his cheeks.

'Penn . . .'

And then Penn was kissing him. It wasn't like the urgent kisses they'd shared on the road in stolen snatches of solitude. It wasn't heated and desperate, like the moment in Hartswood Forest, or later, in the barn, when they'd finally given in to the tension that had been building between them for so long. It was slow and indulgent, and Raff relished the feel of him, the softness of his lips. Raff let Penn guide him down onto the mattress as he slid a leg over Raff's waist, kissing him long and lingering.

Penn moved from his lips to his jaw, his jaw to his throat, trailing a soft line of kisses over his skin. Raff could feel himself lighting up, his lungs squeezing, and when Penn reached the crook of Raff's neck he opened his mouth, pressing his tongue against him. Raff arched against the feather bed, and Penn moved with him, pushing down as he pushed up, grinding against him.

Raff moaned, and felt Penn smile before applying more pressure, the edge of his teeth gliding against Raff's collarbone. His hands snapped instinctively to Penn's hips as he moved, sucking Raff's skin into his mouth, hot and quick and sure to leave a bruise.

Apparently satisfied, Penn edged down towards Raff's nipple, flicking his tongue over the tip. Raff squirmed against the bed, already overwhelmed, and Penn licked again, his hands pressed into Raff's shoulders.

He moved lower still, peppering Raff's stomach with soft, open kisses. When he reached the waistband of his breeches, he rose to his knees, one hand fiddling with the ties and the other palming gently over Raff's aching cock.

'Penn, *God* . . .'

It was supposed to sound like a warning – or a command – but it came out low and needy. Penn grinned, teeth glinting, then swiftly undid the tie and hooked his thumbs beneath the fabric. Together they dispensed with the last of Raff's clothing.

Penn stared down at him, still straddling his hips, expression dark and hungry. Raff could not resist that look. Before Penn could move, Raff heaved himself up, grabbed him around the waist and pulled them both around, slinging Penn onto his back and pinning him between his arms. Penn stared at him, eyes wide, lips wine-dark. He was lovely, even in the dim, flickering light.

Penn lifted himself on his elbows, angling their faces together, but Raff moved back before their lips could meet, eliciting a soft noise of complaint. The low whine mingled into a moan as Raff ducked down, pressing his mouth to Penn's chest, catching one of his nipples between his teeth briefly before moving lower, trailing his lips along the edge of his ribcage.

Raff teased him for as long as he dared before sliding his hands beneath Penn's backside, digging into his woollen breeches. Penn grinned up at him, and Raff made quick work of the ties, tugging both breeches and hose away and to the floor beside the rest of their clothes.

Raff's breath caught as he stared down at him. Penn sprawled on Raff's bed, the furs rumpled beneath him, completely naked. The flickering light of the fire in the hearth danced across his skin.

Weeks on the road had done nothing to help how skinny he was, and Raff couldn't help but ache at the thought of how poor his life had been before his escape. He could fix that, now they were home. Now they were *safe*.

He lowered himself down to the bed beside him, tugging him around so they were lying face to face. Penn's chest was warm, and Raff could feel his pulse beneath his fingers when they came to rest against his neck. He kissed him again, marvelling at the way their bodies fit together, the way their bare legs tangled.

He wanted to feel more of him, feel *all* of him. On the road, he hadn't craved it, too aware of the biting winds and hard ground, the risk that they weren't alone. But now, warm and sheltered with a locked door and several inches of stone between them and the world outside, he did.

'Do you want—' Raff stumbled, trying to find the right way to say it, 'that is, have you been with – before—'

He cut himself off. It was likely a foolish question, considering Penn's relationship with William. But Penn smiled, immediately understanding his fumbling offer.

'Once,' he said, ruefully. 'I took the lead, as we were both inexperienced. But . . .' He faltered.

'You did not enjoy it?'

'It was . . . fairly enjoyable,' Penn said. 'But brief, and risky. Very risky.' His eyes turned stony for just a moment, before he shook his head with a brief, apologetic smile. 'I am not well experienced.'

'I understand.' Raff moved his hand down Penn's arm before taking his hand, threading their fingers together. 'If you do not want to—'

Penn smothered his words under a heated kiss. 'I *do* want to,' he murmured against Raff's lips. 'Very much.'

Raff grinned against his lips, then broke away, sliding from the bed as Penn watched. He moved towards his bags – still unpacked in his haste to settle Penn into the castle – and dug through his things until his fingers brushed against the little stoppered bottle he was searching for. He removed it with a flourish, and Penn raised his eyebrows.

'For blades?' Penn said, recognising it.

'Yes,' Raff said, moving back onto the bed, 'but . . . it has other uses.'

'Is that so?'

'There are many things you learn while training, or on the road. Consider it a poorly kept secret.'

'Is this to be part of *my* training?' grinned Penn. 'The best way to oil a blade?'

'It is an invaluable skill.'

Penn crept forwards, climbing into Raff's lap. 'Then you best show me.'

He attempted to take the bottle from Raff, but Raff managed to stop him, wrapping his free arm around his back.

'Too keen,' he teased. 'Or *is* it that you wish to take the lead?'

Penn shook his head. Raff kissed him again.

'Lie down.'

Penn watched him closely, his legs loose about Raff's waist, as Raff guided him down onto the mattress. He placed the oil on the bed beside him, careful that it would not fall, then grabbed Penn by the hips and tugged him forwards. Penn gasped, but before he could speak Raff bent down and took his prick in his mouth.

Penn writhed beneath him as Raff pressed his thumbs into his hips. Raff moved surely, relishing the way Penn gasped and shuddered beneath him, helpless to the intense attentions of his tongue. When Penn was panting on the mattress, he raised his head, releasing him with a smug smile.

'That is not what I was expecting,' Penn breathed, 'when you talked of *oiling*—'

Now Raff reached for the oil, pulling the cork away with his teeth and dribbling some of the aromatic-smelling liquid over his fingers. He slowly guided his hand over Penn's prick, then lower.

'Is this all right?'

'*Oh*—' Penn lay back. '*Yes*. But what about the bla—'

His teasing faltered as Raff slowly pushed a finger inside him, his breath hitching. Raff was familiar with the sort of fumbling trysts Penn had described, and was intent that this would not be like that.

'Relax,' he coaxed. 'Breathe.'

Penn wriggled beneath him, his body easing, and Raff carefully slid another finger inside before quirking them both forwards. Penn arched on the bed with a loud curse. Raff smiled to himself, placing a hand to Penn's thigh to keep him still before repeating the action. When Penn was keening softly against the furs, he removed his fingers and grabbed the oil again, pouring it liberally over himself.

He clasped Penn's hips, lifting him from the sheets, as Penn used his elbows to push himself forwards. Raff positioned himself against him, waiting.

'Penn?'

'*Please,* Raff.'

He nudged forwards, slowly at first, and Penn stiffened as he eased in, his breath coming in hot gasps. He felt incredible, and Raff released Penn's hip, smoothing his hand over his stomach in slow, calming strokes.

'God—' he muttered, voice low, '*Penn*—'

Penn's lips parted in a low whine as he relaxed around him. Enraptured, Raff lowered himself down so their bodies were flush, capturing Penn's mouth in a kiss. He held himself there a moment, tasting him, *feeling* him, then pushed forwards again, deeper. Penn sighed as Raff began to move faster, taking him in sure, confident thrusts. Penn moved against him, pushing back, and Raff let out a warm breath, his body tensing. He reached between them, keen to for Penn to share in this building, intense pleasure, and wrapped his hand around Penn's cock, matching the rhythm of his hips.

Penn moaned something – it could have been Raff's name, or just a wordless cry.

Penn felt so good, so *right*. He moved against the blankets, arching his back, his eyes tight shut, all his joking and sarcasm and cynicism choked from him as his breath quickened into panting. Like this there was only pleasure as Raff pushed him closer, feeling his own pulse race at the way Penn's hands clutched at him, stuttering his name through kiss-swollen lips.

Raff rutted his hips faster, hastening the attentions of his hand, lost in the delicious noises Penn was making, the way he shuddered against him. He felt him tighten around him again with another groan. Raff made his movements more urgent with a low oath, drawing Penn out with his hand in urgent jerks until he convulsed beneath him, moaning Raff's name into his arm, spending across his stomach and Raff's fingers.

Moving slowly, close to climax himself, Raff was preparing to pull back when Penn wrapped his legs around his waist, trapping him in place.

'Keep going,' he breathed.

'But—'

'Keep going.'

As if to punctuate the remark, Penn tightened his grip, pushing Raff deeper inside him as he did. Raff gasped as Penn's heels dug into his backside, then grabbed his hips and continued to thrust into him. Penn jerked beneath him, keeping pace, stuttering out curses as Raff chased his own pleasure, the tension building in his core.

'Penn—' he managed, 'I – *God,* Penn—'

He hurtled over the edge with a groan. He clung to Penn's trembling hips for a few moments more, feeling his legs around his waist loosening, before gently moving away and collapsing limply on the bed next to him, breathing heavily.

They lay exhausted on the blankets. Penn was desperately warm, his eyes lidded. Raff lowered his cheek to Penn's chest, tracing a hand up and down his arm, dancing in the soft skin of his elbow. Penn shuddered beneath the touch, and when Raff stopped to peer at him, he pulled him up into another kiss.

He tasted of home.

Chapter Eighteen

Raff woke to a bright light behind his eyelids and a cool breeze biting at his exposed skin. He grabbed for the blankets, tugging the thick cover back over his shoulders before extending a hand across the bed beside him.

It was empty.

He opened his eyes.

He was alone. The room was splashed in early snow-bleached sunlight and a cold wind was fluttering in through the open balcony door. He frowned at the space next to him as resignation sank in.

Penn hadn't stayed.

Perhaps Raff had given too much of himself away. Penn had never indicated that he wanted anything more from Raff than safety and the mutual slaking of desire, yet last night it felt like something had changed. There was a pain above Raff's heart like a bruise, too tender to touch.

Penn would have to move on eventually. They couldn't maintain the lie that he was a Lord's brother for ever, and the supposed boar hunt would provide a useful cover for finding Penn somewhere to stay.

That was a *good* thing. It was what Penn truly wanted. Raff tried to remind himself of that as his fingers twitched across the vacant bed beside him.

There was an immense, smothering weight on his chest. He shivered as a gust of wind burst in from the balcony, bringing with it a powdering of snow.

He was about to rise to close the door when a shadow fell across the stone. There – bathed in light and falling snow – was Penn. The rising sun illuminated him, blinding Raff so he had to hold a hand above his eyes to see. He was dressed in a thin linen shirt and nothing else.

'Is that my undershirt?' asked Raff, slowly coming to his senses.

Penn turned to face him. He grinned, the dawn bursting from behind his head in a dazzling halo. Snowflakes clung to his hair.

'I was cold,' he said, spreading his arms. 'And you were not using it.'

Penn lowered his arms with a smirk, and the wide, unlaced neck of the undershirt dropped lower, revealing a swathe of skin. He turned to stare back out across Lord Barden's lands as Raff took a sharp intake of breath, watching the way the fabric hung from his body.

'It's beautiful,' Penn said, his quiet voice carrying in the still air, 'the snow, and the sunrise . . .' He took a deep breath, filling his lungs with crisp winter air. 'I have never seen such a view.'

Raff propped himself up on his hand, watching him. 'Indeed.'

The snow began flurrying down in quick little clouds, slowly building on the handrail and the floor. Penn laughed, pressing it between his fingers, then spun around, face flushed.

'It is also,' he said, breathlessly, '*freezing*.'

With a final glance at the view over his shoulder, he slouched back inside, pushing shut the heavy door. His hair shimmered wetly, the thick flakes melting as he walked back towards the bed. He shivered, rubbing at his arms with his hands, before sliding beneath the covers, slotting in beside Raff and draping a hand across his chest. Raff leaped back with a hiss.

'*Curse you*, you're cold.'

'I mentioned that, yes.'

'Why were you even out there?'

'I wanted to see what it looked like.' Penn shrugged. 'Did you know you've an osprey nesting in the northern wall?'

'I did not.'

Penn wriggled beneath Raff's arm to rest his head on his shoulder, and even though Raff was prepared for the chill of his skin, he still gasped as Penn's frozen feet pressed against his bare legs. They lay like that, for a moment, before Penn spoke again.

'Thank you,' he said, quietly. The whisper tickled at Raff's bare skin, throwing gooseflesh up and down his arms. 'For bringing me here.'

'It was nothing.'

'It wasn't *nothing*. You could have left me where you found me. You *should* have. Anyone else would have, or forced me to return to the keep.'

Raff wanted to argue, but Penn was right: it would take a fool – or a madman – to spirit a servant away from a man well known to be cruel. Instead of responding, he pulled him closer. Penn reached out, sliding his hand down Raff's arm till his fingers rested atop Raff's.

Penn was now thoroughly warmed, and Raff's skin ignited where he was pressed against him. There was something so *soft* about him. It wasn't in his body, not even his *manner*: he was all wit and spikes and barely hidden anger. It ran deeper than that, something about the way he clung to Raff's side, the way he nuzzled close, the way he ran his fingers over Raff's knuckles.

While Raff's invitation to the keep was one he was happy to

extend indefinitely, he knew that it had never been what Penn had asked for. Raff wouldn't stop him when he finally left, no matter how aware he was of the aching space Penn would leave behind him when he did.

This wouldn't last. This *couldn't* last, not in the way he wished.

He glanced down at Penn, who was watching him closely from behind his lashes. This couldn't last, he warned himself again, knowing it was true. But that didn't mean he wasn't able to ask, for once; to give in again to what he wanted and beg for more than just a few sparse days together.

Raff moved his hand upward, carding his fingers through Penn's fringe, brushing the damp hair out of his eyes.

'Penn . . .'

'Mm?'

Raff's hand lingered on the side of his face. Something tightened in his throat, his heart suddenly lodged there. The words stuck.

'You will give yourself a fever if you insist on standing in the snow.'

Penn smiled. 'At least I paused to dress first.'

'In *my* clothes.'

Penn looked down at himself. 'Well,' he huffed, 'if you are so offended . . .' He reached down and began to pull the shirt up.

'That is not—' began Raff, finding the words failing him.

Penn stopped, eyeing him with a cocked brow.

'It doesn't *offend* me,' Raff finished.

'No?'

'It's . . . you . . .' He couldn't find the words – ones that wouldn't damn him.

'Does it suit me?' Penn drawled, with a grin.

You look good. You look like – like mine. Raff quashed that thought, but Penn didn't miss his expression, or the heat in his cheeks.

'I should keep it,' he continued. 'It is a fine shirt, and good for staving off the chill.'

'Is that so?' Raff's hand began to roam up and down Penn's leg, towards his waist, his thumb nestling against his hip.

'I will never take it off.'

Raff let his eyes flick down Penn's body, taking him in. Penn stretched languidly, with a self-satisfied hum.

'Never?' Raff said, then brought his hand up beneath the thin fabric, pushing it away to reveal the supple skin of Penn's torso. His fingers pressed into his flesh, warm beneath his hand. Penn's breath hitched, his pink tongue wetting his lips.

Raff thought of the scars. 'Can I?'

Penn nodded, and Raff tugged the undershirt away, swinging one leg over his hips as he did. He placed one hand either side of Penn's head, nearly pinning him, nearly touching him.

Penn stared up at him, trapped gladly between his arms with parted lips, his breathing heavy. His hair was splayed across the sheet, twisting into tighter curls as it dried. His eyes were bright, the bags that had settled there lightened into nearly nothing. His skin looked temptingly soft in the dawn light, and Raff ached to feel it, to touch him in every place he could reach. Raff realised he was staring. But he couldn't look away, either.

Penn's eyes were wide, but the easy, carefree expression he'd been wearing as he'd joked about Raff's undershirt slipped away.

'Do not . . .' Penn shuffled against the sheets, his cheeks flushing. 'Do not look at me like that.'

Raff leaned back with a frown, running his hands lightly down Penn's chest till they rested at his sternum.

'Like what?'

'Like . . .' Penn swallowed, looking away, 'like I'm *worthy*.'

Raff could feel Penn's quickened heart beneath his palm, as if it were beating just for him. He felt his own heart stutter in his chest, the bruising pain returning. Penn still couldn't meet his eye.

'You *are*,' Raff murmured. 'Of course you are.'

Penn didn't say anything, merely pressed his cheek into the sheet, looking resolutely away. The pain *flared*, opening up, and Raff dropped down to the bed beside him, cupping Penn's face. The teasing expression he'd been wearing had fallen away, and now he seemed uncertain. He still didn't look at Raff, despite how close they were.

'Penn.'

Penn's gaze flicked up. It wavered. Before he could turn away again, Raff surged forwards and kissed him. Penn froze for a moment, then looped his arm around Raff's waist and kissed him back, almost desperately. He *clung*, his fingertips digging into Raff's skin.

Raff released his lips with a sigh, but didn't pull away, pressing their foreheads together.

'You *are*,' he whispered, keeping his eyes shut, feeling the warmth of Penn's breath mingling with his own. 'When . . .' He faltered, as if he was perched on a precipice, ready to fling himself off. 'When you leave, remember that. You *are* worthy.'

He kissed him again, pretending for Penn's sake that he couldn't feel the wetness on his cheeks. Penn huffed a breath against his mouth, a choked half-laugh, before letting go with a sniff. When Raff opened his eyes again, Penn had fixed his expression, his eyes bright if red-rimmed.

'So,' he said, the life returning shakily to his voice as he peered at Raff with lidded eyes, 'did you intend to teach me further how to properly oil a blade?'

The tremor that had been in the back of Penn's throat when he had told Raff not to look at him had vanished. The moment of doubt had passed as soon as it had arrived: or, Raff suspected, it had been forced aside.

He wanted to reach out, to pull Penn close and show him how worthy he was. The night in the alderman's house returned to him, lying helpless to fix a hurt Penn hadn't even named.

But Penn's bold smile had returned. Raff was loath to see it go again, certainly not thanks to his own fumbling words.

He was taking too long. Penn moved closer. 'Well?'

Raff couldn't. He was too weak. He placed his hand on Penn's hip.

'What do you wish to learn?'

Penn smirked, and in a swift movement pushed Raff back onto the bed, heaving himself into his lap and perching atop him. Raff's breath fled, words gone, only able to stare up as Penn lowered himself down till their mouths brushed, chests flush.

'Show me what you did last night,' Penn said. 'Show me how.' He didn't kiss him, just ghosted his lips over Raff's. 'I want you on your back.'

Raff felt himself hardening, heat curling in his belly, struck with the unexpected image of Penn above him, *inside* him, taking him apart.

Penn noticed him hesitating and quickly added— 'If you want it, of course.'

'God,' Raff breathed, '*Yes*—'

Penn grinned, and crashed their lips together with a satisfied hum.

It was late by the time they emerged from Raff's chambers, especially after Raff had called for a bath while Penn returned inconspicuously to the guest room for a change of clothes. He felt as if he were floating, despite his aching limbs. There was a squeeze in his chest, a brightness too intense to look at.

Clean and suitably attired, they'd entered the great hall to find it empty, and had headed down the steep winding stone stairs to the kitchen instead, both ravenous.

Penn introduced himself to the cook with the same story they'd given the rest of the staff, resulting in a long conversation about the merits of wild boar compared to other game. They'd left with their hunger satiated and Penn with the promise that should he return later, he would have first pick of the gingerbread she was making.

According to Raff, this was high praise: the cook had been part of their household staff since he and his siblings were children, and they'd never been given such an opportunity. Penn had simply smiled.

'You cannot fault me for being so charming.'

They headed to the armoury next. With time to spare until his father returned, Raff appeared keen to continue to train.

'I would see you wielding a sword,' he said as they made their way across the courtyard. 'You are quick, and your skills with a dagger are improving, but the sword is the more versatile tool.' He pushed open the door to the armoury, looking around with a practised eye. 'We need to find you something suitable, not too heavy . . .'

Raff continued to muse as he headed deeper into the room. *Blade oil indeed,* Penn thought, peering up at the racks and wondering what Raff intended to do with him.

The armourer was thankfully absent, and avoiding any difficult conversations about why a man apparently set to hunt boar had no skills at swordplay, they spent a long while trying out different weapons. Penn tested the heft of each, swinging them inexpertly as Raff ducked out of his way.

Another snowstorm rolled in from the hills, pushing their lesson short, and they were forced to retire back inside where they found Ash and Cecily lounging in the great hall. Cecily, curled in a high-backed chair by the fire, was mending a sizable hole in the hem of one of her dresses. When Raff had asked her how she came to rip her clothes so thoroughly, she had told him in distinctly unladylike terms to shut his mouth.

Ash had challenged Penn to a game of chess. Having nothing else to do, he agreed, sliding into the seat opposite him with a wily grin, before thoroughly trouncing him three times in a row.

'I still feel we ought to put you to work,' Ash said bitterly, as he reset the board for the fourth time.

Penn shrugged. 'Is beating you at chess not enough work?'

'It certainly doesn't take much effort,' Raff noted, watching from behind Penn's chair.

Penn grinned as Ash sighed at them.

'You are both unbearable,' he sniped. 'Although I suppose this proves that you do enough for the keep.'

'What do you mean?' asked Penn, making his first move.

'I have not seen Raff so content in *years*. If your presence here makes him a tolerable brother, then I would consider that work enough.'

'Is that so?'

'Aye. And it is not an easy job; especially if one spends so much time on his knees.'

Penn felt his face flush, and Ash grinned.

'Raff,' Ash said, peering up at Raff's scowl, 'go and fetch us something to drink, will you? I wish to properly celebrate my new brother.'

Raff rolled his eyes, about to move, but Penn stood first. 'I shall fetch something,' he said. 'Your cook promised me first choice of her gingerbread. Besides, I would not want Raff to be forced to take all those stairs. Especially when his knees are so overworked.'

Leaving both brothers spluttering – and Cecily roaring with laughter – he swiftly made his way from the room and down the steep stairs that led to the kitchen, already able to smell the gingerbread.

Raff took Penn's place opposite his brother, eyeing the board critically. Ash snorted, shook his head, and leaned back in his chair.

'Damn it, Raff.'

'What?'

'You smug bastard.'

Raff looked up, placing his hands in his lap. 'Meaning?'

'Meaning I truly haven't seen you this happy in years.'

'He's right, you know,' said Lily, abandoning her sewing to lean against the arm of Raff's chair. 'It is good to see you like this.'

Raff lowered his head, unsure of what to say. He could feel the back of his neck and ears turning red. Ash laughed.

'You have embarrassed him, Lily.'

'As have you,' she retorted, before glancing at Raff. 'I just hope you know what you're doing.'

Raff turned to her. She looked serious.

'What do you mean?'

She swallowed, her mouth tight. 'You said you will only stay until Father returns. What will you do when he does? *Will* you take him elsewhere?'

Raff's jaw twitched. 'I promised him I would.'

'I know you are a man of your word,' said Ash, beginning to pack the carved chess pieces back into their box. 'But do you not—'

His words were cut off by the crash of the far doors opening.

All three siblings spun around as a powerful gust of wind blew in, sending the candles streaming, bringing with it a flurry of snow and the unmistakable form of their father.

They were on their feet in an instant as he slammed the doors behind him and strode down the long room. His face was red, his riding cloak still tight around his shoulders. He looked furious.

'Raff Barden.' He didn't shout. He didn't need to, as he advanced on Raff with his finger extended. 'What have you *done*?'

Raff froze to the spot, feeling suddenly like a boy being chastised.

'I don't—' Raff began, but his father spoke louder.

'You were *seen*,' he growled, 'in Arlescote, weeks ago.'

Raff's insides turned to ice.

'A Scottish tracker with dark hair, blue eyes, and an inability to keep out of other people's business was spotted travelling north with William de Foucart,' he spat. 'That sounds like you, wouldn't you agree?'

Raff gaped at him. 'I have no idea what this is.'

'Marcus de Foucart thinks you kidnapped his son!' His father *was* shouting, now. 'He's mobilising as we speak, all bluster about "repaying debts" and "offence". He is on the warpath, Raff, intending to head north.'

'I have not *kidnapped* anyone!' Raff shouted back, desperate to be heard. 'I—'

There was the sound of a door shutting behind them. They all turned to see Penn lingering in the doorway that led to the kitchens, an earthenware jug in one hand and a stack of cups in the other. Lord Barden pushed past his son towards him, crossing the room in only a few strides. Penn's face was deathly white, and his hand shook where he held the heavy jug.

'William,' Lord Barden said, looking at him carefully, 'your father is looking for you.'

The jug dropped, shattering in wet shards across the flagstones.

Penn knew he should have been more careful. He should have kept his hood up. Should have waited. Should never have entered Arlescote.

He should never have left his father's keep in the first place.

Everyone was talking at once, but he couldn't focus on what they were saying.

No; not everyone. Raff was staring at him, face blank, his expression broken. He did not speak.

Penn didn't care about Ash's shouting, or Cecily's confusion. He didn't care that the secret was out – the secret of the agreement that had bound himself to his lover's sister. He didn't care that Lord Barden was talking in hurried, low tones about de Foucault's intentions, his plans to come north and seize what was his.

He only cared about Raff, standing still and silent, watching him with that shattered expression.

Penn stepped forwards, reaching for him, 'Raff—'

He took a swift step backwards, wincing. 'No.'

'Please.'

Raff took another step. 'You *lied*. I cannot—' He stared at Penn, eyes burning. It wasn't anger, there, but pain. 'I cannot.'

With that, he turned on his heel and strode from the room, heading through the wide doors and into the raging storm outside.

For a moment, no one moved. Ash opened his mouth to speak, but before he could, Penn pushed past him, rushing after Raff.

It was bitterly cold outside, the high stone walls of the keep doing little to keep out the blizzard. Penn could see Raff's silhouette across the yard and ran towards him, feet skidding across the fresh ice.

'Raff!'

He didn't turn. Penn didn't know if it was the wind muffling his voice, or if Raff simply didn't wish to speak to him.

'Raff, *please*—' He caught up quickly, grabbing his arm.

Raff snatched it away with a grimace. 'Do not assume you can touch me,' he spat. 'Do *not*.'

Penn flinched. Raff's expression was wild, pain and fury mingling like an animal caught in a trap.

'We need to talk,' Penn pleaded, his voice nearly lost to the wind. 'If you would listen to me—'

'What else did you lie about?' Raff demanded, face set. 'I thought . . .' He faltered, but swiftly gathered himself. 'When you spoke about William I thought you loved him. And then I thought you were using him as a means to an end, to meet your own goals. And now . . .' He stared at him through the snow. 'Now I do not know what to think. You *used* me.'

'Raff—'

'No. You just wanted what you could get from me, no more.'

'That is not true. Yes, I wanted to escape. When we met, I would have told you anything, just for your help. But please, Raff, that was so long ago. I did not expect to—'

'To *what*?'

To know you. To care about you. To love you. Penn had tried not to acknowledge it, before. He had tried not to look at it, lest it blind him. But it was true. A sharp, deadly fact. The words caught behind his teeth. They were like the heavy flakes that tumbled around them: they would melt on his tongue in an instant, but too many of them would bury him. Kill him.

'I did not expect any of this. I did not expect for you to bring me to your home. Why would I have followed you here just to leave you or betray you, when I could have left on the road miles ago?'

Raff shook his head. Penn could barely read his expression through the snow. 'You said yourself it was better to be a lord's brother than a servant. You didn't *want* to leave.'

'I didn't want to leave *you*, Raff! I would have stayed even if you *had* taken me on as a servant.'

'How can I believe you?'

'I didn't mean for the lie to last this long. I should have told you—'

'You *should* have told me. You should have told me when we—' Raff sighed, squeezing his eyes shut. 'The first time we were together.'

That stuck. 'Like you did?' Penn shouted. 'Because I do not recall you telling me you were an earl's son before you pinned me to the straw and took my—'

'*Penn.*'

'What? It's the truth! We *both* lied.'

'It's different. You used me. You were supposed to – my *sister*, Penn!' He halted, eyebrows creasing. 'Or is it William, after all?'

Penn shook his head in disbelief. 'I am *Penn*,' he said, furiously. 'I have *always* been Penn. I am your—'

'You are *nothing*.'

Penn went still. So did Raff, his mouth open in horror. 'Penn, I didn't—'

'No.' Penn stepped back again, feet slipping. His lungs were on fire. 'No, I understand. You are right.'

They stared at each other through the snow, the words thrumming between them, taut as a bow string. Penn blinked the flakes from his eyes where they clung to his lashes.

'I will take you across the border tomorrow,' Raff said, breaking the silence. 'My mother's family will take you in, and you can go from there.' He hesitated, expression carefully blank, like a curtain had been drawn over his face. 'You should not stay with them for long.'

Penn remembered what Raff had said the first day they travelled together, about his father consolidating power.

'Raff, no. This is not a doting father searching for his son,' he said desperately. 'He'll come here, and—'

Raff ignored him. 'Be ready to leave in the morning. It will be a difficult journey. Make sure you are prepared.'

Then he turned, and he was gone.

Penn watched him until he vanished, then headed back towards the keep, chest hollow. He heaved open the doors to find Raff's father, Cecily, and Ash still there, gathered around the fire. They wore matching angry expressions. Penn took a rattling breath and walked towards them.

'I know,' he said, feeling nothing at all. 'You can curse me later.' He turned to Lord Barden. 'Tell me what you've heard of my father. What he thinks happened, what his plans are now. I need to know how much danger you are in.'

Chapter Nineteen

The guest rooms were cold and empty despite the fire that had been lit in the grate. Penn fell onto the wide bed with a low groan, longing for the warmth of Raff's chambers.

He had ruined so much. The lie itself, borne for so long, was its own betrayal, but it was because of Penn that Raff and his family found war encroaching on them.

He balled his hands into fists against his eyes, trying to smother the hot pressure behind them.

At least Lord Barden had spoken to him. They still had time. His father had put out several conflicting stories ranging from kidnapping to murder, convoluted tales that spoke of a man wronged, or a brother trying to scupper his sister's wedding. As far as Raff's father could tell, de Foucart had only warned his allies to prepare.

De Foucart had a great many allies, most won through power and wealth. Few of them *liked* him, though, and Penn hoped that the animosity towards him would slow the progress of his neighbouring lords, even with the enticing tale of a lost son.

He'd told them of Raff's decision to head to Scotland. Ash had agreed, telling him to leave. To head beyond the border and hide, to extricate himself from their home. Penn had been forced to bite back a laugh.

'It is not so simple,' he'd tried to explain. 'Father thinks I am here. It does not matter that I will not be. He'll come down on you anyway, with an army.'

None of them had indicated that they believed him. Cecily had asked about Arlescote, and Penn had explained as briefly as he could. She'd looked at him, coolly, and then – much to his surprise – had thanked him for saving her brother's life. Penn had dismissed her.

'He would not have been there were it not for me,' he said. 'I do not deserve your thanks for pulling him from a situation that was my own doing.'

He'd removed himself after that, escaping to the guest chambers and remaining there for the rest of the day. The emptiness of the room pulled at him. In the silence, the argument with Raff still echoed in his head.

You are nothing.

He should have felt pain, or anger. But he didn't: just quiet, familiar resignation. Raff had finally realised what he was.

His scars itched as he rolled onto his side. The bed felt vast around him.

He'd grown used to Raff being close, be it huddled on the ground or sharing a bed. He'd never had such closeness before, and he'd clung to it, unable to let go. He ached in all the places he could no longer feel Raff's touch.

He couldn't face Raff again, couldn't bring himself to confront him properly. It would mean ending this tentative, delicate thing between them for good. This way, at least, he could pretend that Raff still held some regard for him. He wouldn't have to see that hatred reflected in his eyes again – or the hurt.

The hurt hadn't even lasted that long. Raff had looked devastated before his expression had turned blank and he'd decided they'd be heading to Scotland. He'd bent so *easily.* A more brittle man would have snapped and broken in two, but Raff had simply taken the lie and accepted it, made it part of himself. Perhaps this was just what Raff did. He spoke highly of his family, despite taking on so much for them. He appeared to be built on sacrifices, constructed around the needs of others.

Penn sighed into the pillow. That was what he was too: another sacrifice, scaffolding Raff up. He wondered how many burdens one man could carry within him before there was nothing of the man left.

He had no idea how many days it would take to reach Raff's Scottish family, but each one would be marked with pain for them both. It *would* be a difficult journey. Raff was doing what he always did, Penn was realising: throwing himself onto a blade to save another, no matter how much damage he took in the process.

Hot, fierce tears spilled from Penn's eyes, muddling his gaze. He would not let Raff bleed on his account.

Penn's breath hitched as he realised what he had to do. He swiftly rose from the bed towards the chest at the far side of the room, searching through it desperately until he found what he was looking for: parchment, quill and ink.

He rewrote the letter twice – three times, hastily scribbling out a painful '*I love you*' – before admitting that it was all he could do. Without any means of drying the ink, he left it resting on the tabletop then returned to the bed, despite his pounding head. He would need to sleep, if only for a few hours. Tomorrow, he would wake before the rest of the household.

Penn stared at the letter till his eyes slid shut of their own accord.

It was long before dawn when Penn started awake. He'd been dreaming, he was sure, but he couldn't remember of what beyond the unnerving image of his hands stained inky black.

He rose and dressed quickly, grabbed the letter, then slung his pack over his shoulder and made his way down the hallway to Raff's chambers. Raff was typically a sound sleeper; Penn should be able to leave the letter and go without him even knowing he was there.

Penn opened Raff's door carefully, taking its full weight to ensure it didn't creak too loudly or slam behind him. He crept around the antechamber towards the bedroom, his heart in his mouth as he peered in.

Raff was fast asleep, as he'd expected him to be. As Penn edged around the bed, his foot tangled in something on the floor. It was the undershirt he'd stolen from Raff when he'd gone to stand in the snow yesterday morning.

It felt like an age ago. Penn didn't know how he'd been so happy. Barely thinking, he snatched it up and shoved it into his bag with his own things.

He reread the letter, despite having it memorised, then folded it neatly to show where he'd scrawled Raff's name on the underside of the parchment.

He placed it carefully on the table beside the bed, where Raff would be sure to see it when he woke. Still buried beneath blankets, Raff slept soundly, his eyebrows knitted together in an unconscious frown. Penn had to resist the urge to lean down and wake him, or even to kiss him one last time.

Penn rubbed his fingertips together, took a final look at Raff's sleeping form, and fled the room on silent footsteps.

He hurried down the staircase, out through a side door and along the chilly pathway towards the stables. As he entered the warm space, the horses began to stamp at the ground with their hooves, snorting at the intrusion.

'Shh,' he said, approaching his horse, 'shh, boy. We must be quiet.'

He took a saddle from a hook on the wall – a cheaper one that wouldn't be missed – and began to strap it to the horse, soothing him with a calm, low voice. When he was ready, he hefted his bag onto the horse's back, strapping it in place.

'All right,' he murmured, 'let's—'

'Where do you think you're going?'

Ash stood in the open stable doorway, leaning against the frame, arms folded.

'Ash . . .'

'Leaving in a hurry?'

'Ash, *please* . . .'

'He was going to take you to Scotland. Did you even say goodbye? Or did you just get sick of him after he found out you'd lied?'

'Shut your mouth,' Penn snarled, suddenly furious. He dropped the horse's reins and strode towards where Ash stood, his finger outstretched. 'Don't you *dare*—'

'So, what, then? You *are* leaving, even I can see that. Finally going to start your new life?'

White-hot anger bubbled through him, like sizzling oil. 'I'm giving myself up.'

'What?'

'My father—'

'What *about* him?'

'You don't know him like I do. If . . .' he outstretched his arms, looking for the right words, 'if someone hurt Cecily or Raff, what would your father do? What would *you* do?'

Ash huffed, his breath steaming in the cold air. 'I'd kill them.'

'Why?'

'What?'

'*Why?*'

'Because they're my family. Because I love them.'

'My father does not think like that. He does not love me. He'll come for you – for *all* of you, not just Raff – because I'm *his*. This isn't about love, or family. This is just . . . property.'

Ash blinked and uncrossed his arms. He took a step towards Penn, who quickly backed away towards the horse.

'I *have* to go, Ash,' he said. 'As far as he's concerned, I belong to him. Which means he's going to come here, and he's going to bring men, and he's going to take back what's his. No matter who stands in his way.'

'That's madness.'

'We agree on something, then.' Penn ran his hand through his hair. 'You heard your father. He's got half of the southern counties convinced that he's a dedicated father fearful for his lost son. Which means when they agree to join him – which they will, for money, or power, or stupidity – that they won't listen to me. They won't listen to you. They *certainly* won't listen to Raff.'

'So why don't you go to Scotland? Raff's plan—'

'Raff's plan *won't work.*'

'How can you know that?'

'He is the *first* person my father will seek out when they discover I've vanished. It won't matter that I'm gone. He'll come for Raff anyway.'

Ash sighed. 'Raff—' he began, but Penn cut him off.

'He was going to help me leave. We both knew I couldn't remain here for long. He doesn't need me here, Ash. He can go back to his freedom, without me in his way.'

'Penn . . .'

'If I stay here, he'll be killed.'

'You don't know that.'

'You don't know my father. He is cruel, and he is violent, and he is merciless. I—' The words caught. But Penn needed Ash to recognise the danger. 'I have felt his cruelty myself. A hundred times. And I am his *son*. He wouldn't think twice about hurting Raff.'

'If you could just talk to Raff—'

'I *can't*.' Penn's voice, hoarse and worn, cracked.

'So you're just going to leave? Just like that?'

'There is no "just", here. You think this is how I wanted to go? Without even saying goodbye?'

'Then *say* it!'

Penn closed his eyes, resting his forehead against the horse's neck. In silence, he buckled the final strap of the saddle, grabbed the reins and led him towards the doors, where Ash was standing.

Penn blinked as the icy air made his eyes water.

'I *cannot*, Ash.'

'Why not?'

Penn resisted the urge to push past him. 'Because he might ask me to stay.'

Ash's expression softened slightly. There was something like recognition on his face. Penn remembered the conversation he'd overheard so many days ago. Something fell quietly into place. He kept Ash's eye.

'Who is Oliver?'

Ash immediately stiffened. 'What did Raff tell you?'

'Nothing. I overheard you speaking.'

Penn took another step forwards. Ash didn't move.

'Who is Oliver?' he repeated.

Ash's face was unreadable. Thick snowflakes clung to his hair.

'He's dead,' he said, finally.

Penn nodded. His chest felt hollow.

'I am sorry,' he said, somehow sure that it was warranted. 'And I need you to move. *Please.*'

There was a long moment where he thought Ash wouldn't. Where Penn considered the possibility of having to *make* him move. Then he stood back, leaving the doorway empty. Penn led the horse outside into the snow.

'Penn.'

'Yes?'

'Good luck.'

Penn nodded, then swung himself up onto the horse.

'I hope you know what you're doing.'

Penn set his eyes forward, looking down the path that led to the front gates of the keep, and the rising sun.

'So do I,' he said.

He urged the horse forward and was gone, the snow lashing at his face.

Chapter Twenty

When Raff opened his eyes with his arm slung across the empty bed, his first thought was of the balcony. Penn must be out there, enamoured with the landscape that Raff had grown bored of when he was only a boy.

He sighed, pulling up the covers where they'd slipped down in the night, and smiled to himself, already readying himself for the chill of Penn's skin when he returned to steal the heat beneath the blanket.

And then he remembered.

He opened his eyes properly. Penn had not joined him last night.

Penn wasn't even *Penn*.

William de Foucart. Son of Earl Marcus de Foucart, set to inherit land and titles and—

—and marry his sister.

Raff groaned into his hands, wishing he could retreat into the bliss of sleep and hide from the pain that had flared once more in his chest.

The sting of it was sharper than any dagger that Penn could have thrust into his heart. When Raff had begun to suspect that Penn had never loved William, he'd felt no guilt for the betrayed lordling. He'd been happy to ignore the imagined man when the fortunes had fallen in his favour and Penn had fallen into his arms.

But those fortunes had twisted around. He should have known. He'd allowed himself to open up to Penn, exposing himself, making himself vulnerable. He'd given himself more fully than he had to anyone else, assuming that Penn had been giving just as much in return.

But he hadn't, and it had been for nothing. Raff had showed Penn who he really was, and Penn had betrayed him for it. Not just him: his family too.

He sat up with a wince. After leaving Penn in the courtyard the previous evening, Raff had distracted both mind and body in the armoury, throwing himself into training until his arms ached and his head hummed with the clanging of steel. Both of his siblings had come to find him; Ash to inform him that supper had been prepared, and later, Lily, wishing to check on his mood after he had failed to appear in the great hall.

He had told her, sharply, to leave him be. Lily had ignored him, looked around to ensure they were alone, and reached for a sword herself.

Raff had only retired to his chambers when he could no longer hold his weapon steady. He was paying for that now, and the ache in his arms and shoulders mirrored the one between his ribs.

It was just pain. It would pass. Now Raff knew who Penn really was, the need to see his escape to fruition had grown even stronger. He understood why Penn had been so desperate to go. Desperate enough to lie for so long.

In the cold daylight it was all he could imagine: the scars that marred Penn's back, and who had put them there. However much Penn had hurt him, and lied to him, and *used* him till there was nothing left, he would not allow de Foucart to reach him.

He needed to remove Penn – Raff refused to call him William

– from their keep. When the Earl realised his son had fled once more, he would be forced to turn away.

Raff heaved himself from the bed and dressed hastily. He would send Penn to his mother's family, but he had been right to say he couldn't stay long. Aside from the pain of seeing him again, it was far too obvious a hiding place.

He made his way down the hallway, pushed open the door to the guest chambers, and was greeted with an empty room.

Penn must have gone downstairs already, perhaps to speak with Lord Barden about de Foucart's plans. Raff shut the door, then headed down the staircase.

The great hall was empty. The anxiety he'd carried since waking solidified into something heavier as he looked around the vacant room. He headed to the kitchens, where the cook informed him she hadn't seen Penn since the previous day, then dashed through the courtyard and into the armoury. Still he couldn't find him.

He headed back upstairs, hoping that Penn had returned to the guest rooms, or had let himself into Raff's chambers looking for him as well.

Both were empty.

Penn was gone, just like that. All it took was one night, and he'd vanished from Raff's life quicker than he'd appeared.

This was what Raff had offered, an age ago now. He'd planned to find Penn somewhere to thrive without the shadow looming over him that Raff could now see had the shape of his father. It was what he'd still been planning: to take Penn to Scotland and give him his freedom.

But not like this.

Penn hadn't even said goodbye.

He must have decided to continue the journey alone, perhaps returning south to one of the many keeps they had passed on their way to Dunlyn. He had the freedom to go *anywhere,* even if he was forced to make his own way now that the lie was out, and Raff was no longer useful to him.

Raff was about to head to the stables to see if Penn's horse remained, when his eyes fell on something sitting on the table beside the bed. A letter.

Something lurched in his stomach.

He grabbed it and tugged it open, revealing a page full of Penn's precise handwriting. He took a deep breath, and began to read.

Raff,

I'm sorry. I'm sorry for leaving like this, and not saying goodbye. I'm sorry for lying to you. For putting you in danger. For all of it.

I cannot stay here, but I cannot go with you to Scotland either. Your plan will not work. Father will still look for you, even if I am gone. He will come for you, and he may kill you, and I will not let that happen.

I am returning to Oxford. I do not expect Father to understand why I left, or rejoice that I have returned, but I hope that if he has me, he will leave you alone.

No doubt you will see my leaving as cowardly, especially like this. I am cowardly. I hope you will be able to forget me, in time, and the things I brought to you. I hope it is easy for you to forget, and you are not so deceived by the next person you choose to trust.

Thank you for trying to protect me, even though you couldn't.

I will think of you, always.

Penn

Raff read the letter three times. He read it till his eyes burned and the corners tore beneath his hands.

No. Penn was going back.

The anger and the pain fell away, leaving nothing.

The letter grasped in one hand, Raff strode towards the balcony doors and flung them open. The sun had truly risen, the hills beside the castle lit up. Snow fell from the clouds in huge, dangerous flakes. He grabbed the frozen railing and looked down at the ground below, at the road twisting southwards from the keep, the dangerous path marked with steep hills and treacherous, fast-flowing rivers.

God, Penn.

Raff could go after him. If Penn had fled in the night, or early that morning, there was still a chance that Raff could find him on the road and convince him to follow him to Scotland. It hadn't been real, Raff knew, yet the thought of Penn coming to harm at de Foucart's hand still turned his gut.

But it was risky. Both Penn and Lord Barden had warned him of de Foucart's ire. Raff stared out at the snow, head reeling. Surely de Foucart would not turn this into a conflict. Raff had seen proof of how cruel he was, but would he really launch them into war?

Raff didn't know what to do. He needed to speak to his father. If they could assess the true danger of the situation he would be better prepared to act.

With the letter clutched in his fist, the paper crumpled like butterfly wings, he headed back downstairs to the hall. It was now occupied, and he found his father seated at the far end of the long table, the surface covered in ledgers, papers and documents. He looked up as Raff entered, his expression weary.

'You're awake,' he said, looking Raff up and down. 'Join me.'

'What are you doing?' asked Raff, grabbing at a wayward bit of parchment. It showed a map of somewhere Raff didn't recognise.

'Organising,' huffed Lord Barden, taking the map from him and placing it in a stack of others.

'Organising what?'

'I've been considering where our allies lie. The set of the land, which roads are passable this season. This—' he gestured at a leather-bound ledger, 'lists all our provisions set aside for the remainder of winter, along with those in the basements.'

'You sound like you're preparing for war,' said Raff.

His father raised his eyebrows, but said nothing.

'Do you *really* think—'

'I do. Perhaps you should try it yourself, sometime.'

Before he could respond, the doors on the other side of the hall opened and in walked Ash and Lily. The wind scattered Lord Barden's papers.

'Shut that door, will you?' he shouted over his shoulder, as he scrambled to grab at them.

There was a slam, and the wind abated. Suddenly Raff was sharing the bench with his siblings, Lily seating herself beside him and Ash walking around the table to sit opposite.

Lily peered down, curiously. 'What is all this?'

'Unnecessary,' said their father. 'Hopefully.'

Raff sighed, and was about to challenge him again, when Lily spoke.

'Where's Penn?' she asked, picking up a ledger and turning it in her hands. 'I had expected him to be with you.'

'I was about to ask that very question,' added his father, taking the ledger from her and opening it seemingly at random. 'Penn, you call him? Not William?'

'Penn is the name he gave me,' Raff said, uselessly. 'He's . . .'

Gone. It wasn't hard to say. He looked up to where Ash had placed himself on the other side of the table. When their eyes met, he quickly glanced away, an expression Raff didn't quite recognise on his face.

'He left,' said Raff, trying not to let his voice betray his emotions.

'Oh, Raff,' Lily breathed. 'What did he say?'

The letter crinkled in Raff's hand. He couldn't bear to explain it when Lily could read the damn thing herself, so he wordlessly passed it to her. She mouthed the words as she read.

'Oh.'

It appeared to be all she could think of to say. She tried to hand the letter to Ash, but he brushed it aside, so she gave it to their father instead, who read it silently.

It wasn't his father who caught Raff's notice. He stared across the cluttered table at Ash. He kept his face low, refusing to meet Raff's gaze. He looked guilty.

Raff sat up straighter. 'Don't you wish to know why he left?'

'What does it matter?' Ash spoke more to his hands than to his brother. 'He's gone. *That's* what matters.'

'You don't care?'

Ash remained silent, determinedly picking at a loose splinter in the wood. There was something he was refusing to tell them.

'If he displeased you, or you didn't want him here—'

'That's not it.'

'Then why are you being like this?'

Ash suddenly looked up, pushing himself back from the table. 'Because I caught him leaving!'

'*What?*'

'I woke early and heard someone moving around. I found him in the stables, preparing to go.'

'And you *let* him?'

'I was going to stop him—'

'But?'

'But . . .' Ash looked around, looking anywhere but at Raff, 'but he's right to go back, Raff. We all know it.'

Raff stood, furious, the bench screeching across the floor. Beside him, Lily nearly toppled off, but he didn't even notice.

'You should have stopped him!'

Ash rose too. 'And let his father come here and kill us all?'

'We don't know that—'

'*He* did. He told me. He told all of us.' Ash placed his hands on the tabletop, steadying himself. 'We don't know his father. He does. And if he says his father would destroy our family to get to him, then I believe him.'

'But—'

'You can die for him if you wish to, Raff, but I refuse.'

Silence descended, save for the gentle noise of Raff's father turning the pages of his ledger.

The letter sat between them like a curse. Raff reached for it and tucked it into a pocket, standing to go. Before he did, he gestured back to the notes scattered across the table.

'Do you truly think we need all this?' he asked.

Lord Barden shrugged. 'If Penn's risk pays off, then we won't. If he's too late, or his father is unconvinced . . . we shall see.'

The road leading south had become treacherous with ice. Snow was falling thick, and Penn was often forced to dismount while he and the horse slowly made their way through the blizzard. Raff had told him that the steep ridges to the east were merely hills, but in the snow it was easy to believe they were more than that.

The sun, finally risen, struggled against the thick clouds. Penn couldn't help but wonder if Raff had found his letter yet. He'd wondered if he'd found it since the moment he set foot outside the keep. More so, he wondered if Ash had immediately alerted his brother to his disappearance.

After a morning trudging through the snow, no one else had appeared. No one was coming after him. It was a relief – it meant that he wouldn't be waylaid – but it still stung. He was desperate to see Raff one last time, the guilt of leaving so abruptly without having the chance to apologise weighing on him.

It was unforgivable. Penn's actions since that first night had been unforgivable. He'd lied for so long, and brought ruin with him. He'd just wanted an escape, but it had come at too high a cost.

He wrapped his cloak tighter around his shoulders, careful not to let go of his horse's reins as he did. Another betrayal: it was Raff's cloak, and Raff's horse. He was a thief, as well as a liar.

It had taken them weeks to reach Raff's home, but they'd taken a long, winding path. One man, travelling quickly, could probably reach Oxfordshire in ten days. With any luck he'd be spotted sooner than that.

Once he reached the southern counties, he would give his full name whenever he stopped, as well as the direction he was headed. If his father's men passed through any of the same towns or villages in their search for him, they would only need to question a handful of people before learning where he'd been, and where he was going. He hoped it would prevent them travelling any further north.

A second hasty escape meant he had even less money in his purse than before, so he would need to rely on hospitality or makeshift camps rather than inns. At least Raff had taught him how to keep a fire lit and feed himself.

He would be hungry for most of the journey. His feet would blister, his fingertips would purple in the cold. He would deserve it, though, and when he returned to his father's keep, Raff would be safe.

Knowing he was safe would be enough, even though Penn would never see him again. It would *have* to be enough. Perhaps weeks from now – or months, or years – the pain would pass, and he would sleep soundly again. Perhaps Raff's shirt, itching under his own clothes, would be *his*, its history forgotten.

Something had shifted within him. Something had lodged between his ribs and grown there, vines creeping around his bones, into his lungs. He would return to his old life the same, yet incomparably different. Penn had escaped because he had nothing to lose. He was returning, with an echoing cavity in his chest, because he had lost everything.

He had lost it at his own hand. He could not blame his father for his lies. He could not blame his father for the selfish, desperate urge that had stopped him removing himself from Raff's life when he had the chance: when the decision to leave would have left them both whole.

Penn set his face against the wind, and marched onwards.

Chapter Twenty-One

The sky above Dunlyn Castle was tempestuous, and the walls of the keep were pummelled beneath huge, icy raindrops that froze against the stone in glittering icicles.

After speaking to his father, Raff returned to his rooms, the door barred. He still didn't know what to do. He couldn't focus, unable to see through the fog that his thoughts had become.

There was a ringing cavity in his ribs. An ache, nestled around his heart. He lay on his back in the bed, staring up at nothing. They'd only shared the blankets for one night, yet they still smelled of Penn.

Lost in that smell, Raff could only feel grief. Fear or anger he could use: they would fuel him to act. But the grief was directionless, and inescapable.

He'd read the letter so many times that he thought the ink would fade, hoping that he'd been wrong, somehow, and Penn wasn't truly returning to Oxford. He should have burned it or tossed it aside, but he couldn't bring himself to do it. It was covered in Penn's handwriting, smudged with his fingerprints. It was the last thing Penn had touched before spiriting himself from Raff's life for ever. It was the only thing that made it feel real, like he'd even existed.

Hours later, Ash and Lily appeared to inform him the midday

meal had been prepared. His attempts to make them leave were futile, and he found himself being dragged back into the hall.

He forced himself to eat, eyes low, head clouded. He was pickling listlessly at a dripping slice of bacon when his brother spoke.

'Raff.'

Raff looked up. Lily was staring at him too, her face painted with concern.

'What?'

'We have been speaking,' Ash said, nodding towards Lily, 'about this mess. About what Penn said, before he left.'

Raff swallowed heavily. 'And?'

Ash glanced at their sister, then back to Raff.

'Do you think Penn is in danger, returning to his father?' he asked.

Raff clutched at his knife a little harder, feeling himself pale.

'I do.'

Ash's face was set. 'Then you should go after him.'

'But you *said*—'

'I said that I would not die for him. And I stand by that. But we are not talking about what I would do.' Ash rubbed his face. 'He told me he was leaving to keep you safe, but what use is that safety if you simply sit here and waste away? Besides, you will never forgive yourself if he comes to harm.'

'He lied to me,' Raff said, desperately trying to hold onto something he knew was true. 'He *used* me.'

'You lied to him too,' Ash said, eyebrows raised. 'Or have you forgotten begging me not to tell him who you really were?'

Raff looked away. His chest felt hollow.

'Raff, please.' Lily's hand was on his arm. He could have shrugged her off. He didn't. 'Do not pretend that the lie hurts more than losing him, for your sake.'

He stared at her hand. The denial was on his lips, but he couldn't say it.

'And I do not think he used you,' she continued. 'Would he have returned to his father if that were so?'

Raff remembered Penn's pleading in the snowstorm – *why would I come all this way, just to betray you?* Lily was right. If Penn had only been using him to ensure his own freedom, why would he have returned to the place he had fled?

He knew why. Penn had *told* him why, in the letter. He had returned to a cage and a lash to keep Raff safe. No matter the lies, *that* was real. It was a sacrifice that outweighed everything Raff had done for him on the journey north.

Lily sighed, releasing him.

'You do so much for the keep,' she said. 'And for us, too.' She shot a look at Ash. 'You take on our troubles as if they were your own, without considering what it is that *you* want.'

'Lily . . .'

'It's *true*. And you extended that to Penn, too, because you're a good man. But he could have left you weeks ago, just as you could have found him work. Neither of you had good reason to bring him here, except for—'

'The lovely face and a warm body,' Ash cut in, with a snort.

Lily glared at him. 'Ash!'

Ash rolled his eyes, pushed his plate away and leaned back from the table, folding his arms.

'Lily is right,' he said. 'You could have parted long ago. You both chose not to, although I suspect neither of you realised why.' He kept Raff's gaze. 'It is obvious that you are in love with him, and he is with you.'

Raff felt as if the bench had dropped from under him.

'I am not . . .' It was all he could manage before his words dried up.

When he had decided to leave his family after the wedding and seek his own path, he'd been heading towards a future that was uncertain, but his own. He hadn't known what he wanted, then, beyond the chance to free himself from obligation and duty if only for a brief snatch of time.

That vision of his future had changed. It had solidified into something he could hold. The blurred horizon and promise of road and respite had snapped sharply into relief, into gently curling hair and sparkling eyes, into slender fingers and soft lips with Raff's name whispered on them.

He thought of the decision he'd made – even if he'd never managed to voice it out loud – to ask Penn to stay. The understanding of what that decision meant. What it meant *now*, in this new day without Penn in it.

The realisation should have been a shock, like slipping into an icy river. But it wasn't. It was like sinking into a warm bath, so gradual that he hadn't even realised he was drowning till the water was above his head. It was a wonder he hadn't seen it before. Perhaps he had, but had been too afraid to accept it.

Ash raised his eyebrows at him, waiting.

'It's irrelevant,' Raff mumbled. 'My feelings do not matter. Penn does not feel that way.'

His siblings exchanged matching expressions of disbelief over his head.

'He *doesn't*,' Raff repeated. 'If he—' the words felt wrong in his mouth, 'if Penn was in love with me, he would have told me who he was.'

'Or he would have kept the secret,' Lily said, 'afraid that if you found out, you would leave him.'

'I would not have left him.'

'Would you not?' asked Ash, tilting his head. 'If he had told you who he was after this dalliance between you began, would you have stayed by his side?'

'Yes.'

'Would you have still brought him here?'

Raff glanced at Lily. 'I . . .' He dropped his gaze. 'Yes.'

'Why?'

Raff's mind raced. *Because I didn't want him to leave. Because I wanted him to share my bed, and my home. Because he made my family laugh, and he made me laugh. Because of his clever mouth and drifting hands and the noises he made when I took him apart. Because he stood between myself and danger, without being asked. Because there are scars on his back. Because I—*

Raff lowered his head into his hands with a curse. Of course he loved Penn. And Penn—

He didn't know how Penn felt. But Penn's actions spoke for him: he was damning himself, running back to the man at whose hands he'd suffered so much abuse. He would be punished, and every blow he endured would be to protect Raff.

Something had spurred Penn to act. Be it love, or guilt, or simply repaying a debt, Raff didn't know. But he needed to find out.

'What would you do,' he looked at Ash across the table, 'were it Oliver?'

Pain, still raw after all these years, flashed across Ash's face. For once, he did not attempt to hide it. He kept Raff's gaze, though his eyes were shimmering.

'I would have followed already.'

Raff was arranging the final provisions onto his horse's back. The animal stamped at the ground as if afflicted with the same nervous energy that Raff found coursing through himself. It was late in the day, he knew, and soon it would be too dark to ride. But he refused to wait another moment. He had already wasted too much time, trapped by indecision and uncertainty.

He muttered an oath under his breath as he secured the last of the straps. He needed to catch up with Penn on the road before he could throw himself at his father's mercy. Raff knew what would happen if Penn managed to reach de Foucart before he could find him.

Each new scar on his back would be Raff's doing. He had promised that Penn would never be hurt like that again, and he'd been unable to keep that promise for longer than a day; for the handful of days that lay between Penn leaving Dunlyn Castle and arriving at his father's keep.

It had the potential to be a dangerous journey for Raff too. If Lord Barden was correct, the Earl wouldn't be the only one looking for him, and the rumour that Penn had been kidnapped by a disloyal northern lord would be hard to disprove while he remained missing. Raff could be riding directly into a noose.

That wasn't going to stop him. The risk to the Barden family was too great to bring Penn back to Dunlyn Castle, but perhaps he would agree to Raff's plan to find him safety across the border. Raff could even go with him. He would go anywhere, so long as Penn was safe and by his side.

He'd traverse the width and breadth of the country to keep Penn safe, and would do it twice over if that's what Penn wanted. And if he didn't, then Raff had no choice but to accept that. If his siblings were wrong, and Penn had returned to his father out of guilt or fear instead of love, then he would leave.

Lord Barden had been less pleased with Raff's decision. Raff promised he would find some way to appease de Foucart, to find a solution where they could all be safe, but it was clear that his father didn't believe that was possible.

Yet he hadn't stopped him.

Raff's siblings arrived in the stables as he was readying to go. They both looked nervous, wrapped in thick winter cloaks to bid him farewell and good luck.

'You are *sure* you will fare without me?' Raff asked.

Lily gave him a fond, exasperated smile. 'For the last time, Raff. We have done perfectly well in your absence. You do not need to think us incapable.'

'I do not think you are—'

She pulled him into a tight hug, silencing him.

'I know,' she said, clinging to him. 'Stay safe.'

'I will.' Raff was unsure of what else he could say.

He rode out into the storm, his hands stiff in his gloves, his heart pounding as he sped through the blizzard.

By sunset, the snow had stopped.

Penn rode for as long as the horse could manage, every day. When the creature grew too tired, he would walk by its side, alleviating the weight on its back. He considered changing horses so he could push harder, but shame still snapped at him; it was not his horse to trade. He hadn't begun to consider how he would return the animal – and the cloak – but he knew he must, eventually.

The road south was quiet without someone beside him. In his father's keep, he'd been content with solitude, yet over these past weeks he'd become accustomed to constant companionship. He would turn with a comment on his lips only to find himself alone, nothing but cool air and swirling snow beside him. From the corner of his eye, shadows at the far edge of a room or trees at the roadside melded into a familiar set of broad shoulders or a shock of long, dark hair only to twist back into nothing upon a second glance.

He'd come, quietly and gradually, to rely on the reassurance of Raff next to him. To *need* him. It had been a foolish mistake. He had allowed himself to grow attached, despite knowing it would never last. Now he was alone again, and the inevitable silence gnawed at him.

Each day progressed in a repetitive blur. He stopped counting the sunsets, allowing them to pass by unnoticed as the road wended below him. Some roads were familiar, some strange, and on more than one occasion he knew himself to be lost. Still he kept on moving, head low, only stopping when he was forced to.

He curled around himself on the forest floor when he had to, but more often slept on pallets beneath a different stranger's roof every night. As a lone traveller he found it easy to charm people into offering their homes and hearths for the night. He made sure not to arrive too late and always moved on early, leaving only his name behind him. He slept fitfully, burying into the smell of Raff's stolen shirt, heart aching.

Penn didn't realise how far he'd travelled until he spotted the dark, familiar blur on the horizon. Hartswood Forest. It should have felt more welcoming: this was the place he'd fled to, the place he'd met Raff, the place where he'd found his freedom. It was the place where they'd first kissed.

But it held no such intimacy. It looked cold and gloomy, the bare trees the final barrier between himself and his father's court. As the forest grew closer, the darkness bore down on him like a wave. From here, it would take half a day to reach the keep. Behind him, the sun had already begun to set.

He would stop and sleep, and tomorrow would make the final

part of the journey through the forest. There was an inn nearby, but the risks far outweighed the comfort he would find there. He would be recognised immediately. This close, he was determined to return of his own volition, and not at the hand of someone wishing to trade him for a profit.

He made a pitiful camp in a clearing near the edge of the forest, not bothering to light a fire. He still had a few scraps of food in his pack, more than enough to last him till the morning. He tugged Raff's cloak around himself and shuddered, staring ahead at the trees.

Penn could run no longer. There was nowhere left to go but forwards, back to the place he'd vowed never to return to. He would cross the threshold with bloodied feet and an aching back, and it would be as if the past weeks had never even happened, no more than a dream to keep him warm at night.

Dread sank in Penn's stomach, stony and solid, as he listened to the trees move around him. He knew what awaited him in his father's keep. He could already feel the lash on his back, hear de Foucart's words, dripping with venom. Penn had ruined his plans, and he would pay.

The dread hardened. He would pay, and he would take whatever his father deemed a suitable punishment with his shoulders straight and his head high. He would take it, gladly, knowing that he had kept Raff safe.

Penn had all but vanished.

There were traces of him scattered through towns and villages – the whisper of a name Raff knew he didn't use – but nothing more.

There was more than one road south. It could have been just poor luck that their roads had not diverged. That didn't soothe the fear that forced Raff onwards, or calm the frantic way his heart beat every time someone nodded when he asked if they'd seen William de Foucart pass this way.

He took hospitality where he could, desperately hoping he would open the door to an inn and see Penn inside, warming himself by the fire or playing dice with a stranger. But he never did. Often Raff slept beneath the stars, curled around the emptiness beside him.

He moved fast, waking and sleeping early. The roads were quieter in the mornings, and he rose before dawn every day, a lone traveller on frozen paths.

It was on one of these crisp, frost-coated mornings that he finally saw Hartswood Forest ahead of him, the dark treetops mingling with the heavy clouds above, the sky still nearly black.

He was so close. He couldn't believe Penn had managed to evade him. There was a real, terrifying chance that he was already back in his father's keep, taking whatever punishment de Foucart deemed suitable.

More scars to add to the rest.

Even if Penn *had* reached home, Raff would press on. He would march to the gates of the de Foucart keep, a single man with no allies, no useful weaponry and no real plan. He would not give up.

He was riding by an inn on the edge of the forest just after sunrise when he overheard the conversation. A single word caught his ear.

'*William—*'

He came to a halt. Two women were talking, leaning against the low wall around the inn's yard.

'. . .By here, I saw him myself.'

'Surely not.'

'It was him. I would recognise that hair anywhere.'

'But so close! When?'

'This morning,' the first woman said, conspiratorially. 'Dawn. Bless him, Mary, he looked—'

Raff didn't stop to listen any further. *Dawn.* That was no time at all, not with the busy roads and the winding path through the forest. He could catch up, if he rode fast.

He kicked his heels into the horse's flank and was off, throwing up mud behind him.

Chapter Twenty-Two

The trees were a green blur, broken only by snatches of white where the snow had not yet melted. Raff's horse huffed beneath him, sweating. He was pushing too hard, riding too recklessly on the busy road, but he didn't care.

He twisted the horse past a fallen bough and pushed a low-hanging branch out of his way, sending snow flurrying down upon him. He shook his head, and his hood fell loose, revealing his face as he burst from beneath the trees.

The de Foucart keep loomed ahead, as grey and unwelcoming as it had been when he'd arrived for Lily's wedding. There were dozens of people outside the castle, and camps in the fields beside it. De Foucart really *was* intending to mobilise. A stroke of luck: the sheer volume of men meant that he hadn't yet had the chance to do so.

And – there. A lone figure in the centre of it all, standing beside a horse that Raff had purchased himself. He had been led to Penn at the very moment Penn was giving himself up.

He wasn't the only person who had seen him. The gates were already open, and people were streaming out. Guards, by the look of them, or soldiers. Penn was stuck, unmoving, as they gathered around him. One of them took the reins of his horse from his unresisting hand, and something hot flared in Raff's chest.

'Penn!'

His horse complained as he pushed harder, but he didn't stop. He could not stop. He shouted Penn's name again, desperate to be heard.

Penn turned, finally. His eyes widened, but before he could respond he was seized. A guard grabbed him by the arm, hauling him towards the gatehouse. Penn was attempting to pull away, but the man who held him was broader and more practised. He jerked Penn's arm around, pinned it behind his back and shoved him forwards.

This should have been the moment that Raff had prepared him for, the time where he needed to wriggle out of an attacker's grasp and fight back. But Penn was helpless as the guard pushed against him. He didn't even appear to be *attempting* to free himself.

Suddenly, Raff was surrounded. He'd finally been recognised, and the onlookers – all of whom were there to begin the pursuit for the lost heir – began to block his way. He could see the glint of steel as many of them reached for their swords, ready to stop the man who had kidnapped William de Foucart. He ignored them all, shouting over their heads.

'Penn!'

But he was cut off, the men gathered outside the keep too close to either move his horse forwards or dismount. He pulled the reins around, trying to make space. Another guard joined the first, grabbing Penn's forearm, and together they manipulated him into the shadowy space of the gatehouse. Raff pushed forwards, shouting for him, forcing men aside.

But he was too slow.

With an ear-splitting screech, the portcullis dropped. Raff's horse took several panicked steps backwards, sending people scattering as they leaped out of the way of the creature's kicking hooves.

'Penn!'

The heavy wooden gates slammed shut.

He was gone.

The last thing Penn saw before the gates slammed was Raff's startled expression, his violently blue eyes.

Penn was dragged backwards into the yard, heels dragging in the mud. He struggled, but ten days of sleeping poorly and barely eating had taken their toll, and the tentative strength he'd felt under his skin when they'd explored Dunlyn's armoury had left him as suddenly as it had arrived.

He could hear Raff's shouts ringing in his ears, his voice painful in its familiarity. When he'd turned to see Raff speeding down the road towards him, he'd looked like an illusion, like a fragment broken from Penn's imagination. Penn's heart had transformed into fluttering wings.

Now it was a stony, terrified thing. Raff couldn't be here. It wasn't safe.

He pulled against the guard's grasp, cursing him.

'Let me *go*—'

'That will do.'

Penn fell silent. The guard's hand tightened as he turned him to face his father.

De Foucart's expression was entirely blank as he walked past Penn and the guard as if they weren't even there. He called to the soldier who had closed the gates.

'What is happening here?'

'Barden's son, my Lord—'

'I can see that. Why have none of you *done* anything?'

'My Lord?'

'He abducts my son and you and your men simply stand and watch him as he attempts to do so again?'

'No, my Lord, we—'

'Out of my way.'

From the other side of the gates, Penn could still hear shouting. Raff was out there, closer than he'd been in days, yet impossibly far. He watched as his father strode up the stairs towards the wall-walk, pushing onlookers aside. There was a pair of men stationed behind the battlements, both holding crossbows.

Penn's scalp prickled as his father approached the men. One ducked quickly away, lowering his head. The other was not so lucky. De Foucart stood beside him, hands pressed to the stone. Penn couldn't see, but he knew he was looking at Raff below. Weighing him up.

Penn wasn't breathing. He stilled, waiting.

There was complete silence before his father leaned back. His lips moved, but he was too far away for Penn to hear.

The guard readied the bow. He lifted it. He hesitated. De Foucart spun on him. They were arguing, Penn's father shouting and the guard cowering.

Penn had moments – precious seconds, rapidly falling away – to get Raff to leave. He pulled, and the guards held him harder. Above, the dispute was still ongoing. His father was reaching for the crossbow. The guard's face was pale and his hands were shaking but he wasn't letting go.

'Raff!' Penn shouted, desperate to be heard, hoping his voice would somehow carry over the wall. 'Raff!'

He thought of long nights in the woods, his dagger in his hand and Raff at his back. He took a breath, flexed his fingers, then twisted around in a sharp movement, hooking his foot behind the ankle of the man holding him. He wasn't strong enough to bring the guard down, but his grip loosened, and Penn was able to wrench his arm free. He ran towards the gates.

'Raff!' He skidded across the mud, slamming against the wood, hoping his voice was loud enough to reach him. 'For God's sake, go!'

Someone on the wall-walk yelled. And then – a click. A faint whistle, cutting through the air.

The panicked scream of a horse. A thud, heavy and final.

It should have been louder.

No. *No.* He felt a guard slam into him from behind, dragging him back, pulling him away. He was powerless as another guard joined the first, one to each of his arms.

He looked up as they dragged him back into the yard. From the wall-walk, his father was staring down at him. De Foucart's expression was steely. He brushed himself off, shot a final glare at the guard, then made his way back down the staircase.

Silence fell as those who had gathered – soldiers and guards, allies and neighbouring lords – waited to see what would happen next.

His father approached. Perhaps he would be willing to listen. If Penn could get beyond the gates and reach Raff, to see to him, to ensure the wound was not too severe—

He would return, willingly. He would walk into his chambers and lock the door himself if he knew that Raff was all right.

'Please—' he said, breathless and struggling. 'Father, you must let me—'

De Foucart blinked, as if surprised, but his face did not register any emotion.

'I *must*?'

He turned to address the small crowd of onlookers who had gathered around them, raising his voice so they could all hear.

'How wonderful that my son has been returned to me. I regret that it had to end like this, but I am thankful that the person responsible for his disappearance has found retribution so swiftly—' he turned back, catching Penn's eye, 'and so finally.'

No.

Penn went limp. Had the guards not been holding him so surely, he would have fallen. His legs were useless. Bile swirled in his stomach, clogging his throat. Whatever he'd been going to say dissolved into air in his lungs.

There was nothing but silence from beyond the gate.

De Foucart turned to one of his men, hovering nearby.

'Deal with Barden,' he said, glancing towards the gatehouse. 'Quickly.'

The man nodded and hurried away. Penn needed to follow, to *see*—

'Take my son to his chambers.' The grip around his arms tightened once more. 'I want men stationed outside his door. We cannot trust that Barden was alone. His death does not necessarily ensure my son's safety.'

To hear him say it so carelessly was torture. The mud beneath Penn's feet fell away, the guards to either side no more solid than mist. There was an untethered pain, floating inside him, deep and ringing and untouchable. His tongue had turned to stone, turned to lead. He couldn't speak. He couldn't move. He couldn't *breathe*.

He was being pushed again. He went willingly, turning only once to see his father watching him, his chin high.

He thought of the spark that had urged him to run. The flame it became that had made him return.

Now it was nothing more than smoke.

✡

Penn's chambers were much the same as he had left them, but it felt like a stranger's home. After being pushed inside, he rushed to the window, gripping the stone till his fingers bled.

They had opened the gates. First came Raff's horse. Seeing the familiar animal being led across the yard made a hot pressure build behind Penn's eyes. The horse was followed by four men carrying something between them – a bundle, too far away to see. He tried to swallow around the lump in his throat. He didn't need to see. He *knew*.

He vomited noisily into the basin. His nose stung, the pain displaced, as if it were happening to someone else. He hovered beside the bed, unable to return to the window, his legs too stiff to sit.

It had been for nothing. All of it had been worthless; his flight home, the days on the road, carefully seeding his way to stop his father heading north.

It was all his fault. All of it. The broken marriage, the kiss in the woods, the war that his father had threatened to bring to Raff and Raff's decision to bring himself to the frontlines; to ride into danger for—

For what? Penn's legs gave way, and he collapsed onto the bed. Dust exploded around him, clinging to his skin, stinging in his eyes.

Raff had done it for him, that much he could be sure of. Perhaps to curse him or berate him or to make good on his promise to find him somewhere else to go. It couldn't have been the same, blinding urge that had made Penn return to his father; the feeling that had stalked him like a shadow every step of his journey home.

It couldn't have been *love*. It was impossible, and even the thought of it threatened to choke him.

He stared out at the sky beyond his window till the heavy clouds burst, and snow fell.

Chapter Twenty-Three

Johanna came to visit him sometime later, bringing with her food and drink. Penn hadn't moved from his spot on the bed.

'Penn.'

She knelt in front of him, taking his head in her hands. He looked through her, unable to focus. Her words – a babble of reassurances – washed over him, barely even touching him. He let her speak.

Eventually, she perched beside him, hands gripping her skirts.

'You are *sure* you are well?'

Penn thought of bruises on his arms where his father's guards had held him back. The stinging in his nose and throat where he'd vomited – again – on an entirely empty stomach.

He thought about the hole in his chest, dry and raw.

'Yes,' he said, voice hollow, 'I am well.'

'Penn—'

He looked up. The movement sent a flash of pain through his shoulders; he hadn't realised how tightly he'd been holding himself, or for how long. His joints had seized and stiffened. Outside, the sky was dark.

'It is late,' he said. 'I should sleep.'

She left without an argument. She had carried a one-sided

conversation since she had arrived; she must have realised it would be futile to continue. She left the food on the table beside the window.

The chill in the room grew. Finally, he lay on the bed, not bothering to get beneath the covers. They would need airing, he thought vaguely. No one had been anticipating his return enough to prepare the chamber.

There was a guard stationed outside his door. Penn was sure that his father's apparent fears that Raff hadn't been acting alone were nothing more than lies to ensure compliance from his men. Penn had escaped, and de Foucart would not allow him to do so again.

He wondered if they'd discovered the staircase behind the tapestry. Penn had managed to fly once: he could do it again. He could pull the heavy weaving aside and heave open the door and run down the steep stone stairs and—

Even the thought of it exhausted him. He could survive alone beyond his father's walls: he'd proved that on the arduous journey from Dunlyn Castle to Oxford. But he *would* be alone, more palpably and painfully than he ever had been before. The freedom he'd craved had become something rancid.

He *could* go again. He truly *had* lost everything – the worst had happened, the very thing he'd returned to prevent. But his limbs were heavy, his head fogged. He'd turned numb, a carved statue of himself, hewn from wood and left to rot.

Outside, the yard fell silent as the castle descended into sleep. Penn's head echoed with the thrum of crossbow bolts.

A bird darted outside the window. Penn watched as the creature shot to and fro across the neat square of sky, framed by dark stone. The dawn light had not yet reached the foot of his bed, but even then it was near-blinding.

He had not slept. His chest felt like it had been carved out, his head pounding.

When Jo arrived an immeasurable amount of time later, he caught the snatches of a brief conversation between her and the guard outside his door.

'I am still under watch, then,' he said, standing as she entered the room.

'Father is only trying to keep you safe.'

He didn't want to think about their father. 'If you have come here to speak on his behalf, you may leave.'

She abruptly turned on him, her placid expression furious. 'I thought you were *dead*.'

Her sudden ire shocked him into silence, and he took a startled step backwards.

'Father told everyone—' Jo took a breath, her voice catching in her throat. 'You are my brother and we have seen so much together and I thought you had *died*, out there in the forest. We all did.'

'I—'

She spoke over him. 'How did you think I felt, knowing that you were gone? After Henry, and Leo, and Mother, even *Ros*—' Her expression cracked, and there were angry tears rolling down her cheeks. 'Do you think I don't feel their loss too? Every day?'

His stomach lurched. Jo was always so strong. She'd cried with him when they'd received word of Henry's death, and watched with him in mute horror as Leo had been forced from the keep, their father's men close behind. She'd held him in her arms when their mother had died not even three months later.

He'd never seen it till now. He stepped forwards, and before she could push him away he wrapped her in a tight embrace. She sniffed into his chest.

'Forgive me, Jo. I didn't mean—' He stopped. He *had* meant to leave. He'd meant to leave this all behind; including her, the one person he'd been able to rely on. He had never realised that she relied on him too. 'I did not think. I just ran.'

'You were *gone,* Penn. Ros and I thought you'd bolted and would be back within the day. But when you never returned . . .' Her voice wavered. 'I could only think the worst.' She shivered, and her voice cracked. 'Why did you go?'

He pulled away, and looked at her. He wasn't sure she would understand.

'I was looking for freedom.'

She wiped her eyes with her sleeve, shaking her head. 'And instead you were captured by a northern lord.'

He stepped back. 'It was not like that.'

'But Father—'

Anger; hot and tight. He could cling to this, *direct* it.

'Father is *wrong.* Raff saved me. He is—' he choked around the word, 'he *was* a good man. He was my—' He couldn't. 'My—'

She peered at him. The anger dissolved as quickly as it came, leaving behind it that familiar emptiness, the echoing loss. He fell back onto the bed, eyes down.

Jo dropped her voice to a whisper.

'What was he?' she said, slowly. 'What was he to you?'

'He was my *friend,*' Penn finished, uselessly.

It wasn't enough. It didn't properly encompass what Raff had meant to him – what he'd *become,* as the days had passed.

'He found me,' he said, simply. 'He *helped* me. He took me—' he breathed around the words, trying to control himself, 'he took me *home.* He kept me safe. And I ruined that safety by being our father's son. Lord Barden told us that he was bringing an army north, so I returned before he could. I know the sort of man our father is. I knew what he was capable—' Penn stuttered, remembering the sound of the crossbow, the world-ending *thud* that followed. 'What he *is* capable of. But . . .'

'But he followed you. You had no idea?' Penn shook his head morosely, and she continued, 'Father has put out that you were escaping him.'

He frowned. 'What has he been saying?'

'He has been telling his allies that you escaped, and Lord Barden's son—' she fixed herself, 'that *Raff* was in pursuit to recapture you. That there was a scuffle at the gates, so one of the crossbowmen shot him. Father says that the man had only intended to wound him, but he fired poorly, and—' She looked down, and grabbed Penn's hand. 'I am sorry, Penn.'

Penn's breath caught. 'He says the crossbowman shot him?'

'Yes. Why?'

Penn could picture the argument on the battlements with perfect clarity. He'd thought of little else but those frantic moments since he had been locked in his chambers. The tussle between Earl and guard, his father's hands reaching for the weapon—

'Penn?' Jo's worried voice broke him from the memory.

He swallowed, throat stiff and sore. 'It is too much to take in, I think.'

'Of course.' She stood up, straightening her skirts. 'You should rest. Will you join us for this evening's meal? Ellis and Ingrid have been asking after you.'

Penn gave her a weak smile. He had no intentions to attend the lavish meal his father was insisting on; a blatant attempt to maintain favour with his allies.

'Perhaps.'

✡

Penn had never felt so familiar with the walls of his chambers. He slept a lot, and ate little. His sister or a guard would bring him food, and he would only pick at it when he truly had to. He didn't feel hunger, just *pain*, subdued with a mouthful of whatever they had brought him that day.

Jo's visits were regular, but short. The cheer she'd shown when he'd returned had been worn down by his own low mood. He couldn't bring himself to respond to her questions, to laugh at her jokes. She told him that she had sent word to their sister, and gave him Ros's love and apologies that she couldn't be there to see him herself. It was only after Jo had left that he'd even remembered to ask after Ros's health.

Once, Jo asked again about Raff. Penn hadn't been able to answer in any way that was adequate, and she hadn't asked again.

Alone or with her, it all felt the same. Eventually she would stop calling on him, tired of the unpleasant companion he had become.

He refused to attend evening meals. His father appeared, flanked by guards, to berate his absence. Penn had let his admonitions drift past him, nodding when his silence would be tolerated, agreeing when it would not. He could see his father's hand clenched into a fist at his side. He wondered when his temper would snap, and he would receive his real punishment. He suspected it would not be until his father's allies had left, and he was not being watched.

Penn was exhausted by the third day, despite never leaving the room. He watched from the window at the courtyard still full of strangers. Only a few had left, although the number of those preparing to go was rising every day.

The sky had turned a deep red when his sister burst into his chambers, cheeks pink. Penn glanced up from his position beside the window as she pushed the door shut behind her and tugged him away from the sill.

'What—'

'He is alive.'

The next thing Penn knew, he was sitting on the edge of his bed, hands shaking in his lap. His legs had gone numb.

'Are you sure?'

'I heard the guards talking. He is in the cells.'

'And – and is he well?'

Her face fell. 'I cannot say. I only heard them mention that he was there. If I had stayed any longer they would have realised I was listening.'

'You are *sure* he's alive?' he repeated, head reeling.

'Yes, Penn,' Jo laughed, squeezing his hand, 'I am sure.'

Penn looked down at the knotted wooden floor. He thought of Raff's face, the last time they had seen each other – his startled, desperate expression as the gates had slammed.

He thought of the last time he'd truly *looked* at Raff; that crisp, deadly morning when he'd fled Dunlyn Castle. Even asleep, Raff had looked troubled. More than ever, Penn wished that he'd given in and kissed him one last time.

'I must see him.'

Jo's laughing expression dropped away. 'You cannot,' she said, voice low. 'There is a *guard* at your door.'

He let go of her hand and stood, despite the shake in his legs. 'How do you think I left last time?'

'Penn—'

'Yes?'

Her expression was sombre. 'You will be caught. Father will be furious.'

'He will be, yes.'

'But—'

'Has he arranged a meal for this evening?'

'Of course he has.' She frowned. 'Rather – *I* have. He simply sits back and accepts the praise for *my* work.'

Oh. There was a bitter little thrum to her voice that Penn had rarely heard before. An ember of anger, uncovered and unprotected, waiting to be coaxed into a flame.

'Have you been seeing to all the meals?'

'I have been seeing to the running of the keep since he called his allies to arms,' she sniffed. 'Not just the meals. The staff, the food, ensuring we are stocked enough for a dozen lords and *hundreds* of soldiers and servants—' She caught herself. 'It is fine. It is good practice for when I am running a keep of my own.'

'Jo . . .'

She waved him away. 'It is *fine.*' She huffed a breath through her nostrils. 'Why do you ask? Do you finally intend to join us?'

'No,' Penn said, peering from the window to the busy yard below. 'I wish to know when Father will be most distracted.'

The moon hovered above the war-wall of the keep, half-hidden by clouds. The yard was still.

Penn could hear the guards changing beyond the locked door. He took his chance.

The stairway behind the tapestry and the corridor below were empty. Keeping close to the wall, he headed towards the heart of the keep, sticking to the shadows and listening for voices. He slunk through a side door into the yard and edged along the stone until he could see the archway that led to the cells below.

It was a freezing evening, and Penn's breath fogged the air in front of him as he made his way across the courtyard. The trappings of neighbouring lords hung about the yard – banners and discarded weapons. He wished, suddenly, that he was better armed than just the dagger strapped to his hip. He wished he was better trained in using it. More urgently, he wished Raff had never come back for him. He knew, with iron certainty, that he didn't deserve him.

Holding onto that thought, he slid through the archway and stepped into the darkness, his hand pressed against the damp stone wall.

The cells beneath the keep were barely lower than the basements, yet somehow they were danker and gloomier.

There was a faint orange glow from below that grew brighter as he descended the twisting staircase. The guard was allowed a single torch, the light barely enough for one person, let alone the entire room.

Penn jumped the last couple of steps into the low-ceilinged space. The guard who had been sitting on the wooden stool with his legs propped on the table leaped up.

'Master William!' he said, scrambling to attention, 'I, ah, my Lord, but you should not be—'

It was the man from the wall. The guard with the crossbow. Penn pushed him out of the way and grabbed the torch. As he did, he noticed that the guard's sword was hanging beside it, blissfully out of reach.

'Where is he?' Penn spat.

'But you—'

'*Where is he?*'

The startled guard merely pointed towards the final cell in the block; the one furthest away from the light.

Before Penn could walk away from him, he spoke again.

'William, please—' Penn turned. The guard was watching him wide-eyed and trembling. 'I didn't. I swear I didn't.'

Penn swallowed, holding the torch tighter. He'd seen what had happened. He'd heard the story his father had spread.

'I know,' he said, simply.

He spun around and strode down the narrow walkway. His feet echoed wetly on the hard ground. His hand shook around the handle of the torch.

The final cell was worse than the rest. Light hadn't touched this far wall in an age, the stone coated in dust and ancient webs. The bars were slick and rusty. He inched forwards, and the shuddering light spilled into the cramped, rank cell, picking out the pockmarks in the stone, throwing them into irregular patterns.

Hunched against the far wall, his temple pressed to the stone and his back to the door, was Raff.

Penn threw himself forwards against the bars, dropping the torch. It clunked to the floor, the light illuminating the captive from below.

'Raff,' he called, reaching through, 'Raff, it's me.'

Raff was too far away to touch. He didn't even move; didn't register that Penn had spoken at all. Penn strained against the metal, trying to reach him, feeling the bars cut at his shoulder.

'Raff, *please*.'

No response. Penn leaned back, trying to blink back the tears threatening to spill from his eyes. The guard had followed him. He picked up the discarded torch, nervously standing above him.

'William, your father—'

Penn was on his feet in an instant. The man jumped back instinctively. Penn was taller than him, and his sword was still hanging from the far wall. He reached down, hovering his fingers over the hilt of the dagger.

The guard started again. 'William—'

Penn pulled out just enough of the blade to so it would catch the low light. He was glad he'd sharpened it on the road.

'Please,' the guard said, voice quavering, 'they said – your father said he took . . . I was just doing what they said, my Lord, *please*—'

'Give me the keys.'

'But . . .'

'Give me the keys and I'll spare you. And when my father asks why you released his prisoner, you will tell him why.'

The guard blinked, swallowing heavily. He hesitated for a moment, then nodded. With his eyes fixed to Penn's dagger, he slowly reached inside his tunic, took out a key, and handed it over with shaking fingers. Penn smiled. A bead of sweat dripped down the guard's forehead, over an eyebrow, into his eye. Penn pushed the dagger back into the sheath.

'Thank you,' he said, sounding a lot calmer than he felt. The guard turned as if to leave. '*Wait.*' The guard froze. 'You will stay, and hold the torch.'

Penn let his eyes drop to the blade at his hip. He didn't need to say anything else. The guard nodded.

Penn watched him for a moment, then turned his back to him to unlock the cell. The key scraped in the lock and the heavy door creaked open. Raff flinched at the noise.

'Raff,' Penn said again, stepping into the cell, 'it's me. It's Penn.'

Raff shuffled against the stone but didn't turn, didn't speak. Penn reached out and pressed a hand to his arm. Someone had stripped him to his undershirt. It was soaked, clinging to his skin. The once-white fabric was pink with blood. Penn swore under his breath.

'What has he done to you?'

He knelt next to him, uncaring for the uneven floor bruising his knees, and brushed aside Raff's hair so he could better look at his face.

When Penn's fingers made contact with his skin, he gasped. He was on fire, despite the freezing air in the cell.

'Raff . . .'

He used both hands to manoeuvre Raff so he could see him properly. He was covered in a fine sheen of sweat, his eyes unfocused. His breathing was laboured, and as his body slumped back against the brick Penn was struck with the smell of rot. He swallowed, then as gently as he could manage, tugged back the right shoulder of Raff's shirt where the blood bloomed brightest.

Penn hissed through his teeth. Raff didn't even react.

The bolt had struck him in the shoulder. It had been removed, but the wound had turned. The skin was bright red and raw, oozing a foul-smelling pus. It was a disgusting sight, and the urge to vomit was near-overwhelming, but stronger than that – stronger than the urge to recoil – was anger.

Penn thought of Henry, and the messages the family had received only days apart; the first telling them his brother was wounded, the second that the wound had turned, and the third to tell them he was dead.

Raff's glazed eyes peered up at him. He muttered something.

'Raff?'

'Penn . . .'

'I'm here, Raff, I'm here—'

He took a huge, shuddering breath, then leaned his head back against the wall, eyes rolling shut. Beneath Penn's hands, his chest rose and fell in heavy breaths. Penn screwed his eyes shut, just for a moment, before turning to the guard.

'Help me.'

He hooked an arm beneath Raff's wounded shoulder. Raff winced and cried out, and Penn felt a sharp stab of guilt.

'I am sorry,' he whispered into his ear, unsure if Raff could even hear him.

The guard stared.

'Well? What are you waiting for?'

Realising he had no other choice, the guard placed down the torch and entered the cell, hoisting Raff up on the other side.

'We need to get him into a real bed,' Penn said. 'We can take him to my chambers.'

'But, my Lord, your father . . .'

'Damn my father!'

The man stuttered silent. Together, they manoeuvred Raff up the narrow winding staircase and up into the courtyard. Penn sighed, glad to be free of the oppressive air in the cells. Beside him, Raff breathed deeply, his eyes still half-lidded.

It was dark, and quiet. From across the yard, he could see orange light spilling from the great hall and his father's evening feast. Penn swallowed, clutching tighter to Raff's side.

He hadn't thought. All he had known was that he needed to get Raff out. Getting him into Penn's chambers would be impossible: Raff would never make it up the narrow staircase. He was trying to decide the best course of action when there was a shout from across the way.

They'd been spotted. Three guards began to stride over – a fourth rushing away, likely to sound the alarm. Penn swore again, and still balancing Raff on one shoulder reached down and pulled the shining dagger from his belt.

'Don't stand in my way,' he warned. 'Don't you dare.'

The soldier leading the group – an older man Penn recognised as one of his father's more trusted men – stopped with his hand on the hilt of his sword, frowning.

'My Lord William,' he said, confused, 'aren't you – that is, you were—'

'Locked in my chambers? Yes, I was,' said Penn, acridly. 'Clearly I am not anymore.'

The soldier looked between the other men. 'My Lord—'

'You'll need to inform my father. Please do. But if any of you attempt to stop me getting this man—' he shrugged Raff's weight, feeling his shoulder going numb, 'into a real bed, or stop me getting him help, I will kill you where you stand.'

Penn knew that attempting to take on three men was futile. The soldiers knew it too, of course, but he still had the advantage of being the son of the Earl, for however long his father tolerated him. They wouldn't dare kill him.

'But he—'

'Whatever you heard is wrong. This man saved my life. I am repaying his debt. My father cannot begrudge you for following orders. I'm still his son. You do as I say, and I'll tell him the truth: I threatened you, and you felt you had no choice.'

'But—'

'But *nothing*.' He glared, quietly furious, trying to hold back the anger. 'You,' he said, nodding towards the soldier who had yet to speak; younger than himself, eyes wide and horrified. 'Do you know where the nearest physician is? What town?'

The soldier turned to the older one, who nodded. 'A-aye. I mean: yes, my Lord.'

'Is he close?'

He turned to the other man again, clearly his officer.

'I'm speaking to *you*, not him!' Penn barked.

'I . . . he is, I . . .' The boy's voice shook. 'It was . . . y'see, our Marc, he was in the stables, and the horse . . .'

'Speak plainly.'

'Well, my Lord, he's here already, my Lord. The physician.'

Penn let out a long breath. Finally, some luck.

'Go and get him,' he said. 'Bring him to me.' The soldier took one final look at his superior before dashing off. 'You,' Penn nodded back towards the older man, 'help me get him into the castle.'

'Where are you taking him?'

Penn looked down at Raff's grey face. He needed somewhere close, somewhere they could get him without further inflaming the wound.

'The guest chambers,' he decided, 'they're closer.'

The soldier, realising he had no choice, stepped forwards. Together, the three of them picked Raff bodily from the floor. His head lolling, they moved him across the courtyard, heading towards the somewhat smaller wing of the keep where guests stayed, where Raff's father must have slept all those weeks ago.

Penn kept his eyes down, listening to Raff's laboured breathing. As they approached the double doors that lead to the entryway and the guest chambers beyond, there was a shout from behind.

'My Lord!'

Penn turned. The younger soldier was dashing towards them, an older man with olive skin dressed in a dark robe just behind.

'I found him,' he panted, 'but, my Lord—'

'*William!*'

Penn winced. It was a shock that he'd even got this far. He hoisted Raff's shoulders into the arms of the younger soldier and turned to face his approaching father. He raised his chin.

'Father.'

Behind his father, guests had begun to trickle from the great hall, a horrified Jo at their lead. Allies and neighbouring lords, as well as green squires and soldiers. All eyes were on them, watching. Many of them wore matching expressions of shock, several muttering amongst themselves. Clearly word of Raff's survival had not been widely circulated.

'What are you *doing?*' his father spat.

'Can you not tell?'

'That man—'

'That man saved my life. He found me, and he saved me, and you repaid him by shooting him and leaving him to rot in a cell.'

'I commanded he be stopped, for *your* protection.'

Penn shook his head. 'You shot him. You shot him *yourself.*'

'You are hysterical. The guard—'

'I saw you!'

Penn's words hung between them. His father stilled. 'A baseless accusation,' he said, haughtily. 'You are unwell. You do not know what you are talking about.'

Penn took a deep breath. 'I know what I saw. Who else here saw?' He raised his voice, letting it carry in the cool night air. 'Who else saw my father shoot Lord Barden's son? The guard who stood beside you can confirm it, he told me so himself.'

It was not a lie. The guard had given him nothing more than a hasty denial, but it would have to be enough. De Foucart scowled, but no one else spoke. Penn tried again.

'Are you all so cowardly?' he called. 'Dozens of you were there. *All* of you had men stationed beyond the gates. Are you all blind, or have you decided that power and wealth are more important than the truth?'

The crowd began to murmur, but no one moved, their faces unreadable in the low light.

'I see.'

He was about to turn away and get Raff inside, when his father stopped him, grabbing his wrist.

'William, I *demand*—'

Penn wrested his arm away. 'You have *no right!*'

He was shouting, now. He turned his back on his father to face the guards. They were staring at him, but hadn't moved.

'Get Raff into the guest chambers.' His voice shook with a rage that they couldn't miss. '*Now!*'

For a moment, he thought they might disobey him and look to his father instead. But – against all hope – they didn't. Led by the physician, who was peering at Raff with professional horror, they moved inside, the wooden doors slamming behind them.

'William, this is—'

'No!' Penn spun back around, and the fury bubbled over, spilling from him like a flood. 'You cannot tell me what to do!'

His father didn't even flinch.

'This is *enough*,' he said, with the same warning tone that had dogged Penn's childhood.

'You don't get to tell me what's *enough* anymore, Father,' Penn spat.

'I *forbid* you—'

'You forbid me? You cannot stop me!'

'He tried to take you from me—'

'He tried to *save me from you!*'

'You are disobeying—'

'I am!'

And then the dagger was back in his hand, the steel glinting in the light, raised in an arm no longer trembling and pointing directly at his father's throat.

'You do not get to tell me what to do anymore.' Penn marvelled at how steady his own voice was, how clear. 'I am getting him help. And when his wound has healed—' His voice caught. *If his wound heals*. '*When* he heals,' he repeated, 'you are letting him go.'

'William, for God's sake—'

'My name is Penn, Father.' He lowered the dagger. 'My name is *Penn*.'

The dagger hung limply at Penn's side, his palm slick with sweat. The ridges of the hilt had dug neat grooves into his hand, and his fingers were locked into place.

His father was far behind him, like a dream. It was like a dream that he moved through the hall and towards the door that led to the guest chambers, up the stairs, wider and less winding than those that led to his own, and onto the landing above.

He pushed through the door, the dagger dropping from his hand. The men gathered around the bed started as he entered, turning to see the intruder. The guard from the cell – the one whose word he would need to rely on, if he was to prove his father's guilt – and the rest of the soldiers stood nervously to one side, watching him with cautious eyes.

'Leave,' he said.

They didn't need telling twice. They filed out, edging past him without meeting his gaze. When they'd left, shutting the door quietly behind them, Penn moved towards the bed. The physician – a man he recognised but couldn't name – stood aside as he peered down at Raff's still form. He looked smaller, somehow. The physician had removed the wet undershirt, exposing his flushed skin. The wound in his shoulder wept angrily, the edges dark.

'Can you help him?' It was all Penn could manage to say.

'I . . .' There was hesitation in the physician's voice. 'I *think* . . .'

'Yes or no?'

'. . . the bolt was removed, but the wound has been left to fester. We need to cut away the infected skin, wash out the wound, and even then . . .' he sighed, 'we may be too late.'

'But there's still a chance?'

The physician straightened his back. 'There is *always* a chance.'

'Then do what you can. Whatever you need, you'll have it, until my father decides to set his guards on me.'

The physician raised his eyebrows. 'Until then it is,' he said. 'I need my tools: salves, bandages . . . I've something to relieve the pain with me, but the rest I will need to fetch.'

'Is there anything you can do now? Right now?'

'We can clean the wound,' he said, bending to look closer, 'and ease the pain. And then, when I return . . . we shall see.'

That wasn't enough. That wasn't *nearly* enough. But it was all he had. Penn knelt at the bedside, placing one of his shaking hands on Raff's arm. It was far too warm.

Chapter Twenty-Four

The physician, who gave his name as Alsen, moved swiftly whilst Penn mutely assisted. As they heaved Raff up to force the painkiller down his throat, Penn noticed blood crusting in the hair at his nape. He must have hit his head when the horse threw him, stunning him. That would explain why Penn's father had declared him dead so quickly. He must have tossed Raff in the cells as soon as he realised his mistake, hoping his allies wouldn't realise; or that time would finish the job for him.

By the time Alsen cleaned the wound on his shoulder, Raff didn't react at all, the only proof that he still lived the heavy rising and falling of his chest. His skin had taken on a pale, greyish tone that looked even more stark beneath Alsen's darker hands.

They arranged him as best they could on the bed, leaving the lesion bare while Alsen hurried away to fetch the tools he needed to properly tend it. Jo arrived soon after, looking exhausted.

'Father is furious.'

'You think I'm not already aware? Did he send you to chastise me? Because if so—'

'That is not—' She quieted her voice as her gaze fell upon Raff, prone in the bed. 'That is not why I'm here, Penn. I am worried for you.'

'I know.' Penn's voice felt rough in his throat. 'But I will not leave him.'

'How is he?' she said, stepping closer to where he sat at Raff's bedside.

'The wound was left to fester,' he said, reciting what Alsen had told him. 'It has poisoned his blood.'

'Will he live?'

'I—' His voice shuddered. 'I do not know.'

She placed her hand on Penn's shoulder.

'I need to get him out,' Penn said, pushing Raff's hair out of his eyes. 'But I can't fight. I can hold a blade to Father's throat but I can't – I could not see that through.' He sighed, his fingers resting on Raff's temple. He thought of Arlescote. 'And he would not want me to bloody my hands like that, not for him. Not if there was another way.'

'Father will never let him leave,' said Jo. 'He cannot just escape in the night.'

'I know.'

'You need to stop Father from coming after him.'

'I know.'

'What will you do?'

Raff's skin was slick, and far too hot. 'I don't know.'

With a sigh, Penn rose, taking in the room around them. The guest chambers were sparsely but expensively furnished: the low canopied bed upon which Raff had been placed, a fireplace, a table and chairs, a basin in one corner with a jug of water beside. He would need to arrange for a pallet to be brought up; he would not leave Raff's side.

Jo was right. Their father would not simply let Raff go, and he would not be persuaded by force. Penn would have to find a way to leave his father without another choice.

'I cannot do this alone, Jo. I need you.'

'I do not—'

'*Please.* If I am to get him out, I will need your help.'

She rubbed her hands together nervously. Penn didn't push her; she needed to make this choice herself. To stand beside Penn would be to oppose their father.

She stepped forwards, taking Penn's hand.

'Why are you doing this?'

He would have to tell her. She would never tie herself to his ruined fate for a repaid debt, but she might, if she knew the depth of Penn's feelings.

'Because I—' Something inside him urged him to stop, to keep it hidden; safe and protected and untouchable. But he couldn't. 'Because I care for him.'

She gave him a soft, sad smile. 'It is difficult,' she said, 'I imagine . . . without Henry, or Leo—'

'No,' he said quickly, before he could change his mind, 'you do not understand. He is not my brother, or my comrade. I do not—' For once, his words were failing him. He couldn't find the way to make her *see*. 'Do you remember what Ros said, when she arrived for the wedding?'

'She told us how wonderful being married was.' Jo wrinkled her nose. 'Again.'

'What else?'

'I don't understand what that has to do with—'

'She told me I needed someone to love. I thought she was being foolish. She didn't understand. She has Lord Peter, and Robin, and I thought—' He shook his head, sighing. 'She was right.'

His stomach clenched. His heartbeat was deafening. But he had to trust her. He maintained her gaze, never moving from Raff's side.

'I *love* him, Jo.'

It was the first time he'd voiced it out loud, and it *hurt*. He was taking something that wasn't his, that never could be. Raff had followed him, but that didn't mean he felt the same. He *shouldn't*: Penn didn't deserve his love. He didn't deserve the sacrifices Raff had made for him from the moment they had met to the moment the bolt had thrown him from his horse.

He laughed, gasped around a sob.

'I love him.'

Alsen returned quickly, a heavy bag slung over his arm. Penn watched as he neatly sliced away the infected skin. Jo left; she could not stand to see.

He stayed by Raff's side for two days, waiting for him to wake. He slept on a rough pallet placed directly beside the bed. He left only once, seeking out Raff's things: a near-empty pack, his sword, and his knife. No one attempted to stop him as he carried them back to the guest chambers.

Raff was stable, but such stability meant very little when he was not showing signs of recovery, either.

Seated at his side, clutching his hand, Penn thought of the people Raff had left behind; the family he may never see again. The thought that Ash and Cecily would never know what had happened to him made guilt flare in his chest. They would be expecting their brother to return. They would be heartbroken if he never did.

It was that thought that made him realise he'd been too focused on Raff to consider the wider implications of what had happened.

His father had shot and wounded the son of a powerful ally. He had left him to die. It was callous, and cruel. It was a deliberate attack on the Barden family, an attack that hurt all the more for the dissolved betrothal that was still so recent.

Battles had been launched for smaller insults. Wars had been fought for less. And if it *did* come to that, then the rest of his father's allies would be embroiled in it too: men whose biggest crime was their own idiocy in following de Foucart for so long.

Penn knew that his father wasn't popular, that his strength lay in his power, and *that* only held as long as his allies supported him. They would not let him launch a bloody war just because he had the King's favour.

But they would need to see the risk, first. He would need to make them understand how close they were to a cliff edge. He would have to make them desperate for a chance to heal the rift between the families, by any means necessary.

It was a small, desperate chance to barter Raff's freedom, if he lived. But it *was* a chance. When Jo next came to check on him, he begged her for parchment and a quill.

'I know that expression,' she said, watching him. 'You have an idea.'

'I do not know if it will work.' He was shaking. 'Or if Raff will even live to see it out.'

She placed her hands over his, stilling the tremor. 'Let us pray he does.'

Fire licking at him. His lungs full of water. A roiling in his chest and stomach, a pounding in his head. A single, furious centre of pain around his right shoulder.

Raff opened his eyes and was immediately blinded by light. He groaned, trying to lift his hand to shield himself from the glare. Then – a flare of scorching pain, his shoulder screaming at him. He could barely move his fingers, let alone his arm. It dropped uselessly to his side.

The last thing he could remember with any clarity was the hard, damp stone of the cell he'd been thrown into.

No. Not just the stone. A voice. There'd been an argument. A raised voice. A *familiar* voice. It must have been another dream. He'd been plagued with strange dreams since leaving Dunlyn Castle; dreams where he wasn't alone – and dreams where he was.

He twisted, sending another surge of pain shooting down his arm and across his chest, his teeth clenched with the effort of moving. He opened his mouth, but no sound came out; his tongue was dry, lips cracking.

'Raff?'

That voice. He knew that voice, he was sure. There was a distant crash.

'Raff?'

He *did* know that voice. Penn. He was dreaming again. He only heard Penn's voice in his dreams, haunting him every night, calling to him from an unreachable distance. He closed his eyes tighter. If he could slip back into oblivion, perhaps he could see him again.

'Curse it . . .'

There was something cool pressed to his head, followed by a short, harsh swear. The thing fluttered away, the relief gone, and he groaned, attempting to chase the touch.

'Give me a moment. I need—'

Penn's voice faded, as it always did. Raff sank back down, feeling darkness tugging at him already. It would be so easy to let it claim him. Before he could sink into it completely, he heard that voice again, now beside him.

'Stay, Raff. *Stay with me.*'

✡

More dreams. Running through trees, blood between his fingers, black as night. Pain unlike anything Raff had felt before. A voice, lost to the wind. At last, he found his tongue once more.

'Penn.'

A small gasp, the scrape of wood across stone.

'Raff?'

Raff opened his eyes. It took a moment for them to adjust. It was entirely dark, save for orange flickers dancing blurrily across the edges of his vision. For a moment, all was faded, as if looking through murky water.

And then a face appeared through the haze.

'You're awake,' Penn breathed.

He looked exhausted. His hair was an unwashed tangle around his head, dark marks beneath his eyes. He looked very much like he had the second time they met.

Raff tried to look around. He was in a high-ceilinged room, lying on a canopied bed.

'Where—' he managed, before his voice gave out.

'Wait,' Penn said, his eyes wide and solemn. 'You need water. I'm not leaving, Raff. Just wait.'

He vanished from view. Raff was struck with a sudden panic; this was another dream, another vision that was more memory than imagined. But Penn reappeared, a waterskin held in his hands, his brows knotted together.

'This will be easier for you than a cup,' he muttered, uncorking the skin and holding the mouth to Raff's lips.

It was full of fresh water that brought relief to his dry, uncooperative tongue. Penn pulled it away after only a few sips.

'Not too much,' he said. 'If you drink too quickly, you'll vomit. The physician . . .' He sighed, running a hand through his hair. His fingers became tangled, and he winced. 'He told me to only let you sip, if you woke.' He laughed, the sound too loud. '*If*. He was not sure you would. I told him . . .'

His words faltered. Raff moved his tongue around his mouth, willing his lips to work.

'Where am I?'

Penn gave him a grief-stricken look. 'In the de Foucart keep,' he said. 'I am sorry. I wanted to get you out, but the wound . . .'

'Wound?'

'Do you remember what happened?'

'I . . .' The memory was nearly intangible. 'Yes. The crossbow.' Panic bit at him. 'Penn, are you – your father—'

'I am fine,' Penn said quickly. 'You were hit in the shoulder, and thrown from your horse. Father locked you in the cells and the wound turned. When I found you, I thought—' He took a quick breath, and in the yellow light Raff could see his eyes were shimmering.

'Will I live?'

'You *will* live,' Penn said, voice sharp. 'But you must heal, first.'

He lifted the waterskin again, and Raff took a few more sips. His eyes were already drifting shut again.

'Sleep,' Penn commanded. 'You need to rest, or the wound will never mend. I will be here when you wake.'

He sounded so sure. Raff allowed his eyes to close, soothed by Penn's promise that he would remain by his side.

When the physician arrived, Raff was awake again. His eyes had regained some focus, and he could see how truly awful Penn looked – his face pale, jaw stubbled. He'd clearly done nothing but sit by Raff's bedside since dragging him up to the room.

The physician hastily introduced himself, then shooed Penn away before turning to Raff's arm. Penn had resisted, but the older man had won out and Raff had watched from the bed as Penn's miserable face vanished behind the door.

'He hovers,' the physician – Alsen – explained. 'How is your arm?'

Raff spoke as best he could, describing the pain in his shoulder that spread down his arm and back. Alsen nodded, listening, then began the arduous task of tending the injury. There were taut bandages around his chest, looped over his shoulder, and as Alsen unrolled the fabric Raff felt like he could breathe again.

He did not wish to breathe for long. As the final bandage was removed, Raff was hit with a foul smell, which he quickly realised was coming from his own skin. Alsen noticed him wince.

'You are lucky,' he said. 'It was worse when you were brought here. This is healing.'

Raff closed his eyes as Alsen washed the wound, gritting his teeth when he cut away the infected tissue with a sharp blade.

'It could be worse,' he said. 'You will keep the arm.'

When the job was done and the salve applied, he re-wrapped Raff's shoulder then propped him up, pressing a disgusting-smelling liquid to his lips in a small wooden cup.

'This will ease the pain.'

Raff wanted to refuse, but the elderly man was shockingly strong, and Raff found himself giving way. He sipped at the sedating drink, useless against the pillows. It tasted as foul as it smelled.

Alsen pulled a blanket over him before leaving.

'You will feel warm,' he said, 'but they tell me the night will bring snow. Better to sweat out the fever than freeze to death. It would be a shame to succumb to the cold after surviving a wound like that.'

If Raff's tongue hadn't been weighed down with whatever tincture

Alsen had given him, he would have laughed. As it was, he could only grumble a wordless agreement before leaning back against the pillow, breathing heavily.

'Raff?' Penn had returned. Raff hadn't even heard the door open.

'Let him rest,' came Alsen's voice. 'Send someone to fetch me should his condition worsen.'

'Of course.' Penn's voice sounded faint and far away.

Sleep came upon Raff like a wave, dragging him under. The door closed, the noise muffled, and then – after only a moment – there was a cool hand pressed to his own.

Raff fell asleep with Penn's fingers between his.

As the days progressed, Raff's moments of wakefulness were closer together, his eyes focused again. His skin was still too hot, and the wound on his arm was a sight to look at, but Alsen was pleased with his progress. Penn would have to act quickly now Raff's fate seemed more certain.

He told Raff his plan, as vague as it was, early one morning. The need to convince his father's allies that Lord Barden could launch them into war; the urgency with which he needed to describe both Raff's recovery and his eventual freedom.

'Father does not care what I say,' he said, helping Raff awkwardly into his undershirt, 'but if his allies talk, he will have no choice but to listen.'

Raff stared at him with wide eyes.

'Penn—' he began, when Penn finished.

'I know it is unlikely to work,' he said. 'But I fail to see what other choice we have.'

He left as Alsen arrived, leaving Raff in his capable hands. The skies above the keep were cloudy, and Penn could smell rain on the air, the threat of a faraway storm. He stood in the courtyard, breathing it in. It was cool and refreshing outside, especially after spending so long in the guest chamber, clogged with the smell of sickness.

There was a retinue gathered at the side of the yard. The man accompanying them was a short, grey-haired lord that Penn recognised as one of his father's trusted advisors. He was also a compulsive gossip. Secrets left with him – or with a member of his household – did not remain secrets for long.

It was a stroke of luck. Penn wandered over, keeping his eyes up so as not to appear as if he was actively approaching him.

'Greetings, William.'

Penn turned suddenly. 'Oh, Lord Hughes,' he said, as if startled. 'How are you? And John? I heard he was recently returned from France. I trust he is well?'

'As well as can be expected.'

'I always thought he had a particularly strong character,' he said.

'He does,' Lord Hughes agreed. 'I am thankful that he has been returned to us.'

Penn smiled dutifully. 'Of course.'

The last time he had seen John was several years ago, and he remembered him most clearly as a brash, arrogant man who had leered at Jo. Penn did not remind Lord Hughes of this, but glanced up and away across the battlements with an exaggerated sigh.

He could sense Lord Hughes peering at him. 'William?'

'Forgive me,' Penn said, shaking his head. 'I find myself rather distracted this morning.'

'Have I intruded?' Lord Hughes questioned. 'I apologise. I will leave you to your thoughts.'

He turned to go. Penn waited just a moment before calling after him. 'Wait, Lord Hughes!'

The older man hesitated. 'Yes?'

Penn jogged back towards him, lowering his voice. 'Perhaps you could offer me some assistance. I am stuck on a delicate problem, and a man of your stature . . . I would value your advice.'

Lord Hughes immediately straightened. 'Of course.'

Penn looked him up and down, assessing him, then reached into the pouch at his hip and pulled out a folded sheet of parchment. Lord Hughes watched with poorly concealed interest.

'I had intended to write to Lord Barden – Raff's father, the Earl – to inform him of his son's, ah . . .' Penn swallowed, grip tightening on the letter, 'illness,' he finished, the word entirely inadequate. 'Yet I fear I may be too hasty. It could take ten days for word to reach him, even with a fast rider, and by then . . .'

Penn let the implication hang, failing to finish his thought. Part of him couldn't bear to think of it. Part of him was keen for Lord Hughes to be forced to reach the conclusion on his own. Apparently he did, raising his eyebrows as understanding dawned.

'Ah,' he said, 'I see your fear, William. You wish to wait until his future is more certain.'

'I do.' Penn sighed. 'And yet, I do not. Lord Barden is a dedicated father, and he cares for his children. He deserves to know that Raff's life may be at risk.'

'Well—'

'And, of course,' Penn spoke over him, gesturing with the letter, 'there are worrying implications too. Precisely how much should I tell him? Should I detail the exact circumstance of his son's injury, or should I simply tell him that he has been wounded and taken ill? If he knew the full story . . .'

He glanced from the corner of his eye at Lord Hughes, who nodded, lips tight. He had not been there when Raff had appeared at the gates, but half a dozen of his men had been mingling outside. He'd been in the yard when Penn had removed Raff from the cells.

'He would be furious,' Lord Hughes concluded.

'I fear he would. Especially considering the betrothal, and all of this . . .' Penn gestured around the yard at the preparations for war. 'It may not be well-received news.'

Lord Hughes nodded again, seriously. 'It is a difficult decision.'

'It is,' Penn said. 'Frustratingly so. I would ask Raff his opinion on the matter, but he has not yet recovered enough to give me a useful or lucid answer.' He turned. 'Tell me, Lord Hughes. What would you do?'

Lord Hughes peered out across the yard. 'I would send the letter. Lord Barden should—'

'Oh,' Penn cut him off, 'I fear you have misunderstood me. My apologies. I meant: what would you do, were you Lord Barden? If it were John, wounded at the hand of an ally and left without treatment in a cell?'

Something flashed across Lord Hughes' face, barely more than a brief furrow of his brow. Penn noticed his hands tighten around each other where they were clasped behind his back. He did not respond.

'Forgive me,' Penn said, shaking his head. 'I had not intended to burden you with my anxieties. Thank you for lending me your ear, Lord Hughes. I know my father has always trusted your counsel.'

Lord Hughes blinked, as if returning from thought. He was barely listening.

'Ah,' he said, 'of course. You are welcome, William.'

Penn gave him a quick, tight smile and tucked the letter away.

'Why does he call you William?'

Penn paused where he was tending to Raff's shoulder, gently pressing a damp cloth against the jagged ridges of the wound.

'Surely you should ask why I call myself Penn?' he said, wiping away blood in pink-stained circles. 'William is my given name, after all.'

'That, then.'

Penn leaned back, dipping the stained cloth into a bowl of water.

'It is not an exciting story. I have always loved hawking, even when I was small. It was a more suitable hobby than reading, so Father indulged me. My first bird was a peregrine. She was a marvellous creature. I was obsessed, and my siblings used to tease me with the name. It didn't work, of course. Could you imagine, being a bird? I longed for it. Eventually the teasing stopped, but the name stuck.'

'And your father?'

Penn gave him a sharp look. 'It was too fanciful. Besides, he named me William, so William I must remain.'

He could feel Raff watching him as he wrung out the cloth.

'I told you it wasn't an exciting story,' he said. 'But I suppose they can't all be. Come, lean towards me. Alsen will have my head if this is not properly cleaned.'

Raff did as he asked, watching in silence as Penn wiped the rest of the blood away. There was a small, fond smile on his face. It was such a careless, familiar expression that it set talons around Penn's heart: it was too soft a look to turn on a man whose actions had nearly led Raff to his death.

When he was finished, he placed the cloth and bowl aside.

'I will have to leave you, this evening,' he said. 'I must attend Father's feast.'

'How cruel of you,' Raff intoned.

'I do not wish to go. But I am expected to. And I *must,* if I am to make any progress with Father's men.' He knelt by the bed. 'Be thankful you do not have to come with me. You would hate it.'

Raff winced. 'I am sure I would. But your father—'

Penn silenced him with a wave of his hand. 'I have spent twenty-five years riling my father and surviving his ire. I can endure one feast, at least.'

Penn stood, and stared at himself in the mirror above the basin. He'd washed and shaved for the first time in days, his hair loose around his face once more. He felt exhausted – he looked it too – but he would have to act as an earl's son, tonight.

He had returned to his rooms that morning before Raff woke, searching for clothing that would make him look like an heir, not a sickbed attendant. He'd heaved open the heavy door, thankfully unlocked, and his heart had immediately dropped. The tapestry hiding the disused staircase had been torn down, revealing the open door behind it.

Penn would not be allowed to escape again. He hurriedly grabbed fresh clothes and Raff's cloak, where it lay pooled beside the bed, trying to ignore the gap where the tapestry had hung. If remaining trapped was what it took to secure Raff's freedom, he would accept that cost.

Since speaking to Lord Hughes in the yard a week ago, Penn had integrated himself back into his father's court, making himself a fixture in a way he hadn't been before. The keep seemed smaller than Penn remembered it, and he'd made pains to visit every corner: from the Lords and Ladies still mingling in the hall to their squires in the stables. Conversation always drifted towards Raff or Raff's father, guided by Penn's careful words and the others' thirst for information. Dread had begun to creep over the keep, as light and deadly as the ice that frosted across the stone.

He had continued to refuse the evening meals until now, waiting for the best moment to act. Now he could wait no longer.

Raff watched him with a worried expression as he returned to his bedside, straightening the doublet he'd managed to find.

'Rest,' Penn said. 'I will be all right.'

The great hall was packed, as Penn had anticipated. As he entered, he was aware of how many people turned to face him. He suppressed a smile as he realised he was right: Raff would have hated this.

His father, seated at the upper table beside Isabelle and their children, barely registered his entrance. The children did, and Ellis called to him across the hall. Penn returned the greeting, wondering what sort of lies his half-siblings had been fed to explain his absence.

Jo sat at their father's side. There was an empty spot beside her, but instead of heading towards the seat where he belonged, he walked instead to one of the flanking benches where a number of his father's allies were seated. He moved towards a man he recognised from his childhood, sat beside a woman who must have been his wife.

'Lord Thomas,' he said, gesturing to the empty space on his other side, 'would you allow me to join you this evening?'

The lord looked utterly shocked. 'I, well—' He and his wife quickly moved up the bench. 'Of course, William. Please, do join us.' Penn sat, and Lord Thomas summoned for a goblet to be brought to him. 'Wine?'

Penn smiled. 'Please.'

He started to eat, ignoring both the curious looks shot at him from those he was sharing the table with and his father's glaring. Further down the table, a small group of young men were chatting: squires, excitable and unused to the finery of feasting and drinking.

'My Lord William . . .'

Penn turned. The young squire across the way was clearly deep in his cups, his cheeks pink and his lips stained with wine. His expression was keen, matching those worn by the boys beside him.

'Yes?' Penn tried to remember the lad's name, sure he had heard someone address him earlier. 'Calvin, isn't it?'

Calvin grinned. 'Yes,' he said, 'That's right. I, ah – it is . . .' He glanced over his shoulder at his closest friend, who nodded at him. 'I was – *we* were wondering what it was that happened to you. No one knows, y'see, and—'

'And you are curious?'

'Well—'

'*Calvin.*' Lord Thomas cut him off with a scowl. He turned to Penn. 'Forgive him, William,' he said. 'He is an idiot, and a drunkard besides. You do not need to tell him anything.'

His words were sincere, but they did not match his expression. His wife, too, was watching with poorly concealed curiosity.

No one really knew what had happened to Penn beyond the county border. All of them wanted to. Penn set his expression into a false grin.

'There is nothing to forgive.' He resisted the urge to look across the hall at his father, instead turning to Calvin. 'What do you wish to know?'

Penn had returned from the feast flushed. By all accounts, it had been a success. He had told Raff how he'd spread the *true* story of his escape – of his flight from the keep, and Raff's rescue – before adding, sardonically: *Well, not* quite *all.*

Raff watched him feed the fire. Penn peered into the flames, then spoke.

'I considered writing to your father.'

Raff winced as he twisted on the bed to better see him.

'But . . .' Penn turned, brushing down his hands, 'I could not bring myself to do it.'

'Why not?'

'Do you remember what you said to me, when you told my father you were no longer looking for William?'

Raff frowned. 'That I would not tell a father his son was dead unless I . . .' He faltered. 'Unless I held his body in my arms.'

'Precisely. I did not wish to send word until I knew you would live. And I will admit, I feared Ash riding here, ruining my plans and setting us all to battle.'

Raff nodded. Had Penn told his father that his life was hanging in the balance he would have left the keep and returned to Oxfordshire, the wind at his back and a sword strapped to his side. Or, as Penn assumed, it would have been Ash, and the threat of war would have become a promise.

'By the time I am able to write to him, I hope you will be halfway home,' Penn continued.

Raff hesitated. 'You think your father will allow me to leave?'

'I think he will have no choice.'

Penn sat down on the pallet beside the bed and began to remove his boots. He had won a chance for Raff's freedom not on the edge of the blade but the edge of his tongue, just as he had in Arlescote. Perhaps it should have been Penn teaching him all these weeks, instead of the other way around.

It was incredible – *Penn* was incredible – yet the compliment stuck in his mouth as Penn pulled off his stiff doublet to reveal the thin, loose undershirt beneath.

'Is that—' Raff spoke before he realised that he was repeating his own words, 'my undershirt?'

Penn's ears and neck turned red. He swallowed heavily, tangling his hands in the sleeves.

'I . . .' He licked his lips. 'Yes,' he managed. 'You were not using it.'

He looked as if he were waiting for the world to end. Raff's heart was in his throat. The shirt had been left on the floor of his bedchamber the morning his father had returned home. Penn must have taken it when he left the letter.

There was an ache beneath his sternum.

'Penn . . .'

'Yes?'

He wanted to pull Penn up beside him onto the bed, bundle him under the blankets and hold him close. He needed to know that he was *real*, that he was whole and well. He needed to feel his skin pressed against his own and hear his heartbeat.

But – *you will be halfway home*. Penn had said 'you', not 'us'. He intended to stay. Raff had followed to keep Penn safe, but if Penn had chosen to remain in the keep, there was little he could do. There was nothing he could have done *anyway*, not with his wounded arm, surrounded by guards and soldiers.

Raff swallowed down the invitation to join him on the bed.

'Keep the shirt,' he said instead. 'And . . . sleep well.'

The ache expanded, engulfing him.

Penn gave him a soft, sad smile. 'And you.'

Chapter Twenty-Five

The gentle sound of Raff's snores filled the room. Penn had been lying awake for an age, unable to drift away again. He would sleep better at Raff's side, he knew. It would be easy to shrug off the blanket and slide into the bed, looping his arm around Raff's chest and tugging him close, letting his rhythmic breathing lull him to sleep.

But he couldn't, no matter how much he ached for it. He hadn't yet asked why Raff had followed him, using Raff's illness as an excuse not to press the matter, but now he was recovering Penn was realising that he must. He needed to apologise, too, and take responsibility for what had happened to him.

He'd been terrified that when Raff woke he would treat him like *William* – like the son of the man who had tried to kill him. But he hadn't. It was like nothing had changed, and that, somehow, was worse: his soft smiles and easy conversation made it harder for Penn to pretend he wasn't so in love with him.

From beyond the window, he heard a sharp cry, followed by the blast of a horn. A messenger had arrived. They were coming several times a day, thanks to the sheer volume of nobles milling around the de Foucart keep. Penn had made a habit of heading outside whenever there was a messenger at the gates, and leaving Raff asleep he rose, dressed quickly, then headed outside.

He was well aware that his decision to greet the messengers had not gone unnoticed, and could hear the footsteps approaching from behind before he'd even reached the man on horseback.

His father did not stop to speak to him, addressing the rider instead.

'Go,' de Foucart hissed.

'But, my Lord—'

'I said, *go*.'

The messenger hesitated for a second before turning the horse and leaving the way he came. Penn watched him depart, chest tight.

'What is this?' de Foucart demanded, gesturing towards the departing rider.

'A messenger,' Penn said simply, turning to look at his father. 'Many of your men are awaiting letters, I believe.'

'Do not play the fool with me,' his father said. 'I know what you're doing.'

Penn frowned. 'What do you mean?'

'You are sending word to Lord Barden that I—' He stopped himself. 'That his son is unwell. You are deliberately baiting him to act.'

'Baiting him?' said Penn, in feigned surprise. 'Were I to write to him to inform him of Raff's condition, I do not understand how that would be baiting, if indeed it has all been an unfortunate accident.'

His father's face turned red. 'I *forbid* you from writing to Barden, do you understand?'

'You forbid it?'

'I do.'

'Oh.' Penn rubbed his hands together in an attempt to look contrite. He took a step closer and realised, for the first time, that he was taller than his father. 'How unfortunate.'

'Unfortunate?'

Penn sighed. 'I only wish you had informed me sooner,' he said. 'I wrote to Lord Barden five days ago.'

De Foucart's control snapped. He was suddenly an inch from Penn's face, voice raised. People around the yard were staring.

'How dare you?' he shouted, spittle flying. 'How *dare* you? You are bringing *ruin*—'

'You bring ruin to yourself,' Penn countered, not backing away.

'You *insolent* boy,' he hissed. 'I should—'

'What?' Penn said, raising his voice too. 'What should you do, Father? Should you punish me for my insolence? Do you intend to flog me out here where everyone can watch?'

His father's expression cracked. Penn had never seen such hate.

'What did you tell him?' he demanded, pointing a furious finger beneath Penn's chin. 'I demand you tell me! What was in that letter?'

Penn set his shoulders. He didn't step back. He didn't flinch.

'The truth.'

With a curse, his father turned on his heel, and stormed away. Penn felt his shoulders shaking. His knees, which had been locked in place to prevent him running, felt weak. He had no time to recover: their conversation had been watched, and people were rushing over already.

'William.'

He turned, hoping he wouldn't fall. The man who had spoken was one of their closest neighbours – an earl named Lord Godfrey.

'Yes?'

'You wrote to Lord Barden?'

The parchment still lay on the table at Raff's bedside, as blank as it had been when Penn received it.

'I did,' he lied. 'He has a right to know that his son may die. *Any* father has a right to know. I will not be held responsible for his actions after he receives the news.'

'You know the Barden family better than any of us,' Lord Godfrey continued. 'What do you suggest we do?'

Penn held his gaze. 'Pray that Raff recovers.'

'Even if he does,' a neighbouring dowager cut in, a woman who had brought a small army with her, 'the act of aggression will weigh heavily against your father, and any who ally with him.'

'It will,' Penn agreed. 'It is fragile ice we tread upon, especially when war with Scotland is still so fresh. Raff's grandfather is a laird, after all.' He hesitated. Raff had spoken very little of his grandfather. Penn didn't even know if he was still alive. 'I was led to believe that the Scottish seat is a powerful one.'

'So we risk war with the north *and* the Scots,' she said, bitterly. 'And for what?'

Penn bit his tongue. He did not voice out loud what they were all thinking: *for me. For the stolen son.*

'There must be some way we can appease them.' Lord Hughes had extracted himself from the crowd. 'You *know* them, William. Is Barden a reasonable man?'

'He appeared to be,' Penn said. 'He is well established, and is popular in the north. If only there was some way to demonstrate to him that we intend no harm. A show of good faith and trust, to repay the debt.'

'Such as?'

Penn shrugged. 'Money, perhaps. Or Father could re-establish the betrothal, although that would likely be seen as a further insult. Were there anyone suitable, a squire, or a wardship . . . the family has entered such contracts in the past, I know.' There was murmuring around him. He set his shoulders. 'Regardless,' he said, 'there is little we can do now. If Raff—'

'Yes, boy,' a man close behind him spat. 'What if the Barden lad dies?'

Penn spun around to see who had spoken. A red-faced lord he didn't know.

'Well?' the man continued. 'What then?'

'Then return home,' Penn said, coolly. 'Return home, and ensure you and your men are prepared for war. If you would excuse me—'

He pushed past the gaping man and through the crowd. By the time he'd reached the doors that led to the hall, the shouting had started.

He stalked through the dark. *What if the Barden lad dies?* The same question had been plaguing him for days. Raff was recovering well, but it still felt as if he could slip back into illness at any moment and leave him, for ever. He could die never knowing that Penn loved him, still believing that Penn only stayed by his side for his own safety.

Raff had saved him, and risked death for him. And Penn – coward that he was – hadn't even asked why.

He turned towards the staircase, praying that he could be brave.

When Penn returned to Raff's side, he was oddly quiet. He still smiled, still lingered nervously when Alsen came to change the bandages and tut at Raff's wound, cleaning away the last traces of contamination. He still helped him dress, awkwardly pulling Raff's undershirt over his immobilised arm. He still heaved Raff up onto the pillows when food was brought to them, helping him eat to stop him from straining the injury.

But there was something Penn wasn't saying. Raff could see it in his dark eyes every time he glanced at him. It was nearly sunset when Penn finally sat down on the edge of the bed, carefully not touching Raff's side, his hands in his lap. His head was bowed, shoulders up.

'We should talk.'

There was a weight in Raff's chest. Horrible anticipation. 'We should.'

Penn looked at him, face set. 'This is my fault.' Raff tried to speak, but Penn held up a hand, silencing him. 'I lied to you. It was my fault you were hurt.' His mouth was a taut line. 'If it weren't for me, you would be with your family where you belong, not dying under the roof of a man who wouldn't care if you did.'

'I am not dying.'

'But you *were*. And if you had, your blood would have been on my hands.' He unclenched his shaking fingers. 'I'm *sorry*, Raff. For all of it. I don't expect you to forgive me, but you need to know that I never—' He took a breath, chest expanding. 'I didn't want to hurt you. I just wanted you to be safe, and *now* . . .' He laughed, mirthlessly. 'Why did you follow? Did you not read my letter?'

'I did.'

'Then you knew what I intended to do. You were rid of me. Why do it?'

Raff moved higher on the pillows, reaching for him. Penn didn't flinch away, so he placed his fingers gently on his arm.

'I was not rid of you,' he spoke quietly, trailing his fingertips across the fabric of Penn's tunic. 'I have not been rid of you since that first evening in Hartswood Forest. I followed you because I promised I would not allow you to be hurt again. And—' he swallowed heavily, 'I needed to see you again. You didn't even say goodbye.'

'Would *you* have? I was terrified you would curse me for the lies – for bringing ruin to you. That you would . . .' he took a hiccupping breath, 'that you would remind me, again, of what I am.'

'Penn—'

'That is not all. What if you had asked me to stay? I wouldn't have been able to say no. Father would have found me, and killed you, and *that* would have been my fault as well.'

Raff paused for a moment, taking in his words.

'What I said . . .' he started. 'Forgive me. I was hurt. I thought . . . I thought the lie was less in who you were, and more in what you are to me. What *I* am to you.'

'You thought I was using you. Like you thought I used William.'

Raff ducked his head. 'I did. Which would mean that everything that passed between us had been lies too. That *they* were nothing. I followed you because I had to know they weren't.'

Penn's cheeks were ruddy. 'They weren't lies.' He stared at the floor. 'They weren't nothing.'

He was so far away, despite how close he was to him, despite the gentle warmth of his arm beneath Raff's hand. Raff heaved himself up against the pillows, the pain in his arm flaring, making his useless hand tingle and his stomach heave. Penn reacted instantly, placing his hands against his chest.

'You need to lie down—'

Penn's hands were warm, and sure, and *God*, Raff had missed their touch. He spoke without even thinking.

'I love you.'

Penn froze. *Raff* froze. He hadn't meant to say it; he had intended to keep it hidden, to pretend it wasn't true, knowing that Penn had chosen to stay. Yet . . . *They weren't lies.*

Penn's fingertips twitched, but he didn't lean back. He shook his head.

'You . . .' Penn's voice was barely more than a whisper, 'you don't.' He winced, like each word hurt. 'You *can't*.'

'But I do,' Raff said, surer. 'I *love* you, Penn.'

Raff wondered if Penn could feel his heart frantically beating beneath his palms, if the shock in Penn's expression matched his own. Perhaps he'd been wrong, and Penn had never loved him back; perhaps he'd been blinded by the brightness of his own feelings reflecting back at him from those dark eyes.

But Penn closed the gap between them until their lips were brushing. For a moment, they both stilled, breaths mingling. Then Penn moved, and the stillness was broken with an urgent kiss.

Raff found himself being forced against the pile of pillows, Penn's mouth pressing him down. He reached up instinctively with his good arm, resting his hand in the small of Penn's back.

The pain in his shoulder, the horror of where they were, the long-forgiven lie: all were forgotten in the heat of Penn's skin against his own, the quick, hungry movements of his tongue, the grip of his hands. Penn moved fervently, but gently, avoiding the bandages, careful not to push too hard.

When he pulled away, his eyes were sparkling.

'I love you,' he said. It was barely more than a whisper, spoken against Raff's lips. Penn kissed him again, and Raff could feel his smile. *'I love you.'*

Raff gasped against him, tasting the words in his mouth. There was a hot ache around his heart, his skin alight, his body weightless. He tugged Penn closer, hampered by his wounded arm. Penn manoeuvred himself beneath the blankets, lightly trailing his fingers against Raff's chest as he kissed him again, one hand moving to cup the back of Raff's head, tangling in his hair.

The ringing space between Raff's ribs was filled. Yet he was still consumed with the agony of it; missing Penn despite him being so close, wishing they could somehow be closer. He wanted to heave him between his bones and tangle themselves together so they'd never be forced to part again.

He was so lost in the feeling of having Penn back in his arms that he forgot the wound, lifting himself up and wrapping both arms around Penn's body and—

The pain blazed from his shoulder to his back to his fingertips, hot and sudden. He collapsed back upon the pillows with a string of curses as sweat beaded across his forehead.

'Raff—' Penn fell to the bed beside him, 'are you all right?'

Raff took a deep breath. 'I am,' he managed, winded. 'I just—'

Penn placed a hand to his chest, watching him with a worried gaze. 'Breathe,' he said. 'It will pass.'

Raff gripped Penn's wrist with his good hand and breathed through the pain, falling in time with Penn's gentle exhales. When the pain had dulled into a low throb, they nestled beneath the woollen blankets, safe beneath the hanging canopies of the bed.

'We will need to find the best way to travel with your injury,' Penn said, running a slender finger up and down Raff's arm. 'When we return home, we will—' He stuttered to a halt, face paling. 'I – that is—'

'When *we* return home?'

'If that's what you want. Forgive me; I didn't think. I understand that if you do not want me to—'

'No,' Raff quickly spoke over him. 'You wish to return with me?'

'If you still think me worthy. If you will accept me, despite the lies. Despite bringing war to your doorstep.'

'Penn—' He kissed him. 'You have *always* been worthy. I want you to be safe. And I want you with me. Whether that is here, or Dunlyn Castle, or somewhere else. Anywhere else.'

'Anywhere?'

'Anywhere. If it is me you want, and not just the safety of the keep . . .'

Penn silenced him with another kiss. 'I want *you*. Anywhere.

But—' He pulled back, expression clouded. 'But I *cannot* go anywhere. Father will not simply grant me my freedom.'

Raff held Penn tighter, his palm pressed to his back. Despite Raff's fears, de Foucart had not yet disciplined Penn for his perceived wrongdoings. But with Raff gone, and de Foucart's allies returned home, they would finally be alone, and the opportunity would be granted to him.

'I will not leave you here,' he said.

'You may have to.'

'I *will not*,' Raff repeated. A sudden thought struck him, and fear bit at his insides, making him feel even more nauseous. 'Does your father know,' he said, keeping his voice low, 'about . . .' He gestured between the two of them.

'I hope he does not,' said Penn. 'This is *war*. I suspect he thinks we're playing knights, as if you are my king and I your loyal squire. He allowed Mother to raise me on tales of chivalry and loyalty and oaths as strong as steel. He thinks I am acting as Sir Lancelot, and you King Arthur.'

'I would not ask you to follow me like that.'

'I know,' said Penn, edging closer with a yawn. 'Yet I would, if you did.'

Raff watched as Penn's eyes slid shut. *And I you*, he thought.

I love you.

Penn dreamed of strong hands and dark forests, of the smell of straw and sweat.

I love you.

There was an arm wrapped around him. For the first time in weeks, he was safe. He was *home*. He could drift like this for ever, feeling Raff's body beside him, knowing that he was wanted.

I love you.

Raff shifted beside him. And then there was something gentle and fluttering on Penn's lips, a warm breath, the lightest pressure. He lazily opened his eyes just in time to see Raff backing away, an indulgent smile on his face.

'I have wanted to do that since—'

He was interrupted by a violent hammering on the door. Penn had half a mind to tell whoever it was to leave, when there was a shout.

'Penn!' His sister.

He slung himself from the bed, removing himself reluctantly from Raff's side. He was still dressed, thank God, so heaved open the door.

'Father is demanding to see you in his solar,' she said, breathlessly. 'You must come, *now*.'

Penn stood back to let her in as he attempted to tidy his hair, mussed from sleep and Raff's hands.

'What has happened?'

'A party was spotted,' she said, shutting the door behind her, 'carrying Barden banners. They will be here by dawn tomorrow.'

Penn froze. Raff heaved himself upright.

'How?' he said. 'You said you did not send the letter.'

'He didn't,' said Jo, before Penn could speak. '*I* did.'

Penn turned to her, aghast. '*What?*'

She hesitated. And then, to Penn's surprise, she turned to Raff, cheeks pink. 'Your sister is very . . . interesting.'

Raff stared at her, and Jo continued.

'She left a note, before your retinue departed, expressing that it had been a pleasure to meet me and that she was sad we would not be sisters after all. I replied. It was polite, especially after the slight against her.'

'What did you say?'

She frowned at him. 'I do not see how that matters. What *matters* is that she wrote me back. It was a letter sent in haste, telling me you were both returning. She was trying to prevent you coming to harm, Raff, but it arrived the morning after Penn removed you from that cell, and it was too late.'

She looked down, guiltily. 'I wanted to inform them when we thought you had died, but Father said that Penn could still be in danger, and . . .' she looked distraught, 'I didn't know what to do, so I did nothing.'

Penn swiftly stepped forwards, grabbing her hands. 'You tried to ask me,' he said, remembering through the fog of grief.

'I did,' she said. 'I had to know the truth. But you barely even knew I was there.' She gave him a weak smile. 'I should have realised *why*. When I spoke to you, after you saved him. . .' she lifted her head, 'I realised that Father was wrong. I wrote to Cecily the next day. They must have set out soon after receiving the letter.'

'And now they are here,' Raff said, weakly.

'But not, as Father feared, with an army.'

'Not *yet*,' cut in Penn. 'They know Raff is alive?'

She shook her head. 'They do not. They only know that he was wounded, and gravely ill. And . . .' Penn gave her room to speak, 'and they know at whose hand he was wounded.'

So she had told them *all*, taking an unimaginable risk for them. Penn's skin turned cold at the thought of what their father would do if he knew it was *she* who had alerted Lord Barden to Raff's injury, and not him.

'Jo,' he said, 'do not mention the letter to anyone else.'

'But—'

'Father believes I wrote to Lord Barden. I will not have him finding the truth. I will keep you out of this, as much as I can.'

He ran a hand through his tangled hair and turned to Raff.

'With luck, you will be leaving here tomorrow with your family at your side.'

Raff did not seem cheered.

'And what about you?' he asked. 'Where will you be?'

Penn reached out, taking Raff's hand in his. He found his words stuck. He'd be able to guarantee Raff's freedom, but had never considered securing his own. What would he have gained from freedom, when he was so sure Raff didn't want him back? Besides: his single route from the keep had been discovered. If he was to escape, he would need to find another way.

It was still likely they would be parted, after everything.

He squeezed Raff's fingers, and said nothing.

The keep was quiet as Jo and Penn rushed towards the solar. The once-busy yard was empty, save for turned mud and a few fallen banners.

'Has everyone gone?' Penn asked, as they entered the great hall.

'Many have,' Jo replied. 'They fear it is too risky to stay.'

Word had spread, then. Penn wasn't sure how many ears he had whispered in. He was amazed that anyone had listened.

As they made their way up the staircase towards de Foucart's rooms, Penn stopped, aware that they may not get another chance to speak freely.

'Wait—'

Jo hesitated on the step beside him.

'Thank you.' He dropped to a whisper. 'For the letter. It has forced Father's allies to act.'

'Someone had to tell Raff's family.'

'But it did not have to be *you*. The risk—' He couldn't voice it, not so close to his father's chambers. 'I stand by what I said. We will let Father believe it was my doing.'

'Are you sure?'

'I am.' Penn took a breath. 'Why did you do it, Jo?'

She gave him a tight smile. 'Because you love him.'

They hurried up the remainder of the stairs. From the upper landing, they could hear raised voices coming from the solar. They approached the closed door on silent footsteps.

'It is a traditional, *trusted* exchange,' a male voice was shouting. 'Lord Barden would not dare harm him.'

'But he would have no obligation to treat him well!' Penn and Jo glanced at each other. That was Isabelle, their father's wife.

'Better than you have treated *his* son, I am sure!' came the furious reply.

De Foucart spoke next. 'You have no right to—'

'Lord Barden's son will be incapacitated for the rest of his life. He will *never* regain full use of that arm. What will become of him? He will be unsuitable to serve, to pursue knighthood, to *wed* . . .'

Penn took a breath, knocked once on the door, then pushed it open to see his father and Isabelle at the desk, his father's steward behind, and Lord Hughes pacing beside them.

'It is *traditional*,' Lord Hughes insisted again. 'There is no safer place for Ellis.'

'Apart from his *home*,' Isabelle spat. 'We have no reason to trust that they would treat him decently given the rift between our families.'

'What is happening?' Penn said, shutting the door behind them.

Lord Hughes had stopped pacing. 'We are working out this mess, before Lord Barden arrives.'

'Hughes is suggesting an exchange,' Penn's father said, tonelessly. 'An agreement that we will not pursue the issue of your abduction—'

Penn was about to argue, but his father's steely expression had him snapping his mouth shut, 'if they do not seek retribution for their son's injury.'

Jo sat at the desk. Penn placed himself behind her, hands resting on the back of the chair.

'What kind of exchange?'

'He intends to sell off my son as if he were no more than cattle,' Isabelle said, her arms folded across her chest.

'A *wardship*,' Lord Hughes clarified, voice level. 'It is traditional, and Ellis is of the right age. Send him to live with Lord Barden. Establish him as a squire. They will be obligated to keep him well, and it will demonstrate mutual trust.'

Penn nodded, as if thinking. Across the table, his father was refusing to look at him. Penn wondered if word had spread that *he* had suggested a wardship, or if his father assumed his allies had landed upon the idea themselves.

At the time, it had been little more than an attempt to goad his father into acting more rashly. Now, Penn felt something like jealousy pinching at him: if they agreed to Lord Hughes' plan, Ellis would be taken to Dunlyn while Penn remained, trapped.

Yet – he looked across the table at Isabelle. Her eyes were red. She was angry, that much was clear, but more than that: she was scared, just like him.

The thought emerged to him slowly, only half-formed. His fingers held tighter to the carved back of the chair.

'It *is* fair,' he said, '*and* traditional, of course, to bargain for peace with a life. Wardships, squires . . .'

He looked up, meeting Isabelle's eyes. For a single moment, he nearly baulked: this was too bold. Too risky. But it could be his only chance.

'. . . even hostages.'

Isabelle blinked. She had gone very still. De Foucart was still staring resolutely away.

'But if you are unwilling to let Ellis go . . .' Penn look a long, deliberate pause, holding her gaze. 'It is a shame that you are left with no alternative to him.'

'A fair exchange,' she said, slowly. 'A son for a son. But Marcus . . .' De Foucart turned, and she finally looked away, 'you have *two* sons.'

Yes. All eyes snapped to Penn. He forced himself to laugh. 'I am too old to be a ward.'

She tilted her head. 'But you would make a fine hostage.'

Penn kept his expression level. He looked at his father, but could not read his face.

'Trade a hostage for peace?' Lord Hughes looked sombre. 'It may work. But his role would be diminished. The title—'

'Would pass directly to Ellis, yes,' de Foucart finished for him.

There was a sharp glint in his eye. He could regain favour while replacing an unsuitable heir with a more pliant one. His allies would not see the relief: just a father making a sacrifice for the good of them all.

Lord Hughes turned to Penn. 'Would you agree to this?'

'It does not matter,' de Foucart snapped, before Penn could respond. 'He will do is as he is *told*, for once.'

Penn stood straighter. It was a hopeful, desperate chance: one that could grant him his freedom, and a place at Raff's side. But his father would be loath to let him go without punishment, however convenient his removal would be. Penn could only hope that with his allies turned against him, his father's hand would be forced.

'I have no desire to see this come to war any more than you do,' Penn said. 'If by relinquishing my freedom I can guarantee peace for my brother and sisters, as well as men like yourself, Lord Hughes, who have no role in this . . . I would do it.'

He rubbed the lie against the truth. Penn needed to ensure that Jo was safe, but his regard for Ellis and Ingrid was little more than acceptance. He didn't care if his father's allies found themselves embroiled in de Foucart's skirmish. They would deserve it, for allowing his behaviour only until it impacted them.

But he *would* do it. He would do it for Raff, and his freedom, even if that freedom was only from his father's control.

'You need to fix this,' Lord Hughes said finally, addressing de Foucart. 'If bartering a hostage is how you do it, then so be it. We are *all* at risk because of your actions. Anyone who allies himself with you will face war, if it comes to it, not just with the north but with Scotland too.'

'The blame—'

'Lies with *you*.' Lord Hughes leaned over the table. 'You shot that boy yourself, and I have two dozen witnesses willing to attest to your crime. I will take this as far as I must to keep me and mine safe. To the court. To the *King*.' De Foucart visibly paled, as Lord Hughes continued. 'You have never been popular, Marcus. Only powerful. Now you are neither.'

There was a prolonged silence. Penn watched as Lord Hughes straightened, glancing across at him. He tried to keep his expression placid. *It had worked*. Somehow, it had worked. His father was outnumbered by his own men. Raff was guaranteed a way out – any perceived wrong he had committed paled in comparison to the retaliation, especially with Penn's testimony that he had never stolen him in the first place.

His own freedom, he knew, would be trickier to win. His father was being forced to choose.

De Foucart rose, glaring at him. Penn's chest tightened. He was thrown back to the hundreds of times he'd seen that expression; the pain that followed. He stood straighter, staring his father down.

'Get out,' his father muttered.

No one moved.

'I said, *get out!*'

Chapter Twenty-Six

The castle had come to life. Word of the Barden retinue's imminent arrival had spread, and they would need to be greeted appropriately. Rooms would need to be cleared, meals arranged, adequate space made in the stables. It would not do to host them as they had before, forced to camp beyond the walls. They would be welcomed as guests: guests who, if they chose, could ruin them all.

Jo pulled Penn into a quick hug as soon as they were beyond their father's chambers. She was shaking.

'Penn,' she said, 'they seem set. They will use you to bargain for peace.'

'I am not sure I am worth that much.' Penn pursed his lips. 'It does not seem a fair deal.'

She shook her head at him. 'Be *serious*. What will you do?'

'I entered Dunlyn Castle as a servant. I left it as a runaway. Perhaps I will return as a hostage.' He shrugged, lowering his voice. 'There are far worse places to be.'

Jo watched him, nervously.

'You told me you fled seeking freedom,' she said. 'You will never have that, if this agreement is made. You will be just as caged as if you had stayed and wed. More so, given you will be the guarantor for peace. I do not want to see you as a prisoner.'

Penn hesitated. He'd not thought of the implications of the arrangement, focused too much on the prospect of being free of their father and by Raff's side. He *wanted* it – to leave behind the title that had been too heavy for him, and the name that wasn't even his.

But he'd wanted his freedom before. He'd *taken* it, and it had ended in ruin and bloodshed.

'I am sure . . .' he began, feeling suddenly untethered, 'with Raff—'

'What about the family? Will they support this?'

'I hope—' Penn began, before abruptly stopping. 'Perhaps I should ask *your* opinion on the matter,' he said, redirecting with a smirk. 'Seeing as you are so familiar with Cecily?'

Jo scowled at him. 'Yes,' she said, 'we are very alike. We share the burden of having troublesome brothers.' Before he could retort, she set her shoulders, stepping back as a servant rushed past with a basketful of clean linens. 'I must make sure this place is fit for guests,' she said. 'Will you be all right?'

'Of course.'

She gave him a quick kiss to his cheek, then rushed off after the servant. As she rounded the corner, he could hear her telling them where to take the sheets.

For the first time in days, Penn had nothing to do; nowhere he needed to be. There was no vigil to keep, no sickbed to tend. Days of whispers and sowing doubt had come to a head at last, culminating in Jo's letter. He could *rest,* at least until Lord Barden arrived and their fates would be decided.

But weight on his shoulders still threatened to tip him. He *ached,* the ache spreading down his back, through his arms. Added to that, the echo of Jo's words too: what if she was right, and he'd inadvertently walked into another cage?

In the guest chambers, Raff was sitting in the middle of the bed, attempting to sharpen his dagger with his left hand.

'You will rip a hole in the sheets if you continue that,' Penn said, tonelessly.

Raff didn't look up. 'I have *already* ripped a hole in the sheets.'

'Father will shoot you again, you know.'

He grinned. 'Perhaps this time I will be better prepared to duck.' He sheathed the dagger, tossed it aside, then finally glanced up. His smile slipped away as he spotted Penn's expression. 'What happened?'

Penn collapsed down onto the bed beside him. He gave a hasty recount of the conversation, twisting his hands together as he stared up at the canvas.

'A *hostage*?' Raff said. 'It is a common way to broker peace, I suppose. But Penn – would you want that?'

Penn turned to look at him, his cheek brushing against Raff's thigh.

'I want to be away from here,' he said. 'I want to be with *you*. But—' his voice threatened to catch, 'I thought this might be my freedom, but what if it's not? What if I've damned myself? I will not be a guest, not even a servant. I will be a *prisoner*, and—'

'No,' Raff spoke over him. 'Never. If I can speak to Father, and explain . . . If they *do* agree, I swear: I will do all I can to keep you safe. You will be a hostage in name alone.'

Penn stared up at him. The ache in his back began to ease.

'But . . .' Raff continued, frowning down at him, 'even treated well, you would still be forfeiting your freedom. You would be obligated to remain until the agreement ended, which could be *never*. You would be trapped, that much is true.'

'You would be just as trapped,' Penn said. 'You really *would* never be rid of me.'

'I – *no,* Penn—' Raff looked distressed. 'I *want* you with me.'

'For ever?' Penn sat up and forced himself to look at him. 'As you said, the agreement would likely be indefinite. I would gladly stay by your side for all that time, but what if I weigh you down? What if I become a burden to you?'

'You would never be a burden to me. I—' Raff's expression broke, and he surged forwards, catching Penn's mouth in a hard kiss before he could back away. 'I love you. And that will not change.'

'And I love you,' Penn said, sliding his hand to rest on Raff's shoulder. 'But – but you are so *good,* Raff. You deserve better.'

'Damn "deserve",' Raff huffed, not moving away. 'I *want* you. For as long as you will have me, Penn. Yes: for ever.'

It felt like a promise. Like an extended hand; the first light of the rising sun.

'God, Raff . . .' Penn exhaled. 'I have spent days telling anyone who will listen that you may die. I *know* you are well, yet—' He pressed his palms to Raff's shoulders. He was warm, but no longer that awful fever that had gripped him for so long. 'It is too much, even to think about. Add to that the threat of war, and arguments with Father . . .' He sighed, feeling foolish. 'I am so *tired,*' he said, finally. 'And I – I missed you.'

Raff reached out with his good arm, cupping Penn's jaw, tugging him into another soft kiss. Penn relaxed into the touch, breathing him in.

'You are alive,' Penn murmured, resting their heads together.

Raff moved his hand to his waist, sliding around to the small of his back. 'We are *both* alive.'

Raff's breath was hot on Penn's mouth, his hand at his back a grounding pressure. His body beside him was warm and solid and real. An urgent need bubbled in Penn's chest, swirling lower.

He needed to see, needed *proof*. He kissed Raff again, pushing him back onto the bed and slinging a leg over Raff's hips. He trailed his hands down his chest, fingers catching in his undershirt.

'Show me.'

Raff let out a low rumbling sound before sliding his hand beneath Penn's tunic. Together, hampered by the loss of Raff's right hand, they manoeuvred it over Penn's head and onto the floor, swiftly followed by his undershirt.

Beyond the window, the castle was noisy with life. But beneath the hanging canopies of the bed, there was only Raff, and the softness of his skin, and the stuttering of his breath as Penn moved against him.

Far above the courtyard a bird screeched, its wide wings and forked tail stamped against the rolling grey clouds as if it had been cut from them. Raff watched as it flew behind a tower, vanishing from sight. A kite perhaps. He would have to ask Penn, later.

He would have to ask, if he were granted the opportunity.

When Raff woke, it had been with Penn pressed against his back, his arm curled around Raff's middle. Raff had laid there, feeling Penn's heavy breaths in his hair, his feet twitching where their bare legs were tangled together. He'd been muttering in his sleep, as he so often did. Raff had quieted his breathing, listening. Penn had sniffed, clung tighter, and then: Raff's name, little more than a sigh.

Raff wished he could have stayed held in Penn's arms for ever, but it could not last. The sound of servants in the yard outside had roused Penn from his sleep, and they were forced to wake and dress.

Standing side by side, ready to leave the tiny room for the last time, they had bid each other a brief, desperate farewell. There was no time for anything more, even though it could have been their last chance to speak. There was already a guard hammering on the door.

Raff shifted beneath his cloak. Alsen had arrived early that morning, having been informed that Raff would be leaving that day. He had wrapped his arm in a sling, demonstrating to Penn the best way to tie the fabric.

Neither of them had mentioned to Alsen that the lesson may go to waste. There had been no word of a decision from de Foucart, and the longer his silence lasted the surer Raff was that he had decided to risk war, just to keep Penn under lock and key.

They had gathered in the courtyard for his family's arrival. Penn stood several yards away beside his father, wearing the cloak that Raff had lent him all those weeks ago. He had tried to give it back, hands shaking in the wool. Raff had refused to take it, awkwardly hooking it over Penn's shoulders with his good hand.

Now he was alone.

There was a call from the gatehouse. They were here. Raff straightened as best he could as the pain in his shoulder flared, and the gates opened.

His father came first, followed by Ash, and then his sister riding beside a cart. Raff realised how dire the situation had been: for all of them to come, leaving Dunlyn once again empty, meant they truly thought he would die.

Upon seeing him, Lily threw herself from her horse and rushed over. She crashed into him before he could stop her. He cursed, and she immediately let go as he doubled over in pain.

'Oh, Raff—' she stuttered. 'Forgive me, I forgot—'

'It is good to see you too,' he wheezed.

'Perhaps next time you see our brother you could *not* attempt to further wound him?' Ash suggested, still on his horse. 'It has been too long, Raff.'

Raff peered up at him, eyes watering. 'It has.'

Beside Ash, Lord Barden glanced at him. His expression was severe, but his eyes were shining with relief. He turned to de Foucart, looking down at him from his horse.

'You are aware, I hope,' he said in a voice like steel, 'of the position you find yourself in?'

De Foucart tilted his chin higher. 'If we may discuss this—'

'What is there to discuss? You shot my son for a baseless accusation. Afterwards, you locked him in a cell and denied him care. It is only thanks to *your* son—' Lord Barden nodded towards Penn, who quickly looked away, 'that he survived at all. Do you deny it?'

'If we may speak inside . . .'

Lord Barden's expression did not change.

'Very well.' He dismounted the horse, and passed the reins to a waiting servant, then turned to Raff. 'We must speak before I can reach any agreements with the Earl.'

'Of course.'

That was ideal. He would need to tell his father his version of events and warn him not to mention who had really written the letter. Lord Barden gave him a tight smile before turning to Ash.

'See to the retinue,' he said. To Raff's surprise, Ash nodded. 'Be prepared to leave before midday.' He looked from his sons to de Foucart. 'I intend for this to be quick.'

The families were kept apart while their fathers spoke. Raff wished he could have stayed by Penn's side. These could be the last moments they could spend together, and each one that passed felt wasted.

Ash had seen to the retinue, organising the sparse number of servants they had brought with them and seeing to the horses and carts. Raff watched as his brother easily took charge before he headed inside with their father, guiding him to the side chamber in which they had discussed William's disappearance so long ago.

Raff told him as much as he dared as briefly as he could, hoping Lord Barden would understand. Jo's letter had been short through necessity, leaving the family unsure what had transpired. Raff himself was unsure as well: much of the memory was blurred, and he supplemented his recollections with what Penn had told him as he sat by his sickbed.

After his father had gone, shoulders set and expression furious, Ash and Lily entered and he was forced to explain, again, what had happened since leaving Dunlyn Castle. When Raff was finished, Ash leaned back in his chair, looking smug.

'While this *is* a thrilling tale,' he said, 'I must ask: have you told him?'

Lily, too, was watching him. Raff's face flushed.

'Told him what?' he asked, although he was well aware what his brother meant.

'Do not play the fool,' Lily demanded. 'Have you told him, or not? If you haven't, after coming so close to dying, I will be tempted to kill you myself.'

He could feel the smile creeping unbidden across his face. He could not have stopped it, not for anything.

'I have,' he said.

'And?'

He could only grin at them, cheeks burning, as Ash burst into laughter.

Penn leaned against the cold stone wall of the great hall and stared upwards, counting the cobwebs that hung from the rafters. He'd barely reached a dozen when they were scattered by a sudden breeze, his thoughts interrupted by the slam of the far doors opening.

Framed in the doorway, their father looked very small.

'Come, William.'

Penn could only follow as he led him in silence into his solar. De Foucart lingered in the middle of the room in silence, drawing it out, waiting for Penn to snap first. Penn set his shoulders. He wouldn't give him the satisfaction.

Finally, his father relented. He paced the room as he spoke.

'You have brought disgrace to this family,' he said, his tone remarkably even for how severe his words were. 'You brought war to our doorstep. You have actively undermined our family's name, and *my* God-given right—' His voice was rising, and he fixed himself back into cool impassivity. 'You have behaved abhorrently, again and again, and I see now that my attempts punish you have been fruitless. You are senseless, boorish, and entirely unfit to be my heir.'

He peered from the window.

'I am glad your mother is not here. You saw how Leo's conduct affected her. She would be horrified to know what you have done. How *selfish* you have been.'

Penn felt sick. He clenched his hands into fists but did not respond. His father continued.

'By the grace of God, I was granted four sons. Now I have but one. You may say goodbye to your sister, and then you will leave.'

Penn's breath caught, and silence descended. Penn could only stare at him.

'Have you nothing to say?' de Foucart asked, turning to look at him.

There were dozens of things Penn wanted to say to him. A hundred insults, a wild grab for retribution, to make him share Penn's pain. To make him atone for the scars.

'No,' he kept his gaze, 'I have nothing to say to you.'

His father didn't react. 'Very well.'

Jo arrived as his father left. She was smiling, but her face was wet with tears. Before he could speak, she was on him, crushing him beneath a squeezing hug.

'I will miss you,' she gasped.

'Dunlyn Castle is not so far,' Penn said against her hair. 'I am sure you would be welcome there.'

'Would they have me?'

He held her tighter. 'Claim it is an act of diplomacy,' he said, 'checking I am well and thus ensuring the agreement still stands. They will not be able to deny you without looking suspicious.'

She shook her head at him. 'You are too clever for your own good.'

'If I were clever I would not have caused all this harm,' he said, releasing her. 'Will you be all right? Alone, here?'

Jo set her shoulders. 'Of course,' she said. 'I fared well enough in your absence. And you would have left anyway, were you married.'

'Not like this, though.'

'No.' She smiled. 'Not like this.'

They were met by a guard outside the door and joined by two more in the corridor below. Penn and Jo exchanged a knowing glance: he had been deemed an escape risk. He let his fingers drift over the hilt of the dagger strapped to his hip. He wouldn't use it, but it was reassuring beneath his hand.

His father was waiting at the gatehouse in silence. Penn suffered no delusion that he was bidding him a heartfelt farewell; he was only there to ensure Penn made it into the right hands. Penn gave him a curt nod. He had wasted enough words on his father, and he would not grant him any more. The gates opened.

He heard the person beyond the walls before he could see them.

'I am here for the hostage.'

Penn stepped forwards, frowning at the familiar voice. On the other side of the rising portcullis was Ash, still atop his horse. His expression was severe, made more so by the scar, although Penn was quite sure he was trying not to laugh.

One of the guards pushed Penn forwards. 'Do you want him restrained?'

Ash glanced from the guard to Penn. 'No,' he said, finally. 'I am sure I can handle him should he see fit to cause trouble.'

Still with two guards at his side, Penn turned back to Jo. She was alone: their father had vanished. She pulled him into a tight hug, her cheeks wet against his shoulder.

'I will be all right,' he said, pulling back and taking her hands. 'I am useful, at last.'

She gave him a quivering smile. He sighed, and squeezed her hands just once before letting go. He set his shoulders as he walked from the shadow of the gatehouse and out onto the brightly lit road, the guards close behind.

The winter sun hit his face, blinding him. He heard the gate and portcullis slam. He didn't look back, as they began to walk.

'Am I not permitted a horse?' he asked, when they were out of earshot.

Ash looked down at him. He really *was* laughing.

'It would not do to give you a mount only to have you escape on it,' he said.

They made their way down the road that led to Hartswood Forest. Beneath the shadow of the trees was a covered cart and horses, but the rest of the retinue had gone.

'Here,' Ash said, pulling the horse to a stop by the cart and swinging from its back. 'This will be your transport, I am afraid. As I said: they fear you will escape.' He paused, looking back towards the keep. 'Your *father* fears you will escape.'

Penn shrugged. 'I might.'

Ash gave him a long, searching look. 'We shall see.' He handed the reins of his horse to the cart's rider, then – much to Penn's surprise – stalked towards the trees. 'Come,' he called over his shoulder. 'This way.'

Penn hurried after him, feeling the leaf litter crunch underfoot as he followed Ash into a tiny clearing.

'What are we—'

'You've but a minute,' Ash said. 'Any longer will raise suspicion.'

'But—'

Ash silenced him with a raised hand. He nodded – not at Penn, but over his shoulder – then strode back the way he came. Was this their way of allowing Penn an escape? Did *they* not want him either?

'Penn?'

He spun around. Raff was standing on the edge of the clearing, eyes wide. Penn ran to his side, slinging his arms around him in a desperate embrace. Raff buried his face in Penn's shoulder, his breath coming in gasps against his neck.

'You are all right,' Raff said, voice muffled. 'I feared that your father would agree, but refuse to let you go.'

Penn pulled back. Raff's eyes were shimmering, and there were tears glistening on his cheeks. Penn kissed them away.

'I am all right,' he said, lungs tight. 'Truly, I thought Father would refuse myself. Or *yours* would refuse, deeming me unfit . . .'

'You saved my life,' Raff said. 'Of course he would not refuse. And . . .' Raff's expression had turned guilty.

'And what?'

'I threatened to *really* steal you away, if he did.'

'*Raff*.'

'It hardly matters. He agreed, and your father let you go.' Raff hesitated, paling. 'Did he . . .'

He trailed off. Penn caught his implication in the slant of his brows, his worried expression.

'He would not dare, I think,' Penn said. 'Given all that has happened. No: I received the same harsh words I have heard for as long as I can recall. He thinks me a boor. Unsuitable heir, senseless man, selfish son.'

'That is not—'

'Raff.' Penn stopped him. 'My father can think what he wants. I find myself unable to care when he has been forced to let me leave, and I am back by your side.'

Raff's expression cracked into a blinding smile. 'My God, Penn. I have missed you.'

'We have been apart for less than a day.'

'And I have missed you for every moment of it. I thought I might never see you again.'

Penn pressed closer. He could feel Raff's breath on his lips. 'I have missed you too.'

At last, he kissed him. Raff curled his good arm around Penn's middle, holding him. For a moment, Raff was all there was: the grip of his fingers, the softness of his mouth, the press of his chest against Penn's own. He was all Penn *needed,* too.

Eventually, Raff pulled away.

'We should return to the cart,' he said. 'I doubt Ash will have been able to buy us much time.'

Penn frowned. 'You are not riding?'

Raff snorted. 'They claim I am not well enough,' he scowled, 'which may be fair, as I couldn't even get myself onto my *damn* horse.'

'Of course. Raff, I am—'

'No,' he said quickly. 'Do not apologise. You did not fire the crossbow, nor did you force me to ride after you. You *saved* me.'

Penn rested their foreheads together.

'I merely pulled you from that cell. The physician—'

Raff kissed him into silence. 'That is not what I meant.'

His eyes were sparkling. He looked *well*, for the first time in days. He looked like the man Penn had first kissed in the forest.

'Thank you for helping me,' Penn said, sliding his hand beneath Raff's cloak. 'Thank you for *saving* me. For coming after me, and nearly dying for me.' He leaned closer till their lips brushed. 'I wish there was some way I could . . .' he kissed him, '*repay* you.'

Raff clung to him tighter. The treetops swayed above them.

'My Penn,' he sighed, 'you already have.'

Epilogue

Summer

Bright sunshine poured in through the open balcony door, bringing with it the trilling sound of birdsong and the cloying heat. Raff was sorting through their packs once again, ensuring that they were prepared for the journey ahead. He would need to visit the kitchen before they left, and the armoury. He needed to check that their horses were prepared in the stables, that they had been properly fed and watered, that the saddles were in good repair—

'Raff?'

He looked up. Penn had been speaking whilst he'd been lost in thought. 'Ah—'

'You are over-worrying again.'

'I just wish to be *ready*.'

'Ready for the countless bandits we will encounter in Cumberland?' Penn placed the letter he was reading down on the table and walked over. 'Are the mountains truly so dangerous?'

Raff ignored him. 'It pays to be prepared.'

Penn leaned over him, looping his arms around his shoulders and pressing a quick kiss to his cheek. 'I know. But this is supposed to be *enjoyable*, remember.'

Raff sighed, dropping the pack to the floor.

'How is Jo?' he asked, gesturing to the letter.

'She is well,' Penn said, shortly. 'She sends Ros's regards, and Isabelle's. No word from Father, of course, but that is to be expected.'

Raff turned, taking Penn's hands. 'Penn—'

'Jo is busy,' Penn spoke over him, 'as ever. She's taken it upon herself to teach Ellis the intricacies of running a keep, although he is far too young to understand.' He smiled, ruefully. 'I suspect she is trying to counter Father's influence over him.'

'I hope she is successful.'

'As do I.' Penn finally looked up. 'By all accounts, Ellis makes a fine heir, but it sounds exhausting.' His eyes sparkled. 'I think I much prefer being a hostage.'

Raff began to drift his fingers up and down Penn's arms. 'Is that so?'

Penn ghosted their lips together. 'It is.'

Raff closed the final gap, drawing him into a long, languid kiss. Penn smiled against him, and abandoning all pretence of packing, Raff looped his good arm around Penn's waist and pulled them both down onto the bed, savouring the way Penn gasped against his mouth.

He ran his hand up Penn's leg, pressing his fingertips into the soft muscle of his backside, before grabbing the hem of his undershirt and pulling it away. Penn kissed him harder as Raff ran his hand up his back – over the field of scars – and to his nape, tangling in his hair.

Raff was about to reach down with the intention of divesting Penn of his breeches, too, when Penn pushed against him, heaving him onto his back with a knee either side of his hips.

Raff's breath gave out. The light illuminated Penn from behind, making his curling hair glow golden. When they'd first met – when they'd first tumbled into each other's arms – Penn had been a wiry thing: exhausted and underfed, too anxious to even sleep well.

He'd filled out since then, his chest and stomach softer, his arms broadened.

Penn was *strong,* his physical strength coming to match the quieter strength he'd once buried inside.

And he was beautiful. Penn grinned down at him, and Raff realised he was likely reading his thoughts on his face. He felt himself blush.

'How long do we have before we leave?' Penn asked, dragging his fingertips down Raff's chest.

'I intended to set out before midday,' Raff said, shuddering beneath the touch. 'But—' Penn lowered himself down, pressing a line of kisses up his body, 'we are in no great rush.'

He felt Penn's breath flutter across his skin as he laughed. He moved slowly, trailing his lips across Raff's torso, over the aching scar on his shoulder, up his neck. He paused at his mouth.

'Well, then,' Penn murmured.

'Well, then,' Raff agreed.

Penn kissed him again, smiling against his lips as if they had all the time in the world, and the freedom to do as they pleased with it.

At last, Raff supposed, they did.

Acknowledgements

Despite writing a whole book about feelings, I've never been particularly good at having them myself (probably best not to examine that too closely lest we see which of my characters has inherited *that* particular trait). That makes *this sort of thing* - the whole vulnerable business of writing acknowledgements - a little tricky.

We often expect writing to be a hugely isolating experience. A lot of the time, it can be. And it *was*, when I was stuck in the dining room bashing away at my keyboard with my head full of forests and moonlight and pining. But I wouldn't have finished this book or be where I am today without the support, help and love of a huge number of people.

Thank you to my family, especially my parents and grandparents, for believing in me since I was eight years old and decided I was going to be an author. Thank you for nurturing my creativity and encouraging me not to give up on my dream.

Endless thanks to my mum, who was the first person to learn I won the competition (and scared some people going on a walk with her excited yelling). Thank you for believing in me, even when I didn't believe in myself, and for all your love and support. Thank you to my dad, for always encouraging me to do my best. Special thanks to my partner, who put up with my hours of seclusion, demands for chocolate biscuits, and inability to help with the washing up because I was too busy writing.

I want to thank Inber, bearer of the frog and Ash's #1 fan, for her support, guidance, unending patience and invaluable help as I battled my way through the first draft. Without you, this book wouldn't be where it is. It probably wouldn't even exist. Thank you for helping me from the very start of this wild adventure. I'm sorry the Strid got cut.

Thank you to everyone else who supported me through drafting and editing. Special thanks to Grey, who cheered me on through the first draft, and to Dorian, for all his help as I descended into further drafting madness, especially his patience with my infinite fractal edits.

Thank you, everyone, for loving my boys as much as I do, and helping me through the times when I just wanted to hide under the desk. (And, I suppose, thank you to my boys, too. If I'd been writing this for me, I'd never have finished it. Writing it for *them* was different.)

I cannot give enough thanks to everyone who has drawn me art of my boys. Raps, Conny, Nili and Emmett: I get emotional every time I look at my corkboard. There's an interview with Maurice Sendak where he talks about sending a hand-drawn card to a little boy named Jim who loved the card so much that he ate it. It wasn't until I received my first ever art of Raff and Penn (thank you, forever, Raps) that I realised where Jim was coming from. I didn't eat it, but I *did* hold it gently in my mouth like an overgrown labrador.

Conny, thank you for encouraging and enabling my increasingly convoluted ideas as I fell more and more in love with these dudes. There will always be a place in my heart for the vampire and the werewolf. Special thanks also go to Raps and Conny for allowing me to use their gorgeous art in the marketing for *Hartswood*.

I'd like to thank my amazing editor Rebecca Slorach for guiding me through this process and helping me make the finished book the best version of itself it could be (and encouraging me to add more Ash). Thank you to Kate Oakley for her incredible work on the cover. A huge thanks to the whole team at Mills & Boon - especially the judges of the *Romance Includes Everyone* competition - without whom I literally wouldn't be where I am today. Thank you so much for choosing Raff and Penn. I'm so excited to see what happens next.

Finally - and perhaps most importantly - thank you to everyone, those who I know and those who I don't, who have complimented my writing, left me comments, and encouraged me to continue sharing my work. I would never have been brave enough to do this without you and your kind words. I would never have believed that anyone was even slightly interested in my writing without you all. Thank you for your support all these years. I hope you love my boys just as much as I do.

LET'S TALK
Romance

Follow us:

Millsandboon
@MillsandBoon
@MillsandBoonUK
@MillsandBoonUK

For all the latest titles and special offers, sign up to our newsletter:

Millsandboon.co.uk